Should We?

The Blackwood Heirs

Book 1

by Samantha Higgins
& Beth Ann Walker

© 2020 Samantha Higgins and Beth Ann Walker.

All rights reserved. No part of this book may be reproduced or used in any manner without written permission of the copyright owner except for the use of quotations in a book review.

This book is a work of fiction. The names, characters, places, and incidents are products of the writers' imaginations or have been used fictitiously and are not to be construed as real. Any resemblance to persons, living or dead, actual events, locale or organizations is entirely coincidental. The authors do not have any control over and do not assume any responsibility for third-party websites or their content.

ISBN:9798565523546

This story has dark themes and is intended for readers 18+. Contains hetero and LGBTQ relationships, as well as graphic sexual content.

Dedication

This book is dedicated to Jen Harris... you encouraged us from the beginning and were always our biggest fan. We only wish that you were here to see what we've accomplished. We miss you eternally... Always seven with you

Acknowledgements

Thank you to my amazing husband, children, and family for all of the encouragement and support that you have given me. I love you all so much. Also, to my WM girls, you know who you are. I couldn't have done this without the strength that you have provided. Some of the friendships that I have made over the last year will be forever treasured. Beth, I don't know how you have put up with me throughout all of this, but you stuck by me and I am so glad that we did this together.

~ *Sam*

Acknowledgements

Thank you to my wonderful husband Michael, who supports me in every aspect of my life. We're always a team, I Love You! To my family and friends who have encouraged me during this crazy endeavor, especially my cheerleaders Allie, Nicki, and my Eternal Girls. And to Sam, I never imagined that I could write a book. Thank you for listening to my crazy ideas and pushing us to take it to the next level. I'm so grateful that 7 brought us together.

~ *Beth*

Table of Contents

Chapter 1	1
Chapter 2	14
Chapter 3	31
Chapter 4	37
Chapter 5	48
Chapter 6	65
Chapter 7	77
Chapter 8	92
Chapter 9	101
Chapter 10	120
Chapter 11	133
Chapter 12	146

Chapter 13	160
Chapter 14	175
Chapter 15	187
Chapter 16	198
Chapter 17	213
Chapter 18	229
Chapter19	243
Chapter 20	257
Chapter 21	267
Chapter 22	280
Chapter 23	291
Chapter 24	299
Chapter 25	311
Chapter 26	321
Chapter 27	332
Chapter 28	348

Chapter 29	**362**
Chapter 30	**371**
Chapter 31	**380**
Chapter 32	**391**
Chapter 33	**404**
Chapter 34	**409**
Chapter 35	**421**
Chapter 36	**438**
Chapter 37	**448**
Character List	**456**
About the Authors	**458**

Introduction

Welcome to the world of the Blackwood Heirs.

Dalton Blackwood is the Patriarch of the Blackwood family. Born in London to a poor family, Dalton's mother worked as a seamstress, creating beautiful garments for upper-class patrons. From a young age, Dalton assisted his mother, learning to create patterns and to construct everything from suits to evening gowns.

By the time Dalton was a teenager, he was creating his own impeccable designs. As his talent continued to grow, so did Dalton's clientele. His astonishing good looks drew people to him, and the quality of his work kept customers coming back. An established English fashion house took note, hiring Dalton to design for them.

By his early twenties, Dalton had married his long-time love, Mina. Together they started their own fashion company, Blackwood. When his three children were small, the family immigrated to New York City, where Dalton's reputation and wealth continued to grow.

The Blackwood family also continued to grow. Dalton's children had given him five intelligent, handsome grandsons.

As we begin the story of the Blackwood family, Dalton is in his late seventies. His son Alexander, current CEO of Blackwood, is beginning his retirement, and the youngest generation of Blackwoods now

+begin their reign of the family empire.

Thank you for reading Should We? We hope that you will love this family as much as we do and enjoy the surprises that we have in store for you.

Samantha and Beth

Chapter 1

Luca sits in his black leather office chair, his curved rosewood desk piled neatly with stacks of work to be completed. From Luca's computer screen, images of beautiful models stare back at him waiting to be selected for Blackwood's latest ad campaign. Luca, however, can't focus.

He runs his hand through his thick black hair, grasping at the tousled strands. *Fuck.* His head is throbbing. He pulls open his top desk drawer, grabs a bottle of aspirin and shakes two into his palm. He places them on his tongue, washing them down with the sparkling water that sits on his desk. *Get your shit together, Luca.* Acknowledging that he won't get a thing done until the aspirin starts to work, Luca stands and makes his way over to the towering wall of windows.

The New York City skyline is covered in a haze of gray and Luca lets out a little sarcastic laugh, thinking how well it suits his mood these days. Taking off his black-rimmed glasses, he rubs his eyes and presses his forehead onto the cool glass. *Why the fuck can't I get it out of my head?* The images that are burned into his memory just won't go away. He needs them to go away...

Should We?

Scouting locations for the shoot had taken less time than he expected. Luca planned to be gone late into the evening, but the first location had been perfect, and the traffic had been lighter than usual. Luca had instructed his driver, Tony, to take them to Koreatown and Misun's favorite restaurant. He wanted to surprise her with the special dishes that she loved from her childhood. Luca had been working long hours lately, and he couldn't wait for a quiet evening with his girlfriend.

Balancing the take-out bags with his attaché, he punches the code to his apartment into the keypad. Entering quietly, he sets the food and his bag on the kitchen island, glancing around for Misun. Luca hears soft music coming from the bedroom and smiles, pleased to be able to surprise her. He walks towards their bedroom, pausing by the door that's cracked open. With his hand on the knob, Luca tilts his head, positioning his ear close to the small opening when he hears noises. It's the TV, she's watching a movie, please God, let her be watching a movie. *Luca throws the heavy door open. He sees Misun, grasping the headboard of their bed. Her back is arched, her breasts heaving as she pants. A man is on top of her, thrusting between her legs, his muscular back dripping with perspiration. Luca freezes and Misun and the man both turn toward him.*

"Luca!" Misun gasps.

Luca charges at the man, tearing them apart. "YOU! How fucking could you?" he screams in the man's face while gripping his shoulders and shoving him back on the bed. The man grins at him. He fucking smiles at him.

"Luca, Luca please!" Misun shouts, pulling the sheet up over her naked chest.

Luca takes a step back. "Get the fuck out of my house, NOW!" He growls through his clenched teeth at the man.

He turns to Misun, "I'm going into the den. I will give you fifteen minutes to get every bit of your shit packed and go."

Misun pleads with him, "I'm sorry, Luca! Please! Where will I go?" Luca doesn't respond, just turns on his heel and walks away, never looking back.

A quick knock on his door jolts Luca out of his head and into the present. He turns and faces the door as it opens, and sees his cousin leaning past the frame. "Come on in Noah," Luca says. "An unexpected visit from the new CEO, what a pleasure." Luca takes a seat at his desk and gestures for Noah to sit across from him.

"No need for sarcasm, Luca," Noah replies. Luca notes how poised and confident his cousin looks, his tailored suit complimenting his athletic build and making him seem even taller than six-foot-one. Noah unbuttons his fitted jacket and takes a seat in a tufted chesterfield chair. Luca folds his hands on his desk, waiting for his cousin to speak. "Luca, I expected the layouts for the new campaign yesterday. It's not like you to miss a deadline."

"I'm working on it. I apologize for getting behind. I plan on staying late tonight," Luca replies.

"Luca, what's going on? Are you okay?"

"I'm fine." Luca tenses up and adjusts his shirt cuffs. "I'm sorry that I've been distracted."

Noah reaches across the elegant desk to take his hand. He and Luca are very close, all of the cousins are. They've grown up together. He hates seeing him like this, especially after the upbringing he had been forced to endure.

Luca's father, Maxwell, was groomed to become CEO of Blackwood. When he met Luca's mother, she became pregnant with him almost immediately. Her family was well known for ill-reputed business dealings, and Maxwell became entrenched in that world soon after he was born. Luca grew up in a shoddy little house in a rough area, with neglectful alcoholic parents. Maxwell was removed from the family business and his brother Alexander, Noah's father, had become CEO. With Alexander's impending retirement, Noah will be assuming the head of Blackwood.

"Do you want to talk about it?" Noah asks.

Luca gives a slightly forced smile, pulling his hand away. "Thank you, I'll be fine."

"What happened?" Noah persists.

Luca stands up and starts pacing, his body language agitated and stiff. "I don't want to talk about it."

"But Luca, you can't go on like this! Let me help you. It's been weeks since you two broke up. What did she do? What did Misun do to you?"

"There's nothing you can do!" Luca is exasperated, looking out the window to the streets below. "I need to figure this out for myself. It doesn't concern you."

Noah stands and approaches his cousin. "Of course, it concerns me! You're my family, not to mention that this is affecting your work. Our meeting with Grandfather is in two days! He's going to notice your behavior."

"Oh, there it is! And what? He'll assume I'm becoming like my father?" Luca scoffs, glaring at Noah. "He'll be relieved that he's chosen *you* to run the company and not *me?* All because of my stupid fucking father!" Luca gasps, desperately trying to keep in the sobs that have been threatening to escape. He's too humiliated to tell Noah about Misun. Luca takes a deep breath and composes himself. "Fuck it. Let's go get a drink."

Noah can't help but feel almost responsible for his older cousin. He also knows that it's Luca's nature to shut down until he is ready. He'll just have to wait for the fireworks when they happen. Noah nods in response to the offer of the bar, tugging at the knot of his tie. Luca rubs his face with his hands, trying to sweep away the emotions that are consuming his every fiber.

**

Noah runs his hand through his thick brown hair as he steps onto the modern glass elevator. He sets down his briefcase as he pushes the button for the eighteenth floor. After a few drinks with Luca, he had finished up some work at the office. Noah silently thanks his grandfather for having the foresight to purchase the building that is home to Blackwood. Having his apartment in the same building as the offices saves hours of commute time into Midtown Manhattan.

Aunt Bella and his cousins also live in Blackwood Tower, which is convenient for the family business. For the most part, they respect each other's privacy. Noah smiles at the thought of his baby brother Jasper's insistence on keeping his artsy loft in SoHo. He doubts Jasper will ever give that up and will just continue to crash in Noah's spare bedroom after late nights at work.

The elevator chimes the arrival at Noah's floor and the grin doesn't leave his face, despite how tired he is. After entering the security code, Noah steps in and toes off his shoes by the door, dumping his briefcase and suit coat on a nearby chair.

From the full wall of windows, the view of the city in the dwindling daylight is stunning. In

Noah's eyes, his fiancée is even more so. Victoria is facing the windows with her back leaning against the overstuffed sofa. Her earbuds are in, and she's concentrating on her laptop. Psychology books are stacked on the coffee table, and papers are strewn across the floor around her. Noah knows that Victoria hasn't heard him come in, and for a moment he just takes in the sight of her. Her blonde hair is piled messily on top of her head and held in place with a pencil. Face free of makeup and wearing one of his t-shirts hanging loosely off one shoulder, Noah adores seeing her just like this.

Victoria catches Noah watching her from the corner of her eye and pulls out her earbuds. "Well hello handsome, I'm glad you're home."

Noah walks around the couch and slumps into the comfy cushion, leaning back onto one of the dozen colorful throw pillows that Victoria has artfully tossed there.

"I thought you'd be extra late getting ready for your very first meeting, Mr. CEO!" Victoria teases, setting aside her laptop and pulling herself up to sit on his lap. Although she wears a mischievous smile, Noah can tell how proud she is by the look in her gorgeous green eyes.

"Just waiting on a few things from Luca, but I think I'm well prepared," Noah replies while pushing a stray lock of hair off of Victoria's forehead.

"Of course, you are, Noah," she says while stroking his cheeks with her thumbs. "You are a brilliant man. You've prepared well for this role. You studied your ass off at Harvard, graduated with honors, and you've watched how your grandfather and your father have run the business for your entire life!"

Noah smiles at Victoria's confidence in him. "So, speaking of studying asses off, how's it coming?" Noah questions as Victoria loosens his tie and undoes the top buttons of his pristine dress shirt.

"It's coming. Just a little longer and I'll be Victoria Blackwood, Ph.D."

"Well, we need to be married before you're Victoria Blackwood!" Noah twists the emerald ring on her finger. He'd picked it out to match her eyes; an ostentatious diamond would have made Victoria uncomfortable. She is the most down to earth person that Noah has ever met.

Raised in Buffalo, Victoria had come to New York to obtain her degree in child psychology. Noah's aunt, Bella had seen her at a café one day, and had asked her if she'd be interested in modeling. Victoria had done some advertisements for Blackwood and had used the money that she earned for her college tuition. Noah had seen her during a photoshoot while he was home during summer break, working with his father. They were both instantly smitten. They dated whenever Noah was back in New York and continued to get to know each other long-distance during the school year. Noah is completely and utterly in love, as is Victoria.

He proposed a little over a year ago, dropping to one knee at their special spot in Central Park. The last year has been a whirlwind of work, school, and wedding preparations, and they are so ready to begin their life together.

Victoria hops off Noah's lap and pads into the kitchen. "Hey, that reality show Blackwood is sponsoring, Aspire to Design?" she says while pulling the chicken out of the oven. "I've been catching up on episodes! There are some seriously talented designers competing." Victoria plates the dinner and pours two glasses of wine. "A couple of those designers are so funny! And one is dangerously attractive. The company is going to do very well with whoever wins."

Noah pulls out a leather kitchen chair and joins Victoria at the granite breakfast bar. This is their favorite place to eat casual meals together. "Well, I really know nothing about the designers. That's Luca's area of expertise." Noah takes a bite of the chicken marsala. "This is good, thanks for cooking," he continues. "Anyway, Luca was completely distracted today. I tried asking him what was going on with Misun, but he just got angry with me. We got a drink

together today, but he deflected all my questions.

"Well, that bitch did something, I'm sure of it!" Victoria takes a sip of her chardonnay. "Noah, you know that I get along with everyone. I'm usually a non-judgmental person, but something about Misun isn't right. I really tried with her, but she just doesn't seem genuine."

"I know, I know. You've said that since they started dating," Noah says between bites. "We've just got so much going on at work and I need him to pick up the pieces and focus."

Victoria refills her wine glass and continues. "Well, I'm glad they broke up. I just know that Luca will find his perfect person. He's an amazing guy. He just needs to be open to it."

"You're right." Noah takes another sip of wine. "But it's been weeks, and he seems no better! I just hate to see him like this. She was the only one I've ever seen him fall in love with."

Victoria nods, letting out a sigh. The couple continues to chat over their meal, and Noah takes the dishes to the sink when they're finished.

"Go hop in the shower, I've got this. I'm sure you're tired, my love." Victoria noses Noah on the cheek and starts putting the food away.

"Yep I will," he says, kissing her on her cute little nose. "I'm always so happy to come home to you."

Victoria finishes up in the kitchen quickly and heads toward the master bath. She hears the shower running and Noah humming some unknown tune. She strips off her clothes, and quietly opens the bathroom door. The glass doors of the luxurious spa shower are fogged up from steam, but Victoria can still see the broad shoulders and narrow waist of her man. She opens the shower door and slips in. Noah turns to face her.

"Hi," he says with a wide smile, water drips streaming down his forehead onto his pink lips.

"Hi." Victoria stands on tiptoes and swipes her tongue across the droplets. She runs her hands down Noah's muscled back and onto his firm ass.

Noah tips her face up and pulls her into a gentle kiss. The steamy water washes over them, bathing them in comfort as the kiss deepens. Victoria explores Noah's mouth with her tongue and when he gently sucks on it, she lets out a needy groan. She can feel Noah starting to grow hard against the smooth skin of her stomach and she smiles at the feeling. Victoria brings her hand around to caress Noah's erection, which continues to grow with her touch. She rolls her palm over the head of his cock, feeling the pre-come mixing with the water that streams around them.

She looks up into Noah's sparkling blue eyes and drops to her knees. He doesn't take his gaze off his fiancée as she runs her tongue over his tip, swirling around it. Victoria feels Noah gently pull the pencil from her hair that she had forgotten was there. Her damp blonde strands fall in waves down her back. Noah tangles his fingers in it and gently pulls her head closer to his erection.

She runs her tongue along the underside of his cock, feeling the veins and just how hard her lover is. Noah tilts his head back and groans. Victoria continues to move along his hard penis and down to his balls as she twists and strokes along the full length of it. She loves to take care of Noah like this.

Her tongue swirls back up and around as she continues stroking. Finally, Victoria takes the whole head into her mouth, before sinking down to take in as much of his length as she can.

"Oh my god!... Shit, your mouth feels so amazing," Noah says in a deep breathy voice, his eyes fixed on Victoria's mouth around his cock. "You're so good to me, baby, so good."

She starts sucking while continuing to use her tongue to reach around as much of it as she can. Noah wipes the water from her eyes and bites at his bottom lip. Victoria picks up the pace, twisting and stroking the base of his cock as she continues to increase her suction. She feels Noah tense up.

"Fuck... gonna come!" Victoria feels and tastes his release against the inside of her cheeks. She continues to gently stroke him through his orgasm, giving his cock gentle licks and kisses after she pulls off. Victoria runs her tongue across her lips as Noah pulls her up and into a passionate kiss, tasting himself on her tongue. "That was amazing. Thank you, baby." Noah grabs the lavender body wash and starts sudsing Victoria's back.

She takes in the relaxing scent. "You're very welcome, handsome. I love you."

Noah places a gentle kiss on her forehead. "I love you too, Victoria. So, so much. Now let's finish washing up so I can take you to bed.'"

She quickly reaches up to wipe the shampoo off Noah's forehead. "That sounds amazing."

Sometimes Victoria can't believe that she has found Noah. That they have found each other. She can't wait to finish her day curled up in the arms of her amazing man.

Chapter 2

Bella Blackwood admires the Parisian night sky, the Eiffel Tower illuminated in the distance. She leans into her eldest son, squeezing his arm as she sips ice-cold champagne from a crystal flute. "The view never gets old, does it Jayce? I adore Paris."

Jayce nods. "No, it never does, Mum."

"I think it went really well today!" Bella almost shouts to be heard over the booming music and noisy conversation at the rooftop after-show party.

Jayce nods in response. "More successful than last year, I think."

A gorgeous model walks past, winking and tipping his glass toward the pair. Whether he's flirting with Bella or with Jayce, they're not quite sure. Bella looks elegant, as always, but undeniably sexy in her tight red cocktail dress. The creamy skin of one shoulder is bare, while a sleeveless ruffled strap covers the other. Her hemline is fluted below her knees, with a thigh-high slit offering a glimpse of her toned and impossibly long legs. Bella's three-inch stilettos make her the same height as her six-foot-tall son. She had Jayce at twenty-two, and the two have been mistaken for siblings often.

Jayce is the face of Blackwood. Born with stunning deep brown eyes, full lips, and rich dark hair, he has inherited all of Bella's beauty. Having been around the industry with his mother, Jayce has been a model for the company from a young age. Everyone wants him at their events. Tonight, he is wearing black leather pants that fit like a second skin. His burgundy velvet motorcycle-style jacket is embellished with silver zippers. He wears it open with a deep V-neck black tee underneath, revealing his toned chest and the long silver chains that dangle there.

"Ah! Here he is," Bella exclaims, seeing a familiar face in the crowd of people.

Jayce glances away as his mother pulls on the arm of a fellow model. Korian is the next favorite in the fashion ranks after Jayce. He has dark features similar to Jayce's, adorable dimples, and an exotic look that everyone is envious of. Korian works for a different company, much to Bella's annoyance. She gently tugs him over, trying to ignore the stunning woman at his side.

"You promised to come and see me," Bella slurs slightly after one too many glasses of free bubbly, flinging herself into a hug with Korian. He smiles as Bella pouts at him like she's done several times before while flirting. Jayce shuffles his feet awkwardly, trying not to involve himself in the situation.

"I'll come and see you, Bella." He kisses her on the cheek before turning to leave, grasping the hand of his beautiful date. "When we get back, I will." Korian turns towards Jayce, "Nice working with you today."

Jayce nods, a forced smile on his perfect lips.

"Good." She giggles after him. "I will have you, Korian, I can promise you that."

"Mum!" Jayce scolds in embarrassment. "Please."

"Oh," Bella says in her best cutesy voice, clutching her son's cheeks, "I meant to work with, Jayce! Don't make assumptions."

"Stop it." He sighs, pulling away, and sipping his beer.

"You know that you're my number one boy anyway." She laughs. The warm breeze blows Bella's long raven hair onto her face and she sweeps it away.

"I wouldn't let *him* hear you saying that." Jayce tips his beer toward his brother, who is standing against a rustic wall across the rooftop. Decorative cotton bunting is flapping on the bricks above his head.

Harrison is the youngest of the two by a couple of years. Although he's been graced with similarly stunning looks as Jayce, he has no interest in being a model. A polite and charismatic young man, Harrison enjoys making others look good. He has worked his way up the ladder to become one of the head stylists at Blackwood.

With him is Heidi, a junior stylist with the company. She has been enamored with Harrison from the moment she'd been offered a job with Blackwood. Heidi works extra hours to be around him and often travels with them for work. It looks as if her persistence is paying off. They are standing together closely, staring deeply into each other's eyes. Harrison is touching Heidi's cheek gently with his fingers, and she flutters her long eyelashes at him in return.

Jayce smiles, and Bella puts an arm around her eldest son, leaning her head on his shoulder still sipping her tall glass of ice-cold champagne.

"Awww, look at them," she says, much to Jayce's surprise.

"Really?" He raises an eyebrow. "Someone that you think is worthy of your boy?"

She sighs. "I guess so. She's a sweet girl, and I suppose at twenty-six, he has to make his way in the world someday."

Jayce inwardly laughs at his mother's innocent thoughts. She clearly has never seen Harrison picking up girls a few times a week after work. He may be the shyer of the two, but with his looks and charm, Harrison certainly doesn't go short of attention.

Should We?

"So, what was up with you before?" Bella suddenly asks, turning to face him.

"What are you talking about, Mum?" Jayce pretends to have no idea what she's referring to.

"Behave," she says, "I've seen you do that before. Why do you act all strange around Korian?"

Jayce scoffs a little too over the top. "I do not!"

"You have no reason to be jealous, darling," Bella coos. "You'll always be the face of Blackwood. Having Korian with us would just be the cherry on top. You two look amazing working together."

"Hmm, course we do, Mother," Jayce responds, swirling the foam in his glass. "But sometimes we have to be satisfied with what we already have."

Bella takes another gulp of her drink when someone catches her eye.

"Oohhh," Bella hums, bringing Jayce out of his thoughts. "Look at her. She's pretty."

Jayce follows his mother's gaze and sees a model that he recognizes from another company, talking to a group of people. He knows exactly what Bella is thinking. He has seen this too many times.

"Oh, Mum. Not here. Not now."

"What?" she protests, taking her cosmetic mirror out of her clutch and applying another layer of scarlet lipstick in its reflection. "I'm just going to talk to her."

"Hmm," Jayce judges. "I know how your talking goes. You mean you'll end up doing the walk of shame from her room in the early hours of the morning."

"Hey!" Bella's face clouds over. "You just remember who you are speaking to!"

He places a gentle kiss on his mother's cheek. He may not always agree with some of her choices, but he has the utmost respect for her. She is his guiding light.

"Sorry," he falters. "I just don't want you getting hurt, or someone writing something in the press."

"Ah, it will be fine," she says, patting his cheeks affectionately. "I'm a master at this! Besides, Jayce, I've raised you and Harrison alone, and I think that I've done pretty well. It's my time now, *he* can't be having all of the fun."

Jayce laughs as she motions to his little brother who is now enjoying locking lips with Heidi, oblivious to the people mulling around them.

"Maybe this will be you one day?" She kisses the end of his nose. "That you will find your happiness and settle down."

Spraying herself with a little perfume, Bella sets off towards her target for the evening. She hasn't been turned down yet, by any man or woman. Jayce smiles, and shakes his head, turning back towards the tall table next to him, leaning on it with his beer.

He looks around at everyone enjoying themselves, the music echoing around him, almost matching the gentle wind swirling in the air. This site makes all of the hard work and preparation worth it. He loves his job so much. He revels in the attention when he poses for photos or walks down the catwalk, knowing that he is the star of the show. Jayce has always been the center of attention, with women flocking to speak to him and thrusting their phone numbers into his pockets. Like his brother, he's never short of someone to go home with.

"Hey," a small voice says beside him, "I hope you don't mind me coming over."

Jayce rolls his eyes but tries not to let his feelings show. If he had money for every time someone had casually approached him like this, he probably would never have to model again.

He takes in the pretty young woman standing in front of him with a hopeful look in her eyes. He already knows that she'll be in his plush king-size bed within an hour, the two of them having drunken awkward sex that will be filled with regrets in the morning, and that he won't even remember her name.

"Hi." He feigns a smile. "I'm Jayce. Can I get you a drink?"

She gives a flirty giggle and nods, linking arms with him so that they can find someone with another tray of drinks. Jayce avoids Korian's eyes watching him on the way past, making their way through the groups of guests.

**

"Good morning," a gentle voice breaks the silence in the room, making Heidi scrunch up her eyes as the early dawn light floods the room.

"Morning," she croaks back, squinting to see the handsome face in front of her on the adjacent pillow.

She loves going to events with the company, but parties, alcohol, and Paris aren't always the best combination. Especially when they have to be up extremely early the next day. They're due to make their way back to New York soon and have to be ready to go.

"Are you okay?" the sweet voice speaks again, making Heidi blush, memories of the evening before swirling back into her hungover and clouded mind.

She pulls the blanket up towards her chin in unnecessary embarrassment, fully aware of being naked under the crisp, luxurious cotton. Nodding tentatively, she tries not to let her insecurities show. This is something that she's yearned for, and it's happened. She realizes that she was considerably more confident the night before, with a few fizzy Proseccos to do away with her inhibitions.

Harrison stares back softly at her. He can see that the morning after *What have I done?* thoughts are running through her fuzzy head, and he wonders if he's overstepped the mark with what happened. His usual confidence wavers a little.

"Um, sorry," he manages to whisper. "I should have waited until we were sober."

Heidi's eyes widen when she realizes that the situation has become somewhat uncomfortable now. She reaches out from the covers and gently touches his bare arm. He looks amazing laying on his side, the sheet at waist height and his stunning tanned body on display. She needs to pull herself together...quickly. Harrison caught her eye on day one of being hired by Blackwood, and she's tried everything in her power to get him to notice her. Last night, after what seemed like an age of flirting, had been the night. And it was more incredible than she had even imagined.

"No, no," she reassures, teasing her fingers up and down his silky skin. "I just didn't know if you had any regrets?"

Harrison scoffs, snaking his arm over her waist. "No way. It was amazing. What about you?"

Heidi shakes her head, her cheeks flushing bright crimson. "None."

Harrison feels a little better seeing the smile spreading across her face. This is new for him too. Normally he would say goodbye to his date from the previous evening, with the promise of calling, but never did. No one had compelled him to stay interested. Sure, the women had been extremely beautiful and usually kind, but he had never felt a connection to any of them. Until now.

Harrison admired Heidi from afar. He knew that she liked him, but he had tried to distance himself since they work together. He didn't want to be part of ruining her career with Blackwood.

Yet here they are, and he's happy. They both are.

Harrison pulls back a little to pick up his phone from the bedside cabinet. Glancing at it for a moment to let his eyes focus, he huffs at the time.

"We have to get up soon." He sighs, rolling back to face Heidi. "Or Mum will be banging on the door to hurry us up."

Heidi pulls the covers up to stifle her giggles, Harrison grinning in bewilderment at her.

"What? Getting out of bed isn't that funny."

"No, no, It's the mum thing. I still can't get used to you being from an English family."

Harrison lifts his head and rests it on his hand. "Well, I can't help where my family comes from. To me, Mum or Mother is the normal way. Even though I was born in New York, Mom just doesn't seem right to me."

"Isn't it funny?" Heidi observes. "How things are said differently in other countries."

Stroking across the line of her cheekbone, Harrison agrees, giving a wink. "It is, but it certainly makes things interesting!"

Leaning in closer, he lets his lips trace the path he'd traced on her speckled cheek. A slight gasp escapes her and the tiny hairs on her neck stand on end. He starts to pull the material away that is separating them, exposing her bare breasts.

"Harri, do we have time for anything like this?" she whispers. "We have a flight to catch."

He kisses her lips; the sensation feels so natural and comfortable as if they've been together for a long time.

"I can be quick when I want to," he answers, playfully.

"Hmmm." She smiles, reciprocating his affection, teasing her tongue over his eagerly awaiting mouth. "Then get to it!"

Harrison eases Heidi onto her back, his eyes wandering down her chest. He takes in her curves better now that his mind isn't alcohol-fueled like it was the previous night. Harrison looks back up to her shiny red hair splayed out on the pillow. Her turquoise eyes glisten when their gazes meet, and her cheeks flush. He feels a pang in his chest that he's never experienced before. Blushing, Harrison looks away, his ears noticeably red as he tries to ignore the emotions bubbling to his core.

Heidi touches his arm in reassurance, telling him what she thinks he wants to hear. "It's okay you know. Nothing else has to happen between us."

Harrison looks at her lying there, the most beautiful thing he's ever seen, and realizes that he would be a complete and utter fool to let Heidi slip away from him. This possibly could be his chance at a stable sort of happiness. Or at least they could try if she wanted to.

"I want it to," he says. "I just worry. The what-ifs and all that."

Heidi knows this is the best opportunity that she's going to get to stand a chance with this man. She's witnessed many girls hanging around him, acting like they're interested in Harrison as a person and not in his fame and fortune, struggling with her jealousy as it rages inside her. She likes him for who he is, for the personality that matches his beauty.

"The only what-ifs we have to worry about, Harrison, is if we walk away from this and regret not doing anything about it. I know that you feel this pull too. I can tell."

"I do." Harrison grins, pulling her closer. "Now, how much time do we have?"

Heidi laughs against his lips and feels his tongue tease into her mouth. She drapes her leg over his, feeling as his cock twitches through the thin sheet. He tilts his head to allow a better flow of movement between their mouths, small groans escaping them.

Pulling his hand down from her cheek, Harrison glides his fingers over her nipple, a heightened breath escaping her. He continues to move downward until he reaches her thigh that rests against his, tickling it with the slightest pressure causing tiny goosebumps on her skin.

He teases Heidi's leg down and gently lays her back. Pushing up on his elbows, his body hovers above her. Their eyes lock, and Harrison glides his thumb across his own rosy bottom lip, while Heidi twists her red hair playfully around her fingers.

"You are so beautiful," he says, taking in all of her features and admiring her naked figure as she blushes.

"Stop it." She giggles as he moves in front of her, sliding her legs apart and lowering his head. "Harrison, we really don't have time!"

"I need to taste you," he growls, a smirk on his handsome face.

She gasps at the feeling of his lips gliding along the top of her thigh, teasing gently until he reaches her heat. He opens her gently, hungrily twisting his tongue around her clit, nipping and sucking between the gentle strokes.

She starts to whine, the pitch increasing when he slides two of his fingers inside her, curling them up to pleasure her further. He feels how wet she is as her body trembles, and he wants to feel her around his cock.

Harrison pulls away from her, and Heidi groans at the loss of contact, watching him as he reaches for a condom from his wallet. Bella has taught her boys many times about being safe. After rolling it on and discarding the packet, he lays on top of her, pushing inside.

"Hello beautiful," he says as he lowers himself fully on top of her, grasping her hands beside her head.

"Hello handsome," she whispers back, wrapping her legs around his waist, crossing her ankles together.

They move in unison, their kisses soft and slow. Heidi raises her hips to meet his, increasing the friction on her most sensitive spot. She immediately gets close to the edge once more, her groin burning and tingling. "I'm...I'm going to come, Harrison."

"Do it, beautiful. Do it," he responds, squeezing his eyes shut when he feels her muscles clenching on his already aching dick. "Fuck!"

Her noises of pleasure fill the room, her fingers clasping tightly on Harrison's, pushing him over the edge with her. His groans fill the air as his orgasm hits. They kiss their way through it, both coming down from their pleasure, their connection better now that they're completely sober.

"That was even more amazing than last night!" Heidi says, her breathing slowing.

"Even though it was quick?" Harrison says, his self-doubt showing.

She smiles reassuringly and nods, kissing the tip of his nose. They both sigh as there's a sharp knock on the door.

"Ignore it," Harrison whispers. "They may go away."

Remaining almost frozen in the position that they were interrupted in, they pause for what seems like minutes but is only seconds. Hearing nothing else, they resume their embrace, hoping to snatch a little more time together.

"Come on you two," Jayce shouts through the thick wood, knocking slightly harder this time. "You're as bad as Mum."

Heidi snorts into Harrison's arm, and he looks at her in confusion.

"Oh!" he laughs in realization. "So, you find it funny even when *he* says weird English words? Do I have to keep my eye on you two?"

"Behave." She playfully slaps his skin as he lifts off her. "I'll get used to it."

Kneeling up at the end of the bed, he pauses. "So, you're thinking of sticking around with me then, hey?"

"If you'll have me?" she says, getting out of bed and wrapping a sheet around herself.

Harrison grins at her, throwing one of his t-shirts and a pair of his joggers in her direction. Heidi can't go to the airport wearing her dress from the night before. There will be too many people from the press around. She'll just have time to grab her bags from her room and find her sneakers.

The paparazzi often caught girls leaving the hotels after swanky parties and events involving the models. Some of them had even been bold enough to share their stories for a bit of money. Harrison doesn't want too many people to know about Heidi yet. Not because he is ashamed of their new thing, but because he doesn't want anything to spoil it. Being in the public eye can harm relationships.

Smiling to himself at the thought of a future with Heidi, Harrison opens the door to see Jayce standing there glaring at them. Heidi rushes off in bare feet through the corridor to collect her things, her dress in one hand and her heels in the other.

"What?" Harrison protests, turning to throw on his clothes and grab his suitcase rather than stare after Heidi.

Jayce tuts as another door opens, and their mother appears with the beautiful woman that she had encouraged back to her room the night before. The boys screw up their faces as the two embrace passionately, before the other woman makes her way out of the hotel.

Spotting her son's looks of disapproval, she laughs and kisses them both on the cheek, before linking arms with them. "Oh stop it you two. The apple doesn't fall far from the tree you know!" Together, they head down the corridor to meet the cars that will take them to the airport.

Chapter 3

Dalton Blackwood enters the executive board room that he designed many years ago. He is pleased that it looks the same, his family choosing to keep it as it's always been. Three crystal chandeliers hang from the towering ceiling, and the warm wooden walls are accented with matching inlays and crown molding. An enormous oriental rug covers the oak floors, on which is centered the immense teak conference table that he had imported from London. Dalton had wanted mahogany, but Mina had insisted that teak was more durable, and she had been correct, as always. It still looks beautiful. Matching ornate wooden office chairs with caramel nubuck leather surround the table. An imposing Bordeaux colored leather wing back chair sits at the head of the table, the CEO's chair.

Although it's been over a decade since he has run Blackwood, Dalton still has to stop himself from taking a seat in it. He knows that Noah will ask him to, just as Alexander had during his reign as CEO, but Dalton feels that the spot should be occupied by his grandson. It is an honor to sit in that seat, and Noah has earned it. Dalton sits in a chair to one side, as it should be.

Noah enters the room tall and impeccably groomed in his Blackwood custom suit. His broad shoulders remain straight as he exudes the confidence of a man much older than his twenty-seven years. Dalton wells with emotion as his son, Alexander, and his grandsons greet him with love and adoration. *I only wish that Mina was here to see this day.* Memories of his beautiful wife flash through his mind. How he misses caressing Mina's lovely long dark hair and looking into her beautiful eyes. These last few years since her death have been so difficult; he misses her so much.

Building up his fashion and photography company in England back in his younger days hadn't been easy. Moving his young family to New York to expand Blackwood had been even more difficult. Poor Mina was there for him every step of the way. She had supported him through his late-night business meetings and his endless phone calls. She was the reason that Dalton had succeeded in creating the family empire.

Mina had given him the gift of two handsome sons and a beautiful daughter to dote on. And he had. No matter how busy he was, Dalton had always tried to give his family some special attention. He would rush home from meetings to have a quick game of football with the boys, reading his little princess a bedtime story. Sunday afternoons were always spent at home. Mina would cook a big meal, and the family would enjoy relaxing and laughing together.

Isabella, known as Bella, is his angel. Dalton adores his one and only daughter. She is a stunning woman, with all of the looks of her mother. Bella, the creative director of the company and former model, runs the visual side of Blackwood. Dalton tried not to be too disappointed when she got pregnant at a very young age, first with Jayce and then with Harrison. Both boys have the same father, but the man was never involved in their lives. Bella is a strong and independent woman. She raised two amazing young men, and Dalton is proud.

Alexander, his youngest child, is Dalton's double in both features and personality. He is confident with a fair but determined attitude in business. Dalton had always expected his eldest, Maxwell, to follow in his footsteps, however, his choices in life had forced Dalton to remove him from Blackwood. Maxwell's estrangement from the family soon followed.

After discussing pertinent financials, product performance, and current ad campaigns, Noah begins to update everyone about Blackwood's two largest current endeavors. The first, is a well-known charity fashion show in Paris that Bella and her sons are currently participating in. The second, is the TV reality show that Blackwood is the main sponsor for.

"So," Noah says, "the Paris charity event was a success, as expected. I spoke with Aunt Bella earlier, and she said that our designs were well received." Dalton nods as Noah continues. "Jayce was chosen to walk last, which of course is quite an honor and even better publicity for Blackwood. They will all be returning from Paris tomorrow."

Dalton is pleased to see the leadership skills that he has helped pass down as Noah conducts the meeting with ease. His eyes wander toward his eldest grandson Luca, Maxwell's only child. Luca looks somewhat troubled, staring at the table while fiddling with his silver-plated ballpoint pen. Luca's cheeks look pale and drained, his demeanor somewhat uninterested. Dalton knows that Luca has recently split from his girlfriend, and figures that's the reason he's so distracted. It had happened suddenly, not many people knowing why. Luca had met Misun when she was working in a downtown bar. Dalton remembers that, considering it was similar to how Luca's parents had met. Misun is a pretty girl, with parents from South Korea, and Luca had been smitten with her. She wasn't his usual type; she was a bit confident and brash, whereas he is more reserved. Luca resisted at first, but Misun persisted. Soon enough, he had fallen in love with her. The pair splitting up had been a bit of a surprise to everyone.

"Now, regarding Aspire to Design. The finale is this Friday." Noah announces.

"Already?" Alexander huffs, looking at the calendar on his phone. "That's gone quickly."

"It has," Noah responds to his father. "As decided in our previous meetings, the winning designer this year will join us here at

Blackwood." Noah looks at his brother. "Jasper, as you know, you will be taking the photographs at the finale. Are you prepared for that?"

Jasper clears his throat and speaks up. "Yes, I am. I will do my best to represent Blackwood, Noah."

Jasper, Noah's younger brother, is Dalton's youngest grandchild. He has just recently joined the family business. A creative free spirit, he studied photography at NYU and is extremely skilled and talented for a twenty-one-year-old.

"Great," Noah continues. "This is your first big shoot Jasper, and we are counting on you."

Jasper bows his head, trying to appear confident, and glances at his grandfather who nods at him in reassurance.

Noah says. "We are the main sponsors of the show, as you know, and Luca has been announced as the guest judge again this year. Cars have been arranged for Friday. Luca, is your schedule clear?"

"Huh?" Luca says, sitting up slightly and looking around in bewilderment. "Oh, yeah, I'm all set."

Noah frowns and continues to wrap up the meeting, ensuring that all of the details have been finalized. The fashion event and the reality show are two of the biggest things that

Blackwood participates in on an annual basis; their family name held in the highest regard. They have to get things right, and Noah has put himself under a lot of pressure to make that happen. It is his duty now that he is in charge. He really doesn't want to let his father and grandfather down.

After Noah concludes the meeting, Dalton puts a hand on his shoulder. "You did an amazing job, Noah. Your father and I are so proud of you. I know that Grandma Mina is watching over you, just as proud as I am."

Smiling, Noah replies, "Thank you, Grandfather. That means so much to me."

"Blackwood is in good hands. You know that I'm here if you ever need me." Dalton gives his grandson's shoulder a final squeeze before he leaves.

Noah gathers up his papers, and takes a look around the board room, glancing at his imposing chair. With a confident nod, he heads to his new office. He has a lot of work to do.

Chapter 4

Closing the front door, Jaxon tosses his black workout bag onto the floor near a pile of sewing patterns and makes his way over to the slightly tatty couch.

"Ewwww, look at you!" Taylor teases, watching his best friend flop down onto it. "You're all sweaty and stuff after dance practice."

Taylor puts down the fabric that he's sewing on the machine and gets up from his desk, flinging his arms around Jax's shoulders from behind. Jax sighs.

"Shouldn't you be showering so that we can do the final fittings for the show?" Taylor asks.

"Hmm, I'm not sure that this is a good idea," Jax says. "I'm really not model material, you know. I think maybe I should just stick to dancing."

Taylor lets go of Jax's shoulders and makes his way around the couch to sit beside him. They love the view that they have, and often sit staring out the window of their little studio apartment in the Chelsea neighborhood. Taylor had insisted on living here, since it was a short distance from the fabric stores which were essential for furthering his career. Jax was skeptical, given the price, but Taylor sold some of his designs while attending FIT and had saved the money. After Jax was offered a tuition scholarship at a dance company in Manhattan a subway distance away, it made sense for them to live here.

Now Taylor is making enough through his work to pay his half, but Jax still has no option but to take on dance classes, teaching wealthy children various skills. It is a lot of work that has him feeling completely wiped out most evenings, but at least he feels a little comfort that he's paying his own way. Taylor may be his best friend, but he doesn't want to take advantage of him.

"What are you talking about? We have your outfit ready. You can't back out now! You'll be perfect for the show. Wait until the Blackwood's see you all dressed up."

Jax huffs again. That is one of his main concerns. The Blackwood family is so well respected by everyone. Top models the world over are killing themselves to work for Blackwood. How the hell can he walk a runway and be judged by one of them? Taylor had insisted on Jax as his model for the finale of Aspire to Design, and he reluctantly agreed after a few beers. Now the nerves are starting to set in.

"I don't know, Taylor. I just feel a little weird about it all. You know, being on TV, cameras pointing at me, being around lots of people."

Taylor chuckles. Jax is just the same as ever. So much talent and potential yet struggling with his confidence. He's been the same since they were young boys growing up in Ohio together. Attending the same school and living a few streets away from each other, they had been inseparable. When Taylor confided in his best friend that he was gay, Jax had cried. He too had been feeling the same thoughts and emotions dealing with his sexuality. It was a comfort to him that the person he was closest to in the whole world was going through the same thing. They spent hours talking things through, reassuring one another that it was okay.

They had both decided to tell their parents separately, but at the same time one evening. It hadn't gone well. Neither set of parents had accepted what they were told. Especially when they found out that it was both of the boys. They assumed that they were feeding off each other; that it was a phase that they would both grow out of. They didn't.

Taylor collected as much money as he could by selling his designs, and Jax squirreled away as many spare coins as he could earn through working odd jobs. One evening, they both stuffed some clothes into bags and made their way as close to the Big Apple as they could afford.

They are more comfortable to be themselves now; to be at ease with their sexuality. Taylor, with his sandy blond hair and amber eyes, makes friends far more easily than Jax. He's more confident, almost flamboyant, making for some rather interesting ventures out.

Jax, however, likes to spend more time in his own company. He loves to be alone in the dance studio, sweating it out. The grueling moves almost punish his muscles, making them work to the maximum. He likes that feeling, though. As a dancer, he is extremely critical of his own body, constantly examining his features to be sure that they are good enough.

Now that the show is nearing very quickly, Jax is having serious issues with the lines of his figure, feeling certain that people will be judging his physique and writing crude reviews about how he needs to work on his toning.

He feels that his looks aren't as striking as his best friends. Jaxon is extremely handsome but feels self-conscious about his smaller stature and his Asian features. Growing up in Ohio with his Thai heritage had always made him feel like an outsider. He's so thankful that he has always had Tay.

"Oh please!" Taylor whines, snapping Jax back to reality. "You did promise. I need you!"

"You don't need me," he says, pulling away from Taylor and leaning forward onto his knees. "You have plenty of beautiful friends that could do it."

Taylor reaches to pinch the skin on his arm with a playful twist. "*You* are my beautiful friend, you idiot. I want you there."

Jumping up, Taylor makes his way over to one of the many dress forms dotted around the apartment among the yards and yards of fabric. Jax has lost count of the number of times that he's accidentally stepped on a pin during the night, while casually padding through the place for a glass of water.

"Look," he says while dramatically pointing at an almost complete outfit. "This was made for you! This is you!"

Jax can't help but laugh at the person that he's closest too in the world, standing theatrically, glaring at him with pleading eyes.

"Fine." He stands up and grabs a clean towel off the clothes rack near the open window. "Just for you."

**

The late afternoon sun streams through the floor to ceiling windows of Jasper's loft in SoHo. Pools of light gather on the old oak floors and reflect off the camera lenses and tripods, bathing Jasper in warmth. He sits cross-legged amidst the camera bags and equipment strewn about in a semi-organized mess.

Jasper runs his tattooed hand through his wavy dark brown hair. He feels up the back of his neck, almost having forgotten about the undercut he got a few days ago. His fingers travel to his ear and he twists at his multitude of silver hoops as he scans the floor, making a decision on what to pack. Jasper needs to make an impression at the shoot tomorrow. He knows how important this reality show is to Blackwood's reputation. Jasper does not want Noah and Luca to regret choosing him to photograph the finale runway show and the winning designs. He doesn't want to let the family down.

Jasper sighs and grabs his beer off the coffee table. The bottle is starting to sweat, and he finishes off the last of it. Letting the family down, it's what Jasper is always worried about. He's always felt like a bit of a black sheep. Noah's brilliance has always been the shining light in his family, his parents so proud of his Harvard degree and incredible business sense.

Jasper has never favored the mainstream, listening to underground bands, creating edgy art, and struggling through school. He's always been different from his family. He refuses to wear his family's designs, choosing instead to frequent thrift shops to create his own look... pushing boundaries. Jasper got his first tattoo at sixteen, hiding it from his parents. At eighteen, he started expanding his body art, designing most of his own tattoos.

Thankfully when his parents gave him his first camera at thirteen, he fell in love with the way he could express himself through photography. It certainly wasn't his grades that got him into NYU, but his portfolio was impressive, and the prestige of having a Blackwood attend the NYU photography program had assured his acceptance. Jasper excelled there, and he was pleased with his work. His parents were very happy with his accomplishments in photography, and even more so at his decision to work at Blackwood. Jasper, as hard as he has worked to be his own person, still feels like he's not being true to himself.

As he contemplates this, he rubs his eyes in frustration and gets up to get another beer. As he walks toward the kitchen, the door buzzes. Jasper knows who it is; he is expecting her. He swings open the heavy industrial door and takes in the beautiful woman standing there.

"Aunt Bella," he says. "You came."

"Of course, I did, my beautiful boy!" Bella coos, pulling Jasper into a tight hug. She runs her hands down his back, then along his shoulder and bicep. "Jasper, you get more muscles every time I see you. I think you're working out too much!"

"You always say that." He pulls back and looks at Bella. "And thank you for coming. I know you must be exhausted after your flight."

"Don't be ridiculous, sweetheart, I slept on the plane," she says as she walks in, heels clicking on the wood floors. "I'm so sorry that we couldn't meet before I left. I've been worried about you."

Bella kicks off her heels and curls up on the well-worn, deep leather chair, as Jasper pours her a glass of wine and grabs his beer. He sits across from her on his retro corduroy couch.

"I've forgotten how much I love your loft." Bella sips her wine. "Leave it to you to make something stunning from used furniture and thrift shop treasures." She sweeps her hand in front of her. "This brick and the high ceilings! No wonder you wanted to stay here."

"Yeah, I love it here," Jasper replies. He knows that his aunt is making small talk to help him feel more comfortable before their conversation. "I'm grateful that Dad agreed to let me keep it, but I know he expected me to live in the Tower after I graduated."

Bella hums in agreement and leans forward with her wine glass in hand. "Now Jasper, tell me how you're feeling about everything. Last time we met I felt like I did most of the talking."

"No, Aunt Bella. You've been helping me so much," Jasper says peeling the label off his beer. He stops and looks at her. "You're the only one I'm comfortable talking to about this."

"And I'm always here, sweetheart. You and I will always have our special bond." Bella leans back and slings one long leg over the arm of the chair. "Now talk to me."

"I've been thinking a lot about what you said," Jasper starts. "And you're right. All those girls that I dated, it wasn't for me. It was because I didn't want to disappoint my parents...the family." Bella nods as he continues. "They were all beautiful girls, they really were! But I just never felt an attraction to them. It was more like friendship or companionship I guess."

Bella sets her glass on the coffee table, on top of a stack of photography books. "First of all, you could never disappoint us. You are so amazing, Jasper. From the time you were a little boy we were all charmed by your free spirit and joy."

Jasper interrupts, "You were charmed, Auntie. You've always understood me. My parents love me, but never really got me. The real me."

Bella smiles fondly. "Okay let me ask you this. All those girls that you dated, were you sexually attracted to them?'

"Well I did fool around a bit with them, but it never felt right, you know? And I could never, ummm finish." Jasper's cheeks begin to feel warm.

"So, have there been men that you've been attracted to? In a sexual way?"

"There have been. Yes. But I never acted on it." Jasper meets his aunt's eyes.

"Okay." Bella takes a deep breath. "So, I've always had a sexual attraction to both men and women. I've never fought against that; I've always known that I'm bisexual and I'm fine with that," she continues. "It seems fairly obvious that you are only sexually attracted to men. And you need to allow yourself to be comfortable with that." Jasper closes his eyes and takes in what Bella is saying. "It's okay to be gay Jasper, it's who you are. Stop fighting with yourself. You are my amazing, smart, talented handsome boy. And you are gay. And I love all of who you are."

Tears start to fill Jasper's eyes. He looks at his aunt. "But I'm afraid of what Mother and Father will think, and Grandfather."

Bella smiles. "Your grandfather will not bat an eye, Jasper. He's been working with gay designers for years and has many friends in the LGBTQ community." She takes the last sip of her wine. "As for my brother, well Alexander is a bit more conservative that's true. However, he has never judged me for my sexuality. For my choice in partners, yes." She rolls her eyes. "But let's face it, I've never been the best in that area, I admit it."

Jasper laughs. "Aunt Bella, what would I do without you?"

"Live a celibate life, I suppose." Bella strolls over to pour herself more wine. "And I just can't allow that. There's too much for you to explore."

"How do I tell them?" Jasper's teeth tug at his lip ring and he furrows his brow.

"Jasper, don't put so much pressure on yourself." She leans her elbow on the marble counter and brushes her long dark hair over her shoulder. "Just allow yourself to be open to possibilities first. Give yourself a chance to accept who you are. You'll know when you're ready to come out. It might be tomorrow; it might be when you meet someone special." Bella walks over and sits beside her nephew. "It's going to be okay, sweetheart." She softly brushes Jasper's cheek. "Our family will surprise you. You're going to be just fine."

Jasper sits up taller and breathes deeply. "I'm ready. I'm so ready to be who I'm meant to be. Ready to be strong. Ready to love who I'm meant to love."

Bella pulls him into an embrace as he leans into her, resting his head on her shoulder. "You're ready, Jasper, and I'm so proud of you." She cradles his cheeks in her hands. "Now let's make some dinner. I'm starving and I want to hear all about tomorrow."

"Sounds good to me." Jasper kisses his aunt on the cheek. "Thank you, Aunt Bella."

Bella kisses his nose and they walk to the kitchen. "I'm always here, Jasper."

Chapter 5

As the black Mercedes S-Class sits in Midtown traffic, Luca checks his Audemars Piguet watch, fidgeting in his seat. He presses the button lowering the privacy screen and leans forward a little, "How much longer, Tony?" he asks the driver.

"Hopefully we'll arrive in twenty minutes, Mr. Blackwood."

Luca nods and raises the screen again. Eight by ten full-colored headshots and the accompanying biographies of the Aspire to Design contestants sit on his lap and on the seat between him and Jasper.

"So, these are the finalists?" Jasper asks while looking through the pile. He glances at Luca and sees one of the designers smiling from the glossy page in his hand. "Woah," Jasper says.

"Yeah, Woah," Luca replies as he hands over the headshot to Jasper. "He seems really young."

Jasper scans the photo and grabs the biography to skim. "Really young and really hot!"

Luca looks at his cousin with confusion for a moment, then begins to gather the papers and photographs into a pile, placing them back into his bag. "Yeah well, they're all very talented," he says as he massages his temple.

Jasper grabs Luca's shoulder. "Hey, are you okay? I thought I was supposed to be the nervous one."

Luca turns his head and looks at Jasper, letting out a sigh. "I'm alright, just a lot on my mind. I can't fuck this up. I need to focus so that I can choose the designer that will be best for Blackwood."

"You'll pick the right one, Luca. I just hope that these designers have something new to show." Jasper continues, "I'm dying for the company to put out something that *I* actually want to wear."

Luca laughs. "Your aesthetic is definitely different from the lines we've traditionally put out, Jasper. And I agree we need something to appeal to a newer, trendier market." He pats his cousin's thigh. "So, are you ready? This is a big day for you!"

"Yeah, I feel ready. I think that I've prepared well, and I'm actually more excited than nervous." Jasper gives Luca a big smile. "This is my chance to prove to the family that I can be an asset to the company."

"Good for you," Luca says as he tightens the knot of his silk tie and smooths the lapels of his slate-colored pinstripe suit. "I'm proud of you, you know." He peers out the tinted window. "Looks like we're just about there."

**

Backstage is absolute chaos. The final three designers rush around, pinning and tacking any last-minute adjustments to the models' outfits. Taylor is looking over Jax's shoulder at his reflection gazing back at him from the mirror. The makeup artist is applying a dusky shadow to Jax's lid.

"Just smoke it out a little bit more. Yeah, that looks great," Taylor directs the makeup artist as he fluffs Jax's newly dyed hair. "God this looks so good on you, baby. You were made to be a blond."

"I don't even recognize myself." Jax tips his chin up and turns his head, taking in his new look. "Tay, I'm absolutely terrified. What if I fall? What if I completely fuck this up for you?".

Taylor turns the chair around to face him. He leans down so that he can look Jax directly into his eyes, which are adorned with bright blue contact lenses. "Jax, you're a dancer and the most graceful person I know. You're not going to fall."

"How are you so calm?" Jax asks while wiping his sweaty palms with a towel.

"Because I've worked my ass off." Taylor helps Jax up from the makeup chair. "I've done everything I could possibly do. I'm proud of my designs, and if I don't win the contract with Blackwood, well, I'll be okay. This show has gotten my work out there. I'm on my way whether I win or not." He looks Jax up and down, pulling a tiny loose thread off his shoulder. "Perfect."

"I admire you so much, Tay. You're so confident and positive all the time. I'm so honored to be your best friend. I'm going to work that runway like I actually know what I'm doing." Jax takes a deep breath.

"Don't make me cry, now! Then *you'll* start, and this gorgeous face will be ruined." Taylor puts his hand on Jax's lower back and guides him to line up with the other models.

Several assistants nervously elbow through the crowded area backstage. "Five minutes! Five minutes everyone! Models, be ready to walk!"

"This is it! Ready everyone?" Taylor adjusts the fabric on his models, smoothing here and tucking there. He turns to Jax. "You ready?" Jax nods nervously and takes a deep breath.

**

The crew is bustling around making last-minute adjustments during the commercial break. Jasper has his camera in hand, checking the lighting on the runway. He squats down to grab another lens from his camera bag, thick thighs and muscular ass straining against his perfectly fitted slacks. A gorgeous blonde woman stretches out her long legs, the four-inch stilettos making her legs seem even longer. She leans over to Luca, whom she is sitting next to at the judges' table.

"Who is that!" The former supermodel tips her head towards Jasper. She is clearly looking him up and down. "My god, he has tattoos. I am so into tattoos."

"That, Michaela," Luca leans over and whispers to her, "is my cousin Jasper Blackwood. And before you ask for his number, he's only twenty-one which would make him half..."

Michaela cuts him off. "Don't say it, Luca, that would make him just a few...ish years younger than me." She smirks, running her tongue along her blood-red lips. "How the hell can all the men in your family be so damn gorgeous?"

Luca smiles and shakes his head. "Just like my Aunt Bella, aren't you Michaela?" Always eyeing up the young and pretty ones."

Michaela meets Luca's eyes. "Well you're young and pretty Luca, but you're already taken." She obviously hasn't heard that he's single again.

Luca's smile falters at the reminder of his fucked-up life, as the producer gives them the two-minute countdown. "Okay, here we go."

The runway setup is fantastic. Everything is white, save for the Blackwood logo projected above the runway, the elaborate 'B' in black.

Luca is impressed. They clearly spared no expense with this show. No wonder the ratings have been so good.

Each of the three finalists will showcase their final collection, which consists of four designs. The judges will score them based on the originality of the designs, potential to transition into wearable looks, the precision of execution, and most importantly, how each designer has used their concept to convey their message to the world.

The show's host stands on the catwalk as the commercial break ends, and they go live. "Welcome back everyone. It's been a ratings breaking season for us here at Aspire to Design. You've all gotten to know and love our designers and their unprecedented work this season." Images of the three finalists appear below the Blackwood logo, then fade out. "This is the moment we've been waiting for! Our final three will showcase their collections."

The host gestures to the judges as a spotlight sweeps over them. "Our esteemed judges this season will be scoring the designs. Joining them is Luca Blackwood, head of marketing and photography for our sponsor. He is the grandson of iconic designer, Dalton Blackwood." Luca nods and lifts his elegant hand in acknowledgment.

"As you all know," the host continues, "this season, for the first time in Aspire to Design history, our winner will be offered a position as head designer for Blackwood. His or her collection will be the inspiration for their Spring Collection." The host begins to step to the side. "Now let's turn our attention...," he gestures with a sweep of his arm, "...to the runway."

The electronic dance music starts, being played live by a popular DJ set off to the side. White spotlights sweep the stage. Jasper is poised with his camera, ready to go.

The first designer is Alexis Dorsey. Her models start their walk. All four are stunningly tall women. Two are African American, one looks to be Latina, and one is a brunette Caucasian. They are wrapped in exquisite colorful fabrics of African inspired patterns. The designs include an evening look, two dresses, and a pants suit with a long, draping top. Each design has coiled patterned fabric wrapped around the neckline area. The models walk in impossibly high heels.

Luca jots some notes down. The looks are beautiful; however, he doesn't feel they express anything new, and has concerns about whether the looks would transition well to a broad market.

The next designer's models approach the runway. This designer simply calls himself Xavier. All four models are attractive men of different ethnicities. Two are wearing formal suits, two in more casual dress wear. The cut and fabric choices are amazing, but Luca is disappointed. The designer's creativity seems to have been lost in his attempt to appeal to

Blackwood. Luca is looking for something new and different.

The final designs will be those of Taylor King. Luca feels a bit nervous as he remembers that he is the youngest designer of the three, having just finished fashion school. He has low expectations that he will be inspired.

Taylor's first and second models step onto the runway, both are men, and Luca raises his eyebrows. The designs are not what he expected. The fabrics have different textures in various shades of white, tan, and black.

This first model has broad shoulders and an athletic build. He is wearing a casual suit made from shimmery black fabric. The cut is loose and almost baggy, but somehow accentuates his build. A low-cut off-white sheer tee, mid-calf lace-up athletic boots, and raw rope worn as necklaces complete the look.

The second outfit consists of a skirt with a split hemline in off-white, cut from a crisp fabric. The jacket is a more traditionally masculine shape, but the designer has used a sheer draping fabric. Underneath, the male model wears a black flowing tank with a high neckline and high heeled black combat boots.

A woman of average height is the third to step onto the runway. Her hair is shaved on the sides, and her long blonde mohawk is braided. She is not wearing makeup. The pants she wears are high waisted black silk and covered in silver zippers. The tan top is cropped and well fitted, not overly tight. She wears no jewelry, only a rope around her waist as a low-slung belt. Her black combat boots are laced almost up to her knees.

Luca sits back in his chair. This kid is challenging gender norms. Impressive and risky, considering these designs are incredibly different than anything Blackwood has ever done. He expects the fourth model to have started walking by now, but there seems to be a minor delay. Luca impatiently waits.

He finally sees a model wearing all white turn onto the runway. Luca freezes. He can't seem to lower his eyes from the man's face. He is the most beautiful person that Luca has ever seen. His blond hair is tucked behind his left ear, the rest sweeping across his brow and framing his high cheekbones. He appears to be of Asian descent, his monolids swept with smokey shadow that accentuates his almond eyes. His lips are his most defining feature, so full and lush adorned with a shiny pink gloss. The man is small. Probably Luca's height, around five foot eight, but his presence is remarkable.

The final design is an asymmetrically cut white jacket with zippers that falls to mid-thigh. As he walks, or slinks, down the runway, the stunning man rolls his shoulders back. This causes the perfectly cut jacket to drape behind him, showcasing his shoulders and the tank underneath. The shirt dips low, is white and completely sheer with fully cutout sides. The model's dark brown nipples peek through, and Luca can see a silver ring dangling from each. His washboard abs are completely on display. The tank falls below the waistband of the white pants. Although the pants are not fitted, the man's firm thighs and ample ass are visible as he walks. The laces from mid-calf, thick-soled white high tops swing side to side, as do the heavy silver chains around his neck and dangling earrings. The blond reaches the end of the runway and before he turns, his eyes meet Lucas directly. The model blushes and Luca feels butterflies in his stomach and a stirring in his groin.

The models stand on the runway alongside the designers as they wait for the judges' final look at their garments. Luca and the others walk up the steps for a closer look at the quality of the designs. They are all, as expected, impeccable. Luca approaches the angel in white and stops in front of him. He brushes his hand down the sleeve of the white coat, inspecting the seams.

"Taylor, I'd like to see this without the jacket," Michaela requests.

"Of course," Taylor responds. "Jaxon, will you take the jacket off please?" Jax nods and removes the top layer of the outfit.

"Stunning. This is my favorite look, Taylor," Michaela continues. "Your choice of accessories is perfect as usual." She sweeps her hand toward his other models as she speaks.

The other judges voice their agreement, as Alexis and Xavier look nervous.

Luca looks at Taylor and before he can stop himself, he gently runs his fingers up Jax's arm. "Thank you, Jax, you can put the jacket back on." Jaxon nods and looks down at his sneakers as the pink rises in his cheeks.

"Alright, Taylor, Alexis, and Xavier. Well done. Your work is stunning. You all have outdone yourselves." The host addresses the designers. "Now it's time for the judges to make their decision."

Luca joins the other judges and they speak in low voices, comparing the notes they had taken. He then turns back to the designers.

"It appears that we have reached a unanimous decision," Luca announces. "So now, I am pleased to announce that the winning designer is... Taylor King."

Taylor drops to his knees and covers his face, tears streaming down his cheeks. Alexis and Xavier approach him with congratulations. Jax kneels beside him and takes him in his arms, whispering into his ear "You did it, Tay. I'm so proud of you, you did it."

Luca looks away quickly, surprised at the intimate gesture. He sees Jasper capturing the moment with his camera. Jax and Taylor stand up, and Taylor gives his thanks to everyone. Luca approaches him and shakes his hand. "Taylor I'm pleased to offer you a position as a designer for Blackwood. I am blown away by your designs, and I look forward to working with you."

Taylor's smile brightens his entire face. "Thank you, Mr. Blackwood, I am truly honored."

"Please call me Luca. Now I believe that we have a photoshoot to do for the live stream." Luca gestures toward Jasper. "My cousin Jasper will be taking the photographs. Now let's go get set up."

Luca glances at Jax once again, and their eyes meet. This time, Jax doesn't look away.

**

"Annnnnnd cut! Well done everyone," the director shouts. "Five minutes until the after show live stream starts though, people. Get moving and get ready."

He starts to usher the crew around to change positions on the set, pointing in different directions for cameras to move to. Makeup artists and stylists spring into action, grabbing their bags and brushes.

"That went well," Michaela says, slumping into a seat. She pauses to allow one of her staff members to touch up her foundation, while another uses a comb to tease some strands of hair back into place. "Don't you think, Luca?"

Upon getting no response, she swivels her chair towards him, but Luca is focused on the congratulatory group gathering around the winner. Tutting, she turns back to her stylist.

"Mr. Blackwood?" A voice snaps Luca from his thoughts, his shoulders jerking in a slight jump. "Oh, I'm sorry, Sir."

"Huh?" Luca looks down towards the young lady standing next to him who looks increasingly impatient. "My apologies." He follows where she guides him and sits down at a newly placed stage block as instructed. "Here?"

She nods at him and rushes off to place some other people.

"Three minutes!" the director shouts above the bustling noise. "Let's get moving."

Taylor gets swiftly placed beside Luca, and they watch everyone rush around. Two new presenters arrive, and staff bustle to place microphones on their outfits, while others preen with their hair.

"Congratulations again," Luca says to a flustered Taylor who is fanning himself with a bit of paper that he's grabbed from the clipboard of a passing runner.

Smiling sweetly back at him, Taylor puffs his cheeks. "Thank you. Like seriously, I can't believe it."

Luca pats his knee. "You really deserve it. Your designs are incredible."

"Oh, I absolutely agree," Michaela says, positioning herself on the other side of Taylor. "You have done exceptionally well."

Luca rolls his eyes, a slight grin forming as he watches Michaela place her hand on Taylor's. He politely pulls it away, nodding his gratitude.

"One minute!" The director's voice is agitated and impatient as he waves his hands around. "Places everyone."

The last of the guests that attended the show get hurriedly shuffled out of the side exits, leaving the judges, designers, models, and a few others left and ready.

Everybody gets prepared as they are counted in and the red lights on the cameras start to shine, indicating that the show has started. The presenters recite their well-rehearsed scripts, mentioning how grateful the production is for the amazing sponsorship from Blackwood, and how wonderful it is to have members of the family in attendance this evening.

From that, they go straight to Luca who gives a very impressive thank you to everyone that has contributed to the production of the show, his fellow judges, and most of all to the designers and the models that made the show amazing.

Jasper watches his cousin from behind the camera with nothing but admiration. He monitors how Luca professionally adjusts his glasses while talking, his hand gestures displaying the confidence of someone who has been in the business for a while. He marvels at how well he presents himself in his specially tailored suit, his black hair swept perfectly away from his eyes. Jasper takes a few photos of him to capture the moment.

After Luca finishes, the female presenter turns her attention to the two losing designers. She offers her commiserations to them both, and reassures them that by being a finalist, many doors will be open for them in the future. They both talk about how much they have enjoyed participating, and what an amazing opportunity it has been for them. She asks them a little about their designs, and what has inspired them, a round of applause from everyone left filling the air after they've finished talking.

As the noise settles, the male presenter approaches Taylor, congratulating him on his win. Taylor's cheeks flush crimson while he mumbles that it still hasn't become a reality in his mind yet.

"So," the presenter says, heading toward Taylor's four models, "tell us a little about your styling, and why you have pushed the boundaries of norms."

Jasper starts to take some snaps of the winner, zooming in with his lens, taking in the beauty of this designer and his stunning work. He finds himself smiling at how attractive Taylor King is, the words of his Aunt Bella ringing through his mind. She is right, he knows it for sure.

Luca, out of frame for the cameras whirring away nearby, steps back and watches as

Taylor points out all of the details on each of the individual outfits, describing the intricate work that he's put in with his team, and the meaning behind it all.

When they get to the blond, Luca is completely mesmerized, his eyes fixed on Taylor's hands pulling at the material that's clinging to the lines of his defined body. Luca can't help but watch as Taylor pulls the sheer top up a little, exposing the skin underneath, causing Luca to gasp a bit too loudly. The cameraman turns to look at him.

Gesturing with a wave that he's fine, Luca pulls his phone out of his pocket to distract himself for a moment. His stomach flips when he sees a text from Misun. He hasn't spoken to her in the month since they split, so he's completely bewildered by what she could possibly want. He doesn't open the message, but he can see it displayed on his screen.

We need to talk.

Sighing, his heart thudding in his chest, Luca flicks the button to darken the screen and thrusts his phone back into his jacket pocket. He can't deal with her right now. He had no reason to deal with her ever again.

He virtually growls at himself, annoyed that he let his own emotions start to surface again. A hiss pulls him from his anger. "Mr. Blackwood...the photoshoot."

Turning to see the same agitated assistant glaring at him, obviously annoyed, he realizes that it was nearly his cue to get back in front of the cameras. Pulling himself together and pushing Misun to the darkest depths of his mind again, he makes his way towards the newly set backdrop.

Michaela links arms with him as the judges strike various respectable poses for the cameras. Luca winks at Jasper, who's taking his job quite seriously, ducking and twisting into angles to capture his best shots.

When they're done, the designers join them for a few more clicks of the camera, followed by more shots of Taylor alone. The live photoshoot streams to many fans around the country who are eager to get a glimpse of the exquisite new designs, as well as members of the famous Blackwood family.

"Okay," the female presenter suddenly pipes up from the sidelines. "How about we have Luca posing with the models, considering his name *is* on the wall there."

Before Luca can even answer, the other judges have been ushered away, and the models are quickly instructed into place. He soon becomes aware of the blond standing directly next to him, his neck tilted so that his head is extremely close to Luca's.

His face drains pale as his nose soaks up the aroma of Jax's cologne, mixed with copious amounts of hair sprays and gels. Glancing to the side, Luca is stunned by his features up close. He is truly beautiful.

Chapter 6

Noah stands in front of the towering windows of his new office. It's a bit overcast, but he can still take in the view of the bustling streets below. He is still getting used to the fact that this is his office now, the CEO's office. He's spent his childhood coming in here when it was his father sitting in the tall leather chair. Alexander would take him and Jasper over to the windows and lift them up to show them the skyline.

"Boys, look at the view of New York City!" Alexander would say. "When I was your age, Grandfather Dalton and Grandma Mina brought Aunt Bella, Uncle Maxwell, and me to live here all the way from London."

"That's so far away, isn't it Father?" Jasper asked.

"Yes, it is very far away. We flew on a big airplane for a very long time to get here." Alexander continued his story. "All of our toys and even our furniture had to travel over the ocean on a ship to get to us."

The boys were always fascinated by stories of their family's immigration to New York.

Noah comes back to the present and turns around to face Luca, who is standing on the opposite side of the enormous mahogany desk.

"So, everything went fantastic with the show." Luca gestures to the eleven by fourteen photographs neatly sorted on the desk. "You can see from these shots that Jasper did an amazing job with the photography."

The photographs are from the runway, as well as from the post-show live stream. Various creative angles and filters make a change from the usual formal, boring shots.

"He did," Noah responds, picking up a few of the photographs for a closer look. "I am so impressed with him."

Luca looks at his cousin. "Make sure that you tell him that, Noah. Remember how young he is, and how much he looks up to you."

Noah rubs his brow and returns the photographs he's holding to his desk, only to pick up another for closer inspection. "You're right. I don't tell him enough how much I respect him. Lord knows he didn't hear it from our father. He was always too busy worrying about preparing me to run the company."

"Jasper is coming into his own, and starting to gain a bit of confidence," Luca says as he sits down, removing his black-rimmed glasses and placing them next to the photographs. "I try to encourage him the best I can, but it will mean so much more coming from his brother."

Noah nods and sits down as well. "The ratings from the show and the live stream were through the roof." He leans back, locking his hands behind his head. "America loves Taylor. His personality is infectious, and I couldn't be more impressed with his designs. You chose well."

"The direction he went was really like nothing we've done before," Luca says. "He didn't sell out trying to gain the position."

Noah nods in agreement. "Jasper has always said we need to change things up. Try to appeal to a clientele more like him. Now that I see these designs, I completely agree with him." Noah looks closely at one of the photographs and turns it around to show Luca. "Who is this model?"

Luca's eyes widen as he takes in the image of the gorgeous blond. "His name is Jaxon Somsi." He leans back. "He's not a model, he's a dancer and he's Taylor's best friend, maybe even his partner. That's all that I know."

"Well, we need him." Noah tosses the photo down and grabs another showing Jax. "When Bella sees these, she's going to want him. He's a completely different representation of masculinity than Jayce."

"I agree, Noah, but I'm not sure that he'll be interested." Luca walks over to the built-in bar and pours himself some water from the crystal carafe. "He absolutely slayed the runway, but he seemed quite self-conscious during the photoshoot with Jasper, and..."

A knock on Noah's door causes the men to stop their conversation.

"Come in," Noah says melodically. The door cracks open and Taylor sticks his wavy, sand-colored head in the room, a brilliant smile on his handsome face.

"Oh, I'm sorry, am I interrupting? Your secretary just told me to knock," Taylor asks, as his smile falters a bit.

"No, no Taylor, not at all. I told him to send you right in when you came to see me." Noah guides him into the spacious office.

"Luca, hi, great to see you! Wow, Mr. Blackwood, your office is unreal!" Taylor's enthusiasm is contagious.

"Call me Noah, and yes, I'm still getting used to it myself!" Noah gestures at his desk. "Take a look at these, Taylor. Luca and I were just discussing how well you're going to fit in here at Blackwood."

Taylor scans the photographs on the desk. "These came out amazing. Better than I ever imagined!" He picks up an image of his best friend. "Jax looks stunning, I still can't get over seeing him like this!"

"Yes, we were discussing Jaxon as well. Please, have a seat." Noah gestures towards another expensive leather chair. "Are you getting settled in? I hope that everyone has been welcoming."

"Everyone has been wonderful. I met Harrison and he gave me a tour of my design studio." Taylor is bubbling with excitement. "I never imagined that I would have a space like that. It's like a dream! The technology, the worktables, the equipment! I've been sewing in my cramped apartment for so long; it's a bit overwhelming.

Noah and Luca exchange glances and they both laugh.

"Well, you have earned it, Taylor. We were just discussing how amazed we are by your collection," Luca tells him. "We look forward to expanding it and taking the company in a new direction."

Noah continues where Luca left off. "Luca informs me that you have an interesting background. You're from Ohio, correct?"

Taylor nods as he responds. "Yes, Jax and I are from a small town. We left when we were teenagers and never looked back."

"Well, people are fascinated by you Taylor, and they love your work." Taylor blushes at Noah's complement. "The photographs that Jasper took turned out fantastic as you can see." Noah hands a few to Taylor, who nods. "We've decided that we are going to do a big spread in Blackwood Magazine introducing you and featuring these photographs."

"What?" Taylor glances between Luca and Noah. "Are you sure? I thought it would just be the designs featured!"

"People want to know more about you, Taylor," Luca tells him. "The show just piqued their interest. And let's face it, you are gorgeous enough to be a model yourself."

Taylor blushes as Noah continues, "I'd like to learn more about you. We will all be working closely together. We're done for the day. Let's continue this over drinks, if you're free."

"Yeah, that sounds great." Taylor has a look on his face that's a bit bewildered.

"Luca, you'll join, yes?" Luca nods, and Noah reaches for his phone. "I'll call Jasper. I'd like him there to talk about the magazine spread. Do you think that Jaxon will join us? He seems like a big part of your life, and I think people would love to learn more about your relationship. Especially since he is featured in the photographs."

Taylor glances at the clock. "He should be done with his dance classes within the hour. I'll text him. He can never say no to me, so I'm sure he'll be there."

"Perfect," Noah says, standing from his chair.

Luca tries to ignore the butterflies in his stomach, reaching for his glasses from the desk. "Yeah, perfect."

**

Luca fiddles with the placemat, pulling off little scraps of paper and rolling them in between his thumb and finger until Jasper sets a bottle of beer in front of him.

"Shit, what's up with your face?" he says, perching on a stool beside him.

Noah appears soon after and joins them. "What's going on?"

"Nothing." Jasper sips his drink. "I just asked Luca what the matter was."

Looking at his cousin, Noah can sense a little agitation from him, almost nervousness. He looks him up and down. "Wait. Did you go home and change?"

Luca's cheeks flush crimson as he straightens his black leather jacket, wiping his clammy palms on his fresh jeans. "Yeah, well, I wanted to get out of my suit."

"But." Jasper leans in closer to him. "You've put contacts in instead of your glasses." Turning to Noah, he shrugs. "Told you, something is up with him."

Noah squints over the small round silver table they're sitting at. "You're right. He has!"

"Fuck off you two." Luca angles away from them, grabbing his bottle.

"Oohhh okay," Jasper teases. "That's rather uncouth for a high-flying New York businessman!"

The brothers continue to laugh, when Taylor appears at the table. "Am I interrupting something?" He sits beside Noah. "Is it a private joke?"

Noah shakes his head, composing himself, a sly grin still poised on his lips. "No, it's fine, sorry. We're just having a little fun."

"At my expense!" Luca scoffs, causing Jasper and Noah to chuckle again.

"Sorry, Luca," Jasper says, patting him on the arm. "I think that it's great that you're putting yourself back out there. You know, after..."

"Yeah," Noah says more seriously, "I agree. Forget her. Find yourself a nice girl that will treat you right."

Luca suddenly feels increasingly uncomfortable at this conversation. Even more so than when they were mocking his change of clothes. Yes, he had gone home to freshen up. That's all it was, a quick shower and outfit swap. Nothing to draw attention to.

Taylor leans towards Noah and whispers, "I'm guessing he's been shit on by a girl?"

Noah nods his head. "Yes. Recently too."

"Okay, okay," Luca interrupts the gossip and puts on his more professional demeanor. "We aren't here to talk about me and my crap relationship skills."

"Hi," another voice says from behind Luca, making the others look up. Luca remains staring at the drink in his hand but mumbles a greeting in return.

Out of the corner of his eye, he watches Jaxon make his way around the table to sit on a stool next to Taylor. He notes that Jax grasps hold of Taylor's fingers on his lap, while picking up the spare bottle of beer in his other hand.

The group of men talk, yet it seems a distant noise to Luca as he finds himself closely fixating his gaze on the newest member of the table.

Jaxon's blond hair is less dramatically placed, the gels and sprays washed out, leaving it softly settled on his brow. His face is natural with no makeup at all, yet his skin still glows almost perfectly, the silver metal of his dangling earring reflecting on his chiseled jawline.

"Luca?"

Startling himself, Luca becomes aware that Jax is staring right back at him. He gives him a gentle smile, and Luca clears his throat. "Hmm?"

"The photos," Noah repeats. "Jasper did a good job of them."

"Oh," Luca says, sitting up straighter. "Yes, they're amazing. You should come and look at them some time." He realizes that he's still looking in Jax's direction and glances around flustered. "If you like?"

"Yeah, we will," Taylor answers. "I would love to see your work again, Jasper." He winks at the young photographer. "I'll come over to see you with Jax so he can check them out himself, yeah?"

Jasper finds a confidence with men that he didn't realize he had and clinks his bottle on Taylor's. "Sure, I look forward to seeing you."

Noah's puzzled look distracts the attention away from Jax for a moment. "Um, so," he says, "I hope that you settle in well with Blackwood."

Taylor flashes a flirty glance in Jasper's direction. "I'm sure that I will."

Jasper grins and asks a passing server for another round of drinks, when a lady in a smart tweed suit appears. "Pardon me for interrupting," she says in a well-mannered and upmarket tone. "My name Glenda Montrose. I do an entertainment column for The Express."

"Yes, I've heard of your articles," Noah says, bowing his head politely. "Can we help you with something?"

Glenda guffaws in an exaggerated way, throwing her head back in largely faked laughter. Luca and Noah glance at each other.

"Nothing bad, I presume?" She flirts with Noah. "I like to write honest and read-worthy items." Turning to Luca, she taps him lightly on the shoulder. "How fantastic were you on Aspire to Design? I watched it all."

"Thank you," Luca says with a smile. "I was just doing my job."

"And you!" she exclaims in Taylor's direction, ignoring Luca's response. "How incredibly amazing are your designs? You are going to be a star."

Jasper does a pretend vomit face to Noah out of view at the sheer over-the-top way she lays on the compliments. Noah stifles a laugh.

"I'm sorry," he says, clearing his throat. "We are just having a bit of an informal get-together. Is there anything that we can do for you?"

"Oh, my apologies." Glenda starts rooting through her beige designer handbag and pulls out her phone, before pointing to Luca and Taylor. "Is it possible to have a photo for tomorrow's column of you both? Just so I can get a little one over on the other columnists. You know how it is."

Luca looks at Noah, who shrugs and tilts his head. "Sure," he says to her. "Where do you want me?"

She laughs again in flirty insinuation and instructs him to stand by Taylor. When Luca is in place, she opens her camera and holds it up towards them.

She lowers it again and frowns. "Hmmm, we can't have this without the model too." She waves her hand at Jax, who obliges and leans in towards Luca.

Her shutter sound makes a couple of clicks, and she says her goodbyes. The men all look at each other with stunned yet amused looks on their faces as she bustles away.

Chapter 7

Luca's sigh echoes around his office as he leans his head in his hands. He realizes that the extra shots that he'd been persuaded to do after copious amounts of beer hadn't been the greatest idea ever.

The gentle tap on his door makes him look up, his assistant entering before the grimacing expression on her face says it all. "Oh my," she says, setting a cup of coffee and some painkillers in front of Luca. "You look like shit."

"Yes, thanks for that, Sacha," he groans. "Like I need reminding!"

She laughs, putting down the morning newspapers beside him, and heads to the nearby bar to pour him a glass of water.

Passing it to him, she pauses to watch him swallow the tablets, taking in his disheveled state. "What time did you go to bed? Have you even *been* to bed yet?"

Luca forces another big gulp of water, before setting the glass on the coaster. Sacha hands him his coffee knowing that by the look of him, he needs it.

"Um, Luca... Misun called here this morning to speak to you." Sacha uses her words gently, knowing how messed up he's been over recent weeks. "She said she wants to talk to you."

Luca bows his head in his hands again, thinking about his phone buzzing in his pocket the previous evening. She had messaged him then too, but he was too busy enjoying himself with the others and winding down after the stress of the show.

"What does she want from me?" he asks with an inkling of desperation in his voice.

"Probably more money," Sacha sniffs indignantly. "As if she's not had enough from you."

Luca raises his eyes to look at her. Sacha is a friend as well as his personal assistant. He knows that she's right. Misun always did come creeping around when she wanted something. Sacha had lost count of the times that she'd turned up at Luca's office when they were together, putting on the charm until he gave her his credit card.

"Sorry," Sacha says, heading to open the blinds hanging from the big glass windows to let some light in. "I'm just fed up with seeing her use you for her own gains."

"I know, I know," he groans. The desk phone rings, and Luca picks it up, taking a deep breath. "Luca Blackwood."

He speaks for a few seconds before hanging up the receiver. "Noah was checking that I was at work. Apparently, Jasper is nowhere to be seen today."

"I'm not one-bit surprised judging by the state of you this morning," Sacha laughs. "Can I get you anything else, Luca?"

Luca shakes his head. "No thanks. You brought me the papers, right?" She points to the stack next to him. "Oh yeah, great. Noah says that I have to look at the column Glenda wrote. But I'll read it when my eyes can focus a little more."

"Glenda? Isn't she the one from The Express that does those flamboyant articles?" Sacha asks, and Luca nods.

"I'm guessing that it's the same person. We saw her out last night."

"Well, good luck with reading that!" Sacha laughs, heading out of the office and closing the heavy wooden door behind her.

Luca takes a deep breath of dehumidified office air and stands to look out the window. Squinting at the sun, he sees Manhattan traffic bustling below him, horns beeping impatiently as people cross a few seconds after the light. Smiling, he tries to remember as much as he can from the night before.

Even though he hates to admit it, Luca had enjoyed himself. It was the first time that he'd been out to socialize since Misun. It had been

Should We?

nice to relax and forget about things, despite the text that he ignored again. Luca had especially enjoyed the company he'd been with. He always got along well with his cousins, but having Taylor and Jaxon there just made for a more pleasurable evening. A bit too enjoyable judging by how he feels right now.

Taking his seat again, Luca thumbs through the pile of papers until he finds The Express. He takes a few sips of his coffee and slouches back in his seat. Flicking the pages over, he spots Glenda's name and stretches the sheets open.

Gasping, he all but chokes on the remnants of coffee in his mouth as he sits up, placing the paper on his desk in front of him. Staring up at him is a picture of himself and Jax. No Taylor, he was cut out of it, just those two.

He skims the article to see what Glenda has written. She talks about Aspire to Design and how amazing it was, how Taylor will be an amazing asset to Blackwood, and what a breath of fresh air his designs are in today's fashion industry.

She starts to talk about bumping into them the evening before, and how pleasant and sweet they all had been, allowing her to take a photo for her article. The breath catches in Luca's chest as he reads the next line.

I had originally taken a photograph with more members of the group in it, but after looking at it in my office, and this my gorgeous readers, is just my opinion, but don't you think that they make a cute couple? I do!

Luca can feel the sweat beads starting to form on his forehead. He pushes the newspaper away, resting his elbow on the wood and his chin on the palm of his hand.

A knock on the door makes him squeeze his eyes shut. "Noah, if you've come to make fun of me, this really isn't a good time..."

A familiar and soft voice carries across the room making Luca open his eyes quickly. "Sorry to disturb you. Your secretary let me in after some persuasion."

"Jax. Hi," Luca stutters, standing to address him. "What are you doing here?"

"I came to see if you're okay," he says, stepping into the office and closer to the desk. He's wearing a simple black pair of jeans and a black t-shirt. Jax pulls a pair of sunglasses away from his eyes. He glances at the open pages with their picture largely filling a quarter of the paper. "So, you've seen it then?"

Luca nods, his cheeks flushing in embarrassment. "I'm sorry. I'll get them to retract it."

Jax laughs, waving his hands in reassurance. "No, honestly. It's fine. I think that it's a nice picture."

Luca motions him to sit in the chair on the other side of the desk. "Really?"

Jax shrugs his shoulders. "Don't you?"

Luca takes his seat and peers down at the article again. "I didn't look at it too closely."

"Oh, well that's nice!" Jax laughs.

Luca joins him in his laughter, his awkwardness fading slightly. "No, I didn't mean it like that!"

"I'm kidding." Jax smiles. "How's the hangover?"

"I feel like shit!" Luca groans, making Jax chuckle out loud, clutching his stomach. Luca grins. "Coffee?"

Jax shakes his head. "Nah, I'm good thanks. I just had a donut and latte on the way over."

"How do you get away with eating donuts with a physique like that?" Luca asks. "I'd be huge if I ate that for breakfast."

Jax gets up and makes his way over to the window. "It's an occasional hangover treat," he says. "It's nice to know that you're keeping an eye on my body!" Luca blushes. "Wow! What a view."

Luca smiles, watching him stand by the bunched-up blinds, one of his hands shoved in his pocket and his hair perfectly placed. Luca becomes suddenly aware of how scruffy he looks this morning and starts to try and straighten some of his strands of hair that are sticking up.

Jax turns and makes his way back towards the desk, but perches on the edge of it next to Luca. "Do you think Noah will make fun of you? That was what you meant, wasn't it?"

Luca's face clouds over thinking about the taunting that his cousins will give him. "I think they'll have a few things to say about it, but it will blow over. One article won't have too much of an impact."

"Ah," Jax says, hooking his sunglasses over the top rim of his t-shirt. "So you haven't seen the rest then."

"The rest?"

Jax nods. "Apparently it's in all of the gossip columns about how good we are together," Luca notes the smirk on Jax's lips. "Well, that's what Taylor told me anyway."

"You haven't seen?" Luca asks him, leaning forward on the desk fully aware of how close he is to Jax's thigh.

"No, Taylor woke me up to tell me, shoving this picture in my face." Jax points to the open paper. "So, I got dressed and came here."

"How was Taylor over it? Not too upset I hope?"

Jax looks confused. "Why would he be upset?"

Luca tries to maintain eye contact. "Isn't he your partner?"

Jax laughs out loud. "My partner? You mean my boyfriend?" Luca shrugs. "Oh no, he's just my friend. Like a brother really. I'd be lost without him."

Sighing with more relief than he should, Luca glances at the pile of papers on the other side of the desk and turns to Jax. "Do you want to have a look at the rest of them?"

Jax's cheeks flush and he nervously giggles. "Together? If you want. I mean, it might be fun." Luca nods, and Jax jumps off the desk almost running around for the other chair, wheeling it beside Luca. "Are you sure about this?"

Luca bows his head again, sliding the rest of the pile in front of them both. Turning to the man next to him, he smiles. "Should we?"

**

Luca slumps back into his chair and puffs his cheeks. "Well, at least it was all positive, I guess."

Jax slouches into his seat beside Luca. "True, I suppose. I wasn't expecting it though."

"And you think that I was?" Luca laughs. "Not so long ago I was just a judge on a design show, with a fucked-up love life hanging over my head. With a woman, I might add!" He holds his hands up in exaggerated desperation. "Now I'm splashed in every paper with them asking if the rumors are true, that I'm seeing a beautiful model."

Jax nudges his arm. "Oh yeah," he says, playfully sweeping his hair. "So, you think that I'm beautiful?"

Luca huffs, his ears burning as he becomes shy. "Stop that!" He gets up and makes his way over to the water and pours them both a glass, before sitting and swiveling his chair towards Jax. "I'm just quoting what the papers said."

Jax takes the glass from him, fully aware of their fingers brushing gently together. He rests his elbows on his knees, glancing back towards the abundance of newspapers spread all over the full length of the desk. He glances at Luca who is also casting his eyes over the articles again

"What did you think about what they wrote?" Jaxon asks, surprising himself with how bold he is being. He is normally more reserved, but the fact that he even had the balls to go to Luca's office in the first place, is a big deal for him. "About what they *actually* said about us"

Luca gives a little nervous cough and sips his water, turning to rest his arms against the wood, instantly regretting placing his elbows on the black ink of the paper. Scanning over the articles, his heart flutters at the photos. There were even some from the show where he stood with Jax. They did look amazing, and everyone had been so positive with what they had written.

Adjusting his glasses back up his nose, Luca shrugs. "Yeah, well these people know what they're doing to gain readers."

Jax puts his drink down and grabs at the arm of Luca's chair, spinning it to face him again. The paper sticks to Luca's elbows and his water spills over the rim of his crystal glass.

"Easy!" Luca laughs, using some of the papers to mop up the spillage, spreading black ink down his forearm. "What are you trying to do?" He pauses as he sees Jax's serious expression looking at him. "Are you okay?"

"Luca, I want to know what you think. Not the columnists, *you*."

Instantly realizing that he's overstepping the mark with Luca, Jaxon pulls back, holding his hands up apologetically. He's trying so hard to keep in mind that this is his best friend's boss. Or one of them. He can't screw this up for Taylor. He has worked so hard for this opportunity.

Getting up quickly, he steps back. "I'm sorry. I shouldn't have asked."

Turning on his heel, Jax heads swiftly towards the office door. As he reaches out for the handle, he is suddenly aware of Luca directly behind him. Luca's fingers reach for his own, resting on the metal.

Jaxon takes a sharp intake of breath, aware that Luca is interlocking their hands and standing closely behind him. So close that the hairs on his neck are raised.

"Luca?" he whispers, trying to keep his composure. "What are you doing?"

"I have no fucking idea," Luca whispers back, his voice shaky and nervous. "What am I doing? I've never touched a man like this in my life!"

Jax closes his eyes, feeling Luca's breath sweep across his jawline. "Yet you're still doing it." He can feel Luca's body trembling where it rests against his back. "I thought that you were into women."

"I am." Luca laughs. "But you..."

Jax twists his head, grazing his cheek against Luca's. "You, what?" The words barely make it out of his mouth, as he tries to ignore the stirring in Luca's trousers against the top of his thigh.

"Just you," Luca mumbles, snaking his left arm around Jax's waist, hooking his thumb onto the silver belt buckle at the front.

The pause in the room is encased in a sexual tension that is almost suffocating. Jax doesn't know whether it's the best idea to flee from the room or to do something about this first move that Luca has made. His mind is swirling. Luca is straight. Or so he thought, the talk of an ex-girlfriend. It's all a little confusing.

He places his left hand on Luca's. "Is this a good idea?"

"Probably not," Luca says. Jax can feel a small smile. "Maybe I'm still drunk."

Jax gasps playfully and turns to face the man that's so close to him, Luca's arm still around his waist, and the other on the door behind his head. "Oh, I see how it is. I'll have you know Mr. Blackwood, that I'm simply not..." He pauses watching Luca's eyes narrow, their faces close. "What?"

"Say that again," Luca instructs, his fingers sliding into Jax's blond strands, twisting them.

"I'll have you know..." Jax starts, and Luca shakes his head. Their eyes stay fixated on each other, their breathing deepening. Jax realizes what he's being asked. "Mr. Blackwood."

Luca catches a gasp in his throat like it's almost painful. "Again."

"Mr. Blackwo..."

Luca plunges forward quickly pushing his mouth onto Jax's, not aggressively, but as if he desperately needs him. Jax quickly responds, pushing his tongue in between Luca's lips. Their hitching breath and frustration fill the room as their hands run almost uncontrollably around each other's bodies.

Luca is practically drugged by the scent drifting from Jax combined with the sweetness of his taste. It doesn't even feel strange that he's a man. Something that is very, very new to him, yet so natural right now. He wants to keep hold of Jax and never let him go.

They both stumble until Jax is leaning fully against the door. Luca uses his grip to push their waists together, Jax's leg slotting in between his thighs. *Fuck, his cock is against mine. His cock. A fucking man's cock.* He keeps repeating in his head, an experience that he never imagined would ever happen to him.

But he likes it, and inches himself as close as he possibly can, the pair simultaneously grinding against each other, their erections growing. Luca groans at the ache running through his body, letting his tongue naturally go to where it wants to taste. Jax matches his sounds, and Luca is relieved that he's enjoying it just as much.

Luca pulls back a little, the sound of their lips detaching clicking in the air. The two men pause, panting, their dicks still hard and pressed against each other. "Fuck," is all that he can manage to say.

"I know!" Jax smiles. "Are you sure that this is what you want?"

Luca nods. "How about you? Do you want this?" Jax leans in to run his tongue along

Luca's bottom lip slowly. "I'll presume that's a yes."

Jax follows it up by watching Luca's reaction as he nibbles on the delicate skin where he's just licked, humming at Luca's eyes glistening. Luca sweeps his tongue to meet with Jax's before drawing him in to lock together in a kiss again, grasping at his hair.

Luca's pocket starts to buzz, breaking them begrudgingly apart. "I hope that's your cell and not your cock?" Jaxon laughs.

Pulling his phone out of his pocket, Luca smiles while looking at it. "It's Jasper," he says. "Probably wants to make excuses for not coming in today. I have to call him back."

The two men reluctantly let go of each other and brush themselves down. "It's okay, I have to go and see Taylor anyway."

"Wait," Luca exclaims, interrupting as Jax tries for the door handle a second time that day. "Let me take you out."

"Like on a date?" Jax asks, glancing down to make sure his erection has subsided before he leaves.

"Sure. The press has made their mind up anyway, let's give them what they want. I'll call you. I'll get your number from Taylor or something."

"Or I could give it to you while you have your cell in your hand?" Jax laughs.

"Fuck, I forgot about my phone!" Luca blushes, handing it to Jax. "I'm such an idiot."

Jax inputs his number and gives it back. "But you're a handsome idiot."

As the door shuts behind him, Luca almost squeals in a mixture of excitement and disbelief. *Did all of that just happen?*

He virtually floats back to his desk, collapsing in his chair shaking his head. He grins at the photos, still staring up at him, and sips some of the remaining unspilled water. *Glenda is absolutely right. We do make a cute couple.*

Chapter 8

Taylor sits at one of the endlessly long tables in his new work studio. His leather loafers have been kicked off under the table, and his bare feet are curled up beneath him on the tall, high backed stool. He is using a stylus to sketch on an enormous tablet that sits in front of him. He glances over his shoulder and sees that his new assistants are busy organizing a huge quantity of expensive fabrics, notions, and anything he could possibly need to execute his designs.

As he returns to his sketching, a familiar voice breaks his concentration. "Hi, Tay."

"Jaxon! What are you doing here?" Taylor gestures to the stool beside him and Jax takes a seat. "What the hell! Did you take the stairs? You're all flushed!"

Jax shakes his head and touches his full pout, which is noticeably puffier than usual. "I just came from seeing Luca and I wanted to check out your new space!" Jax looks around, taking it all in. "Oh my god, Tay, this is amazing! Does this mean we can get all of your shit out of our living room?"

Taylor laughs and fingers through his long waves. "You know that I can't part with my machine, but I'll declutter just for you." Jaxon giggles and nods, looking into Taylor's amber eyes. "Spill it," Taylor says. "You're acting weird. Did you go to see Luca?"

Jaxon spins the stool around with his feet and returns to meet Taylor's gaze again. "I did. About the articles."

"Hmmmmmmm. What did he say? Had he seen them?" Taylor raises one heavy brow as he leans toward his best friend.

"Well, he had seen the one." Jax sighs. "But he hadn't seen all of them."

"Don't keep me in suspense!" Taylor says excitedly. "How did he react?"

"He apologized and said that he'd have it retracted." Jaxon picks at something invisible on the worktable. "But then we looked through all of the other articles together."

"Annnnnddd?" Taylor makes a 'come here' gesture with his long fingers, trying to get Jax to elaborate.

"Well, he kissed me." Jaxon puts his small hands against his cheeks, which are becoming increasingly red. "More than that actually, things got pretty heated."

Taylor leans in and puts his hands on Jaxon's knees. "What are you saying? How did this happen? I thought he was straight?"

"I don't know, Tay, I'm still trying to process it myself. I mean there was definitely some attraction between us last night when we went out. Sexual tension, something, I don't really know how to describe it." Jax becomes anxious as he spits out his words." I thought he was straight too. I mean he says that he's only ever dated women. But we are just drawn to each other. Like a magnetic pull or some shit like you read about." Taylor rubs his hand up his friend's arms trying to calm him. "He asked me out, Tay. I mean he said that he wants us to date."

Taylor squeezes Jax's arms. "Baby, slow down. This is not like you at all. You're the cautious one, the one who never brings anyone home. You're waiting for the real thing, remember?"

"But, Tay, what if this *is* the real thing?" Jaxon grabs Taylor's arms that are still comforting him and squeezes. "What if he's the one."

"I'm just worried. What if he's just bi-curious? I can't bear the thought of him using you just to test out being with a man." Taylor gazes into his friend's eyes, reflecting on the worry that he's feeling. "What if he decides that he wants to be with a woman and leaves you heartbroken? I mean, you just met each other!"

Jax puts his hands on his best friend's cheeks. "Tay, I want to do this. I need to do this. It's just a feeling I have. I can't explain it." He can't stop the tears from welling up in his eyes.

Taylor gives his arms one more squeeze. "Okay. I trust you, and I'm always here for you."

"And you always have been. You're my only family, Tay." Jax pulls him into an embrace.

"Oh my god, we are so fucked," Taylor says as he pulls away from Jaxon. "What are these Blackwood men doing to us?"

"You are so into Jasper. Could you be more obvious?" Jax plops back onto the stool, which almost rolls away from him. "I was distracted as hell, but I still picked up on your flirting!"

"Well, you know that I'm naturally flirtatious!" Taylor says as he straightens his friend on the stool. Jaxon raises an eyebrow at him. "Not like anything is going to happen anyway. I work for the company. He's technically my employer, so I'm sure HR would have something to say about it."

"Noah is technically your employer, Tay. I wouldn't worry too much." Jax tries to reassure him. "Jasper is totally your type. You love those bad boys."

"Well he might look like a bad boy, but he's actually quite shy. We stayed and drank together after you all left."

"Ummm hmmm, I know. And you got home really late."

"Yeah well, nothing happened. We talked a lot. He's only twenty-one, Jax. He does seem to like me? I mean he was shy when I flirted, but he did touch my hand a lot. He leaned his head close to mine when we were talking."

"It definitely sounds like he's interested," Jaxon encourages.

"He did confide in me. He's not confident in himself." Taylor looks around to make sure their conversation is still private. "He's just trying to be comfortable with his sexuality, and he's not out yet. I don't want it to seem like I'm taking advantage of him."

"It's not like that, Taylor." Jax strokes his hand. "Everyone needs to have someone to help guide them. We had each other, but we just muddled through it together. Jasper could use someone who's been there. Don't give up before you've even started. He can use a good friend, at least."

Taylor sighs. "I want more."

"I know you do, but there's no need to rush," Jaxon says, in the soothing voice he often uses with his oldest friend.

Taylor tips his head back, letting out a loud laugh. "Says the man who's in love after one day!"

"Point taken!" Jaxon joins him in laughter and gets to his feet. "Okay, I need to get going. I have classes that start soon. Get back to work, Mr. Designer."

"I'm really excited. Isabella is supposed to come and meet me today." Taylor gets up as well and walks Jaxon toward the door.

"Oh shit, she's so intimidating!" Jaxon grabs Taylor's hand. "I think that I'd pass out in her presence. She's like a goddess!"

Taylor laughs again as he hugs Jax goodbye. "See you at home later."

Once Jax has gone, Taylor busies himself sorting through fabrics with the help of his assistants.

"Taylor, darling!" He hears a loud voice in an English accent. He turns to see Isabella striding over in a gorgeous cornflower blue silk pantsuit, her ever-present stilettos clicking across the studio floor.

"I have been dying to meet you! Our new designer whom the world adores," Bella coos.

Taylor greets her with a kiss on each cheek. "Ms. Blackwood, it's such an honor."

"Oh stop, darling. Please call me Bella. We will be working closely together, after all." Taylor bows his head a bit in grateful acknowledgment. "Now show me what you're working on. I am obsessed with the collection that you presented on Aspire to Design. Absolutely stunning and just what we need," Bella says, as they walk towards Taylor's worktable.

Taylor gestures to the tablet. "I've just started sketching a few new ideas to expand the collection," he says, while swiping through the images.

"These are wonderful. Truly inspired," Bella compliments, tapping on the tablet.

"Thank you, Bella. That means so much, but I've only just started with these," Taylor says, continuing to show her more sketches.

"You know, Taylor," Bella starts while sitting down on the stool, hooking her heel over the metal bar, "that my son Jayce will be modeling some of these designs once the line is released." Taylor nods as she continues. "I honestly feel that we need to show some unknown faces in the ad campaign as well. This line is so different, and we need to show that diversity." Bella leans her elbows onto the worktable, propping her chin in her hands. "I am very interested in your blond male model. Jaxon, I believe his name is?"

"Yes, Jax. He's my best friend and he's not really a model," Taylor explains.

"Yes, yes, Noah told me that. He said he is a dancer, am I right?" Taylor nods as she continues. "I saw the photos that Jasper took from the show. I was immediately drawn to him. Do you think that he would consider meeting with me?"

"Actually, you just missed him! He stopped in to see me." Bella pouts as Taylor continues. "Honestly, I wouldn't get your hopes up, Bella." Taylor leans on the table as well, meeting her eyes. "He only did the show as a favor to me, and I pretty much guilted him into it. He is not very confident about his looks."

"That's utterly ridiculous," Bella tuts. "That man is stunning. It's worth a try anyway, ask him to meet me."

"Yes, I will Bella, I will," Taylor sighs.

"Well, you and Jasper can come with him, if he'll feel more comfortable." Taylor blushes and leans back as Bella reaches out to him, grasping his hand in hers. "Jasper tells me that you all get on quite well. He seems especially taken with you, Taylor." Taylor just stares at Isabella for a long moment until she breaks the silence. "Don't look so surprised, darling. Jasper and I have a very close relationship. He tells me everything."

Taylor looks down at his shoes. "Oh, well okay. I didn't know that. We've really just started to get to know each other."

"And I hope that you continue to do so. Jasper is an amazing young man, and obviously." Bella sweeps her arm around her indicating the work studio. "You are too, Taylor." She stands up smoothing out the silk of her outfit. "Well, I'm off. Packed schedule as usual."

Taylor stands as well, grasping her hands and kissing each cheek again as she gets up to leave. "It was such a pleasure meeting you, Bella. I appreciate your kind words."

"And it's a pleasure having you here at Blackwood, Taylor. Please let me know about your friend." Taylor nods, and Bella squeezes his hands before gliding out the door.

Taylor walks back to his stool, pushing his tablet aside. He folds his arms on the table and dramatically drops his head onto them. "Well, I wasn't expecting that!" He mumbles to himself into his folded arms. Taylor takes a deep breath and sits up, getting back to work.

Chapter 9

Taylor looks up from his machine and grins to himself, before going back to his sewing. "Jax, you look incredible as always."

Jaxon takes a deep breath and looks himself up and down in the full-length contemporary mirror by the door. Leaning in to examine his hair for what seems like the hundredth time, he sighs. "Oh, Tay, I don't think that I can do this. What if I screw it up? What if I..."

Smiling again, Taylor puts down the fabric and makes his way over to his friend, who is still straightening his jacket. He turns Jax to face him and gently grasps the top of both arms. "Wow, you really like this one, don't you?"

Jax looks back at him, his face strained with worry. "I do, Taylor. I don't know what it is, but I really do. But what if it doesn't work out?"

"Why wouldn't it?" Taylor laughs. "He thinks the same of you, right?"

Jax nods, his cheeks flushing, remembering some of the flirty messages that have passed between them. "I think so. He acts that way."

He sighs, releasing himself from Taylor's grip and slumping back onto the wall behind him. "But I might fuck it up, and then that makes it awkward for you at work."

"Jax! You will not fuck this up. I have a good feeling about this one."

Turning back to the mirror again, Jax takes a big, deep breath through his nose. "Me too, Tay. That's why I don't want anything to go wrong."

Taylor grasps onto his shoulders, the two boys staring at their reflection in the glass. "Look," he says, "just go and have fun. I'm sure that it will all go just fine. Look at you... you're the most stunningly beautiful person on the planet."

"Oh stop it!" Jax smiles, crossing an arm over his chest and grabbing Taylor's hand. "What would I do without you?"

Taylor squeezes his fingers. "I don't know, but I think that you'd be a little lost!"

The two men burst into laughter together, when there's a slight tap on the door causing Jax's face to crumple into a completely panicked look again. "Oh shit, Tay, I can't do this!"

Pulling him away from the mirror, Taylor turns Jax to face him and brushes him down. Stroking his cheek, he says, "Yes you can. Just go and enjoy yourself. Just be you. That's who he likes. You've got this."

Jax takes another deep breath and opens the door. He immediately relaxes seeing Luca standing there in his pale blue ripped jeans and black leather jacket, although he does feel a little overdressed in comparison, wearing tight black jeans, a tucked-in white shirt, and a black fitted jacket.

"Wow, you look incredible!" Luca gasps, Jax's cheeks burning red at the compliment. Turning to Taylor, he smiles. "Hi, Taylor."

"Not too dressy then?" Jaxon says, as Luca shakes his head, grabbing him by the hand.

"No, you look simply beautiful." He glances down at his own attire. "Maybe I should have made more effort."

Jax pulls him closer, drawing him in for a hug. "I love seeing you without the suit on."

"Slow down," Luca jokes. "I don't think that we've hit that stage just yet!"

"Oh fuck, no, shit... I didn't mean... damn it." Jax stumbles back and throws his hands up to his face to hide his embarrassment, wishing that the ground would open and swallow him up. "I am so sorry."

Taylor laughs hysterically behind him, finding his best friend's blunder highly amusing, while Luca removes Jax's hands and kisses him on the lips. "It was funny," he says, pulling him towards the door. "Let's get going."

Waving goodbye to Taylor, Jax and Luca head down to the waiting car, Jax still mumbling about how shocked he is and how silly he feels. Luca can do no more than tell him that it's fine in between his sniggering.

Arriving at the small restaurant, Jax takes in the quaint, European-looking stone front. Hanging vines surround the windows, with pretty red flowers lining boxes on the sills, and dainty metal tables and chairs are set outside. Luca climbs out of the car first, turning to grab Jax's hand to help him out.

"Look at you being all chivalrous." Jax smiles, facing Luca and grazes their lips together. His eyes widen looking around at the customers nearby. "Sorry. I didn't know if…"

"If I wanted people to see?" Luca asks. "Don't get me wrong, Jax, this is a little different for me, I'm not going to lie." He pulls Jax in to kiss him, locking their lips together for a moment. "But I'm not ashamed of us. People will find out soon enough."

Jax's eyes well slightly at the words that he has been wanting to hear. "Us."

Luca smiles, interlocking his fingers with Jax's, leading them both into the building. After being shown to their seats in a secluded corner, the couple orders a bottle of wine.

"You've been here before?" Jax asks as the staff greet Luca like a regular, one of them pouring glasses of full-bodied red.

Luca takes a sip of his drink. "Clients, yes. We bring them here because it's less formal." He picks up the menu to browse and glances up to see Jax looking at him with a raised eyebrow. "Oh! You mean women? Nah. It isn't Misun's style."

Jax shrugs. "Sorry, I was just curious. I'm not a jealous type, don't worry about that!"

Luca smiles and gestures for Jax to order his food and then relays his own choice. Handing the menus back, Luca sits back in his chair with his glass. He can't help but stare at Jax and his stunning looks.

Jax breaks the silence. "So, what happened with her?"

Luca shifts in his seat with a little discomfort. "Misun?" Jax nods. "Ah, you don't want to hear about all of that."

Jax, without thinking, grabs Luca's hand. "I do if you want to tell me?"

"There isn't much to tell really," Luca says. "She did a shitty thing to me. We split up. The end. I'll tell you more about it another time." He squeezes Jax's fingers. "But right now, she's gone from my life for good, and I have you."

A flush rises in Jaxon's cheeks and he touches two fingers to his plump lips. "Do you want to keep me?" he asks Luca coyly.

Luca can't help but fall for the man looking back at him. The personality that draws him

Should We?

in, looks that he could just watch for hours on end. He lowers Jax's fingers from his lips, taking them into his own. "Jax, I've said this before. It is all new to me. I would never in a million years have thought that I would have a boyfriend. I mean, fuck Jax, I've never touched another man's dick in my life! I have no idea what to do!"

Jaxon belly laughs at Luca's innocence, throwing his head back hysterically. "Oh Luca," he says when he has calmed, "I happen to be a good teacher if you want?"

Luca leans in closer to him. "Yes. Show me."

**

After an afternoon of flirty conversation and getting to know each other a little better, plus the playful fight over who was paying the check, Luca puts his wallet back into his pocket and stands up.

"Seriously, Luca, you should have let me pay half," Jax pouts, slipping on his jacket.

Luca straightens his sleeves and slides his arm around his new boyfriend's waist, pulling him closer. "It was my treat for you allowing me into your life, Angel."

"Angel! Hmmm, I like that." Jax drapes his arms around Luca's neck, sliding his fingers into his hair.

"Well from the moment I saw you on that runway, all in white," Luca whispers against his ear, "I thought you were an angel. Sent here just for me."

Jax pulls him even closer. "I am so glad to have you in my life, too. I'm the happiest that I've been in a long time."

Luca hums in agreement, giving him a quick peck as they start out of the restaurant, when a familiar posh voice fills the air. "Oh my gosh!"

"Glenda!" Luca says, as they see the lady at the table that they were just passing. "How lovely to see you again."

She eyes the two of them arm in arm, pointing her fork back and forth between them. "Is this what I think it is?"

"Yes Glenda, it is. Jaxon is now my boyfriend," Luca says, before the two of them head towards the door.

"See," they hear Glenda say, "I told you that they're cute."

**

They both decide to walk for a while, Luca joking that he isn't used to eating lobster during the day, and Jax pointing out that he isn't used to eating it at any time.

"Are you sure that was a good idea?" Jax motions back towards the direction of the restaurant. "Saying that to Glenda?"

Luca tilts his head. "Everyone has to find out sometime that we're together." He glances over at Jax and blushes. "It still seems strange saying that." Jax links an arm with him. "Besides, I'm seeing a lot of my family later. Aunt Bella has summoned us all. I'll tell them then."

"What about your parents? Will they be bothered by it?"

Luca shrugs, his face darkening. "I don't give a shit what they say. I have nothing to do with either of them."

Jax can see that it isn't wise to push the subject, judging by the look in Luca's eye. "So," he says, changing the subject, "What do you want to do now?"

"I wouldn't mind doing some more of that amazing kissing that you do." Luca winks at him, pulling him into a small side street, and pushing him up against a wall.

The sounds around them fade into the background as they stare into each other's eyes, their breathing heavy with anticipation. Luca leans into him, gasping gently at the feel of Jax's dick against his, fully aware that he was making it twitch.

"This is becoming a bit of a habit, you pushing me against things," Jaxon says, his voice raspy.

Luca smirks, his newfound confidence burning inside him. "What are you teaching me first?"

Jax raises his eyebrows and smiles. He teases his fingers in between Luca's, drawing his lips forward until both sets touch. Moving their mouths slowly, they tease their tongues together.

Tilting his chest to sway Luca away from his body, Jax tightens his grip on Luca's fingers. "Do you want to try something new?"

Luca scoffs briefly, the nerves tickling his stomach and sending butterflies throughout him. He mumbles a "Yes," letting Jax lead him.

"It's okay." Jaxon moves their hands towards his jeans. "Unfasten them."

Luca pauses before shakily undoing the button and zipper, revealing Jax's black briefs, an urge that he's never felt before engulfing him. "Can I?" he whispers.

Gaining consent from Jax who uses his head to move him in for a kiss again, Luca tries to concentrate on sliding his hand into the fabric. Grasping Jax's cock in his hand, he exhales deeply, the veiny, hard skin feels amazing in his hand, especially when Jax lets out a small whimper.

As much as Jax is almost desperate for more, he knows that this isn't the right place, so uses Luca's jacket sleeve to pull his hand out. "I know, I know," he says seeing Luca's disappointed face, "I want it too. Like really want it. We will do it and more. Soon."

Luca sighs, knowing that he's right. "Still, I've finally touched one!"

Jax finishes adjusting his clothes and links arms with Luca again as the pair set off to continue their walk. He smiles coyly. "Yep, I've taken your penis virginity."

**

Isabella pads barefoot toward the kitchen of her luxurious penthouse apartment. She lifts the lid of a few pots simmering on the stove, grabbing a large spoon off of the sprawling marble countertop and stirring them. Next, she walks to the huge wall oven, opening it and checking on the roast that she is preparing for dinner. Satisfied that the dishes will be perfectly timed, she grabs her wine glass and heads to the white leather sectional sofa to put her feet up. The sofa takes up almost the entirety of the room; Bella had it custom-made for the space when she moved in.

The hidden stereo surround system plays classic seventies rock, and she gazes around the home that she adores. Bella is thankful that her father hadn't made a fuss when she changed his dark English Tudor style decor. In her mind, it had done nothing to accentuate the openness of the space or the towering windows that surround her. Dalton, however, had favored it. He said it brought back memories of their old home in London. Now her father resides full time in his Connecticut estate, which Isabella thinks looks like it was transported directly from the English countryside. Her brother Alexander and his wife have recently moved to the estate as well, for which she is grateful. She hates the idea of Dalton living alone. Bella, however, loves The City and adores her work. Dalton was pleased that his daughter wanted to move into the larger apartment that he had called home during his workweek.

Bella has transformed the penthouse into a light and modern space, featuring light gray wood floors and white walls which make the towering ceilings seem even higher. Her decor, however, is still comfortable and cozy, and her boys Jayce and Harrison loved it so much that they decided to continue living with her. The penthouse has four bedrooms, each with its own ensuite bath. The size of the space and the distance between their respective bedrooms allow for privacy, even when one or more of them entertain overnight guests.

The door buzzes and Bella looks over her shoulder to see Jasper coming in. His dark hair is ruffled, and he is wearing a black hoodie, baggy black pants with buckles, and combat boots. Jasper drops his backpack and camera bag by the door.

"Boots off!" Bella says, and Jasper nods.

"I know, Aunt Bella, how many times have I been here?" he replies, untying and placing his boots next to his bags.

"Yes, yes, sweetheart. I'm glad that you came a bit early." Jasper walks over to the built-in fridge and grabs a beer. He twists off the cap and comes to sit down next to his aunt. He places a kiss on her cheek, and she stretches her legs across his lap.

"Smells good! You're cooking?" Jasper raises his eyebrows.

"Don't look so surprised! I thought a family tea was a good excuse to put my fabulous kitchen to good use!"

Jasper squeezes her manicured toes. "Thanks for doing this, Aunt Bella."

"Are you sure about this, sweetheart? Are you sure that you're feeling comfortable?"

"Yes, I think so. I didn't expect to meet someone that I'm interested in this soon, though. Since he works for the company, I don't want things to become complicated. I want to let everyone know."

Bella nods and takes a sip of her wine. "I met Taylor; you know. I stopped by his work studio."

Jasper laughs. "Couldn't help yourself, Aunt Bella? I knew I should've waited to call you!"

Bella giggles as well. "Well I needed to meet him for work, but I will admit that I was curious!" She swings her feet to the floor, ready to get up to refill her wine.

Jasper jumps up. "I'll grab the bottle." He walks back to the kitchen, grabbing the wine as well as another beer. "So, what did you think?"

Bella nods as Jasper refills her glass. "Well, I think that he is gorgeous, talented, and charming. Basically perfect."

Jasper rubs his face in his hands. "He is, he really is. He's so confident and experienced though, Aunt Bella. And I'm neither of those things."

"Take your time. Get to know him."

Noise at the door ends their conversation. Noah and Harrison step in, toeing off their shoes. Noah has clearly gone home to change after work, as he is wearing jeans and a casual shirt.

Harrison heads to the sofa, kissing Bella on the forehead. "Hey, Mum, good day?"

"Productive," Bella hums. "Go change, darling, and let Jayce know that everyone is here."

Noah claps his brother Jasper on the shoulder and heads off to make a drink. "Bella, you're cooking for us? I thought we were ordering." He pours some Jameson over ice and strolls into the great room. "What's the special occasion?"

Bella catches Jayce from the corner of her eye, heading over to join them. "It's just been a while since all you boys had a meal together. It's easy to get distracted by work, and I want all the youngest Blackwoods to remember to stay connected."

"Jayce, grab a drink." Bella points her glass his way. "Can you get another bottle from the wine fridge for me?"

Jayce nods, running his fingers through his still-wet hair. "Where's Luca?" he says, as he opens the door to the six-foot-tall restaurant-grade wine fridge, scanning the labels.

"On his way, he just finished up a couple things for work," Noah says over his shoulder, helping his aunt chop vegetables for the salad.

"Does Victoria have classes tonight?" Jasper addresses his brother.

"She does," Noah replies, "but she's missing you. You two are overdue for a coffee date."

"I'll text her," Jasper says, as he puts silverware around the table.

Harrison appears in sweatpants and a white tank top, approaching the door to open it when he hears the keypad is pressed. "Hey," he says to Luca, opening the door wide to let him in.

"Hey," Luca replies, as he loosens his tie and removes his suit coat, hanging it by the door.

Jayce opens the wine that he has selected with ease, refilling his mother's glass and pouring three others. Luca and Harrison grab a glass each, as does Jayce, and they tip their glasses toward each other before taking a sip.

It's easy and comfortable, the men all being together. They've grown up together and know each other so well. Bella takes in the sight of all of her boys as they chat with each other. She hopes that they will always remain this close. "Let's get everything on the table and sit for tea," she announces.

"Mum, you know we call it dinner here," Harrison teases.

"Well it's dinner where I am from in England too, but tea from the North of England is so much more fun. It will always be tea for me," Bella responds, as the boys all take a seat while laughing to themselves.

As they pass the meat and side dishes between them, they share a comfortable conversation about Paris, politics, and just general bullshit.

Noah raises his voice a bit above the din. "Everyone," he begins, "I'd like to let my brother know just how proud I am of the work that he's done with the reality show." He turns toward his brother. "Jasper, I've always known what a talented photographer you are. However, you have exceeded my expectations. Your shots are amazing, and you've represented Blackwood well. I'm proud of you."

Jasper meets Bella's eyes across the table and then looks down at his plate as his family whoops and applauds. He raises his eyes to meet Noah's. "That means more than you know, Noah." He ups the tone in his voice a bit. "Actually," Jasper begins as everyone quiets down, "I asked Aunt Bella to host this dinner so that I could talk to all of you." Jasper takes a deep breath. "I've been struggling with something for a while now and Bella has been really helping me." The men share glances at each other across the table but remain silent. "I know that this isn't something that I have to do with everyone here, but I wanted to. For me." Bella nods her encouragement and Jasper sits up straighter in his seat, squaring his shoulders. He takes a deep breath. "I'm gay."

Everyone around the table releases a collective sigh. Noah gets up and goes to his brother, pulling him into an embrace. A few tears trickle down Jasper's cheeks.

"Jesus, kid," Harrison says. "I thought you were going to tell us that you have an incurable disease!" Jasper smiles.

"Congratulations" Harrison continues. "That's good, really good. You'll be fine."

Jayce addresses his cousin. "Jasper, I'm sure I speak for everyone when I say that you have our full support." The men all nod in agreement. "Are you seeing someone?" Jayce asks.

"Well no, but I've met someone that I want to get to know better. I wanted to tell all of you because, well, you know him." Jasper nervously picks at his salad. "It's Taylor. Taylor King." He turns toward Noah. "I wanted to talk to you because he works for the company and I didn't want things to get, well, complicated."

Across the table, Luca rests his head in his hands, massaging his temples.

"I think that it will be fine, kiddo," Noah addresses Jasper. "If things start to get serious, we'll all talk about it."

"Thanks, Noah," Jasper sighs, his relief obvious. Bella comes over and gives him a huge hug.

"Umm, everyone?" Luca coughs. "I have a bit of an announcement as well." He turns to Jasper. "I don't want you to think that I took this moment from you, but it's important."

Jasper smiles and nods. "Luca, it's fine I've said what I needed to, go ahead."

From the coffee table a phone pings, and a few of the men look in that direction.

"Okay." Luca takes a deep breath and lets his words spill out. "I'm dating Jaxon".

"Jaxon?" Jasper says with a surprised look. "As in Jaxon, model Jaxon, Taylor's best friend Jaxon?"

Another ping from the coffee table breaks the silence.

"Wait a minute," Jayce begins. "I saw those articles and thought it was all bullshit. You're telling me it's true?"

"It is bullshit. I mean it was!" Luca stumbles over his words and Harrison refills his wine glass. "It's complicated."

"Luca..." Noah begins, as yet again, the phone alerts in the next room.

Jayce walks over to see who's phone it is.

Noah folds his hands on the table and looks toward his cousin. "...we all support you, just like we do Jasper, but I'm confused," he continues. "You have never dated a man, only women. Are you sure about this?"

Jayce walks back to the table holding Luca's phone.

"Noah, I'm sure. I can't explain it, but I'm sure," Luca states with conviction.

"Luca, I'm sorry but it's your phone." Jayce hands the phone to his cousin. "Misun keeps texting you. She says it's urgent."

Luca sighs, looking down at the messages. He runs his hand through his hair and his eyes meet Noah's. He shakes his head.

"Well!" Bella begins, "I'd say this was an enlightening family get together!" She raises her wine glass for a toast. "To the Blackwoods."

The men all raise their glasses and join in the toast. "To the Blackwoods." They clink glasses and each takes a sip of their drinks.

Luca glances down at his phone once more, tossing it aside on the table. *Why the fuck can't she leave me alone?*

Chapter 10

Luca smiles at the message. If he is honest with himself, his face lights up every time his phone pings and the name Jaxon flashes onto the screen. The computer sits on his desk, full of work for him to complete, yet he can't seem to focus properly. He feels like an infatuated teenager, with the world's biggest crush.

The picture attached to the message is a simple photo of Jax smiling, his hair scruffy and swept to one side. His chest is bare in the photo, having clearly just woken up. Luca can't tear himself away from staring at it. He tries to reason with himself that he's a grown man, and should be acting like one, but he really has never seen anyone in his entire life that's as beautiful as Jax.

He realizes that he is falling for him. And hard. It scares him a little, he must admit, what people may say or think. But then he could never imagine not having Jax in his life. He hasn't had him in his life for very long but knows that he is worth everything.

Especially now that he has his cousins and family behind him for support. They've been amazing about it. A little shocked still, but great. Jasper even jokes about them going on a double date when he finally makes his move with Taylor. He will tell his grandfather and uncle soon, although he suspects that word will have traveled fast.

Luca's face clouds over remembering his father. He knows that there is no way that he will approve of his relationship. Not in any way. But he doesn't matter. He isn't even relevant in his life anymore.

Taking a deep breath, he shakes his head cursing to himself for being distracted while he's so busy. He puts his phone to one side, and begins his work, smirking to himself when he hears his phone buzz again. He knows that it will be Jax, but he has to try and at least type a few words.

A knock on the door disturbs him from his concentration again. "I'm sorry, Luca," Sacha says, stepping in, looking slightly agitated. "There is someone here to see you, and they are extremely persistent."

"Who?" Luca sits back in his chair before the door is flung open wider and his heart sinks.

"Me," the person in question bellows, striding brashly into the office. "Why won't you fucking answer me, Luca?"

Luca nods at Sacha to signal that he can handle this, and motions to the chair in front of his desk. "What do you want, Misun?" He watches her take a seat, trying to ignore the nauseating feeling building inside his stomach.

"Well," she sneers, "If you had answered me at some point, then I wouldn't have had to come down here."

Luca rolls his eyes, folding his arms on his desk in front of him. "We have nothing more to say to each other, Mi. You made that choice."

He realizes that he has a newfound strength inside him that he didn't even know that he had. He figures that Jax played a part in that. Misun looks different to him now. He still thinks that she's attractive with her Korean heritage, her long dark hair, and piercing brown eyes, but he doesn't feel that love anymore. Strange really, considering he had imagined at one point that they would be married and have a family. Now he just sees her as an old someone.

Misun glances up from her bag and sees her ex-boyfriend watching her. "Why didn't you answer me?" She pauses, checking her phone, and placing it on the desk.

"Misun." Luca sighs. "Why are you here?"

"Oh, I'm sorry," she says sarcastically. "Am I distracting you from the new boyfriend?" She stops Luca as he tries to speak. "Really, Luca? A boyfriend? Yeah, I saw it in the press. I've had people messaging me to tell me, too. Did I put you off women for life?"

"Don't flatter yourself!" Luca scoffs, his posture becoming upright and rigid. "The relationship between Jax and me has absolutely nothing to do with you!"

Misun laughs out loud. "A relationship? Are you for real? With a guy?" She shakes her head in disbelief. "Fuck off, Luca, you know it's just rebound shit."

"What's wrong with me being with a man, Misun?" Luca's anger is apparent in his tone. "He makes me happy. More than you did." He realizes that he's getting louder, and takes a breath, rubbing his temples with his fingers. "I'm not talking to you about this."

"Do you actually touch this guy's dick? 'Cause I'm trying to imagine you with one in your hand, and the image is pretty disgusting, to be honest."

Luca practically jumps out of his seat, slamming his hands on his desk. "Misun. Enough. What do you wa..." Her phone vibrating in between them, stops him. Luca sees the name flashing on the screen. "Jayce? Why is my cousin calling you?"

She grabs the phone, and clicks the red button, throwing it into her bag. Shrugging, she looks at him. "I wanted to get in touch with you because you weren't answering, so I found his number instead." She gets up and heads to the window. "I always did love this view. You can see so much. Do you remember when we had sex on your desk for all to see?"

Luca grimaces at the topic of conversation. He isn't comfortable with it anymore. "Will you please tell me why you are so desperate to speak to me, Misun?" This is getting to be a joke now."

Her shoulders slump, still facing the glass. Luca can't help but see a small inkling of vulnerability about her persona now. "Is anything wrong? Do you need anything from me? Money?"

She shakes her head and sits on the edge of his desk, her legs swinging back and forth. "No, Luca, nothing is wrong." Her face is serious now. "But I do have something pretty important to discuss with you."

**

Why is this happening to me? Luca has his elbows resting on his knees and his head in his hands. His suit coat and tie are carelessly tossed on the leather seat next to him.

"Everything okay, Mr. Blackwood?" Tony says as he weaves through traffic on the way to Chelsea.

Luca doesn't respond. He rubs his hands through his tousled black hair, finally lifting his head. He meets his driver's eyes in the rearview mirror, and that's enough for the man to see that, no, everything is not alright.

"We'll be there shortly, sir," Tony tells Luca, and he hands him an icy bottle of water over his shoulder.

"Thank you." Luca takes a long drink of it as he stares out the window without really seeing. Lost in thought, he barely registers the fact that the car has stopped until Tony comes around to open the car door for him.

"Here we are Mr. Blackwood. Just text me when you're ready." The driver shuts the door behind him.

Luca stands staring at the building looming in front of him. He nods to Tony as the car pulls away.

As he rounds the corner, Tony picks up his phone and presses the call button. "Yes, sir, I just dropped him off," Tony responds to the man on the other end of the call. "Yes, he was definitely upset...No. No, sir, I'm not sure." Tony nods as he listens. "I don't think so. He said he'll call me when he's done...Will do, I'll let you know." Tony disconnects the call, continuing to drive through mid-day traffic.

Luca slowly approaches the building, manicured finger hovering at the intercom. *This is it, I need to do this. He's going to end us before we even get started.* Luca takes a deep breath and pushes the button to Jaxon's apartment, the shrill buzzer almost painful to hear.

He only waits a minute until he hears Jaxon's voice. "Luca, is it you?"

"Yes, it's me, Jax," Luca anxiously replies.

"Kay, I'm buzzing you in, come on up." Luca nods, even though Jax can't see him.

Luca feels the pit in his stomach grow larger with each floor that ticks by, but he doesn't hesitate when the elevator doors open. He walks with purpose to Jaxon's door and knocks. He needs to see him.

The door opens and Jaxon pulls Luca inside and into a tight embrace. Luca rests his head against his shoulder and inhales the scent of him, vanilla and honey. Jaxon's hair is wet and his body warm, having just showered after his dance classes.

"Come on, Luca, come and sit down." Jax leads Luca over to his well-worn couch, the one that he and Taylor love spending nights stargazing from. "You sounded so upset on the phone, I'm not sure what to think."

Luca nods grasping Jax's small hands in his own. "Are we alone?"

Jaxon rubs his fingers in Luca's palms, trying to reassure him. "Yes, we're alone, Taylor won't be home for a couple of hours. Luca, what's going on?"

Luca meets Jaxon's gaze. He can see the fear and uncertainty in his beautiful eyes, now their natural golden brown, and it makes his heart hurt. "Misun came to see me at work today. She barged in."

"Okay, why would she do that?" Jax asks, still holding Luca's hands.

Luca takes a deep breath. "She has been messaging me all week, and I haven't responded. She had something important to discuss with me."

Jaxon starts to speak, but Luca stops him. "Jax, let me just get this out, I need to tell you what she said."

Jaxon lets go of Luca's hands, moving slightly away from him. He's preparing himself for the inevitable. *Taylor was right.* He waits for Luca to speak.

Luca rubs his eyes, then reaches for Jaxon, who keeps his hands resting on his muscular thighs. "She's pregnant, Jaxon, Misun is pregnant."

Jaxon sits perfectly still, perfectly silent, just looking at Luca.

Luca's eyes begin to fill with tears as he continues. "I was done with her. I never wanted to see her again, and now she's pregnant."

"When was the last time you slept with her, Luca?" Jaxon asks, with barely a change to his flat facial expression.

"It's been almost three months. She showed me the blood test results from her doctor." Luca reaches for Jax and pulls him close so that their foreheads are touching. "I don't want to do this with her, Jax. I want you. I know this is new, but you're everything. I feel everything with you that I've ever wanted to feel for another person."

Jaxon relaxes and grasps Luca's cheeks. "I feel it too, Luca, I do. But you're going to have a baby with her."

"Jax, you don't understand!" Luca starts getting more emotional, and puts his own hands on top of Jaxon's, still caressing his cheeks. "She insists that this baby is mine, but I don't know! I can't know until it's born!' Luca pulls back a bit so that he can meet Jaxon's eyes. "I caught her in bed with another man. It's what broke me." Jaxon sighs deeply as Luca continues. "I can't ask you to wait until I know for sure. I can't ask you to get involved in this mess. I'm so sorry." Luca lowers his gaze.

A few minutes of silence pass, then Jaxon speaks. "Luca, look at me." Luca meets Jaxon's eyes once more. "If this baby is yours, will you want Misun? Do you want to be a family?"

"Never," Luca responds with certainty. "We will have to learn to co-parent, but she will never be my family."

Jaxon brushes a strand of Luca's hair from his brow. "Well, then you don't have to ask me. I'm not going anywhere."

Luca grabs Jax and kisses his full lips. "What?" he says between kisses. "You still want me? Are you sure?" It's so much to ask of you!"

Jax kisses Luca's forehead. "I'm sure Luca. I've been waiting so long to feel this way about someone. I've been waiting for my person." Luca just smiles and Jax continues. "I know that this relationship is new, and yes, this is a lot. But I think that you're my person, Luca."

Luca gives Jaxon gentle kisses. First, one on each eyelid as he runs a finger down Jax's cheek. He then moves to his nose and each cheek, lightly brushing his lips on the soft skin. When he reaches Jaxon's full lips, he lets his lips linger there, tasting him. Luca can't believe that this beautiful man is real. "Thank you, Angel," he whispers. "Thank you for believing in me."

Jaxon runs his tongue along Luca's lower lip, sighing as he deepens their kiss. He wraps his arms around Luca's neck, pulling him closer, and Luca responds by running his hands up and down Jaxon's back. Luca's hand slips under Jaxon's white t-shirt, his fingers trailing circles on Jax's lower back before lifting it up and over his head.

Jaxon unfastens the buttons of Luca's dress shirt, kissing and running his tongue along his neck, nipping and sucking at his collarbone and trailing down his chest. Luca tips his head to the side, completely overwhelmed by the feeling of his boyfriend's tongue against his skin. He feels his cock hardening in his slacks, and Jaxon runs his hand down over the zipper lightly touching him there. Jaxon pulls his head back, a seductive smile on his lips, as he guides Luca's hand to the front of his tightening jeans. They continue to kiss and explore each other's mouths and skin with their tongues, as they touch each other through their clothing.

Jaxon starts to unbuckle Luca's belt, reaching for the button of his pants. "This okay?" he whispers against Luca's ear.

Luca nods, and traces his fingers around Jaxon's belly button, and follows the faint trail of hair toward his jeans. He looks at Jaxon.

"Yes, yeah good." The air is hot around them, and the room is silent except for the heavy breathing of the men as they kiss and caress each other. Luca pushes Jax gently back on the sofa and places a throw pillow under his head. He begins to rub himself against Jaxon, feeling their cocks against each other through too much fabric. Jaxon wants to feel Luca's skin. He lifts his hips, lowering his jeans.

Luca lightly touches Jaxon's erection with more confidence this time, looking down and smiling. "No underwear, hmmm?"

"Easier access!" Jax pushes Luca's slacks and boxer briefs toward his knees.

The men continue to touch each other, kissing, licking, and sucking at necks and chests. Jaxon takes his hand and wraps it around both of their cocks, running his palm over their heads and the pre-come dripping there. "Still okay?" He asks Luca, who groans in response, and places his larger hand over Jaxon's circling them together. They begin to move as one, panting into each other's mouths as they kiss and rub their erections together.

Luca can't believe how good it feels like this, being so intimate with his boyfriend. Touching him. Being touched. Luca whispers "I'm close Jax, so close."

"Go ahead, come for me," Jaxon pants, and feels Luca's release, continuing to stroke him through his orgasm while getting so close to his own. Luca's come coats both of them, and the feeling of it pushes Jax over the edge, tensing and shaking with both of their hands still circling their lengths.

Luca collapses down onto Jax, panting into his shoulder. "That was, wow. Another new experience for me!"

Jaxon kisses the silky skin of his exposed shoulder; Luca's dress shirt having fallen to his elbows. "I hope it wasn't too much. I know we agreed to go slow."

"Angel, I want more of you. All of you." Luca rubs his nose on Jax's cheek. "Can I stay tonight?"

Jaxon runs his fingers through Luca's messy hair. "Not tonight, Luca. It's too soon. You have a lot to think about, and so do I." Luca nods as Jax continues. "I'm not going anywhere, so we have plenty of time."

Luca lowers his head to Jax, nose to nose. "You're right. I just love being with you." He pushes up off the sofa. "Now let's get cleaned up and I'll go."

Twenty minutes later, they share a tender kiss by the door and Luca heads home. Jaxon makes himself a mug of tea and heads back over to the sofa. He lays down, pulling a soft fleece blanket over himself, and looks at the night sky. *I hope that I'm doing the right thing. I hope that he doesn't change his mind.* So many thoughts come rushing into Jaxon's head. His tears start falling, and he can't seem to stop them.

Chapter 11

"Sheesh, Taylor." Jax laughs as he watches his best friend rearrange the assortment of fresh flowers in the vase for the fifth time. "Now it's your turn to be all nervous and flustered!" He finishes setting the table by placing the folded napkins on mismatched but artfully coordinated plates. Taylor walks to the table, setting the centerpiece down. Jax gently stops him from adjusting the flowers once again and faces them together. He pushes a lock of Taylor's wavy hair from his clammy brow. "Now then, take a deep breath."

Taylor does just that and lets out a groan in his deep baritone voice. "What on earth are these Blackwood men doing to us?"

Jax shakes his head. "I don't know, but they've certainly drawn us in." The two embrace in reassurance. "They'll be here any minute, you go and freshen up."

"Are you sure that you're okay? You know, with everything?"

Jax nods and points in the direction of the

bathroom. He watches as Taylor follows his instruction, and inhales. He feels nervous this time. Things are a bit different than before, and he is still adjusting to his thoughts. Tucking his shirt neatly into his jeans, he brushes himself down and heads to the fridge for a beer. The intercom buzzes, startling both men even though they were expecting it.

Taylor runs from the bathroom, wiping his face with a towel, and presses the button to let them in. He looks at Jax who stifles his laughter with his hand. Taylor's nervousness is so unusual yet endearing. He opens the door to allow Luca and Jasper to enter.

Jax immediately heads over to Luca, throwing his arms lazily over his shoulders. He noses at his neck inhaling his familiar scent, raising his lips to initiate a passionate kiss. Jasper and Taylor glance at each other awkwardly, not really knowing how to act around each other.

"Um, come in," Taylor eventually says, motioning him to follow. Luca and Jaxon trail behind, hand in hand. "Let me take your jacket, and you can have a seat." Taylor takes Jasper's leather biker jacket from him, while Jasper plops down on the well-worn cozy chair by the couch. Taylor hangs his jacket by the door, using the moment to compose himself. *Shit, he had to wear that tight shirt with his tattoos showing just to kill me.* He grabs beers from the kitchen, knowing

Jasper's preferred drink.

"Did you order the food?" Luca asks Jax, who nods. He starts to pull his wallet from his pocket.

"No, no." Taylor waves in his direction, walking over to join them. "It's on me for everything that Blackwood has done for me." He looks at Jax. "For us."

Luca smiles, sliding it back into his jeans. "Okay, if you're sure. But believe me, you're an asset to the team, and we're the grateful ones." He turns to Jax, pecking him on the lips again. "I've missed you."

Taylor hands everyone a beer and the men make easy flowing conversation. The food arrives and the four of them move to the nicely set table to enjoy it, even though it's far too much for them all. Jax informs the Blackwood men that Taylor always orders way too much, because he likes to eat the takeout leftovers the following day.

"Ugh." Luca grimaces while opening some of the cartons. "I can't do day-old takeout." He tips his drink towards his cousin. "But Jasper's fridge is always full of leftovers."

Jax bursts into laughter. "Match made in heaven then," he teases, causing Taylor to glare at him in embarrassment.

Jasper's cheeks flush too. "I really like your place here." He looks around, changing the subject. "I love how you've decorated."

"Oh, yeah," Luca says, dishing some rice onto his plate. "I forgot that this is your first time here."

"It's mostly Taylor, he is the designer, after all." Jaxon squeezes Taylor's shoulder and continues. "At least you can see our floor now that he's working from his studio!"

Jasper nods. "It's cool." Turning to Taylor, he smiles. "Maybe you could come over to my place one day to give me some style tips?"

Jax giggles, leaning into Luca. "Is that what they're calling it now?" Luca joins in with the laughter, and Jasper playfully punches him on the arm.

The meal passes smoothly, and the four make conversation until the dishes have been cleared away, Luca still grumbling about how vile leftovers are as he puts them in the fridge.

All of the men head to the sitting area to continue the evening. Luca curls up in the corner of the sofa resting his back against the arm. Jax snuggles against him and Luca twirls strands of his hair between his fingers. Taylor and Jasper sprawl out on the floor, relaxing on the many brightly covered cushions that Taylor had sewn.

"I can't get over this view!" Jasper exclaims, rolling on to his front to stare out of the windows, sipping his beer.

Taylor shuffles closer and lays beside him. He notices goosebumps develop on the skin of Jasper's arm as they briefly touch. "I love this view so much." He turns to look at Jasper, who shyly glances towards him. "This one isn't too bad either."

Luca smiles as Jax raises an eyebrow at the two of them flirting. "Oh, just get it on you two!" Jax teases again.

"Will you stop it!" Taylor orders his friend, a tiny smirk developing on his lips. He turns back to Jasper, realizing that their faces are so close. Closer than they have ever been. He can feel Jasper's elevated breath on his cheek.

Taking this chance, he leans in and places a long, lingering kiss on a slightly surprised Jasper's lips. He doesn't pull away; he closes his eyes at the soft feeling. They don't move, just let the moment stay as gentle as it is.

The mood is broken by a familiar voice. "Finally," Luca says. "You two took your time."

"Stop teasing them." Jax snickers. "But I also agree."

"Who would have thought it?" Luca smiles as Taylor and Jax sit up, glancing at each other coyly. "Because of Taylor entering Aspire to

Design, the four of us would have ended up like this."

"Before the show, neither of us were even out as gay," Jasper says.

Luca waves his hands. "I'm not gay. I can't be. I must be bi, I think. Well, I'm happy where I am." He kisses Jax on the head.

"True." Jasper tilts his beer bottle towards him. "You are having a baby after all."

Luca's face drains, "Yes, Jasper. Thanks for the reminder."

Jasper scrunches his face up in regret for his words. "Sorry Luca, I didn't mean to..."

"It's fine, honestly." Luca reassures, sighing. "I have to face it at some point."

Jax lifts Luca's arm and kisses the skin. "And we're here for you every step of the way."

The men on the floor nod their heads and mumble in agreement. "We are," Jasper says. "It will all be okay."

Taylor gets up and makes his way to the fridge for more drinks. "What about you, Jax?" He knows that his best friend is still struggling with the whole baby situation, so swerves the topic away. "Your meeting with Bella. Are you ready for it?"

Jax puffs his cheeks at the thought of his interview, even though he keeps getting reassurance that it is just an informal chat. Bella Blackwood is such a high-profile woman in the fashion and design industry, the thought of being in front of her terrifies him.

"Hmm, maybe," he says. "I still don't know why she wants me. I'm a dancer first and foremost."

Sitting back next to Jasper, a little closer than before, Taylor hands him a bottle. "But, like, have you seen your face, Jax? You are fucking stunning, man."

"I'm biased anyway," Luca quips. "But I one hundred percent agree there."

Taylor pats Jax on the knee and smiles, turning back towards Jasper who's watching him. "You will be just fine. These Blackwood's aren't that scary."

**

Jaxon rubs his eyes a little harder than he should and immediately curses himself. Taking his phone out of his pocket, he flicks the camera on to selfie mode to see if he's made his face red.

Clicking it off, he smiles at the text of encouragement from Taylor, reminding him that he's in the same building, that he's thinking of him, and to stop by his studio when he's done.

"You can go into the office now," Noah's assistant says, breaking him from his thoughts.

Jax thanks him and stands, smoothing down his fitted black suit and white ruffled shirt. He is suddenly feeling a little too dressed up for this. Taking a big deep breath in, he runs his hand through his styled blond hair that he spent far too long on, and heads into the office.

"Jaxon, darling!" Bella's bellowing voice echoes around the room, pulling him into an embrace, allowing him to kiss her on each cheek. "Come. Sit."

Doing as he's instructed, Jax can't help but notice how exuberant and different she is from the Blackwood men in the family. With her tall stiletto heels, her tight-fitting black dress, and long colorful over-shirt, she is certainly the brightest out of them all.

She leans against the desk, and Noah shakes Jaxon's hand before he settles into his chair. Noah offers him a drink, and Jax politely declines with instant regret considering how dry his mouth and lips are.

"So," Bella continues, "you've met my nephew Noah, but I'm not sure if you have met my son Jayce?" She looks over at her eldest, who is completely distracted messaging on his phone. She clears her throat loud enough to get his attention. "Jayce?"

He sits up in surprise, setting his phone onto the shelf next to him. He leans over to shake Jax's hand himself. "Please excuse my ignorance," he says trying to ignore his mother glaring at him from the side. "I'm Jayce, also a model."

Jax blushes, feeling shy. "Well, I'm not really a model, I was literally just doing it as a favor for my best friend."

"Yes," Bella says. "The beautiful Taylor. I've heard all about your friendship from him, and that just makes us want you as part of Blackwood even more. Not to mention how close you are to Luca. It makes perfect sense for you to join us here." She strides behind Jax, her shirt swishing as she moves. As she places her hands on his shoulders, Jax is a little surprised at how friendly and affectionate she is. "You will fit in perfectly."

Noah finally speaks. "Looking at the photographs that Jasper took for Aspire to Design, we can see that you have something special. We would really love to have you on board."

Jayce nods in agreement. "It's true, the camera loves you. I'd like it if you would come and join our team. We'll give you all the help and guidance that you need."

"But, my dancing really is my first passion..."

Jax starts.

"We know, and we fully appreciate that. We would never want you to give that up," Noah says.

"Which is why," Bella coos, proudly, "we plan to make an addition of a Blackwood Dance School within the company, and we would like to offer you the position of head dance teacher if you are willing to accept."

Noah continues where his aunt left off. "Yes, we already have studio space as part of our on-site athletic facilities. We currently offer yoga and Pilates classes and have had inquiries regarding dance classes." Noah leans back in his chair and continues to address Jax. "We would like to offer classes to our employees and their families. If all goes well, we are in a position to be able to expand to the general public."

Jaxon sits open-mouthed at the proposal as Noah hands him some papers that read *Contract,* his mind swirling in utter surprise. "Um," he says, trying to stop his hands from shaking as he spots the salary figures jumping out among the black printed ink. All he can think about is the fact that he could stop teaching the low paid dance lessons. No more struggling to pay half of the rent every month, and being able to begin modeling while also continuing to teach? This is a dream come true.

Bella can see the shock by his paled cheeks

and smiles sweetly. "It's okay, darling, you really don't need to make a decision now. Go away and think about it. Read the contract and see what you think. There really is no pressure."

"I don't need to think about it," Jax mumbles quietly. "Could I please have some water?" Jayce pours him a glass. "I'd love to accept it. A job like this would be crazy to turn down. If you'll have me, then I'll take it."

Bella shrieks in excitement, clapping her hands together. "Yes! That's fabulous. I still want you to take that away and have a good read of it before you sign anything. Okay?"

Jax nods, his hands trying to hold the glass steady as he takes a sip. Noah leans forward onto the desk. "Not to discuss too much about your personal life, as that is your business. But, of course, we are aware of your relationship with Luca. Not to mention this situation with Misun, and firstly I want to personally thank you for being there for him and for making him happy." Jax blushes, feeling a little uncomfortable with three of his boyfriend's family members staring at him. "Secondly, we appreciate that as well as things are going now, sometimes situations may change." Jax presumes that he means if they break up. "So, what I'm trying to say is that your life with Luca is completely separate from your work life here, and nothing will affect that."

"Thank you, I appreciate that," Jax replies.

Jayce stands up and extends a hand to Jaxon. "Now how about I walk you down to the athletic facility and have the manager show you around? "

"That sounds amazing." Jax smiles widely, getting up to kiss Bella on both cheeks and shake Noah's hand. "I can't thank you enough for this opportunity."

**

Hurriedly rushing down the corridor, Jax can't wipe the smile from his face. Bursting through the door, Taylor shrieks as he's startled. "Jesus, Jaxon, what the hell is wrong with you?" he says, sucking the blood from his finger that he's just caught with a needle. "You never heard of knocking?"

door a bit more gently than the way he came in. "Guess what?"

"Well," Taylor says, placing the samples down and swiveling in his seat to face his friend, "I'm kind of guessing that the meeting went well?"

"Went well?" Jax exclaims. "Went well? It went better than that."

He thrusts the contract papers into Taylor's hands, his face all flushed and his eyes glistening with excitement. Taylor smiles fondly, taking a look at the document. "Wow, look at this for a model's salary." He keeps reading, as Jax bounces impatiently, waiting for him to spot it. The wait seems like forever as he watches him scan the papers. "Wait..." Taylor stands up slowly from the stool and looks at his friend. "A dance school?"

"Mhhhmm!" Jax grins. "And they want me to

run it."

"Oh shit!" Taylor flings his arms around Jax. "I am so happy for you."

Jax's eyes start well at the thought of having a stable career. "I can't believe it."

Taylor hands him his contract back. "Look at you." He rubs Jax's arm. "New boyfriend and not one, but two new jobs."

"Oh!" Jax says, "I need to go and see Luca tell him. He's stuck with me now."

Taylor shakes his head laughing as Jax runs out of the office as quickly as he came in.

Chapter 12

"What time did they say they're coming?" Victoria asks Noah as she crosses her long legs and takes a sip of her lemon drop martini. She meets her fiancé's eyes as she runs her tongue along the rim of the glass, licking up a bit of sugar.

Noah raises his eyebrows and gulps his drink. Jameson on the rocks, as always. "Behave," he says. "They're on the way."

"Can't help it." Victoria sets down her glass and twists her blonde hair into a bun before letting it fall onto her shoulders again. She rarely wears her hair down these days. "I'm just so glad to have a night free of classes and away from my laptop."

The couple intertwines their fingers with their elbows resting on the table. Noah brings Victoria's hand to his lips, giving it several soft kisses. "You've been working so hard, babe. I can't wait to help you relax tonight." Victoria rests her head on Noah's shoulder. "But for now, let's enjoy a little time out."

Victoria sips at her cocktail. "I've met Heidi quite a few times at Blackwood, but we don't really know each other. She seems really sweet. Smart, too."

"Ah, here they are." Noah stands as Harrison and Heidi approach their table. The cousins pat each other on the shoulder, and Harrison leans in to kiss Victoria on the cheek. Noah gives Heidi a quick embrace, and the women face each other, grasping hands.

"Heidi, I'm so happy that you came! I'm looking forward to getting to know you better," Victoria says with a genuine smile on her beautiful face.

"Me too." Heidi smiles back squeezing Victoria's hands.

The four of them sit, and the cocktail waitress comes right over. The Blackwoods frequent the quiet little jazz bar often, and she knows how well they tip. "Another round. Mr. Blackwood?" Noah nods at the waitress' question, and Harrison orders a cabernet for him and Heidi.

"Actually," Heidi addresses the server. "Could I have one of those?" She gestures to Victoria's glass.

"I think we'll get along just fine!" Victoria giggles and Heidi joins in. "I was just telling Noah how excited I am to get to know you better."

"I feel the same way," Heidi replies. "Harrison and I just started our relationship, but I already know so much of the family from work." Harrison grasps her hand across the table. "It kind of seems like I already know you, Victoria, from hearing so much about you from the boys."

The waitress brings the drinks to the table, and the four clink their glasses together. "Good things, I hope." Victoria smiles while sipping on her fresh drink and leans in towards Heidi.

"Of course. All good things." Heidi releases Harrison's hand. "Unlike, Misun," she says under her breath. Everyone at the table quiets, and Noah takes a deep breath. "I'm so sorry. I shouldn't have said that." Heidi rubs at her temples and looks at her boyfriend.

"I just told Heidi the news." Harrison sighs, and Noah grasps his arm in reassurance. "I just can't fucking believe it."

"Oh, I believe it!" Victoria's face flushes, her anger apparent to all of them. "I was so relieved when he got rid of that bitch. Now, this? I know damn well that she planned it all." Victoria tips back the rest of her drink and slams her glass onto the table, signaling to the waitress for another.

Heidi puts her hands on top of Victoria's. "I really shouldn't have brought it up, but I'm furious too. I take it you feel the same way that I do about Misun?"

"Woman's intuition, whatever it is. I knew when they first started dating that she was trouble," Victoria says.

Noah finally speaks up, "Babe, I know how you feel, and we've talked about this before. Luca is a grown man and he's always been free to make his own decisions."

"Yeah," Harrison adds, "but when it comes to Misun, Luca has always made shit decisions."

Heidi pushes her pretty red fringe off from her freckled forehead. "Well from what I've heard from Harrison and Luca, he seems very happy with Jax. I just hope that it works out for them."

"Well we were all surprised about their relationship, but Luca really seems enamored with Jaxon." Harrison raises an eyebrow.

"Jaxon is an amazing and genuine person, from what I've seen so far." Noah sips at his whiskey. "He's agreed to stay with Luca through all of this."

Victoria reaches over to stroke Noah's hand. "I can't wait to meet him. I just hope that Misun doesn't ruin it. Now that she's having Luca's baby, he's never going to get rid of her."

"Well, all that we can do is support Luca through this," Noah says. "That's what family is for."

"I agree." Harrison nods as he sips at his wine. "We'll all be here for him."

"Now tell me about you two!" Victoria tries to lighten the mood. "How is it going, working together now that you're in a relationship?"

"Really well actually," Heidi says. "All of that tension between us is gone, so it makes it easier."

The men order some appetizers to soak up the alcohol, as Heidi and Victoria chat. "That's wonderful." Victoria smiles. "You two seem great together."

"Well we've been working as a team for so long, it just kind of carries over into our relationship." Heidi leans forward into Victoria's space. "I'm so happy, Victoria, I really am."

Victoria squeezes Heidi. "Love is in the air at Blackwood! What did you put in the water coolers, Noah?"

Noah and Harrison both laugh, enjoying the sight of their girls getting along so well.

"Speaking of that," Victoria adds. "Jasper finally texted me about getting coffee. I can't wait to hear all about Taylor! He can't possibly be as adorable as he was on Aspire to Design, I practically fell in love with him myself!"

"Hey!" Noah says, causing everyone to laugh.

"Ummmm, he is, Victoria, he totally is." Heidi blushes slightly, placing a hand over her soft pink lips. "Absolutely gorgeous, funny, quirky, and talented?" Oh my god."

"I know, right?" Victoria swoons. "His designs for the finale? I thought I would die."

"You should see the sketches he's working on for the rest of the collection!" Heidi giggles again, and the women lean together until their foreheads almost touch.

Noah drains his glass as Harrison looks at Heidi, then at Victoria, then at his cousin. "What the fuck is happening here?"

"Looks like a meeting of the Taylor King fan club!" Noah says as another round of drinks is passed around. "Thank god he's gay or we'd be screwed."

"Can't help it if we're jealous of Jasper!" Victoria giggles again, feeling the effects of her martinis.

"So you two," Heidi addresses Noah and Victoria, changing the subject again before their men get too irritated. "Tell me about your wedding!"

"It's not for another ten months," Noah says. "Victoria is so busy with school, and so am I with my new position."

"How's the planning going, though?" Heidi questions.

"Well, Noah's mother is taking care of that. She has a wedding planner, and it's not really my thing, so..." Victoria explains, and looks at her fiancé.

"Victoria would rather just elope! She's really doing this for my family, for my Mum," Noah says.

"Yeah, I barely survived the engagement party!" Victoria gasps, recalling the elaborate affair.

Harrison joins in. "Yeah, my aunt loves throwing those fancy as fuck parties. Uncle Alexander just lets her do her thing."

"I do still need to find a dress though." Victoria grabs Heidi's hand. "Maybe you could help me? I could use your expertise!"

Heidi grabs Victoria's hands. "Yes, yes, yes! I'd love to!" Heidi pauses for a moment, looking at her boyfriend, then back at her new friend. "Victoria, what if we asked Taylor to design one for you?"

Victoria clasps her hand over her open mouth, and both women hug each other excitedly.

"Here we go again!" Harrison sighs jokingly, leaning back in his chair.

"Well," Noah says, turning to Harrison. "I'm sure it will be a wedding to remember!"

"You're right about that!" Harrison clinks glasses with his cousin, "It certainly will be."

**

Luca smiles as he steps into the door of the studio. Leaning against the wall beside it, he brushes his jacket back and thrusts his hands into his pants pocket, watching the scene before him.

Jax is sitting at the desk in the corner, filing through some papers. His headphones are in and he's humming away to the music. Looking around the place, Luca can already see that in just a couple weeks since being offered the position, his boyfriend has put his stamp on the studio. Dance posters are pinned to the notice boards, and extra full-length mirrors line the walls.

He stares endearingly at Jaxon, who runs his hands through his fluffy, unstyled hair. His wide-neck crisp white t-shirt hangs loosely on one side, showing off his toned shoulder and defining collarbone. Sighing contentedly, Luca waits for Jax to look up and notice him.

"Oh hey!" Jaxon jumps up pulling his headphones out and flinging them down with the papers. Running over to Luca, he throws his arms around him, drawing him in for a cuddle. "How long have you been here?"

Luca pulls him by the waist closer, kissing his lips softly, a groan escaping him as he does. "Not long. It was fun just watching you look all handsome and mine."

"Stop it." Jax blushes, playfully slapping Luca's arm. "You know that makes me embarrassed when you say things like that."

Fondly stroking Jax's cheek with the back of his forefinger, Luca grins and gazes into his man's sparkling eyes. "It's true. I've never seen anyone so beautiful."

Jax pecks him on the lips again. "You are too sweet." He grabs his hand and leads him into the room more. "Come and look at this,"

"I have been into this studio before," Luca laughs. "It *is* owned by Blackwood."

Chuckling, Jax stops him in the middle of the shiny wooden floor, and faces him, holding both of his hands. "I know, I know. But I'm here now."

"And just look at you!" Luca squeezes his fingers. "Here, a dance teacher and a model. I am so proud of you." Jaxon's ears turn as red as his face at the compliments, shuffling his feet on the floor. "You deserve it, Jax. You do."

"I wouldn't have been able to do it without you, though. And everyone else at Blackwood." He smiles. "And let's not forget my main man, Taylor."

"Main man?" Luca teases. "Oh, I see how it is!" He pretends to try and struggle away from Jax, who throws his head back laughing.

Jax pulls Luca over to the desk and grabs the documents he had been holding before, bringing them up to show him. "Look. Look at how busy the classes are."

Luca scans all of the class schedules for the next few weeks. "Well, the classes *are* being taught by an amazing and inspiring dancer. One that is also a handsome model who wore the winning designs on Aspire to Design. Who wouldn't want that?"

Luca's facial features falter, the sparkle in his eyes fading as his hand drops to his side. Jax holds his shoulders. "Hey. What's wrong?"

Luca shrugs, placing the forms back onto the desk. "I just wish that I could be here for opening day tomorrow."

Jax wraps him in his arms, holding him close. "I know, me too. But you know that you have to go to that appointment, don't you?"

Nodding, Luca sniffs into Jax's shoulder, breathing in the comforting scent of vanilla that he is accustomed to now. "I do. I know I do." He pulls away in frustration. "It's just so fucked up all of this."

"Look." Jax sighs. "I know that it's not ideal and that the timing is shit with us just getting together. But the fact is that Misun is pregnant, and it could be yours." He pulls Luca's face up to look at him. "It needs to be dealt with regardless. I know that you'll do the right thing. You are just that sort of person. Let's just take it one day at a time, right?" Luca nods his head at him. "Go to the sonogram tomorrow with her, and then when the next appointment comes, we can deal with that too. We can do this together." Bringing his thumb and finger under Luca's chin, he smiles. "Right?"

"Right." The corners of Luca's lips turn up more at the support from Jax. Looking over at the sound system in the far corner, he motions towards it. "Does that work?"

Frowning, Jax turns to where Luca is directing them. "The music? Sure." He faces Luca again. "Why?"

Luca starts from Jax's hair and trails his fingers down his jawline, tracing over his exposed collarbones and gliding down his arms until their hands are gently caressing each other. "Dance for me," he whispers.

"Now?" Jax stutters, and Luca hums in acknowledgment. "Oh! Okay." He makes his way over to the high tech set up and presses a few buttons to start it up.

Luca leans back against the table, resting his hands behind him. He crosses one leg over the other and tells Jax to pick whatever he wants. He presses a few more buttons and heads towards the center of the dance floor.

Jaxon places himself in his starting dance position, and the music starts up filling the air in the entire studio. Luca tilts his head to one side, taking in the sight before him. He has seen Jax dance before briefly, but this is the first time he has taken it in properly.

Jax still manages to glide around the space in his ripped blue jeans and white shirt, his black leather boots making virtually no sound on the flooring below him. Luca can't believe how graceful he looks. His movements are almost hypnotic, making Luca hold his breath as he watches.

The song finishes with Jax lying on the floor, his eyes closed and his breathing heavy. Luca has to pull himself out of his trance. Making his way over to Jax, he kneels beside him. Jaxon opens his eyes, beads of sweat pooling on his forehead and attaching to strands of his hair. He turns his head to face Luca.

"Was that what you wanted?" he pants, his hand on his fast-rising chest.

"It was perfect, Angel." Luca lowers himself to kiss Jax's lips, not caring about the perspiration collected there. "Absolutely perfect."

Jax wraps his arms around Luca's neck, pulling him to rest on his chest. Luca catches their reflection in the mirror. "We look pretty good together, don't we?"

Chuckling, Jax tilts up and follows Luca's gaze. They spend a moment just taking in their reflection until Luca softly speaks. "Jax?"

Jaxon's stomach flips in anticipation. "Yeah?" he asks, trying to stay calm.

Luca takes a deep breath. "I just want to say something. I know that things are weird right now, but you still want to be with me, don't you?"

"Of course, I do, Luca. More than anything," Jax reassures him.

"Good... because, Jax... I'm..." His cheeks flare crimson, "I..." Jax tries to speak, but Luca covers his lips with his finger. "Please let me get this out. Jax, I'm sorry if this is too soon. I didn't even know you a month ago. But... I'm falling for you."

Jax gasps, grabbing Luca's hand against his mouth, drawing it away slowly. "You... you are?" Luca bows his head, and Jax's eyes fill with tears.

"Please tell me that these," he says, wiping at the tears trickling down Jax's cheeks, "are because you're happy?"

"Yes!" Jax tumbles them both over, ending up with Luca on his back and Jax on top of him. "Me too, Luca, me too."

Luca looks up at Jax's tear-stained face and thinks that he could never be as attracted to anyone the way he is to Jax. "Say it to me," he whispers. "Tell me how you feel."

Jax kisses Luca's lips, sliding his leg in between Luca's thighs. "I love you, Mr. Blackwood." He feels Luca's heart pumping fiercely against his chest at his words.

Luca teases his fingers through Jax's hair, drawing his face closer. They kiss passionately, their tongues tasting each other, conveying the emotion that they both feel. Jax pecks tiny touches with his lips around Luca's cheeks before slowly nibbling his bottom lip. He can feel Luca's cock becoming erect through his slacks, as he teases his thigh against it.

Groaning out, Luca uses his strength to flip them both over. He takes another glance at their reflection in the mirror, before looking back at Jax. "I love you too."

Chapter 13

Luca has never felt so out of place before. He looks around the waiting room, posters on the wall showing different stages of fetal development; baby care magazines stacked on the coffee table in front of him. He glances over at Misun who is sitting next to him. Her shiny black hair conceals her face as she bends forward, texting. Her phone has been pinging relentlessly signaling incoming messages.

"I need to make a quick call," Misun says while standing to step into the hall.

What the fuck? Luca waits a few seconds, then goes to the door, cracking it open and easing out after Misun.

She has her back to him and is loudly whispering to someone on the phone. "I told you to stop messaging me! No... I'm absolutely sure. Yes, I know...stop talking and listen to me! This is not your baby, it's Luca's baby...Stop. Just stop...don't call me again." Misun ends the call and sighs, turning around, shocked to see Luca.

"You have got to be kidding me Misun! What the fuck? Was that *him*?" Luca run's his hands through his dark hair and steps directly in front of Misun. "How do you even know that I'm the father. This baby could very well belong to that bastard!"

Misun puts her hands on Luca's shoulders and looks into his eyes. "It's yours, Luca. I used protection except with you."

Luca pulls away from her. "Yeah, and you were supposed to be on the pill, Misun! Jesus!"

"I was, Luca! I must have missed a day or two!" Misun looks at him innocently.

"Like I'm supposed to believe that, Mi." Luca shakes his head and turns to open the door. "Let's go back in so we don't miss this damn appointment."

**

Misun lays on the exam table with her head propped up on a pillow. "I'm Laura, and I'll be performing your exam today." The technician tells them. "Are you ready to see your baby?" Laura says while lifting Misun's shirt and draping a sheet over her lower waist.

"Yes, I'm ready," Misun says, glancing at Luca.

"How about you, Dad, are you excited?" the technician says to Luca, who doesn't reply. He sits back in his seat taking a deep breath. "This is just a warm gel that I will be putting on your belly," she continues, and Misun nods. "Okay here we go!" Laura runs the sonogram wand over Misun's stomach while looking at the screen. "Ahhh okay, there's your baby! Can you see the heartbeat?"

Luca removes his glasses and leans towards the screen. He sees a tiny heart beating. "Right there?"

Laura nods. "The heartbeat is strong, and the rate is just as it should be."

"Are those fingers?" Luca asks, pointing to the image.

"Yes, those are fingers, and I see five on each hand. Perfect," Laura says enthusiastically while moving the wand a bit. "And here are some toes!"

"Misun, are you seeing this?" Luca grins excitedly while grabbing her hand. Misun is looking at Luca but briefly shifts her gaze to the screen.

"Yes, I see it," Misun replies, looking again at Luca, who can't take his eyes off the grainy display.

Laura continues to point out areas in the sonogram image. "Here you can see the head and the spine. Everything is looking great."

"Can you tell if it's a boy or girl?" Luca asks, putting his glasses back on.

"No, not yet, it's a bit early. Looks like the baby is about fifteen or sixteen weeks, according to the measurements," the technician says and looks at Misun. "Mom, you doing okay? You've been quiet. I know it can be overwhelming."

"No, I'm fine. It's very exciting," Misun answers in a rather flat tone.

Luca brushes back Misun's hair and rubs her cheek. "Mi, look at that! A perfect baby. It's so tiny in there, but it's already moving!"

"I can't feel it moving," Misun replies. "All that I feel is nauseous."

"Well the nausea is normal, as you know," Laura tells Misun, "and you won't feel the baby move for another few weeks. Your doctor will give you more information at your next appointment." She puts the wand down and wipes the gel from Misun's belly. "Everything looks amazing. Congratulations to both of you. I'm printing out some pictures for you."

Luca takes the pictures, a wide smile on his face. "Thank you so much."

**

Luca pulls into traffic in his Audi, Misun relaxing in the passenger seat. "Do you want the seat heater on?" he asks Misun.

"Oh, Luca, so sweet, are you worried about me?" Misun replies in a saccharine tone.

Luca glances at her. "Misun, you're pregnant. You know I won't let you do this alone."

Should We?

"So generous of you, Luca, but how will you have time for me with your new *boyfriend?* What's his name again? Jason?"

"It's Jaxon, Misun. You know that. Please don't start." Luca raises his tone. "You just saw your baby for the first time, and this is how you're acting?"

"It's your baby too, Luca. And now you're going to be too preoccupied sucking dick to take care of us."

"Need I remind you that *you're* the one that cheated on *me?* You broke my heart Misun. And with *him* of all people." Luca is almost yelling, the fury evident in his voice.

The rest of the drive is quiet. Misun looks out the window while Luca grips the steering wheel tightly, gritting his teeth. He pulls into Misun's parking spot at her apartment complex, still staring straight ahead.

Misun sighs and rubs Luca's shoulder, breaking the silence. "It was a mistake, Luca. A terrible mistake." Luca turns to look at her with a tear running down his cheek. "Can you please walk me up so we can discuss things?" Luca doesn't say a word. He gets out of his car and walks around to open Misun's door. They remain in silence until they enter Misun's apartment.

"I have nothing to say Misun. I will support you and the baby, but I'm in love with Jax and we plan on staying together."

"In love with him?" Misun laughs. "You just met him, Luca, and he's a *man!*" She steps closer to Luca, wrapping her arms around his neck. "Do you honestly think he'll stick around after the baby is born? Would you tie him down like that?" Misun gently wipes the tears away that are running down Luca's cheeks. "Luca, you still love me. I know you do. Look at this." Misun takes the sonogram photo from Luca's shirt pocket, showing it to him. "It's our baby." Misun begins brushing her lips over Luca's, whispering to him. "We belong together, Luca, as a family." She starts to kiss Luca, pressing her body against his. Luca begins to respond to the kiss, taking in her familiar taste and scent. "No one can make you feel as good as I can Luca." Misun takes his hand pulling him toward her bedroom.

Luca suddenly draws his hand away. "Stop it, Misun. This is not happening! I do not love you anymore. I will support you and be a father to the baby, but we will never be a family!" Luca can't believe that he almost fell under Misun's spell once again.

Misun pushes him back. "Okay, Luca, I understand. But here's something for *you* to understand." The look in Misun's eyes sends shivers up Luca's neck. "I am *not* keeping this baby." She holds up the sonogram photo once again for Luca to see.

"What? What are you saying, Misun?" Luca grabs her shoulders squeezing tightly.

Misun pulls herself out of Luca's grip. "You heard me; I'm not going to have this baby." She walks to the kitchen and pours herself a glass of wine. "It's what, sixteen weeks? That's still early enough, I'll find a doctor."

Luca strides over grabbing the wine out of Misun's hand, dumping it down the drain. "You wouldn't. You saw that baby moving, Mi. It's part of you. That's your child!"

Misun grabs his face in her hands. "Yes, Luca, and if you want it to be born, if you want to find out if it's your child too, then you're going to have to do something for me."

Luca is close to panicking. He cannot believe that this is the woman that he used to love; that this beautiful woman could be saying such ugly words. He grasps his head in his hands before looking Misun in the eyes. "What is it, Misun? What do you want from me?"

**

Putting his key into the door of his apartment, Taylor stops to take in the face standing next to him. "I've had such a good time this evening." He smiles.

Jasper returns a fond expression and kisses his lips. "Me too." He sighs. "Thank you for inviting me up."

Taylor brushes a lock of Jasper's hair from in front of his blue eyes and lets them both into the apartment. Stepping inside laughing together with their arms lazily draped around each other, they immediately stop when they see a worried-looking Jax pacing around with his phone in his hand.

Letting go of Jasper, Taylor rushes over to his friend. "What's wrong?" he says. "Is everything okay?"

Jax shrugs his shoulders and presses the green icon on his phone, placing it to his ear. Sighing, he clicks it off again when he hears the voicemail message that he's been hearing all evening.

"I thought that you were meeting Luca tonight?" Jasper says from behind Taylor.

"Yeah, me too," Taylor adds, looking Jax up and down. Noting that he is in clothes suitable for an evening out, he frowns and pulls Jax to face him. "What's happened?"

Jax's eyes start to pool with tears hearing his friend's soothing tone. "I don't know, Tay. We were supposed to meet at the bar, but he didn't show. I waited for an hour, and he's not picking up his phone."

Taylor glances at Jasper, who shakes his head before speaking to Jax again. "He had that sonogram today with Misun, right?" Jax nods. "Have you spoken to him since then?"

"No," Jax says. "I've haven't heard from him since this morning." He tries to call Luca again to no avail.

Jasper pulls his own phone from his pocket and calls his brother, while Taylor pulls Jax in for a comforting hug, telling him that he's sure that everything is fine.

Ending the call, Jasper shakes his head. "Noah hasn't heard anything from him either. He said if we meet him, he'll help us look for Luca."

Grabbing Jax's hand, Taylor leads the three of them out of the apartment, all of their evening's plans put on hold.

**

Noah had just finished his shower when Jasper called. He runs his hands through his damp hair, addressing the group that has just met at his apartment. "Okay. So, he's not at the bar where he was supposed to meet Jax." He motions towards Jasper. "And he's not in his apartment?"

"No, he's not there," Jasper says. "He won't pick up his phone either."

Noah groans, rubbing his eyes. "Okay. Well, I'm not sure what else to suggest."

"He's not still going to be with Misun, is he?" Jasper asks.

"I hope not!" scoffs Noah. "I doubt it."

Taylor looks at Jaxon whose face is ashen with worry, and slips an arm around his shoulder, pulling him in tightly. "Could he be at

Blackwood? It's the only place that we haven't been."

Jasper and Noah exchange glances. "At work?" Noah says. "It is pretty late now. I suppose that we should check."

The four men exit the elevator and enter through the glass doors of Blackwood. They make their way to the black marble front desk where security greets them.

"Good evening, Mr. Blackwood." He nods towards Noah. "It's late. Can I help you?"

"Has Luca been in?" Jax blurts out before Noah can answer.

Noah pats Jax's arm. "Yes, we are looking for my cousin. I know he had the day off, but have you seen him?"

The man behind the desk nods. "Yes," he says, the smile fading from his lips, "he came in a couple of hours ago. He's upstairs. He didn't look in a good way, to be honest."

Thanking him for his help, the men set off for the offices. Taylor stops Jax from sprinting. They reach Luca's door at the end of the corridor and file into the room. The sensor switches on the main lighting. They all look around at the empty room, before glancing at each other.

"He's not here!" Jaxon cries out in desperation, throwing his hands up in the air. "Why is he not here?"

Taylor grips his hand. "It's okay, Jax. He has to be around somewhere. He hasn't left the building."

Noah takes a few steps forward and faces the other three. "Right, he's here somewhere. Let's all go and have a look around. We all have our phones, call if you find him."

Setting off, they go from room to room looking. Taylor bumps into Jax coming out of one of the offices looking frustrated and slamming the door.

"Hey, hey," he says, rushing to his best friend. "We'll find him."

Jaxon can't stop the tears from flowing as he leans against the wall and slides down to sit on the floor. Burying his head in his hands, he sobs. "Something is wrong, Tay. I just know it."

Taylor squats next to him, placing a hand on his shuddering shoulder. "Jax, come on. I agree that something seems strange about him disappearing, but we need to be there for him. We need to find him." He stands and pulls Jax's arm. "Jax?"

A beep makes Jax pause. Taylors draws his phone from his pocket, reads the message, and then looks at Jax. "Jasper has found him."

Jax stands straight, his eyes wide. "Where?"

"The main conference room. He's locked himself in."

"Fuck," Jaxon says, racing off in that direction.

They get there at the same time as Noah. Jasper is by the door trying the handle; light shines from under it indicating that someone is inside.

"He's in there?" Noah asks. "Are you sure?"

"He has to be," Jasper says. "I don't think that there's anyone else in the building.".

Noah makes his way to the front of them all and knocks. "Luca?" There is a pause, silence filling the air. He tries again. "Luca, it's Noah. Are you in there?"

"Go away, Noah," Luca's voice bellows from the other side of the wood.

The men on the outside all look at each other, Taylor squeezes Jax's hand. "See, I told you that we would find him," he whispers.

Noah tries the handle for himself. "Luca, please. Let us in."

They lean in as they hear movement and a clink of a glass, yet still, he doesn't unlock the door.

"What is he doing?" Jasper asks, and Noah shrugs.

Banging on the door a little harder, Noah shouts. "Luca. Whatever it is. Let us help you."

Another agonizing pause passes before the lock clicks and Luca tentatively opens the door, stepping aside to let the men enter. His face drains when he makes eye contact with his boyfriend. "Jaxon," he gasps, stumbling backward until he reaches the table.

Slumping down on a high back leather chair, Noah takes in the scene in front of him while Jax runs to kneel on the floor in front of Luca, his hands on his thighs.

"Now I see why you've been in here," Noah says, spotting a glass of bourbon clasped in Luca's hand. It was clear that he had purposely sought out the alcohol. "Luca, what's the matter?"

"Is the baby okay?" Jax asks, rubbing his legs.

Luca squeezes his eyes shut, before looking at his boyfriend. "The baby is amazing," he slurs. "I saw it on the screen. A little person. It was amazing."

Jaxon looks up at Taylor, confused. Noah heads to the crystal decanters on the sideboard and pours himself a whiskey. "So, what's all this about?" he asks, taking a big gulp.

Sitting forward, Luca rests his forehead against Jax's who can smell the strong alcohol on his breath. "I'm such a fucking idiot," he whispers. "I've fucked up everything."

He sits back and goes to take another sip, but Jax stops his arm. "What is it, Luca? Let us help you."

Jasper and Taylor quietly watch from near the door as Luca starts to explain. Noah sits back down, wheeling the chair closer to his cousin.

Tears start to pour from Luca's eyes. "She wanted me to sleep with her."

Jax's heart starts to pound in his chest. "And did you?" He could hardly say the words, his entire world slowly starting to crash down in front of him. Luca shakes his head, and Jaxon breathes out. "Thank fuck for that."

Luca abruptly stands up, causing Jax to fall backward with a slight thud. Taylor rushes to him as Luca starts to walk around the room, gulping back the drink that he'd grabbed. Letting out a tortured sound, Luca flings the glass tumbler, shattering it against the wall. Alcohol drips down, staining the wooden wall.

"Jesus fucking Christ, Luca!" Jasper shouts, having dodged the flying glass. "What is fucking wrong with you?"

Noah jumps to his feet, grabbing hold of his cousin. "Luca. What the hell is the problem?"

Luca starts to sob, and Taylor helps Jax up. "She... she said that she can't do this alone." He can't control his breathing, almost hyperventilating. "She said she will not have this baby and be a single mother."

"What do you mean, she won't be a single mom?" Jaxon says with a tremor in his voice, not liking where this conversation is going. "What are you trying to say?"

Releasing himself from Noah's grasp, Luca turns to the man that has become his world. The man that he's in love with. "I am so sorry, Jax. I've agreed to marry her."

Chapter 14

"Luca?" a voice says, snapping him out of his tortured daydream.

Looking up, Luca can see Noah staring at him with a concerned expression on his face. "Oh, sorry." He sits up in his chair, clearing his throat, glancing around the conference room trying to regain his bearings. "What were you saying?"

Noah touches his arm. "You have to snap out of this, Luca. We have so much work to get through. Everyone else has gone."

"I know." Luca clicks his pen as though he is ready to get back to work. "I apologize. I've not been sleeping very well. Please carry on."

Noah sighs, and gets up to pour them both a coffee while Luca looks through the papers having no clue where he left off. Setting a cup down next to his cousin, Noah tilts his head feeling sorry for him.

"Luca look..." he starts, and Luca holds his hand up. "I know that you don't want to talk about it. But just know that I'm here if you do."

Should We?

Luca nods his head, and takes a sip of his coffee, his hands shaking.

"Are you still drinking every night?" Noah asks, observing this.

"So, what if I am?" Luca snaps, throwing his pen down. "I need it to get me through the evenings." Noah goes to say something else, but Luca interrupts. "Believe me, Noah. I know what everyone is thinking. But I've made my choice."

"You don't have to marry her to be a father, you idiot. You know that." Noah snaps.

"I do. And anyway, it's all under planning now. My relationship with Jax is over, I'm back with my girlfriend, and we are getting married. Not to mention the fact that we are having a baby." Luca's face is dark, with big circles under his eyes.

"If it's yours!" Noah points out. "What if it's not and you've married her?"

Luca rubs his temples in frustration. "Well, I'll deal with that then."

Noah lets out a sigh for a second time and picks up the documents in front of him. "Well, you know what I think. What we all think as a family. But we will support you." Noah stands up, and Luca doesn't take his eyes away from his coffee, too ashamed to look at him. "There's no point in us doing this right now. I think you need some space to think."

He pats Luca on the shoulder, who slips into his trance-like swirl of despair, before leaving him to his thoughts. Luca doesn't even hear the door click shut behind his cousin, the room falling empty.

Noticing the cleaned up but still visible stain on the wall, Luca's heart shatters once more remembering that night. Jax's cries of devastation, sitting on the floor in front of him, begging him not to make the wrong decision. Jasper trying to clear the glass from the floor while Taylor attempted to console Jax. Noah had been the more levelheaded one of the evening, but even he hadn't been able to make Luca see sense.

Luca had tried to explain his decision, but even as he was saying it out loud, he could hear how crazy it sounded. Getting back together with someone that he couldn't even bear to be around, let alone marry her. It was madness. It still is.

He sits forward, grasping tufts of hair tightly in his fists, and rests his elbows onto his knees. Breathing in deeply, Luca shudders over how life has been recently. Misun insists on affection which he is struggling to provide. She is getting extremely impatient with the lack of sex, even blaming him for having a boyfriend.

She doesn't believe that the two men haven't slept together yet and keeps telling him how wrong it is. She says that she's saved him from making a mistake, the biggest of his life, in her words. Luca sits back and rubs his eyes. He knows the true mistake that's happening but feels powerless to do anything about it now. Like life is running away from him and there is absolutely nothing that he can do about it.

His memory flashes back to that day a few months earlier. Walking in from work to discover that Misun was cheating; that she was sleeping with somebody else. It had destroyed Luca. His entire world had come crashing down in an instant.

Now he is back here, living the nightmare that he was slowly recovering from. It has taken him so long to open himself up to anyone. To trust someone. He had that with Jax. He really thought that Jax was the one. But he blew it.

The door opens and a figure steps inside, freezing when he locks eyes with Luca, who is just as startled. He closes the door slowly.

"Um, sorry," Jaxon whispers, looking awkward and uncomfortable, shuffling his feet as he stares down. "I didn't realize that anyone was in here."

Luca stands up, his heart twisting in his chest looking at the man that he is so incredibly in love with yet can't go near. Jax stands there in his tight-fitting black slacks and simple lemon colored t-shirt, his hair swept to the side. Luca tries not to let the emotion that is rising show on his face. "It's fine." He picks up his things clumsily. "I was just leaving anyway."

Luca's arms are shaking, and Jaxon steps forward to help him. He places a few documents onto the top of the pile that Luca is balancing, and the pair lock eyes for a moment, close enough to lean in for a kiss. Luca internally screams at the sight of his beautiful face.

"How are you?" Jax mumbles, trying to ignore the tension building in the small gap between their bodies.

"I'm fine." Luca lies, trying to fake a small smile. "You?"

Jax touches Luca's sleeve, and Luca is powerless to stop him with his arms full. "I miss you," he whispers.

Luca bites his lip, unable to stop the pools of tears filling his eyes. "Jax..."

"I know." Jaxon nods, admitting defeat and inhaling deeply. "I know."

He turns to open the handle and swings the door open for Luca, who virtually sprints from the room. Closing it behind him, Jax also looks at the just visible stain on the wall, a reminder of losing the best thing that had ever happened to him. He has tried so hard to accept Luca's decision and to understand why, but it is killing him inside. He sinks to his knees with tears streaming down his cheeks wondering how he is ever going to live without him.

**

Luca cringes as his office door opens and the voice of his once again girlfriend fills the room. "Hey, babe," she says with a wave.

He glances up from the computer, watching her gently rubbing her small baby bump, and forces a smile. "Hi, what's up."

She glides around the desk and drapes her arms around his shoulders from behind him, resting her chin on his head. "Am I not allowed to just stop in and see my boyfriend?" She holds her left hand up in front of his face and the sparkly ring catches his eye. He can sense just by looking at it how much his bank account must have been drained by the purchase. "Although this doesn't mean boyfriend anymore," she says, moving to straddle his lap, facing him.

"So you picked one then?" Luca asks, trying to avoid eye contact and keep the conversation light.

"Yeah." She pouts, pecking him on the lips. "But I would have preferred it if you had picked it for me instead. You know, like going out shopping and choosing one for me."

"You know that I've been busy, Mi. And you know what you like anyway, so it was easier for you to decide on one." Luca makes excuses as she pulls his hands around her waist.

"I know," she puts on her best whiny voice, fluttering her eyelashes at him. "It's okay, I may consider forgiving you if my baby does something for me." She wriggles herself on his knee, giving him a seductive look.

"Mi, I have work to do." Luca tries to put her off.

She pulls herself closer to him. "I know you want me," she whispers, brushing her lips over his. "Stop trying to resist it."

Flicking her tongue into his mouth, Luca responds, tilting his head to ease the angle of the kiss. She moans out as they get more passionate, grinding herself slowly on his lap.

"It's me and you, Luca," she says in between panting breaths, their kisses getting more frantic. "We have each other. We don't need anyone else."

She guides his hands upwards and into her top, letting the straps fall off her shoulders, encouraging him to slide his fingers inside her bra, a gasp escaping his lips at the touch of her soft nipple. "That's it, that's my Luca. You are the only person who knows exactly what I like."

She tilts her head back, closing her eyes, while Luca trails small kisses down her neck, gently blowing her long dark hair from her shoulder, and grazing over her collarbone with his tongue.

Lifting herself to face him again, she watches the pleasure on his face as she unbuckles his belt, followed by the button on his slacks. Plunging her hand into his underwear, she grasps his already semi-erect cock, and starts to twist her fingers around it.

As he moans out, she smirks. "See," she purrs with a smug tone, "you only need me, my love." She squeezes a little harder as he grows in her palm. "You don't need a man. You don't need Jax."

Luca freezes at the sound of his name, snapping himself out of this momentary lapse of reality. He can't believe that she still has this hold over him.

She groans in frustration, feeling his erection start to soften. "For fucks sake, Luca." She pulls her hand out and straightens her clothes before climbing off him. "You really need to get that guy out of your head, or this..." She points between the two of them. "This will never work. You have to think about us now, and us only."

Silently fastening up his pants, Luca can feel nothing but shame. He knows that Misun isn't who he wants, yet he can't seem to get out from under her spell.

Misun strokes his shoulder. "It's okay, Luca," she says. "We will have sex soon enough. I'm going to be your wife before you know it." She rubs her baby bump. "And we will be a family."

Luca sighs and stands up. "I have work to do, Mi."

She picks up her bag from the desk, doing the last button on her dress. "Fine, I get the message. I'll go and do some more wedding shopping."

He walks her out of his office, ignoring Sacha's disapproving look that he can see from the corner of his eye as they pass her desk. Once out in the corridor, she pauses to face him.

"I love you," she says, tilting her head and pouting.

"Ah, Noah!" Luca exclaims with a little too much enthusiasm, so grateful for the interruption.

"Oh!" Noah gasps, looking up from his papers towards Luca, grinding to a halt. "I was just coming to find you." He spots the woman next to him. "Hello, Misun, how are you?"

She smiles back at him. "Hey, Noah. I'm very well, thanks. How is the beautiful Victoria?"

"She's fine, thank you." Noah makes polite conversation back.

"Good, good," she giggles. "I presume that the wedding plans are going okay?" Noah nods. "And I hope that she doesn't think that I'm stealing her thunder by doing ours first." She points to her swollen belly. "But, you know, we were a little bit quicker off the mark."

She laughs out loud, Luca and Noah exchanging glances of annoyance. "Oh, babe," she says, turning back to Luca, remembering the real reason that she came to see him. "Can I have your credit card again, please? I have some things that I need to go and buy for myself."

Noah raises an eyebrow and puffs his cheeks as Luca takes his wallet out of his pocket without saying a word. He hands over his card and she kisses him on the cheek, before quickly putting it into her purse.

Taylor appears from around the corner and Luca's eyes open wide when he sees Jax following him with his head bowed to the floor. Noah can see the look of horror on Luca's face.

"Taylor!" Misun bellows, Noah eyeing the awkwardness of the crowd now gathered in the corridor. She draws him into a hug as though they are close friends. "Have you found any time in your busy schedule yet for me?"

Taylor shakes his head. "Sorry, Misun, I'm too busy to do your dress in such a short period." He lies, glancing at his heartbroken best friend.

"Awww that's a shame. If you get an open window, give me a call. Luca has my cell number." She looks over Taylor's shoulder at the figure trying to stay out of the way as much as possible. "And you are Jaxon, right?"

"Mi..." Luca starts, clasping her arm as she steps towards him.

"Oh, it's okay, Luca," she scoffs, shrugging off Luca's grasp. "I'm not going to say anything bad. I'm actually going to thank him."

"Thank him?" Luca asks in surprise. "What for?"

She turns back towards Luca, brushing his cheek with the back of her hand. Taylor hears his best friend take a sharp intake of breath from behind him.

"For looking after you while we've been apart." She giggles and Noah rolls his eyes. She peers over at Jax again. "And I'm kind of hoping that you have taught him some new tricks for the bedroom."

"Misun!" Luca says, firmly. "Stop it."

"What?" She exclaims, throwing her hands up in protest. "I'm just saying. He may have taught you some things that us women don't know about."

Luca grabs her arm tightly. "That is enough!" he says through gritted teeth. Noah shakes his head.

Smiling back at Luca, feeling smug at getting a sly dig in, she kisses his cheek. "Fine, I'll behave."

"I have to go," Jax says, pushing past Taylor while avoiding Luca's gaze, and fleeing off through the corridor.

"Ohhh," Misun mocks, watching him leave. "I was just kinda saying."

Taylor shakes his head and follows after Jaxon. Luca rubs his eyes while Noah squeezes his arm in reassurance.

"Misun, what are you doing?" Luca asks.

She throws her arms around his neck. "I'm sorry." She tries to kiss his lips, but he pulls away from her. "I'll just say it's a little bit of jealousy. Blame the pregnancy hormones."

Noah huffs quietly to himself, knowing full well that she has this sort of character without being pregnant. "Luca," he says, trying to help his cousin out. "We really do have some work to get through."

Misun tuts and throws her bag over her shoulder. "I'll take that as a big hint for me to leave then." She kisses Luca, who lets her this time, not having the mental energy to keep fighting with it.

As she sets off towards the elevator, she turns back briefly. "Goodbye to you both." She laughs and runs her hand over her bump. "From baby Blackwood, and the future Mrs. Blackwood."

Luca sighs, and Noah throws his arm around him, leading him back to his office.

Chapter 15

Luca leans forward placing his head into his hands. *How the fuck did it get to this point?* He reaches over to the lighted limo bar and pours himself a bourbon, draining the crystal glass, then pours another. He gazes out the tinted window, watching as Noah, Victoria, Heidi, and Harrison make their way up the steps and into the small church. It's only been a month, but Misun has thrown together an elaborate wedding, much to Luca's dismay. He had wanted to go to the courthouse for a private civil ceremony. Misun had refused, thriving on the attention and publicity that a Blackwood wedding would garner.

Luca sits back and adjusts his bowtie, knowing that he cannot put off going inside much longer. There will be no bridesmaids and no groomsmen. Misun has no family or close friends as far as he knows, and Luca is very aware that his cousins do not agree with his decision to marry Misun, although they respect it. Luca shakes his head at the thought. *I wonder what they'd think if they knew that she threatened to terminate the pregnancy if I didn't marry her?*

"Mr. Blackwood, the paparazzi are here." His driver's voice brings Luca back to reality. Luca sees the press with their cameras gathering around the church steps. *Just fucking fabulous.*

"Of course, they are, Tony. What sells more papers than a Blackwood wedding?" Luca replies as he finishes the rest of his drink.

Tony answers with a laugh. "Well a Blackwood scandal, of course."

Luca lets out his own bitter laugh in agreement. "You should know, Tony. We've been together for a long time."

"That we have, Mr. Blackwood. Let me escort you to the door," Tony says, as he gets ready to help Luca out of the car.

"No, I'm okay. I'm going to do this alone." Luca steps out of the limo and straightens his tux.

Flashbulbs go off in his face as he quickly strides toward his unwanted destiny. As Luca approaches the church doors, he watches as the press rushes toward someone ascending the steps behind him. Luca turns and sees Taylor, arms wrapped around a stunned Jaxon, trying to shield him from the onslaught of the media taking pictures and aggressively yelling questions in his direction.

Luca runs back down a few steps, grabbing Jaxon's hand in his, placing his other on Jax's lower back. Luca doesn't think about what the papers will say the next day; doesn't think about what Misun's reaction will be. All he can think about is protecting Jax at that moment. Luca quickly guides him up the steps, and off to the side of the vestibule.

He is visibly shaken, and Taylor pulls him into a tight hug, whispering into his ear, "Are you okay, baby? We can leave right now. I told you that you don't have to do this."

Jax answers in a shaky voice, "I'm okay Tay. I'll be okay, just give me a minute and I'll join you inside." Taylor nods and opens the doors to the sanctuary.

**

Taylor looks around, sighing at the sight of the elaborate floral displays that adorn the pews. Almost every available space is consumed by them. He takes a deep breath while looking around, and the overwhelming smell of flowers turns his stomach. It reminds him more of a funeral than a supposedly joyous occasion.

Jasper stands to get Taylor's attention, looking absolutely gorgeous, albeit a bit uncomfortable, wearing his custom black suit. Taylor sighs again and approaches Jasper, thinking that black is an appropriate color for the occasion. Jasper reaches his hand to Taylor, and they sit down together. Taylor traces his long fingers over the thick silver rings that adorn Jasper's fingers and trails them up to the tattoos that peak out from his shirt cuff.

"Hey, are you okay?" Jasper asks.

"No, not really," Taylor answers, looking into Jasper's beautiful blue eyes, his own welling up with tears at the thought of what Jax just went through.

Jasper raises his hand to brush his finger along Taylor's jaw, feeling an uncharacteristic bit of stubble there. "I thought Jax was coming with you. I'm glad he changed his mind."

Taylor shakes his head as he responds to Jasper. "Oh no, he came." Taylor raises his hand to his own head, grasping at his waves and pushing them behind his ear. "We just got bombarded by the press. They were sticking cameras right in his face."

Jasper opens his eyes wide. "Oh, no. You've got to be kidding me. Those bastards can never leave us alone. Where is he now?"

Taylor looks toward the vestibule where he knows that his best friend is probably falling apart right now. "He's with Luca."

**

Luca stands taking in the sight of Jaxon in front of him. He is stunning, as always, in tight-fitting pressed slacks and a pink silk shirt. Luca feels his chest tighten. He hasn't been this close to Jax in a month, having only had awkward encounters with him at the office.

He enters Jaxon's space, briefly tracing his fingers down his flushed cheek. "I'm so sorry Angel. So, so sorry. You shouldn't put yourself through this."

Jaxon winces hearing Luca utter that name and takes a small step back. "I wanted to be here, Luca. I wanted to support you. I still love you, and if I can't have you in the way that I want, at least I can be here as your friend."

Luca once again steps closer to Jax. He can't believe how amazing this man is, and Luca is breaking his heart. Luca can't stop himself from rubbing his nose against Jaxon's neck, taking in the sweet smell that always draws him in.

He is torn from the moment when Jax gently pushes him back. "Friends, Luca, it's all we'll ever be. You are marrying someone else."

Jax turns and leaves him standing there, walking through the heavy wooden doors. Luca is left trying to compose himself, taking deep breaths. *I need to do this,* he repeats to himself, *for my child.*

**

Misun stands in front of the full-length mirror in the bridal room, running her hands over her curves. She admires the way her full breasts fill out the bodice of her dress, with plenty of cleavage on display, accented by the low curved neckline. *Being pregnant has its advantages.*

Turning to the side a bit, Misun sees how the beautiful beaded satin of her dress clings to her protruding belly. The tight mermaid fit, and her towering satin heels will make her walk down the aisle a bit precarious, but Misun's not worried. She knows that the look on Luca's face when he sees how stunning she is will make it all worthwhile. A knock on the door pulls Misun away from her reflection. The door opens, revealing the man standing there.

"Wow, you look gorgeous," he says.

"I know," Misun says in annoyance. "What are you doing here?"

He takes a step toward the bride. "I just thought that you could use a friend right now. I came to check on you."

Misun tips her head to the side and scoffs. "A friend? I don't have any friends, Jayce. You should know that." She hands him a few bobby pins and turns to face the mirror again. "Here, help me with this."

Jayce stands behind her, securing an elbow-length veil into her cascading black waves. "Are you sure about this, Mi? You don't have to do this you know."

Misun turns around, glaring at him. "What are you saying, Jayce? You know how long I've wanted this. My baby is a Blackwood, and it deserves a mother who's a Blackwood too."

Jayce lowers his head and takes a deep breath. "If you say so, Misun. I just hope that you're making the right decision." Jayce turns and leaves the way he came.

**

Jaxon grips his best friend's hand so tightly that it threatens to cut off his circulation. "Deep breaths, baby. That's right." Taylor can tell that Jax is going to break down any minute. "Let's just leave, Jax. It's crazy being here. I can't bear to watch you go through this."

Jaxon straightens up and looks at Taylor, then at Jasper. "No. I'm going to do this. I have to accept it, and I'm going to see Luca at work anyway. There's no running away from this situation," Jax continues, his voice shaking as he speaks. "Besides, those cameras are still out there, and I can't face that again."

Jasper speaks up, "Listen, Jax, let's just go. I'll sneak you out the back to avoid the cameras."

"No," Jax says firmly. "I need to be here so that I can move on. I'm staying."

Taylor and Jasper look at each other for a moment, and they can tell what the other is thinking.

I hope that he makes it through this.

Noah grasps Victoria's hand giving it a squeeze as they wait for the ceremony to begin. "Did you talk to Luca today?" Victoria whispers to her fiancé.

"No, he didn't respond to my calls or texts," Noah sighs as he replies. He looks over his shoulder, spotting his brother sitting with Taylor. "Jax is here. I can't believe it. He's sitting with Jasper and Taylor."

Victoria turns around, spotting the men, and lifts her hand in a small wave. She turns back to Noah, shaking her head. "I can't believe it either. He's a lot stronger than I would be."

They hear a noise as Taylor stands to take Jaxon out of the church after admitting defeat. He knows that he can't do it. The feeling of deep sadness and devastation consuming his whole being.

Heidi squeezes Victoria's shoulder to get her attention. "Look! It's Misun!" Heidi nods her head toward the back of the church. Misun is looking around, clearly to see if Luca has arrived yet. She quickly disappears again into the room to the side of the church. "Oh my god!" Heidi says. "I can't even believe that she's wearing that! Although I must say that she is a beautiful woman."

"Yes, she certainly is beautiful," Victoria replies, shaking her head. "And she certainly is looking forward to having all eyes on her."

"Here comes Luca!" Harrison tells them as they all direct their attention to the man headed toward the altar. Luca looks handsome as always, his Blackwood tuxedo perfectly fitting his toned body. His black hair is slightly messy, cheeks pink, and he has a blank look on his face.

Luca walks toward the front of the church, barely registering the faces of his family around him. He purposely avoids looking towards where Taylor and Jasper are sitting, knowing that seeing Jaxon again will break him. Instead, he focuses on the glistening candles and large floral displays that cover the altar behind where the minister stands. When he reaches the front of the church, Luca can't help but scan the room.

Luca barely registers the fact that Misun has entered the sanctuary, ready for her moment. He is too busy trying to find Jaxon among the crowd of people. Whispers from the guests draw Luca's attention back to Misun as she starts slowly walking toward him. He looks at his bride, stunning in her dazzling gown, and then at the man that escorts her, Misun's arm interlocked with his.

This can't be happening; this cannot be fucking happening. Luca stands staring, unable to move as the two approach him.

The music stops, and Misun takes her place by Luca's side. The man offers his hand to Luca. "I'm here to give you your bride. Congratulations, Son."

Luca stands frozen in place, silence all around him. The man slowly lowers his hand, aware that Luca has no intention of shaking it. "How dare you?" Luca spits out, looking at Misun, and then back to the man in front of him; the man he despises because of how he has been treated. "Misun, how fucking could you?" The minister places a hand on Luca's shoulder, and he shrugs it off. "My father of all fucking people, Misun?"

Misun looks stunned as Maxwell speaks. "That's right, I'm your father, Luca. Of course, I should be here to celebrate your union with the beautiful Misun."

Luca lurches forward, grabbing his father by his shoulders, throwing him back. Noah and Harrison jump up and run to the front of the church, as Luca plants punch after punch on his father's face. Maxwell hits back, landing a few on Luca's cheek. Harrison grabs Luca, pulling him back as Noah drags his uncle toward the back of the church. Jayce joins his cousin, grabbing Maxwell's other arm to escort him out.

"Can't say that I'm happy to see you, Uncle," Jayce says, as Maxwell shrugs off his nephews and exits the church. People are whispering loudly, unsure of what to do.

The room goes silent as Luca turns to Misun. "I'm done with you Misun. It's over."

"You wouldn't dare, Luca." She glares at him while she speaks. "You can't leave me. What about our baby?" Luca turns from her, tears running down his cheeks.

As he walks away, he hears Misun calling after him. "Luca! Luca, don't you leave me standing here. You'll regret this, Luca Blackwood!"

I only regret one thing. Luca thinks as he gets to the back of the church, looking over to where Jaxon had been sitting. Of course, he's not there. He's gone. It's done.

Chapter 16

Luca sits in his office, papers strewn across his desk displaying evidence of his disastrous wedding. *How ironic.* He thinks, remembering how just two months ago, this was how his relationship had started with Jax. He walks over to his built-in bar, grabs a couple of ice cubes and wraps them in a napkin. He holds it up to his purple and swollen cheek, returning to sit at his desk.

The press has not been kind. Luca had expected the onslaught of nasty publicity; he had practically handed them the dirt on a silver platter. What he did not expect, was that Jaxon would be painted as a homewrecker. The papers, which gushed over their relationship just a couple of months ago, had completely turned on him. Pictures of Luca leading Jaxon into the church were placed next to photos of Misun, visibly pregnant, standing at the altar. Someone had taken cell phone photos at the church and had given them to the press, undoubtedly making a pretty penny in the process. It was insinuated that Jaxon had stolen Luca not once, but twice from Misun. Poor pregnant Misun, left at the altar while her fiancé cavorts with a beautiful man. Luca's head is throbbing as he thinks about what Jaxon must be going through. Jax will not answer his calls, and Luca can't blame him. All Jax had ever done was support him and look at what he had received in return.

The intercom to his office buzzes, and he hears Sacha's voice. "Luca, I'm sorry to tell you this, but your grandfather is on the phone."

Fuck! Luca has been expecting this call, but he was hoping that it wouldn't come this soon. "Alright, Sasha. Put him through." He takes a deep breath and gets ready to pick up the phone.

"Hello, Grandfather." Luca prepares himself for the conversation that he has been dreading.

"Luca," Dalton says, his voice firm, "Noah and I have been dealing with this situation since Saturday evening. I know that you're going through a difficult time, but we must discuss this."

"I know, Grandfather. I'm so sorry. I've made a mess of everything, and the company is suffering from it." Luca has worked so hard to make Dalton proud. He can't imagine how disappointed his grandfather is.

"Luca, Blackwood will be just fine. We've been through bad publicity before, and we always get through it," Dalton continues. "We've been in touch with the company counsel, and they've determined who leaked the photos.

Thankfully we've taken care of it, and none of the photos of the altercation with your father will be published."

Luca breathes a sigh of relief. *Thank god.*

"Luca, I need to know what happened with Maxwell. I know that he's not the ideal father, but what in the bloody hell was that about?" Luca can hear the strain in his grandfather's voice.

"I wasn't expecting him to be there." Luca tries to keep his voice steady. "None of us have seen him in god knows how long, and there he was walking Misun down the aisle. I was overwhelmed with the entire situation, and I just snapped. I'm so sorry, Grandfather, you don't need this stress."

"Well, you have a complicated relationship with your father. I understand that, Luca." Dalton reassures him. "It hasn't been easy for you," Luca says a silent prayer that his grandfather won't press the issue further. Thankfully, he changes the subject. "Now about this Misun. I wish you would have come to me, Luca. If you boys would just keep it in your trousers, we could avoid these situations!"

Luca laughs a bit as his grandfather continues. "Noah has told me about Jaxon and what a good man he is. It's up to you to handle this situation now. I trust you to do the right thing."

"I'm trying." Luca sighs. "I have quite a mess to clean up."

"Try not to worry too much about the press. They'll be on to the next thing in a day or two. That's how it works."

"Thank you for your support, Grandfather." Luca is so grateful to him.

Dalton responds in a matter-of-fact tone: "We're a family. It's what we do."

After he hangs up with his grandfather, Luca looks at the mountain of work in front of him. He folds the offensive newspaper articles, shoving them into his desk drawer, and checks his watch. Forty-five minutes until his scheduled meeting with Noah. He sighs and gets to work.

**

Luca taps his knuckles on Noah's solid mahogany office door before pushing it open. Noah looks up from his expansive desk, coffee cup in hand. "Hey, Luca, come on in."

Luca nods, taking a seat across from Noah, and leans forward. "Noah," Luca addresses his cousin, who closes his computer and folds his hands on his desk, waiting for Luca to continue. "I just want to thank you, for everything." Noah opens his mouth to reply, but Luca cuts him off. "I mean it, Noah. This entire thing has been one huge disaster. You tried to offer me your advice before it got to this point, and then you had to deal with the

Should We?

aftermath. I can't tell you how much I appreciate it."

"Well Luca, it wasn't ideal, I'll say that." Noah rubs his forehead as he responds. "I think that Grandfather and I have handled the worst of it."

"Yes, I spoke with Grandfather earlier." Luca shakes his head and stands up to pour himself some coffee. "He's being very supportive, surprisingly."

"You know him. He's dealt with worse than this over the years, he can handle it. He just wants you to be happy." Noah joins Luca, holding out his cup for Luca to refill. "You look awful, by the way." Noah adds a bit of cream to his coffee, stirring it while he takes in Luca's appearance.

Luca reaches up, tentatively touching his swollen cheek. "Yeah, no shit. I haven't slept, and that bastard landed a couple of punches."

"Yeah well, you know how strong Maxwell is. He still looks like he's in his thirties." Noah regrets his words when he sees Luca's pained expression. "You want to tell me what happened? I didn't think that you invited him."

"Oh, I didn't invite him." Luca doesn't elaborate. "What did Uncle Alexander say about it?"

"Well, Dad and Mum are both worried about you. Dad just kept shaking his head, you know how he feels about Maxwell."

"Perfect brother, perfect son, perfect father," Luca says bitterly.

Noah steers the subject toward another unsavory topic. "I'm sorry to ask, Luca, but have you heard from Misun?"

"Nope, not a word." Luca's tone is extremely bitter. "I'll deal with that when I have to. It's too late in the pregnancy for her to do anything now. I'm sure she's reveling in the fact that the media has painted her as the victim."

Noah sighs, sitting back down in his desk chair. "Well, I've handled it for now. She's signed a unilateral nondisclosure agreement. She won't be going to the press."

"And what does she get out of it?" Luca rubs at his eyes with his thumb and forefinger, grimacing when pain shoots down his cheekbone. "Let me guess. How much did you give her?"

"Enough to keep her quiet." Noah hands Luca a copy of the document. "And if she violates the agreement, she forfeits any future child support payments."

Luca glances over the papers and sees Misun's signature at the bottom. He places them into his leather attaché to review later and nods gratefully to Noah. The men hear their aunt's voice as the office door swings open. "Knock, knock!" Bella says while gliding inside, Jayce is directly behind her. Both are perfectly styled, as usual. Bella is wearing a gray pencil skirt with a fitted white cotton blouse. Her collar is open, and a colorful silk scarf printed with the Blackwood logo is knotted at her neck. Her long bare legs are smooth and shiny; red pumps complementing both her scarf and her red lipstick. Jayce, always playing the part, has on his Blackwood aviators, even indoors. His ripped jeans are rolled at the ankle, and he wears white leather sneakers. A graphic tee and satin bomber jacket accentuate his incredibly broad shoulders.

Bella places a kiss on Luca's cheek. "What are you even doing here, darling, you look like absolute rubbish."

Luca responds with a deep breath, "I'm well aware, Aunt Bella. Thanks for the reminder though."

"Stop. You know that I'm just worried. You should've taken the day off, Luca," Bella says while rubbing her nephew's shoulder.

"Well, there's no point in staying home and dwelling on my shitty decisions." Luca busies himself making his aunt's tea. He knows how she likes it, strong with sugar and a splash of cream. "The paparazzi are camped out there. Tony snuck me out the back of my apartment, and in here through the back door."

Bella nods and accepts the cup from Luca. "Poor Jaxon," she says while sipping her tea. "I can't believe that they portrayed him that way. Like he is the villain, and Misun is completely innocent in this situation."

Jayce sits back in his chair "Well let's not forget that she *is* pregnant. And she *was* left at the altar," he says, while tipping his glasses up, holding his dark hair back with them.

Bella whips her head in her son's direction. "Jayce, are you mad? Do you even know what that girl has done to Luca?" Jayce looks at his hands in his lap, and Luca closes his eyes, as Bella continues. "To actually threaten to terminate her child; to use that baby as a pawn. It's unthinkable."

Jayce meets eyes with Luca, surprise apparent in his gaze. "I didn't know," Jayce says, elbows on his knees and head in his hands.

Noah speaks up before too much more is said. "Well I, for one, am glad that the marriage did not happen. Luca deserves to be happy."

"I agree," Bella says.

Jayce meets Luca's gaze once again as he speaks under his breath. "Yes, we all deserve to be happy."

"Now," Noah says, "we do have business to discuss. Bella?"

Bella places her teacup on the side table next to the comfortable chair she sits in. "Yes, regarding the Spring Collection. Taylor is doing amazing work here at Blackwood. His transition here has been seamless."

"No pun intended." Jayce chimes in.

Luca gives his cousin an annoyed look while Bella continues. "He is already working to expand the line. Of course, it is based around his existing winning designs. He is keeping with the androgynous feel and using the same color pallet." Bella looks toward her nephew. "Luca, Taylor and I have chosen some possible fabrics for the collection. He just wanted your input."

"I will stop by his studio today," Luca says, as he jots down some notes. "Has Harrison consulted with him about styling?"

Bella responds. "He has. They are planning on continuing with the rope and chain theme that Taylor used with his existing designs and expanding on that. Harrison is working with him to design footwear specifically for this collection."

Noah nods, speaking up, "Jayce, you are working with Bella to choose some different models for the new collection?"

"Absolutely," Jayce replies, nodding. "Taylor wants to continue with the theme of some gender non-conforming models. Jax will be the face of this collection. He already has a large following on social media because of Aspire to Design." Jayce looks toward Luca as he continues. "Unfortunately, the recent negative publicity is a worry."

Luca squeezes his hand into fists but remains quiet. Noah speaks up, "Yes, I've thought about that. We have an article set to be published in Blackwood Magazine next month. It is an interview with Taylor discussing his designs, featuring Jasper's photos from the show." Noah leans back in his chair as he continues. "We touched on Taylor's relationship with Jax in the article, but I think that we should do a separate companion piece on Jaxon."

"That's wonderful, Noah. We can introduce him as our new model and showcase his work at the dance school." Bella crosses her long legs and claps her hands together. "He is such a gentle soul; we need to capture his personality."

Luca leans forward clasping his hands on his knees. "Yes, that's an amazing idea, Noah." He addresses his cousin. "Jax deserves the chance to leave this bad publicity behind. I'll arrange the interview and talk with Jasper about taking some new shots. Let's get the publication date pushed up as well."

"I'm working with Jax this afternoon," Jayce says. "We're doing some test shots to get him comfortable in front of the camera. I can talk to him about the article if you'd like?"

Noah nods toward Jayce. "That sounds great. Just let him know that I'll be calling him to discuss the details." Noah stands up, concluding the meeting. "Okay everyone, thank you. I'm pleased with our progress."

**

Tapping his foot as the elevator descends toward Taylor's studio, Luca lets out a heavy sigh. It takes all his self-control not to press the button that will lead him to the dance studio. He knows that Jax has classes right now, and he wants nothing more than to watch the beautiful man dance. Luca closes his eyes imagining the sight of him moving as one with the music, a sheen of perspiration covering his toned muscles. The elevator doors open, pulling Luca back to reality. He sighs again, stepping forward and heading off to see Taylor.

Taylor is holding his tablet, talking with his assistant designers while looking at different fabrics. He looks up when he sees Luca approaching. "Luca, hi! Perfect timing. I wanted you to take a look at these." The two men discuss the fabric choices, swiping through Taylor's designs while Luca voices his opinion. The staff busies themselves per Taylor's directions, while Luca and Taylor head to the worktable to sit.

Taylor wheels himself closer to Luca, grasping his hands. "So, I think we should talk," he says.

Luca nods, squeezing Taylor's hands. "He won't talk to me, Taylor. I've ruined it. I'm not sure what to say."

"He's hurt, Luca, and confused. He's been broken-hearted from the moment that you told him you were marrying Misun. He cried until he had no more tears left. You never even offered him an explanation."

Luca nods, his tears threatening to fall. "I know. I fucked up. I didn't see any choice but to marry Misun."

Taylor tips his head to the side, a confused look on his face. "I'm not really sure what you mean, Luca."

"She threatened to get rid of the baby, Taylor. And I knew that she'd do it." Luca wipes his eyes and continues. "I'm not sure what I was thinking. I don't love her. I should have found another way."

"Jesus, Luca. Why didn't you just tell Jax what was happening?" Taylor says, clearly shocked at the revelation.

"I didn't tell anyone. I thought that I was doing the right thing." Luca stands up and begins to pace.

Taylor rises, turning Luca to face him. "Well, you need to fix this. Jaxon is a mess. He's gotten threatening letters telling him to stay away from you."

"What?" Luca is shocked. "Why didn't you call me!"

"He refused to allow it, Luca! And I'm sorry, but my loyalty is to Jax, not to you," Taylor replies with obvious anger. "Especially after what you've done. I called the police about the letters. They said it was to be expected after those articles were printed. Apparently, when you're in the public eye, crazy people can do what they want to you." Taylor is clearly worried.

"Well, I want you to show me those letters, Taylor. This is all my fault."

"Listen, Luca, enough of this pity party. You've got to get your shit together and figure this out. Right now, Jaxon feels like if he takes you back, he'll just be left broken-hearted after the baby is born and you decide to take Misun back, *again*."

"Taylor, I don't want Misun. I want Jax. Even after the baby comes, it will only be Jax."

"Well, Luca." Taylor sighs. "Then you better convince him of that."

**

"I'm afraid I won't know how to move right," Jax says as Heidi adjusts his belt and rolls up the sleeves of the light blue silk shirt that Harrison put him in. She leaves it tucked in the front, loose in the back.

"Don't worry Jax," Jayce reassures him. "We don't expect you to be perfect. This is just to practice, and I'm right here to help you."

Jaxon nods and wiggles a bit against the black leather pants that are clinging to his ass and thighs. "God, Harrison. Are you sure these aren't too tight?"

Heidi chimes in, "Are you kidding? With that ass? You look good enough to eat."

Jaxon blushes, and Harrison raises an eyebrow toward his girlfriend. "Really, Heidi? But she's right, Jax. They look perfect." Harrison bends down and clips the buckles on the black motorcycle boots he has chosen for this look. "Okay, perfect."

Jasper fusses with the lights and changes the lens of his camera. He decided against using assistants today, knowing that Jaxon will be nervous. "Okay, Jax, I'm ready to start. Just stand right there for a few test shots." With the lights shining on him, Jaxon does not see Luca, who has quietly come in to stand next to Harrison.

Jasper takes a few photographs and checks the screen. "Perfect. Now let's try a few poses."

Jaxon sways a bit awkwardly in front of the white background. Jayce walks forward to guide him through a few different positions. "Now try putting your arm up over your forehead, yeah just like that. Great." Jaxon copies what Jayce has shown him, moving slowly while gazing into the lens of the camera.

"Looks beautiful, Jax, now turn around and look over your shoulder," Jasper says. "Perfect."

Jayce stands to the side, giving Jaxon some tips when he looks nervous. Before long, he gets a feel for what to do and moves fluidly while Jasper takes his shots. "Amazing Jax, this looks fantastic," Jasper encourages him.

Harrison leans over to whisper in Luca's ear. "Looks like he's a natural."

Luca nods his head, unable to take his eyes off the stunning man in front of the camera. "He certainly is," he responds. "He's a star."

Chapter 17

"Is he still there?" Jax asks, pretending not to care, fingering through the hair at the nape of his neck.

Taylor nods as he peers out of the apartment window onto the crowded street below. Jaxon manages a small smile as he watches his friend standing there in his white t-shirt and blue checkered shorts. His wavy hair is still damp from his shower. He honestly doesn't know what he would have done without him during the last month.

Jax's phone starts to ring again, Luca's name flashing on the screen. Taylor glances over his shoulder at his friend and rolls his eyes. "You can't ignore him forever, you know."

"Yes, I can," Jax says, indignantly, crossing his legs up onto the sofa. "I don't want to speak to him, and he knows it."

Taylor sighs in frustration and makes his way over to Jax, curling up beside him and snuggling into his body. Jax wraps his arms around Taylor's shoulders and rests his cheek on the top of Taylor's head.

The pair sit and look at the darkening sky in front of them, the lights starting to flicker on in adjacent apartment windows. Jax turns on the lamp on the small side table next to them, the orange glow shedding a little illumination around them both.

Jax's phone pings, the message tone breaking the silence. Taylor waits to see if Jax picks it up. He continues to ignore the phone, so Taylor picks it up himself.

"He said that he's going to sit out there all night until you talk to him," Taylor says, tossing the phone down on the couch beside them.

He feels Jax's shoulder shrug. "So? He can do that if he wants. I'm not letting him in."

"Oh, come on!" Taylor snorts. "Stop being so stubborn and just talk it through with him."

"What's the point, Tay?" Jax sits up, his body stiffening, which pushes Taylor off him. Jax looks at him. "He made his choice."

"Exactly! He chose not to marry her!"

"But he was *going* to." Jax folds his arms like a petulant child. "He picked her."

"Shut the fuck up." Taylor's agitation shows. "You know as much as anyone that he wasn't marrying her because he loved her. He was doing right by his kid, Jaxon."

Jax lifts himself from the sofa and wanders over towards the window, trying to act casual as he peers down. Taylor throws his arm along the back of the chair, his fingers toying with the threads on the cushions. "Besides, you've seen how hard Luca is trying. He knows what a horrible mistake he made."

Biting the inside of his cheek, Jax faces his friend. "You're supposed to be on *my* side," he says.

Taylor laughs. "I *am* on your side, you fool! Why do you think I'm doing this?"

Jax's phone begins to ring again and Taylor holds it up. "Shall I?"

Reluctantly, Jax nods, crossing his arms in front of his chest. Taylor answers it and tells Luca that he will buzz him in. Clicking the red icon, he inwardly smiles at Jax discreetly checking himself out in the mirror to make sure that he looks decent enough.

Taylor heads over and presses the button for the main door, before grabbing a pair of sweatpants from the laundry pile and flinging them on over his shorts.

Jax starts to pace back and forth. "What am I doing, Tay?" he mumbles.

Rubbing his arm, Taylor smiles. "The right thing, Jax. That's exactly what you're doing."

Jax clenches his fists and breathes out heavily when a knock from the other side of the door fills the room. Taylor gives Jax a quick hug. "It will all be okay," he says, pulling at the handle.

Luca shifts awkwardly on the other side of the frame, before looking up at Jaxon. "Hi," he says.

Taylor slips his feet into his sneakers and grabs a jacket from the hook. "Come in." He pulls Luca by the arm. "I'm going out to Jasper's. Give you two some space."

Jax looks at him with pleading eyes as Taylor blows him a kiss and leaves, closing the door behind him. Now alone, the air is thick with tension.

"Come in." Jax breaks the silence, pointing to the seating area.

Luca makes his way past him and Jax follows, inhaling the familiar scent of Luca's cologne deeply. They sit next to each other on the couch, and Jax pulls one of the cushions onto his lap for comfort. He examines Luca. He looks tired and unhappy. His clothes don't seem as pristine as usual, and dark circles are beneath his beautiful gray eyes.

"Thank you for seeing me," Luca says. "It seems like forever since we talked."

It does." Jax pulls the cuffs of his sleeves over his hands and cuddles into the cushion. "A lot has changed."

"I heard about the threats that you received," Luca says with worry, taking off his glasses and putting them on the coffee table.

"And I was assured that threats are just random, one of the things that can happen when in the public eye."

Luca turns to the right to face Jax, bending his leg and resting on the sofa. Jaxon can see that the muscle definition on his thigh is different; he's clearly lost some weight recently.

Touching Jax's arm, Luca smiles. "Not everything has changed. My feelings for you haven't."

Jax pulls his arm away. "How can you say that? Look what the press said about me! I'm a homewrecker." Luca tries to speak, but Jax cuts him off. "You were going to marry someone else."

"For my baby!" Luca says in frustration. "I did it because I thought that I was doing the right thing. Jax, I was wrong. And the press is taken care of. They will move on to something else soon enough. Look, I made a terrible mistake. I love you, and only you. Please forgive me."

Jax sighs. "I don't know what to think, Luca. I try to understand what you did, but you also have to realize that you tore my heart to shreds that night."

Luca leans forward closer to Jax and grabs his hands. "I know. I really do. I did it to myself too. I ruined things for us both. But I want to be with you." He looks fully into Jax's eyes that are glazed with impending tears. "I need you, Angel."

Jaxon's tears start to brim over when he hears Luca use that name. "What about her?"

Using his thumb, Luca brushes one of the drops across Jax's cheek before gently placing his hand on the back of his neck, teasing the little hairs on his nape to stand on end. Luca leans in closer. "I'll be there for my baby if it is mine. But that's it as far as she goes. I want to be with you. I love you."

Being so close, Jax can feel the labored and nervous swirls of Luca's breath near his lips. "Is there anything else that I need to know?" Jax questions and Luca looks away guiltily, his hand sliding to Jax's shoulder.

"I slept with her," he murmurs, struggling to say the words. Jaxon makes a noise of peak devastation, tears flowing down his drained face. "It was once. The night before the wedding. I hated it." He was speaking so fast, determined to justify his actions. "I swear it was only once. It was over quickly."

Jax sits forward and Luca copies, rubbing his back. "I feel sick," he whimpers.

"I'm sorry, I am so, so sorry." Luca keeps repeating it over and over.

"Is that everything?" Jax looks at him, his eyes puffy and red.

Luca nods and Jaxon can see the shame on his face. He knows that he has no right to be angry with Luca considering they weren't together and that he was in a relationship with Misun at the time, yet it still doesn't stop the heart-wrenching knot in his chest.

He slides himself off the couch and crawls in front of Luca's knees. Suddenly having flashbacks of that night in the conference room where he ended things with Jax, Luca's tears start to fall.

Jax's lip wobbles as the men just look at each other for a moment, both feeling each other's pain. "I am so sorry," Luca struggles to get out.

Jax places his hands on Luca's thighs and lifts himself to sit on his heels, closer to Luca's face. "I love you too," he says and leans in for a kiss.

Luca can hardly believe it as their lips slowly brush together, the tender feel of Jaxon's plump lips against his, both ignoring the wet remnants of their despair still dropping from their eyes.

Jax trails his fingers along the collar of Luca's jacket teasing his hairline until Luca sits back, pulling Jax to kneel in between his thighs. Their lips remain fixed together, tasting each other in eager desperation. Jaxon takes Luca's hand and gently pulls him towards his bedroom.

The lights of the city illuminate the room dimly, shadows playing across Jaxon's face. He walks to his dresser and side table, lighting some candles. The warm glow flickers off the walls and soft bedding, and Jax beckons Luca to him. Luca sweeps Jaxon's blond hair gently to the side and touches their foreheads together. He places a tender kiss on each of Jaxon's cheeks and his nose before leaning in to taste his lips once again. Their kisses become more desperate as they try to become part of one another.

Luca finally breaks the kiss and stretches to reach the hem of Jax's sweater, lifting it over his head. "Fuck." Is all that he can get out when he sees Jax's firm abs and reaches to tease his small, brown nipples and the shiny rings dangling from them.

Smirking at Luca's reaction, Jaxon's sadness begins to fade. He drags Luca's jacket down the length of his arms slowly, flinging it to the side, before entwining their fingers together.

Goosebumps form on Luca's arm from Jax's warm breath as he teases his lips on the inside of his wrist. He touches his tongue tenderly along Luca's arm and up his bare skin to the sleeve of his t-shirt.

They come face to face again, their bodies trembling in anticipation and nerves. Luca holds Jax's chin with his thumb and forefinger, taking in the features that he's missed and craved so desperately over the past month. The sultry look in Jax's eyes indicates to Luca that he wants this too.

"Don't ever leave me again," Jax whispers, sweeping a fallen eyelash from Luca's cheek. He holds it up. "Make a wish."

Luca closes his eyes briefly and breathes gently, the tiny strand blowing away with the wish that Luca has asked for.

Jax nuzzles his nose into Luca's neck, taking in his scent again like an addiction that he doesn't want to control. Luca runs his fingertips along Jax's back, stirring in his jeans at the feel of the toned lines of his shoulders.

"I'm not going anywhere. Ever." Luca sighs.

Jax starts to unfasten Luca's pants, glancing at him for permission. Luca nods, tilting his body up so that he can pull his clothes down with ease.

Luca gasps out as soon as Jaxon encases his erection with his hand, twisting it smoothly up and down the length encouraging the juices to trickle from the end. Luca lays back on the bed, gripping the down comforter as he squeezes his eyes shut. "Oh my god," he says, appreciating the touch that he had resigned himself to never having again.

"Can I taste you?" Jax asks.

Luca nods eagerly. "Please. Please do." It is like he is begging to be pleasured by the person that he loves most in the world. "I need you to."

Jaxon wastes no more time before sinking his full, rosy lips down Luca's shaft, his tongue lapping up the bitter droplets. Luca groans out at the feel of it running along his length, occasionally darting to the head.

"Fuck. Fuck." Luca can hardly control the sounds escaping his lips, his knuckles whitening from clutching the bedding so hard. Being with Jaxon in this moment feels more incredible than he ever could have hoped for. Jax's experience with other men was evident in his movements.

With his thighs burning and the thrusting of his hips to push himself in further, Luca is afraid that he will climax too soon. He isn't ready for it to end just yet and touches Jax's cheeks, pulling him smoothly off.

The noise of his lips disconnecting fills the air, as Jax looks up at Luca to make sure that nothing is wrong. "Are you okay?" he asks, wiping his mouth with the back of his hand.

Luca nods. "I'm perfect." He smiles. "I just want us to..." He pauses, waiting for it to register in Jax's head. "I think that we need to."

"Are you sure that you're ready for that?" Jax tilts his head, not expecting to hear this.

"I am." Luca sits up, brushing Jax's dampened fringe back from his forehead. "I'm ready. I want to be inside you. Well, I want to try."

"Okay," Jax says. "If you're absolutely positive that you want to do this."

"Well," Luca laughs, his face flushing in embarrassment. "I'm ready to do it to *you*. I think it will be a long while before it's my turn."

Jax smiles, before reaching into his side table drawer. Luca watches as he takes out a condom and a bottle of lube. Jax pulls off his sweatpants and boxers, leaving him completely naked. Luca leans his back against the headboard, taking in the incredible sight in front of him as Jaxon straddles his lap.

"Does this mean that you're mine again?" Luca asks, hopefully.

"Hmmm." Jax teases, rubbing his chin. "It depends how good you are at this."

"Oh, no pressure then!" Luca laughs.

The mood suddenly goes quiet as the realization of what they're about to do for the first-time hits. "Are you sure about this?" Jaxon asks him again, praying that his little joke hasn't unintentionally put Luca off the idea.

Luca drapes his arms around Jax's neck, pulling him closer. "I am surer of this than I've ever been of anything. But you're going to have to tell me what to do."

Jax grins. "You are having a baby," he says, pointing to Luca's still erect cock. "I'm sure that you know how *that* works."

Laughing, Luca pinches his cheeks playfully, grateful that Jax is putting him at ease. "Yeah, okay. You have a point." He takes a big, nervous breath. "Okay, I'm ready."

He guides Jax's face closer, their pink lips searching for each other's. Luca shuts his eyes, wanting to embrace the feel of Jax's tongue against his, and relaxes into the feeling of safety and love that is surrounding them.

Jax clicks open the bottle to prepare himself, but Luca shakes his head. "Let me," he whispers, taking it from him, allowing their fingers to glide together. He squirts some on his fingertips, probably a little more than necessary. "Is this enough?" Jaxon smiles, nodding in confirmation.

Renewing their kiss, Jax guides Luca's hand to reach behind him. "You know what to do," he says. Luca slides a finger in slowly. Jax moans out at the feeling, his sounds indicating that he needs more. Luca gently pushes in another finger, stretching him out, loving the sensation of Jax moving his hips to get the pressure right.

"Open your fingers a little more, Luca. Ohhh, that's good. Now add one more." Drops of perspiration begin to form on Jaxon's forehead. Luca pushes his fingers gently into Jax, and pulls them slowly back out, repeating the motion as he watches his lover's face. "Now curl them up, baby. Toward my belly button." Luca does as instructed, and the most erotic sound he's ever heard escapes Jax's lips. "Right there, Luca. Rub right there." Luca is lost in watching Jaxon's pleasure, his erection becoming impossibly hard.

"That's so good Luca, but I want you in me now. I'm ready." Luca is suddenly aware of Jax ripping open a packet. He rolls a condom down the length of Luca's cock, before reaching back to remove his fingers. Jax needs to feel Luca inside him. Grasping Luca's erection in his hand, Jax tilts his body up and guides it into him. The two of them keep their eyes locked together as he lowers himself.

Hissing through slightly gritted teeth, Luca freezes at the sight of Jax wincing. "Jax? I don't want to hurt you, Angel. We can stop."

Jax kisses Luca's lips, and his face relaxes a bit. "No, it's fine. It's been a while. I'll be okay soon."

Luca waits, his body desperate to move at the feeling of Jax wrapped tightly around him, the urge strong to push deep inside. Trying to ignore the intense aching in this groin, he lays a small peck on Jaxon's cheeks as he rests into his arms.

Sitting up, Jaxon breathes deeply as the stinging subsides. He starts tilting his hips in a rhythm that satisfies them both, and Luca grips his hips to ease himself a little bit deeper.

Jax begins to move, raising himself and gently lowering down onto Luca, his face blissed out as he moves his dancer's hips in circles. Luca continues to stare into his lover's eyes, not wanting to miss a moment of the pleasure on his face. The sounds of their lovemaking echo throughout the apartment, only increasing Luca's desire.

Running his fingers through Luca's hair, Jax moves faster, his pre-come leaking onto Luca's stomach. Luca feels the warm liquid on his skin and takes Jax's cock in his hand, twisting it in his palm, the juices making it easier to glide over his veins. Jax buries his head into Luca's neck, grasping his shoulders and teasing kisses along his earlobe.

Luca knows that he can't take much more, the intensity of their lovemaking overwhelming him. His forehead is getting a film of sweat from Jax's beading shoulder. "Jax, I'm...I'm close."

"I know," Jax says into Luca's cheek. "Me too."

Trying to concentrate on pleasuring Jax as well as focusing on his own pleasure, Luca grips harder with one hand, and pulls Jax's hip with the other, his fingertips digging into his skin.

"Come for me," Jax says through labored breaths. "I want to feel it."

Thrusting upward to match Jax's movements, Luca cries out, his body erupting into a trembling wreck. His eyes screw shut to the point of seeing stars, his hand movements pause temporarily as he forgets about everything except the feeling that engulfs him.

Jax moves at a gentler pace, watching the pleasure on his lover's face, having never witnessed anything so beautiful in his life before. Luca's cheeks are rosy red and tiny gasps are leaving his lips.

"Sorry," Luca says, gathering himself back to reality and continuing to pleasure Jax, who smiles at his sweet reaction.

He takes over from Luca and tugs himself a few times before streaming lines of come onto Luca's front, grunting as he does. They stay joined together, panting as their bodies recover, placing gentle kisses on each other's cheeks and shoulders as they catch their breath. Luca presses Jaxon even closer, pulling his head in for a deep and languid kiss.

When they gently end the kiss, Luca traces his finger down Jaxon's cheek. "I love you so much, Angel. Thank you for coming back to me."

Jax lays his head on Luca's shoulder. "I love you too, Luca. So much."

Jax finally lifts himself off Luca and disposes of the condom. Luca watches him from the bed, his head tilted back onto the pillows, hands dropped lazily by his side. Jaxon reaches out for him, intertwining their fingers. He pulls him up to guide him toward the shower, whispering to Luca. "Stay with me tonight?"

Luca kisses his lover's shoulder, squeezing his hand. "I'll stay with you forever."

Chapter 18

Jaxon looks over his shoulder into the full-length mirror, checking out his outfit. He takes in the sight of his full, muscular ass, which is accentuated by his tight-fitting black jeans. He sighs. He's always been self-conscious of his looks, his petite frame adorned with well-defined muscles from his years of dancing. His ass has always attracted attention, both wanted and unwanted. Today, however, he admits that he looks good... that he *feels* good. His confidence is growing, thanks to all the positive remarks that he's received from his photographs.

The test shots that Jasper had taken had turned out well. So well, in fact, that some were used for the article in Blackwood Magazine. He still looks at the pictures and sees a stranger looking back at him sometimes. His exotic looks seem to photograph well, his brown almond eyes accented with liner and shadow. He knows how to move his body, and it has translated well into his new job as a model for Blackwood.

Jaxon's thoughts are interrupted by the intercom buzzing, and Luca's voice. "I'm here, Angel. Want me to come up?"

"No, Luca, I'm ready. I'll just head down," Jax replies.

He takes one more quick look in the mirror, adding some clear gloss to his lips before he heads down to meet his boyfriend.

Luca is waiting for Jax outside the wooden doors of his building. "Hi!" Jax says, throwing himself into Luca's arms. "What a nice surprise to have lunch together today!"

"Hmmmmm," Luca growls into Jax's ear. "Well you had the day off, so I thought it would be a nice treat. You smell delicious." Luca nips at Jaxon's silver hoop with his teeth. "And you look delicious. The shirt looks amazing on you, just like I knew it would."

Jax pulls back from Luca and smooths over the red silk. He is wearing the two top buttons open, and a black satin choker around his neck." Thank you, Luca," he says coyly. "But you didn't have to buy me clothes, you know."

"Well I wanted to," Luca replies while helping Jax into the back of the Mercedes. "We need to expand your Blackwood wardrobe, considering your new position." Luca walks around the back of the car, sliding into the seat next to Jax. He grasps Jaxon's hand, intertwining their fingers.

"Good afternoon, Mr. Somsi." Tony tips his head toward Jaxon. "You look stunning, as always."

Jaxon blushes a bit. "Thank you, Tony. And please call me Jax."

"Very well, Jax. Mr. Blackwood has a lovely restaurant picked out for you today," Tony says, and then raises the privacy screen.

"Are you sure that you can afford time away from work?" Jax asks while he uses his available hand to tease Luca's knee and then smooth down his ornate necktie.

"Of course. I wanted us to celebrate your article. This was the best-selling issue of Blackwood Magazine that we've ever released. People love you."

"People love Taylor and his designs!" Jax chuckles. "But I was really pleased that I got a chance to show the real me. Not just the homewrecker everyone assumed me to be."

Luca brings their intertwined fingers to his lips, placing gentle kisses on his boyfriend's soft hand. "Those dancing shots that Jasper took of you? My god, I can't even look at them without getting hard."

"Luca!" Jax exclaims, pulling his hand away to swat at Luca's shoulder.

When they arrive at the restaurant, Tony walks around and helps Jaxon out of the car. "Here we are, Jax. Mr. Blackwood, I'll be waiting for your text."

"We are planning on having a long, leisurely lunch, Tony," Luca says, taking Jaxon's hand to lead him inside.

"Very good, sir. Enjoy yourselves." Tony drives away, back the way he came from.

**

The black Mercedes makes its way into Chelsea, stopping at a twenty-four-hour parking garage. Tony takes off his suit jacket, pulling on a gray hoodie, baseball hat, and sunglasses. He walks out onto the street, fingering the device in his pocket as he heads toward Eleventh Avenue. Rounding the corner, Tony sees Jaxon's building a few blocks ahead. Checking his watch, he slows down his pace as he approaches.

Tony takes out a cigarette, lighting it and inhaling deeply as he lingers on the sidewalk. Before long, he hears the buzzing of the lock to the front doors, a man exiting while talking excitedly on his phone. Tony eases his way toward the door, slipping inside behind the distracted man before it closes. He enters the stairwell, fully aware that there are no security cameras in the building. He pulls his hood tighter and approaches Jaxon's apartment door. Quickly looking around, he pulls the electric lock gun from his pocket, disabling the lock in a few seconds. Tony steps inside, knowing he will only be there for a few short minutes.

Back in the car, hoodie and hat placed securely in the trunk, Tony pulls out his phone to make a call. "It's done. Yep. I'm aware... I hope you know what you're doing boss...No, sir. I'm not questioning you...Yes, sir." Tony ends the call and pulls out of the parking garage, headed back toward the restaurant.

**

Luca and Jax share a tender kiss outside when Tony pulls up. Luca has his hand gently threaded through Jaxon's blond locks, and Jax trails his fingers down his cheek.

"Thank you for an amazing lunch together, Mr. Blackwood," Jax says as they touch their foreheads together.

"Stop now. You know that I have a meeting to attend." Luca sighs deeply.

Tony opens the door, and the men slide into their seats once again. "Tony," Luca says, "would you mind taking me to the office first, then dropping off Jaxon?" Luca turns to Jax. "Is that okay? I don't want to arrive late to the meeting."

"It's fine, Luca. I think I'll take a hot bath and relax this afternoon." Jax says as Luca places a tender kiss onto his forehead.

When they arrive at Blackwood and Luca heads inside, Tony begins the drive towards Chelsea once again. "You look very happy, Jaxon," Tony says, looking into the rearview mirror.

"I am happy, Tony. Luca is really someone special." He responds.

Tony nods. "Yes. Well' I'm pleased to see you together again."

Jax leans back and closes his eyes, relaxing as he reflects on his wonderful afternoon. He must have dozed a bit, awakening to Tony's voice. "Jax, you're home." He opens his eyes and sees that they have stopped in front of his place. Tony helps Jax from the car. "Until next time," he says, and watches closely as he enters the building.

**

Jaxon turns on the faucet to the old clawfoot tub, making sure that the water is nice and hot. He sprinkles in some bath salts and unbuttons his new shirt while walking toward the sitting area. He steps with bare feet toward the coffee table to grab some magazines to read while soaking and stops. He tips his head to the side. Lying separate from the pile is his issue of Blackwood Magazine. He was sure that he had put it on the pile earlier. Shrugging, he picks it up along with a few others and heads back to the bathroom.

Jax strips down and eases into the tub, loving the way the warm water relaxes him. He grabs his favorite honey and vanilla body wash, taking his time to suds himself everywhere. He washes his hair and submerges himself under water to rinse out the soap. He stays under longer than is needed, enjoying the weightless feeling and the hot water around him.

When he resurfaces, Jax dries his hands on a towel and grabs a magazine from the stool next to the tub. He leans back and flips through the pages, studying the models and their effortless poses. He wants to do his best to represent Blackwood and imagines himself recreating the postures from the pages. Tossing the magazine aside, he grabs his issue of Blackwood Magazine. Jaxon smiles at his best friend's face grinning at him from the cover, and flips to Taylor's article. He can't believe how far that they've come from their shitty lives back in Ohio. He is so incredibly proud of his friend.

Jax continues to turn the pages until he gets to his featured article and freezes. He stares down at his picture on the page, expecting to meet his own eyes. Instead, he sees two gaping holes in the page. He flips to the next picture and the next. In each picture, his eyes have been cut out. Jax sets the magazine on a stool and reaches for his towel with shaking hands. He wraps himself up in the cotton but doesn't dry himself. He grabs the magazine and walks, dripping water, into his room and sits on the bed.

Jax opens the magazine again and finds every picture of himself. The eyes are gone from every single image. Taking a deep breath, he reassures himself that this is just a silly joke. He tries to imagine Taylor with his sewing scissors, cutting out his eyes. Tears trail down his cheeks mixing with the dripping tub water. *It's just a joke. Just Tay trying to be funny. I'm sure that's it.* Jaxon grabs his phone and messages his best friend.

**

"I just absolutely love this studio," Heidi says, trailing her hand along the fabric patterns strewn along the old bench by the window. Twisting the fingers of her other hand through her springy red curls, she picks up a set of material swatches. She rests her elbows on the wood and flicks through the elaborate fabrics, mumbling to herself. "Wow!"

Victoria grins at Taylor who sits down on a facing stool. She looks over at her friend. "Um, Heidi. We are here for a reason, remember?"

"Oh, crap," she says, rushing to join the other two. She pulls out an old mahogany stool that Taylor has seated with a cute patterned cushion, and plops down. "Yeah sorry. I just adore this place."

Victoria hands her one of the glass bottles of water from the tray, before turning to Taylor. "Thanks for doing this, Tay. I do appreciate it."

He nods his head at her, shrugging his shoulders. "Of course. How could I not make the wedding dress of the century? Mr. Blackwood marrying his beautiful bride."

Victoria flushes crimson and waves her hand in front of him. "Oh, stop it." She covers her face in embarrassment to hide her blushing cheeks. "You'll make me all shy!"

"Pfft, you, shy?" scoffs Heidi, playfully screwing off the lid and gulping back the clear liquid. "Ewwww, you didn't tell me that this was sparkling!" She shudders and puts the bottle down next to her with a face of absolute disgust, staring at the bubbles.

"Can we begin now?" Taylor laughs at Victoria's playfully irritated expression and rustles a few sketches that he has in his hand. Setting the leather folder down beside him, he passes a few of the pages to Victoria. "What do you think? I hope that you like some of them. If not, I can work on some more."

The two women browse over the designs, both making approving noises as they scan through the pages. Taylor knows that he's good at designing what people specifically ask for, yet he still gets nervous when showing his clients his ideas.

Heidi points to one of the sketches. "I really like this one."

Victoria nods in agreement, turning the page and holding it up for Taylor to see. "This one," she says. "This is absolutely the most perfect thing. Far better than I could have imagined. You've captured exactly what I asked for. You are amazing, Tay, really you are."

Taylor grins as she passes it over. "I'm glad that you like it. I was hoping that you'd pick this one. I think that this is my favorite too."

Putting the others back into the folder, he explains the finer details to both girls who sit and eagerly listen. The dress will be an A-line drop with a long court train; the materials of a tulle and lace design. The tulle will be full length, but without the skirt being too big and princess-like. Around the waist will be a pretty lace overlay with a few added sparkly diamantés. The top will feature a sleeveless bodice with a plunging neckline to accentuate her chest line. Heidi howls with laughter at Victoria's embarrassment when Taylor mentions her breasts. It doesn't help that they both have a crush on the young man sitting with them. After they compose themselves, he goes on to further explain that the bodice will have the same lace pattern that will be on the skirt.

"It's a very 'fairy in the woods' type of design, isn't it?" Heidi says.

Victoria takes the paper again to have another look. "It really is. I can just imagine it."

"Ohhh." Heidi starts bunching up strands of Victoria's straight, blonde hair. "I can just picture it styled up loosely like this, with little flowers or sparkles placed in it."

"Well, that's your job to help me with." She laughs at her friend.

"I agree," Taylor says. "I think that will really suit you and match the theme." He jumps off his stool and puts the paper on to his desk. "Are you okay with the color though? I thought something a little less traditional would be nice."

"It's champagne color, right?" she asks him, and he verifies. "Yes, I love it. A little unusual."

Taylor grabs a few samples of tulle and shows the girls, who equally approve of the shade. Victoria states that it looks even better than she expected. After showing them some lace samples, they're all happy with their decisions. Victoria's face is glowing with excitement.

She lets out a big sigh of relief as Taylor adds those pieces to the design board, ready to get started with the construction. "We will have to book an appointment for final measurements and then I can get started," he says.

Heidi claps her hands in excitement. "I can't wait. It will be so amazing to have a Blackwood wedding."

"Well," Victoria raises an eyebrow. "Let's not forget that there's already been one. Or there almost was."

"Gah." Heidi snorts, flicking her hair back. "What an absolute shit show that was. I am so glad that Luca saw sense." She turns to Victoria. "And I am so, so pleased that your dress is going to be nowhere near as elaborate and garish as hers was."

"That's because Taylor didn't make it," Victoria laughs.

Taylor rolls his eyes. "Oh, she wanted me to. She messaged me a dozen times about it. I just couldn't. You know, with Jax and everything?"

Heidi folds her arms with an indignant look on her face. "Well, what an absolute nerve she has! But it doesn't surprise me one bit."

Victoria hums along with Taylor. "She has balls, that's for sure." She pats him on the arm. "How is Jax doing? Are things okay with Luca now?"

Taylor's face lights up. "Yes," he says. "They seem to be back on track, thankfully." His phone starts to buzz on the table, and he gestures to Heidi and Victoria. "May I?"

They indicate that they have no objections, and he heads over to look at it. The two women continue to express their thoughts about Misun and the whole situation, enjoying their little gossip about the whole situation. Thanking the stars above, that Misun will no longer be in their circle of Blackwood partners.

"Tay?" Victoria pauses and watches as Taylor frantically messages something back, with a flustered and upset look on his face. She slides off her stool and crosses the studio with Heidi closely following. "Are you okay?"

He looks up at them having almost forgotten that they were in the room. "Oh, sorry." Taylor is flustered and thrusts his phone into his pocket. "It was Jax."

"Is there something wrong?" Heidi asks him.

"Umm," he says, "I'm not sure. I think so. I just worry about him."

Heidi and Victoria give each other a confused look before turning back to Taylor. Victoria rubs his arm. "Can we do anything to help?"

Taylor takes a deep breath and places his hand over Victoria's. "Jaxon just got another threat."

The girls look at each other before Heidi speaks to him. "What kind of threat?"

Taylor shrugs his shoulders. "I don't know. But he seems pretty shaken up. He asked if I'd played a prank on him with scissors? He said he would talk to me about it when I get home."

"I see," Victoria says, drawing him in for a hug. "You know that these people are usually just opportunist assholes who have nothing better to do, don't you?"

"Yeah," Heidi chimes in. "Those who get a kick out of hurting people in the public eye. Vile people."

Taylor bows his head. "I know. I can't help but stress over him. He's like my family, you know?"

She gives him another squeeze. "Make sure he tells Luca, and then Noah. They will keep an eye on things. I'm sure it's nothing serious."

He smiles at them both, not realizing the severity of the situation. "I will. Thank you both." He throws his hands up in the air, changing the subject. "Now we have a dress to finish planning`, ladies!"

Chapter 19

Luca rushes past the police officers and over to Jaxon, who is standing teary-eyed and barefoot in loose white tee and sweatpants. The officer talking to him steps aside, and Luca sweeps the back of his fingers down Jaxon's cheek, wiping away a few stray tears.

Luca turns to the officers. "What the hell happened? Someone broke in?"

"Doesn't appear so. No sign of forced entry," the officer says, in a somewhat put-out tone.

"Mr. Somsi, are you sure this wasn't some kind of joke? Done by someone you know?"

"No, no of course not. Why would someone do that?" Jax stutters.

"I don't know, Mr. Somsi, jealousy? You've made quite a name for yourself in the papers," the officer speaks to him condescendingly.

Luca approaches the police officer, standing directly in front of his face. "I don't like the way you're speaking to my boyfriend, sir. Just what are you insinuating?" Luca clenches his teeth, attempting to remain in control. "Mr. Somsi has already obtained some threatening letters, now this. What are you doing about it?"

"Well, Mr. Blackwood, *sir*, we haven't found anything, and Mr. Somsi hasn't had any physical threats from anyone." The man turns toward Jax. "Have you noticed anyone following you?"

Jaxon shakes his head as the officer continues. "I'm sure it's nothing to worry about. I'll take the magazine to forensics and file a report."

"No," Luca says firmly. "You have the letters, and we haven't heard one word of followup from you. Not one returned call..."

The officer cuts Luca off. "Mr. Blackwood, this is New York City. We have murders, rapes, and assaults to deal with on a daily basis, as I'm sure you're aware."

Luca grabs the officer, escorting him toward the door, his partner following. "Yes," he says, firmly. "Well, the Blackwoods won't be bothering you anymore. I will handle this from now on. Good afternoon gentlemen." Luca grabs the bagged magazine from the officer and slams the door.

"Luca." Jaxon approaches his boyfriend. "I'm sure that he's right. Don't get so upset. It could have been a prank before the magazines were delivered here or something."

Luca pulls Jaxon into a tight embrace, whispering in his ear, "Well, I'm not taking any chances. I'm not going to let anything happen to you." Jaxon gently pulls away and walks to the kitchen to pour them both a glass of wine. He hands Luca the glass, and Luca continues. "I want you to stay at my place tonight. I'm going to have Blackwood security replace the lock and put up cameras. I'll message Taylor. He should stay with Jasper tonight."

"Luca, I just wonder why?" Jaxon sips his wine and grabs an overnight bag to throw some things into. "Everyone has been so supportive since the article! I've received so many nice messages on social media."

Luca helps Jax gather some clothes and toiletries as he responds. "I don't know, Angel. I'll figure it out. It will be just fine." Luca doesn't mention the one name that keeps entering his mind. *Misun.*

**

Running the towel over the rim of the glass, Misun lets out a big sigh. The rundown, backstreet bar that she works in is bustling with men talking loudly about how crap their jobs are, or the last time that their wives nagged at them for doing something that wasn't their fault.

She turns and sets the glass on a shelf behind her and runs her hand over her swollen stomach, smiling to herself at the feeling of the swift kicks. She *is* happy about the baby; it's just not how she had planned it.

Leaning her elbow on the bar, she rests her chin on her palm, still clutching the towel, and reflects on the past few months. Yes, she had lied to Luca. The pregnancy wasn't an accident like she had claimed. She had stopped taking her pill a couple of months earlier and had gotten pregnant very quickly.

This isn't how it's supposed to be. She lets out another sigh, knowing that she's fucked up. *What am I going to do now?*

"I'll have a beer please, Sunshine," a voice says, making her freeze.

He is here. She was expecting him to show up at some point. Turning to face him, she places the towel on the wooden bar in front of her and forces a smile. "Hey. I was wondering when I would see you."

Pouring him a drink, she watches out of the corner of her eye as he pulls off his blue cap, running his fingers through his thick dark waves before replacing it. He sits on one of the bar stools and she places a napkin down, setting his beer in front of him.

"Now I know what you're going to say..." she begins.

"I wasn't going to say a thing, Sunshine," he says with a smug smile. "I just came out to enjoy an evening by myself."

She knows him better than that. Misun fully expects him to change his persona at any time and tries to avoid him as much as possible. He watches her constantly. She knows that his intimidating stare is a sign of things to come.

By the time that he's had his fourth beer, the man is chatting to some locals that he has befriended for the evening; the group of them are loud and spewing profanities.

"Hey." One of the men points at her as she walks by with a tray. "Aren't you her? From that expensive wedding that was in the news?"

She tries to continue on her journey past, but the man with the blue cap grabs her arm. "Now, Misun, let's not be rude to this kind gent." He indicates to those sneering at her with him. "Answer him."

Misun knows better than to disobey him. She nods her head, feeling his grip tighten around her arm as she tries not to drop the tray.

"Damnnnn!" the guy says, waving his free hand in the air, the movement spilling his beer down his other wrist. "That was brutal, man." He points to her bump. "Leaving you stranded there in that condition."

She bows her head as the man with a hold on her laughs. "Right? She couldn't even keep hold of him while pregnant. And what's even worse, she lost him to a gay guy! I certainly haven't taught her very well, have I?"

"Oh my god, no!" the other man says, showing his homophobic side. "Another man? That's just nasty."

"I mean, look though," the blue cap guy says, glancing her up and down. "Look at how she's dressed!" Misun looks down at her bump squeezed into a skirt that's far too short, and a shirt with a few buttons unfastened for the wandering eye. "No wonder a classy guy like that didn't stick around."

Misun feels her arm being released after their humiliating taunting dies down. She rushes back behind the bar, cursing herself for letting him affect her this much. Setting the tray down, one of the girls that she's working with notices her shaking hands as the glasses rattle.

"Are you okay?" she says, blowing a bubble with her gum. "Isn't that the guy you always talk to? Isn't he like, your boyfriend or something?"

"I'm fine." Misun snaps. "Just let me get back to work."

The girl scoffs at Misun's rudeness and walks away. Misun can feel tears welling in her eyes but refuses to let them fall knowing that he's watching her. She breathes a sigh of relief when he eventually leaves.

**

Stepping outside at the end of her shift, Misun pauses and leans against the wall. She slips off her shoe and massages her foot with her free hand, cursing to herself about wearing heels when pregnant and on her feet for hours.

She hears a noise nearby and her heart sinks. She knows exactly who's been waiting for her to finish. She'd hoped that her ride would be here by now, but it isn't.

"Hey, Sunshine," the man in the blue cap slurs, sliding his arm around her waist. She brushes him off. "Ohhh now. Someone is a little feisty this evening."

"Do we have to do this now?" She sighs, putting her shoe back on. "I'm so tired."

He laughs. "Well you wouldn't be if you hadn't screwed up and lost Luca. You'd be living a nice, comfortable life. We both would be."

"What do you want me to do?" She practically pleads with him, the tears starting to finally fall from her eyes. "I didn't mean for him to find out that I was cheating."

"Exactly," he says, shrugging his shoulders. "If he hadn't found out, then he wouldn't have fallen for that, what's his name? The gay one?"

"Jaxon," she whispers, her head bowed.

"That's it!" He shouts out. "Gay boy Jaxon. Now Luca is the same and it's disgusting." He leans in towards her, a sneer on his face. "Don't you think it's disgusting? And just think, he's been inside you. Hmm."

"So have you!" she snaps back.

"True," he says. "Still nasty, though." He stumbles a little before touching her hand, giving her a familiar look, which indicates that he wants something. "Look, Mi, you know that you have to get him on your good side again. Now that you aren't going to be his wife, you need to get as much money out of him as you can for the kid. You know that don't you?"

She nods in agreement, knowing that most of the money won't even be for the baby, but for the man standing in front of her. He smiles and kisses her cheek, the smell of alcohol on his breath turning her stomach. "I'll be in touch, Sunshine," he says before staggering away.

Misun tries to compose herself while she waits for her ride. She wishes she could just run away, but she knows that the man will find her wherever she goes. She wipes her eyes on her jacket sleeve, avoiding the headlights as the car pulls up beside her. She opens the door and slips into the passenger seat.

"Thanks for picking me up, Jayce," she says to the driver. "Sorry for calling you, I didn't feel like walking home."

"Yeah, well, if anyone sees us together, can you imagine?" he says, pulling out. "We've had enough Blackwood scandal involving you, Misun."

"I know, Jayce and I'm sorry. I just didn't feel safe." She can't tell him why.

Jayce raises his brow, and she prepares herself for his usual lecture. "Well, you know if you speak to Luca, he may be able to figure something out. You shouldn't be working here. Especially not in your condition."

"I know that! I just don't want to talk to him yet. I message him about baby things and that's it!"

Jayce sighs. "Misun, Luca is my cousin, right? I know that he'll help you. Stop being so stubborn."

"He left me at the altar!" she screeches dramatically at him, pointing to her bump. "Like this!"

"Mi, you didn't even want to marry him anyway. Stop kidding yourself!" Jayce says as she pulls some napkins out of the glove compartment and dabs at the makeup smudges on her cheeks. "I don't know what it is that you're trying to do, what game you're trying to play, but right now you need help. And Luca can do that."

**

Jax cuddles up to Luca on the sofa, a big fluffy blanket draped over them. Candles are lit around the room, flickering shadows dancing across the crisp white walls in the dusky light of the evening. "If it wasn't for Taylor," he murmurs in a contented tone, "then I wouldn't want to go home."

Luca grins resting his head on top of Jax's, breathing in the scent of his hair, freshly washed after their steamy lovemaking session earlier. "I know, I don't want you to go." He lifts their intertwined hands and kisses the back of Jax's hand. "I could just stay like this forever."

Their peace is disturbed as the intercom buzzes, echoing around Luca's apartment. Jax looks up at Luca who shrugs his shoulders. "I'm not expecting anyone," he says, lifting Jax's relaxed body off him enough to slide off the sofa. Jax groans and curls up under the blanket.

Answering the intercom, Luca pauses. "Hi... Yeah, come up." He presses the button to open the main door and turns to his boyfriend with a confused look. "It's Misun."

Jax sits up straighter. "Oh," is all that he can say, fully aware that he is sitting there in just a pair of shorts with no t-shirt. He pulls the blanket tighter around himself. "Is she okay?" He tries not to let his dislike for her show, even though his boyfriend is about to have a baby with her.

Luca shrugs. "I literally have no idea. We haven't actually spoken since the wedding, and even when we do communicate it's just messages about doctor appointments."

"Do you want me to go and sit in the bedroom or something?" Jax asks, but Luca shakes his head.

There is a gentle tap on the door, and Luca swings it open, inviting Misun in. "Is everything alright?" he asks.

"Everything is fine," she says, stepping into her former home that feels strange and awkward now. She notices Jax on the sofa, as he wraps himself up more into the fabric. "Oh, sorry. I didn't realize that you had company."

Luca walks further into the room, and she follows. "Yeah, Jax is staying here for a while until his apartment is more secure."

She glances at Jax. "Secure? Has something happened?"

Luca huffs. "Are you trying to tell me that you don't know anything about it?"

Looking in confusion between the two men, Misun frowns. "About what, Luca?"

Luca scoffs in disbelief. "Oh, come on, Mi! Who else would break into Jax's apartment and do what they did? Who else has such a grudge against him?" He can't help the dark emotions bubbling up inside him at the thought of someone threatening the man he loves.

Her eyes are wide, and Jax grasps Luca's hand, exposing the top of his bare chest as the blanket falls. "What?" she exclaims. "Luca, I have no idea what you're talking about. Really I don't."

Jax squeezes his lover's fingers. "I think she's telling the truth, Luca."

Misun glances over at Jax, her eyes wander down to his skin and she realizes that they were having an intimate moment. "Oh, sorry, I didn't mean to disturb you both."

She turns to head back towards the door, but Luca steps away from Jax and stops her from leaving. "Okay, I believe you," he says. He turns Misun to face him. "We need to start getting along, Mi." Touching her bump, he feels some movement. "For this little one if it's mine."

Sighing, she bows her head to the floor. "It is Luca." She is so tired of being doubted, but considering that she cheated on him, she can understand why. Looking back up to face her former partner, the tears start to roll down her cheeks. "I need your help."

He gently guides her towards the sofa, and Jax moves his legs and makes room for her to sit. Luca has seen her manipulative tears, but this time he can see that she's vulnerable. He sits between the two of them.

"What can I do?" he asks, eyeing her closely. He isn't used to seeing her out wearing no makeup. Her clothes are loose and dull; this isn't like her at all.

"I'm struggling to work at the bar." She rubs her eyes with her hands. "I'm like, more tired than I can even describe, Luca. And I'm so mentally drained from all of the fighting. I want us to get along as well." She turns to Jax. "All of us."

Luca and Jax exchange glances as she continues. "I can see how much you love each other, and I was wrong to try and get in the way of that. I'm sorry."

Jax pulls a tissue from the metallic box on the coffee table and hands it to her. Luca takes hold of one of her hands while she wipes her eyes with the other.

"Misun," he says. "I have an idea." He pauses to let her blow her nose. "I'll give you the equivalent of your weekly wages so you can leave that place."

She shakes her head firmly. "No, Luca. I can't let you do that."

"But I want to," he says. "You can leave that nasty place and get some rest. After the baby is born, depending on what the test says, we can talk about a suitable amount for the two of you."

"Are you sure?" She smiles at him as he nods. "Thank you, Luca. I appreciate it so much. You have no idea."

She spends a little more time talking to the two men, before reminding Luca about their appointment the following week. Thanking them for their kindness, she leaves the apartment to make her way home. Luca offered to call Tony to give her a ride, but she explained that it was still early, and some fresh air would be good for her.

Once outside, she walks away from the building with her hands in her pocket, a smile etched on her lips. As soon as she knows that she's out of sight of Luca, possibly watching her from the window, she pulls her phone from her bag and dials a number.

After a few rings, he answers. "Hi," she says into the handset. "I've got Luca on my side. It's working."

Chapter 20

"What are you doing here?" Noah looks up from his desk and a large grin spreads over his face when he sees his beautiful fiancée gliding into his office.

She smiles back and places a wicker basket in front of him. "I needed to get out for a while." He watches as she brushes her blonde hair behind her ears, sweeping the stray strands away from her eyes. "Besides," she says, pulling items out of the basket, "I thought you might be hungry, so I made some food."

Noah makes some approving noises as she sets it out for them, the smell of the picnic snacks floating around the room. He starts to pick at the olives in one container, and sits back in his chair, keeping his gaze on her as she pours the lemonade that she's made herself.

Handing him the glass, Victoria becomes aware of him watching her and blushes. "What?"

"I just love looking at my wife-to-be," he says, reaching for a small slice of bruschetta topped with his favorite blue cheese and Parma ham, before resting back into the luxurious leather.

Victoria slips off her shoes and sits on the edge of the desk, her legs dangling along with her long, flowing skirt. She clinks her glass with Noah's.

"I needed some brightness, Noah," she says. "This thesis is hard going."

"How are you doing with it?" he asks. "Making progress?"

She sighs, grabbing a strawberry and taking a bite before throwing the stem onto her plate. "It's developing well, thankfully. It's just so sad reviewing those cases all day."

"I bet it is," Noah says. "Knowing that those kids were abused is absolutely horrible."

"You're right. And some of them have had no help or therapy to get their lives back on track. It's really hard, because then they go on to make some bad decisions later in life. It's tough."

"I can't even begin to imagine," Noah says, thinking about how good his life has been and feeling grateful to have the parents that he does. "It must be so difficult going through life like that, with such horrendous memories plaguing you."

He holds her hand and pulls her gently toward him. She's still sitting on the desk, but

The Blackwood Heirs Book 1

with her feet resting on his thighs. She scrunches up her toes feeling the soft, expensive material on her skin.

"It will be worth it," he says, setting his glass down and trailing his fingers up her calves.

"I hope so, Noah, or I've been working at this for a long time and it will all amount to nothing!" She nervously laughs and leans her elbows on her knees so that her face is close to his. "Which is why I wanted to get out of our place and come and see you, my love."

Noah runs his hands under her skirt and rests them on the outside of her thighs. "Well, I'm glad that you did." He loses himself in her eyes for a moment longer, before pressing the button on his intercom to his assistant. "Yeah, hi. No one is to disturb me for a while, okay?"

His assistant agrees, and Victoria raises an eyebrow as he stands, positioning himself between her thighs. She lazily drapes her arms on his shoulders.

"Hello, Mr. B.," she says, looking longingly at him. "I love you."

"I love you too." He leans in to kiss her, moving his lips slowly over hers.

She responds, their eyes closing in unison as they fall into the moment. He can taste the food that she has graciously prepared for him, and he fully embraces the sweetness of strawberries on her tongue.

Running her fingers through his thick hair, she pulls him closer, sliding her way to the edge of the desk. Victoria feels his semi-hard cock, and moans as she feels him pushing against her.

Noah gently lays her back on the desk, pushing some of the food to one side, carefully brushing her hair away from the dishes as she rests her head back.

She watches as he unbuttons his sleeves and begins to roll them up to his elbows. "Oh, this looks serious," she says to tease him.

Laughing, he hitches up the material of her skirt, tracing his fingers over the top of her lace panties, watching as her eyes flicker shut at his gentle touch. Noah looks adoringly at the stunning sight in front of him, fully appreciating how lucky he is to have Victoria. She moves her hand up to the base of Luca's cock and gently massages it. Noah pulls her panties to one side, stroking his fingers along her velvety skin. He finds her clit, flicking and circling it. Victoria lets out a quiet groan as he increases the pressure, slipping a long finger into her. Noah unzips his pants, releasing his erection. He pushes himself carefully inside her, and a gasp escapes her. She spreads her legs wider, hooking them over his arms as he rests his palms on his desk to steady himself.

Victoria places her hands beside her head, knocking off one of the dishes. Her eyes shoot open, and she tries to see how much of a mess she's made. "Oh shit, Noah I'm sorry."

He smiles at her and starts to move slowly. "Don't worry about it," he says in a relaxed tone. Nothing can distract him from the amazing feeling of being inside her.

Still feeling a little apprehensive, Victoria tries to allow her body to relax. She rests her head back again, watching the pleasure overtake Noah's face as he gazes at her with adoration.

Moving faster and a little harder, he can tell that Victoria is trying to keep her noises to a minimum. "Let me hear you," he commands with a deep whisper.

"But, ah..." Victoria struggles to get her words out. "Others will hear me too."

Noah shrugs, an expression on his face showing that he doesn't care. "I want you to forget about everyone else, and where we are."

She closes her eyes, allowing herself to get lost in the moment, her body starting to tingle. Their breaths get deeper and faster, their noises filling the room as he slides in and out of her at a steady pace.

Gripping at his shirt on his shoulder, her body begins to tremble with her orgasm taking hold. "Noah, I..., Noah...!" she shouts out, unable to control herself.

Feeling her gripping and pulsing over his dick, Noah can't control himself any longer and comes inside her, thrusting deeply as he grunts through his own orgasm and it ebbs away.

Releasing his arms from under her legs, he stands up straight and grabs one of the napkins that Victoria has added to their little picnic. He dabs his beading forehead with it before sliding out of her, cleaning her up and fastening his clothes.

She adjusts herself and sits up, trying to make her hair a little more presentable. "I only came to bring you some food." She laughs and jumps off the desk picking up the plate she had dropped and grabbing some more of the serviettes to try and clean up the spill. "This will stain, Noah."

He takes her arm and pulls her up to face him. Placing his hands on her waist, she stands there with a dish in one hand and wet napkins in the other. "Leave it, I will get it cleaned up."

He kisses her on the lips to taste more of the strawberries.

**

Turning the corner Misun gasps as she collides with Luca who is waiting on the other side of the wall. Feeling flustered, she glances back over her shoulder to make sure Jayce is gone. She doesn't want Luca to know that his cousin has dropped her off at the hospital.

"Oh, you're here already?" she says, trying to act normally, brushing her jacket down.

The Blackwood Heirs Book 1

"Yeah, I just finished a meeting so thought I'd make my way over," Luca tells her as they start to make their way through the sliding doors and down the corridors towards their appointment. "Did you walk here?"

She shakes her head. "No, I took the subway," she lies to him.

Luca tuts at her. "I told you that I'd send Tony to pick you up. I hope that you'll let me help you."

"You already do enough, Luca," she says, touching his arms softly. "And I'm so grateful."

And she is. Genuinely. She knows that she's hiding a lot from her ex-partner and father of her child, but to be able to leave her job and take care of herself better is something that she is truly thankful for. She hates all of this sneaking around and lying to him, but she doesn't feel that she has much choice with *him* around.

Sitting down on the waiting room chairs, Luca can see that she has gone very quiet. "Are you okay?"

She takes a deep breath and nods her head. "I'm fine." She bends the truth again. "I'm just a little nervous since this is the last appointment, which means that it's nearly time for this little one to arrive."

She runs her hand over her swollen belly, and Luca places his own there too. "Look, whatever happens, I'll be here to help you. And so will Jax when you are ready to allow him to be around."

Needing all the support that she can get, she nervously smiles at Luca, wondering if it's time to tell him everything. "Luca..." she begins.

"Misun?" A voice pulls her away from her confession, indicating that it's time for her appointment. "You can come in now."

Luca allows her to go in first for her internal examination. Even though they possibly made the baby together, he doesn't feel that it's right to be there for something so intimate. Sitting and waiting, he reflects on everything that's happened in the past months, and how many things have changed. He smiles and pulls out his phone, sending Jaxon a quick good luck message for his photoshoot, telling him that he will be there as soon as he can.

A few minutes pass before Luca is called in, and he takes his place next to Misun in the room. He sits and listens to all of the information given, Misun asking questions about her labor and delivering the baby. He's impressed at how knowledgeable she is about it and wishes that he had looked up some information for himself.

"So, will the father be present?" Luca is asked, but he shakes his head.

"No, I don't think that..." he begins.

"Yes," Misun says. "He will be there." Luca turns to her, and she nods at him. "Please Luca, I want you there."

He scoffs nervously. "Actually there? Like in with you?"

She laughs at how flustered he is. "Yes! If you want to be? You've been amazing to me recently. I know that we've had our struggles, but I want that in the past now. This is your baby too."

**

Once outside, Luca turns to Misun. "I'm heading over to the Brooklyn Bridge shoot, do you want me to call Tony for you?"

"No," she says. "I'm meeting up with someone, I'll be fine. But thanks, Luca."

He touches her arm affectionately. "No, Misun, it's me that should be thanking you. Are you absolutely sure that you want me in there with you?" She reassures him that she does. "I really appreciate it." His eyes well with tears. "You don't know how much that means."

She playfully slaps his arm and laughs. "Stop that! I'm supposed to be the emotional one."

"Okay, okay." He smiles at her. "Right, well I have to go. Are you sure that you don't want any help getting somewhere?"

"I told you," she says. "I'm only going around the corner and then I won't be on my own."

As long as he's known Misun, he has always been aware that she's a bit of a loner without any close friends, despite her loud and confident nature. Luca eyes her with a hint of suspicion as she walks away and turns the corner.

Chapter 21

It's cold. Jaxon rubs his hands together, blowing warm air into them.

"Oh, Jax, you'll get used to it soon enough," Jayce says. "Outdoor shoots can be tough when it's cold out, but we need to act like it's a warm summer day for the photos."

"How the hell do we do that? Aren't you freezing?" Jax replies. He is sitting on a director's chair while the makeup artist touches up his lips and liner.

"Here, hold on." Jayce waves over an assistant, who gives Jaxon a hand warmer and drapes a fleece blanket around his shoulders.

"Don't mess up his hair!" Heidi shouts from a few feet away, where she's adjusting silver necklaces on their female model, Treeva. Taylor is standing with her, making sure that his new design for the Spring Collection looks perfect.

It's late autumn, and Blackwood is doing a few teaser shots for the Spring Collection. The runway show for Taylor's full collection will be in a month or so. Luca arranged the photoshoot today on the Brooklyn Bridge; the iconic spot will create the perfect backdrop to showcase Taylor's designs. Jaxon looks around, a bit overwhelmed at the enormity of the preparations going on. The area has been blocked off, and Blackwood security is there to ensure that anyone gathering to watch stays behind the barricades.

A couple of NYC police officers are lingering around, having checked that the permits and paperwork are in order. Jasper is directing his photography assistants and technicians in setting up the lighting and proper equipment in the first spot for the shoot. There are large privacy screens set up so that stylists, hair, and makeup artists can work on the models without anyone sneaking photos with their phones.

Jaxon is starting to warm up a bit, but still shivers from nervousness. *I wish that Luca was here.* Jax knows that he'd be more relaxed with some reassurance from his boyfriend, but Luca is with Misun at her pre-delivery doctor's appointment. The time is getting close, and he knows that Luca must be there. Hopefully, he will make it to at least part of the shoot.

Bella is elegantly dressed, as usual. Her tight-fitting black skirt falls just below her knees, and she struts beside Harrison in knee-high black leather stiletto boots. A tight black turtleneck accentuates her long neck, and she wears a white fox fur vest, much to Harrison's dismay. Her son scolds her every time she wears real fur, but what can she say, old habits die hard. Bella thinks that the fox would be pleased with how gorgeous she looks.

She observes her son and Heidi as they bicker about the best way to wrap the mile-long laces on the sneakers that he and Taylor had designed. *They're adorable.* Bella grins, taking a sip of her tea when she feels her phone buzz in her vest pocket. She pulls it out, her smile growing when she sees the name on the screen. "Darling! This is a surprise!" she coos. Heidi glances her way, and Bella walks away for some privacy. "I'm so pleased to hear your voice!"

"Hello, Bella. I'm in town for a few days for a meeting. I wanted to see you, and I have a few hours free today." The voice on the other end of the call is a bit difficult to hear, the New York traffic audible in the background.

"Well we're doing a shoot today, darling, so I can't break away for lunch. Would you be interested in coming here?" Bella asks.

"Sure, I'd love to. I have a driver, just let me know your location."

When Bella finishes her call, she checks in with Jasper to make sure that everything is ready. "How's it going, Jasper, everything all set up?"

"Hi Auntie, yes I'm ready. How's this spot to start?" Jasper knows that his aunt has an amazing eye.

"I think it's perfect, sweetheart. The Manhattan skyline is always stunning here," Bella replies. "Just double-check with Taylor. You must respect his vision."

"Of course." Jasper smiles thinking of how talented Taylor is. "Would you mind checking on the models and sending Taylor over when he's ready?"

"On my way," Bella replies. She observes the crowd growing behind the barricade as she heads back toward the privacy screen. Police officers escort people who want to cross the bridge past the set. They'll have to wait to cross once Jasper begins. When she arrives at the styling area, everyone is bustling with last-minute preparations.

Heidi is finishing up with Treeva. She is a stunning African American woman with high cheekbones and hair shorn close to her head. She stands about five foot eleven, and Taylor has dressed her in his ivory linen harem style pants. They have zippers at the bottom, enabling them to be unzipped and snapped up into a shorter style. All of Taylor's new designs can be worn by any sex, and many can be converted into multiple looks. On top, Treeva has a thin silk jacket adorned with a diagonal zipper, the color a slightly lighter shade of ivory. Her ebony skin is visible through the fabric, as are the dark nipples of her small high breasts. Mid-calf ivory sneakers with laces that wrap around her ankles complete the look. Treeva has on very minimal makeup, with only smudged black liner under her eyes.

Jayce is relaxing in a chair, texting. The hairstylist is applying a light mist of spray to his raven hair. It is swept forward toward his face, covering his brows and accentuating his full lips. His outfit consists of a sheer white tee with cap sleeves and a deep V-neck. The pants almost look like sweatpants but are made of thin leather and adorned with multiple zippers. A jacket of the same material falls to Jayce's mid-thigh, and he wears black leather boots, unzipped. He also wears black eyeliner. Bella pats his thigh as she passes by, and he looks up briefly at his mother.

Bella sees Taylor finishing up with Jaxon as she approaches. Jax looks visibly nervous, shaking his leg as Taylor fusses over him. "Please stop moving, Jax!" Taylor says. "Stand up for me." Jaxon obediently stands, and Taylor finishes his adjustments. Jaxon is wearing a white shirt similar to Jayce's. His pants are also white, with zippers running the length of the front and back of each leg. The pants can be converted into a skirt by unfastening the crotch panel and attaching two flat panels in its place. His jacket is a cropped version of Jayce's, but a bit more fitted and without zippers. His sneakers are like Treeva's, but shorter.

"Taylor, Jasper is ready to start shooting," Bella says, placing a hand on his shoulder. "He'd like to talk with you before I send the models over." Taylor nods and places a kiss on Jax's cheek before he walks over to Jasper. "Jaxon. You look stunning. You'll be perfect." Bella reassures him. Jax is wearing the same black smudged liner under his eyes, and his blond hair has been gelled back off his face. The only jewelry he wears is a pair of dangling silver chain earrings.

"Thank you, Bella, I hope so. I can't believe how relaxed Jayce is! I'm freaking out over here!" Jax says.

"He's been doing this forever, darling. You'll be that relaxed in no time. Now head over with the others. I'll be right there." Bella instructs Harrison to take the models over to Jasper. She then heads over toward security to see if her guest has arrived. She sees him standing by the barricade, tall and handsome in a jean jacket and aviators. Several people have recognized him, and Bella sees him posing politely for a few selfies. The guard sees Bella approaching, and gets the man's attention, extracting him from his fans. Bella grabs his hands, pulling him in for a hug. "Korian. I'm so very pleased to see you. You kept your promise."

"Of course, I did, beautiful. I'm a man of my word." Korian offers Bella his arm and they continue to talk as they head toward the shoot.

"Korian, why don't you stay with me tonight?" No need for a nasty hotel. You and I can have a quiet dinner and discuss you joining us at Blackwood." Bella strokes her free hand down Korian's arm, silently admiring his muscular bicep.

"Oh, Bella. That's so sweet of you. But I can't. I have late meetings this evening, and I fly back to LA tomorrow. It's a short trip this time." They arrive to stand behind Jasper and off to the side, observing as the models pose for a few test shots. "Your son is perfection, as usual, I see." Korian tips his head toward Jayce.

"Did you expect anything less? He *is* my son, after all." Bella giggles a bit. "That could be you out there, Korian. We need you when we introduce the full collection."

"Bella, I'm already completely booked, this season and next," Korian replies. "And you know that Jayce doesn't like sharing the spotlight."

Jayce pauses as Jasper makes some adjustments and notices his mother. *Really, Mum?* Jayce sighs and nods his head at Korian, who is watching him. *She's at it again. Why the hell didn't she tell me that he was coming here?* Jayce sighs, and returns his attention to his job.

"Korian, look." Bella gestures toward Jax. "Jayce has no problem working with Jaxon."

"Let me rephrase then, Bella," Korian says. "Jayce doesn't like sharing the spotlight with *me*."

"Jasper hold on a second please," Taylor says while looking at the test shots. "I'm not happy with how this looks, both Jayce and Jax in the white shirts. Give me a minute." Taylor approaches his best friend. "Jax, I need to make an adjustment." He calls over Harrison and whispers something in his ear. Harrison rushes off.

"Taylor, am I doing something wrong?" Jaxon's anxiety is building.

"No, baby, you're perfect. But I need you to take the shirt off." Taylor says while tugging at the sleeves of the jacket.

"What?" Jaxon asks while Taylor is pulling the shirt over his head, careful to avoid Jax's styled hair.

Harrison returns, handing something to Taylor. "Here, you can do the honors." Jax looks between the two and feels a tugging at his nipple.

"What the fuck! Tay, I'm going to kill you later!" Jax whispers to his best friend as he looks down and sees a silver chain connecting his nipple rings.

"Put the jacket back on and we're good to go," Taylor says, heading to stand next to Jasper as his best friend glares at him.

Jasper directs the three models seamlessly through various poses on the bridge. When he's ready to take individual shots, Jayce goes first.

He, as always, breezes through his solo shots in no time. When he finishes, he walks off to grab a drink and looks for his mother. He expects to see her hanging all over his rival model, but when he finds Bella, Korian is gone.

As Jasper works with Treeva, Jax steps to the side to get his hair and makeup touched up. While more gel is added to his hair, he looks at the crowd gathering to watch the photoshoot. He's surprised how many people there are.

As he scans through people's faces, he meets the eyes of a man that is staring at him. The man has thick dark hair and sunglasses perched on his head. Jax really can't see him very clearly with the sun in his eyes, but the way he is looking at him makes Jax uncomfortable. The man will not avert his eyes. As Jax continues to stare back, the man slowly raises two of his fingers to point at his own eyes, then slowly turns his hand to point them toward Jax. A sick feeling bubbles up in Jax's stomach as he sees the man smirk at him.

"Jax, we're ready for you." Jasper calls him over for his solo shots. He tries to ignore what just happened as he gets back to work. "Ok, Jaxon, I'm going to try something a bit different," Jasper says. "We're going to utilize your dance skills."

"Um, okay. Just tell me what to do," he replies.

"See this white line on the bridge?" Jasper says, and Jax nods. "Okay, first I'm going to take some shots without your jacket. I just want you to stay on that line and do a few dance moves. Just whatever you're comfortable with. Turning, swaying, use your arms and legs."

Jax glances at the barricade, and the man is still watching him. He runs through a simple routine, pushing thoughts of the man to the back of his mind.

"Perfect. That was amazing." Jasper praises him. "Now I want you to leap over the line, as high as you can while tilting your head back," he instructs. Jax does the move a few times until Jasper is satisfied.

"Okay great job everyone! Models, we're going to convert Taylor's designs and move under the towers for the last few shots," Jasper announces.

Staff starts rushing to move the equipment under the suspension cables, as Jax dabs a few beads of sweat from his forehead. He's warm now despite the cool temperature. He heads over to get his makeup touched up when two arms circle him from behind. Jax tenses immediately, thinking of the staring man, until he smells Luca's cologne.

"Hi, that was amazing!" Luca nuzzles his nose into Jax's neck.

Jax spins around, embracing his boyfriend. "Luca! You're here!"

"I am! And you're so beautiful, Angel," Luca says. "But you're shaking! What's wrong?"

Jax looks over to the barricade, but the man is gone. Luca follows his gaze. "I know. Lots of people. But you'll get used to it."

"No, Luca, there was a creepy man that kept staring at me," Jax says, squeezing Luca's arms.

"You're gorgeous, Jaxon. Lots of people stare at you," Luca replies.

Jax shakes his head. "No Luca, I'm serious. This was different. I was scared."

Luca takes a step back and grabs Jaxon's hands. "What did he look like, did you recognize him?"

Jax replies, shaking his head. "No. I don't think so. It was hard to see with the sun."

"Okay. You go get ready for the next shots, and I'll talk to security," Luca reassures him. "And by the way," Luca teases, tugging at the silver chain connecting Jax's nipples. "Tell my cousin that we're taking this for later." Luca winks as Jax lets out a little squeal, heading off to get changed.

Luca walks over toward the Blackwood security guards, and a few people in the crowd whisper and wave at him. He pulls the men aside, asking if they noticed anyone suspicious. They assure Luca that no one stood out, but that lots of people have come and gone. Luca nods, telling the men to let him know if anything changes, when he hears someone call his name.

"Mr. Blackwood? Excuse me, Mr. Blackwood!" Security follows Luca to the barricade where a woman is trying to get his attention. "I'm sorry to bother you, but I found this on the ground a little while ago." The woman hands Luca an envelope that used to be white but is currently marred by dirt and footprints. Jaxon's name is typed across it.

"Did you see who left this here?" he asks the woman.

"No, I'm sorry, I didn't. I just noticed it on the ground. People were stepping on it and I thought it was trash until I saw the name on the front," she responds.

What the hell is this? Luca nods and thanks her, placing the envelope into the inside pocket of his suit coat. Before he heads over to watch the second part of the shoot, he finds a private spot to open the envelope. Luca pries at the seal, praying that it's not what he thinks it will be. His stomach drops when he removes the contents. Inside are several of the articles that were printed after the Misun wedding debacle. The articles contain photographs of Luca and Jaxon. In each one, Jax's eyes have been carefully cut out, just like in the magazine.

Luca inhales deeply, and with shaky hands thrusts the articles back in the envelope and into his pocket. He bends forward, placing his hands on his knees. *Fuck.* Luca knows now that this is a serious threat, and that the man was *here*. He was watching Jaxon. Luca takes a few more moments to compose himself. He cannot let Jaxon see this. *I will handle this.* Already deciding what steps he needs to take to keep his boyfriend safe, Luca heads over to watch him work, trying to hide the fear encompassing him.

Chapter 22

"Where to now?" Jax links arms with Luca after wandering around a few shops. He looks at the bags filling Luca's hands. "You really don't have to buy me things, I do earn more money now, thanks to Blackwood. I can afford it."

Luca kisses his cheek. "I know but like I've said before, I enjoy spoiling you. I believe that you deserve everything and the world." They pause for a moment while Luca looks around, thinking. "Should we get a coffee somewhere?"

Jaxon grins as the couple heads towards a quaint little café on the corner, sitting outside at a tiny metal table for two. As Luca bends down to put the packages at their feet, an envelope falls from his pocket, fluttering to the ground. Jax picks it up and notices Luca's eyes open wide.

"What's this?" he says, turning it over and seeing the typing on the front. "It has my name on it."

The awkward pause between the pair sits in the air for a while; Luca doesn't know what to say. Upon receiving no answer, Jax looks in the already opened envelope. He flicks through the threatening images, his face paling at the sight of more disturbing photos.

"I'm so sorry." Luca clasps Jax's wrist. "I didn't want you to see those. I had no intention of letting you look at them. I promise you that we will get to the bottom of this and I will do everything in my power to protect you."

"But I don't understand," Jax whispers. "When?"

"On the bridge. When you were doing the photo shoot." Luca admits. "Someone left it." He pulls the envelope from Jaxon's hands and clutches his fingers. "Jax, please look at me. I will handle this. I really will."

"That man, staring at me. It had to be him!" Jaxon meets his boyfriend's pleading gaze. "You should have told me."

Luca nods. "I should have, yes. I'm sorry. I just didn't want you to be worried. I just wanted to protect you."

"Please don't keep things from me again. I don't want secrets between us."

Bowing his head down, Luca agrees but knows that he has things that he's kept from his love. The waitress approaches the table and asks for their order. After she has left, Luca takes a deep breath. "Jax, there is something else that you should know."

Jaxon rubs his eyes. "Have there been other threats?"

"No, no, this is from before you came into my life. About Misun and the baby."

Jaxon sits up straighter and listens carefully. He's been waiting for this moment, for Luca to finally open up about this situation. He knows how much it has affected him. He has seen how much it has upset Luca.

"We split because she was cheating, obviously," says Luca. "And he could be the father of the baby. But it wasn't just some random stranger."

"Okay?" Jax says slowly, preparing himself for what he's about to hear.

"It was someone that I know, Jax. I caught her in bed with part of my own family." Luca sighs.

Jaxon's mouth drops open. "What? Someone in your family?"

"Yes," Luca shrugs. "So even if this isn't my child, it will still be a Blackwood," he says matter-of-factly.

"That is seriously messed up, Luca." Jax sits back in his chair. The waitress places their drinks on the table. "I mean, I don't know what to say."

Luca takes a sip of his coffee. "There isn't anything to say. It is what it is."

"Luca, who was it? Who was sleeping with Misun?"

Luca gives a bitter laugh and begins to stir his coffee. "You won't believe it when I tell you, Jax." Luca's phone starts to ring in his pocket.

Pulling it out, he scoffs, turning the screen to show Jax. "Speaking of! I wonder what she wants?" He answers the call and pauses to hear what she has to say. "What? Okay, I'll be right there."

Plunging his phone back into his jacket, he takes another big gulp of his coffee and begins to gather the bags up. "It's time," he says, his voice panicky. "The baby is on its way. I need to go."

"Oh shit," Jaxon says, helping him. "What do you want me to do?"

Luca takes a deep breath to calm himself and faces Jaxon. "I would really, really like you there, if you want to be?"

"There? Not in the room!" Jax is confused.

"Not *there*, there!" Luca laughs. "But at the hospital, I mean. Or would you rather not?"

Jax kisses Luca on the lips. "I'm with you one hundred percent whenever you need me. Always." He takes the bags from Luca. "You get to the hospital, I'll take these home, and then I'll head over there to meet you."

Luca smiles. "Thank you."

**

Heading down the hospital corridor, Jaxon checks his phone again, scrolling to the message where Luca has given him the number of the waiting room. Looking up at the signs, he turns to the left, through some double doors, and up a flight of stairs to the correct wing.

He stops at a vending machine and bends to look at all the options. Standing up, he freezes at the reflection in the glass. A man standing behind him with the same creepy eyes that were staring at him on the bridge that day. Jax spins to face him.

"Oh, don't look so petrified, Jaxon," he grins. "I'm not here to scare you."

He places a hand on Jaxon's shoulder, who quickly brushes it off. "Leave me alone," he says, and tries to walk away, but the man stops him. "What do you want from me?"

The man holds his hands up. "Okay, okay." He takes a step backward. "I only wanted to see you up close. Your stunning eyes," he taunts.

Jaxon flees from him as quickly as he can, rushing through the waiting room door. Luca is there since he is expecting Jax to arrive, but the smile fades from his face seeing Jaxon looking so distressed.

He runs over and grasps his shoulders. "What is it? What's wrong?"

"He was here," he whispers, struggling to get the words out.

"Who?" Luca asks before the realization hits him. He runs to the door and looks up and down the corridor. Seeing no one there, he races back to Jax. "Are you okay? Did he do anything?" He sits Jax onto one of the plastic chairs.

"No, I'm fine, honestly. How's Misun?" He changes the subject.

Luca sweeps Jax's hair from his eyes. "She's fine. Nearly there. It's moving fast."

"You had better get back in there then!" Jax puts on a smile, ignoring the thudding in his chest. "I'll be fine here."

"Are you sure?" Luca says. "I'm worried about you now. Why was he even here? Was he following you?"

Jax shrugs his shoulders. "No idea, but I will be just fine. Any issues and I will call you." He gives Luca a gentle, lingering kiss. "I'll be right here waiting for you."

Luca nods, torn about leaving Jax alone, and heads off back to Misun. Jax waits until he's out of sight and closes the waiting room door so that he can't be easily seen.

**

Jax jumps in fright when the door flings open, but Luca doesn't notice. He has a big smile on his face. "It's a girl, Jax. A beautiful little girl."

Jax stands, wrapping his arms around Luca. "Congratulations," he says. "I am so happy for you. Are they both well?"

Luca pulls him down and sits next to him. "Yes, they are both fine. Misun is tired, but she is doing okay." His face is flushed pink with happiness. "I'm trying not to get my hopes up, Jax. I know that she may not be mine, but it was amazing."

Jax can see how smitten he is. Luca has an expression that he's never seen on him before...pure elation. "She is still your family, regardless. It's wonderful news, Luca. Does she have a name?"

Turning to face Jax, Luca places his hands on his boyfriend's knees. "She does. Misun wanted me to name her."

"Well?" Jaxon laughs.

"I decided to keep it Korean after Misun's heritage, so I picked Dasom. It means love. What do you think?"

"That is a beautiful name." Jax intertwines his fingers with Luca's. "And no matter what the test results say, I know that you will have an amazing bond with her."

"I hope so." Luca can't stop smiling. "And you too, when everyone is ready."

Jaxon nods at him. "You should get back to them."

Luca takes his phone from his jeans. "I will, I just have to call Noah and tell him the news. He will pass it on to everyone else." He holds it up in the air, trying to get a signal. "Fucks sake, there is literally no service here."

"Go outside, I'll stay here," Jax says.

Luca rushes off to make the call, and Jaxon slumps back into his seat, saying a thankful prayer to himself that everything has gone well. Noise by the door makes him look up. The man is standing there with a sinister smile.

"Why are you here?" Jaxon tries to act like he isn't concerned but is secretly hoping that Luca will be back soon.

"Oh, you know. I was just passing," he says with an arrogant tone, sitting on the chair opposite Jax. He glares at Jaxon. "You know, I can see what Luca sees in you. You are rather pretty."

Jaxon squirms in his chair, pleading internally for Luca to hurry. The man looks familiar, and his accent is strange, but he is still intimidating to someone like Jaxon who usually shies away from confrontation. "Luca will be back here any minute," he says, hoping that it will scare the man off.

"I know," he shrugs. "I'm hoping to speak to him too."

"Well, that's the family told..." Luca walks back into the room. He stops when he sees the other person with Jax, then he rushes over to his boyfriend. "Are you okay?" Jax nods but is noticeably shaken. He turns to face the man, his face contorted with anger. "What are you doing here?"

The man sits back onto his chair and pulls his blue cap off. "It's a public place. I'm allowed to be here." He looks up at Luca. "And you're wrong, you haven't told *all* of the family, have you?"

Jax looks in confusion at Luca, who slumps his shoulders. "What do you want from me?" he sighs.

"Has Misun had the baby?" the man asks.

"You know Misun?" Jax frowns.

Laughing, the man leans back into his chair. "Oh, come on, Jaxon. You have the beauty, but clearly not the brains."

Luca squares up to him, his body rigid. "Don't you dare speak to him ever again, Dad."

"Dad?" Jax questions, his mouth open, looking between the two. "But..."

"Yes, Jaxon, has the penny finally dropped?" he says, smugly. "How many English people do you know?" He holds his hand out to shake Jaxon's hand, a smirk on his face. "I'm Maxwell Blackwood, Luca's father."

Luca grabs his father by the collar and drags him to stand up. Staring into his eyes, he speaks through gritted teeth. "You are no father of mine."

Max laughs. "Fine, be like that. Has she had the baby or not? I have a right to know."

"She had a girl," Luca says quietly.

Max claps his hands together. "Great, let's get this test done so that I can find out if I have a granddaughter or a daughter."

"Oh, fuck off!" Luca blurts out. "She will be nothing to you, regardless of the results."

Jaxon, who has been quiet all this time, trying to process everything, turns to Max. "But, why were you stalking me on the bridge during the shoot?"

Luca looks at his boyfriend and points in his father's direction. "Him? It was him?" Jax nods and Luca looks at the man that partly created him with such hatred. "Is it *you* that has been threatening Jaxon?"

Max laughs out loud again. "Stop it, Luca! Threat? No. Just a bit of, I guess that you could say, fun."

"Fun?" Luca spits. "You think that breaking into someone's apartment and stalking them is fun?"

Max shrugs. "Stop being so dramatic, Luca. I have to do something to pass the time now that I've been pushed out of the company by my brother and your cousin."

"You pushed yourself out by acting like a dick," Luca says. "Stop blaming other people for your actions and take responsibility."

The look on Max's face darkens. "Responsibility?" he hisses. "Like saying that my own son is now shacked up with another man. How embarrassing, and quite frankly, disgusting."

Luca sees red, pushing his father back against the wall with some force. "Don't you ever, EVER, go near Jaxon again. Do you understand me?" Jax tries to pull Luca back, but the rage has sent the adrenalin surging through his body. "I want nothing more to do with you!"

"Excuse me!" A voice interrupts the fight. A passing nurse has heard the commotion. "I'm calling security! This is a hospital. Babies are being born a few yards away. Have some respect."

"My apologies," Max says, brushing Luca's hands off. "I clearly didn't teach my son any manners. I'll leave." He turns to Jaxon before he leaves the room. "I'll be seeing you around, pretty, pretty boy."

Chapter 23

Jaxon cannot believe what he's just heard; what he's just seen. "Luca. Luca! Look at me. Breathe!" Jax places his hands on Luca's cheeks to try to bring him back from his shock. Jax's hands are shaking, and he tries to calm himself for Luca's sake. Luca finally meets his boyfriend's eyes, his own welling with tears.

He grabs Jaxon in a tight embrace, sobbing into his shoulder. "I'm so sorry. I'm so, so sorry. This is all my fault."

"Luca, stop. Please stop saying that. This is *not* your fault." Jaxon tries to reassure him, pushing his anxiety aside for the moment. "Your father did this, not you. *Your father.*" Jax grabs Luca's shoulders trying to ground him.

"Exactly, Jax! My own fucking Father! First, he fucks Misun, now I find out he's the one threatening you? It's too much Jax, too much to deal with." Luca tenses up with anger again, and Jax knows that he has to do something.

"Luca, we *will* deal with it. Your family will help us. We will call Noah, and he'll help us figure this out." Jaxon's calming tone is helping Luca to compose himself. "But right now, we have Misun and the baby to worry about." Luca looks shocked, like he's just remembering where he is and what he's there for.

Luca takes a few deep breaths. "Okay. Okay, right. I'm going to go back in to check on them," he says. "Jax, come in with me. I don't want you out here alone."

"He's gone, Luca. He's not coming back here, it's late and security won't let him back in now." Jaxon says. "Besides, you need a little time with the baby. I'll be right here." Luca nods, placing a gentle kiss on Jax's cheek, and goes to make sure that Misun and the baby are settled.

Jaxon sits in the waiting room, his elbows on his knees and head bent, trying to compose himself. He can hardly believe the drastic changes to his life over the last few months. Things were simpler when he was just a dance teacher. He was happy with his quiet life, just he and Taylor. He takes deep breaths, thinking about his life before he met Luca. *Would I go back if I could?* Jaxon has waited his whole life for true love, for someone who touches his soul. At twenty-five, he's never had anything even close to that. Taylor is the closest thing he's ever had to a soulmate, but they are friends; brothers. They have never even considered something more than that. When he met Luca, Jax thought he'd found his fairy tale. He never could have imagined how complicated his life would become.

Luca quietly walks down the hospital corridor and sits down next to Jax on the uncomfortable chairs. He traces the back of his fingers softly down his lover's cheek, and Jaxon raises his eyes to meet Luca's. At that moment, Jax knows. *I would never go back. I would never give up having Luca in my life.*

"How's the little princess?" Jaxon's voice is a bit hoarse from fatigue.

"She's beautiful, Jax. Perfect. A headful of black hair and little dimples like Misun's. I can't wait for you to meet her." Luca looks exhausted, but he gives Jax a sweet smile.

"I'll meet her soon, Luca. Are you okay?"

"Tired, but fine. Happy. Let's go. Let's get some food and talk. There's a café around the corner. I'll have Tony pick us up there." Luca places a lingering kiss on Jaxon's head, and they walk hand in hand to the elevator.

The night air is chilly when they exit the back door but feels good after being in the stuffy hospital. It immediately makes Luca more alert. He texts Tony to meet them at the café, and the men walk together, pinkies intertwined.

"I'm calling Noah when I get home," Luca says. "We need to get my father out of our lives for good."

"Why didn't you tell me, Luca? That it was your father with Misun?" Jax looks down at the sidewalk as he asks the question.

"I was ashamed. Humiliated. That man of all people, Jax! I didn't tell anyone." Luca turns toward him, and their eyes meet. "No more secrets, Jax. I promise. I'll put my father in jail and we can be happy."

Jaxon nods. "Okay, Luca. I'm just scared."

Luca stops walking and pulls Jaxon into an embrace. "He's never going to hurt you again. I promise."

"I believe you," he says. They walk in silence for a while, until Jaxon speaks again. "Luca? I'm sorry to ask, but did they do the paternity test?"

Luca nods. "It's done. Paperwork is signed and it's gone to the lab. Jax, what am I going to do if she's my father's? How can I look at that child if she's his?"

They walk through a quiet alley next to the cafe, when Jaxon stops. He turns to face Luca. "Hey, that baby should not be punished for this, Luca. Either way, she's your family. A Blackwood. Your father clearly cannot be a parent to her." Luca wraps his arms around Jax and draws him closer. "We'll figure it all out Luca, I'm here."

Luca brushes his lips against Jaxon's, the feeling of being home overwhelming him. Jax responds by pulling his boyfriend's head closer and teasing his tongue onto his top lip. Luca opens his mouth to taste him, so familiar, so perfect. They kiss lazily and deeply, communicating that they are there for each other, without words.

Jax is ripped away from Luca's lips by a hand on his shoulder. "Aww, this is so romantic! Look at the two of you." The deep voice is tainted by alcohol, words slurring.

"Get your fucking hands off him you piece of shit!" Luca pulls Jaxon away and stands protectively in front of him. Jaxon sees Luca's father and freezes.

"What's wrong, Luca, don't want to share your boyfriend with me?" Maxwell is right in Luca's face, spitting out filth. "Sharing Misun was such fun though, wasn't it?" Maxwell turns his attention back to Jax, grabbing him and pulling him close, his nose on Jaxon's neck. "Luca, he smells so good, so sweet." Luca's father runs his hand through Jax's hair pulling his head back as he speaks." Luca lunges at his father, but even in his drunken state, Maxwell moves back quickly, Jaxon still in his arms. "He's so pretty, Son. Beautiful. I can almost forgive you for being a faggot...almost." Maxwell slowly traces his tongue down the side of Jaxon's face, the putrid stench of alcohol making Jax gag.

Jaxon keeps his eyes on Luca, and things seem like they're moving in slow motion. Jaxon has never in his life seen absolute rage in someone's eyes before, but his lover is lunging toward his father, eyes consumed by a hatred that Jaxon didn't know was possible. Luca rips Maxwell away from him, shoving the man back. Luca is fueled by adrenaline, hands shaky as he pushes Jaxon to safety. He seizes his father's shoulders, shaking him violently as Jaxon watches in shock.

"You put your filthy hands on him." Luca doesn't yell; he practically growls in Maxwell's face. "You will go to jail for the rest of your pitiful life." Luca jerks his father's arm behind his back to restrain him and calls to Jax. "Call the police." Jaxon is already fumbling with his phone.

"The police? Funny, Luca. You think they're going to do anything? I have my people everywhere." Maxwell smirks, not an ounce of fear on his face. "Why do you think they never helped your little boy toy?' As Luca's father looks toward Jax, he uses Luca's momentary shock to pull himself around. He grips Luca by the front of his shirt, using his other fist to land punch after punch into Luca's stomach.

Luca groans and gasps for air when Jax throws himself at Maxwell, knocking him onto the worn and cracked asphalt. He crouches over the vile man, trying to restrain his arms. Despite Jax's strength, Maxwell overpowers him, flipping them over. Jax feels Maxwell's hands on his neck, and he digs his nails into them as hard as he can. He is starting to feel dizzy, unable to inhale. Just as Jaxon is about to lose consciousness, the pressure is gone. Luca is on top of his father. Without a word or a sound from his lips, Luca pounds his head over and over.

"Luca! Luca stop!" Jaxon yells. *Why has no one heard us?*

Luca hears nothing. Sees nothing. Just the rage that consumes him. Jaxon sees Luca's phone lighting up on the ground next to him. He grabs it pushing the button. "Tony! Tony the alley! We're in the alley! Hurry!" Jax throws down the phone and tries to pull Luca off Maxwell, as he slams his father's head into the asphalt.

Tony comes running to their location, his suit coat open and his tie flying behind him. Together with Jaxon, he pulls Luca away from his father. Jaxon grabs Luca and stares into his eyes. Nothing. He must be in shock. Jaxon then sees Tony hovering over Maxwell, checking his pulse. "Call an ambulance!" Jax yells at him.

Tony looks at him and shakes his head. "He's gone, Jax. He's dead."

"Call someone! He attacked us! The police, Tony. Get someone!" Jaxon is panicked.

"No, no. I'm going to take care of this." Tony turns to Luca and shakes him. "Mr. Blackwood ... Luca!" It's the first time that he has ever used Luca's first name to address him.

Luca looks at him, then over to his lifeless father on the ground. "I killed him. I fucking killed him. He was going to kill Jax."

"Luca listen to me. I'm going to pull the car to the end of the alley. You need to help me put him in the car." Tony scans the alley, looking up and down the dilapidated buildings. "There are no cameras here. No windows. We'll put him in the car, and I'll take care of this." Luca is nodding, still looking at his father. "Once he's in the car, you and Jax straighten yourselves up, walk a few blocks, and take a cab home."

Jaxon grabs onto Luca, turning him away from his father and holding him. As Tony walks away, they hear him on the phone. "Yeah, listen. We have a problem…"

Chapter 24

The Persian rug in Luca's living room is covered in pieces of baby equipment. Jax is squinting at the instructions trying to make sense of the parts that Luca has in his hands.

"How the hell are we going to assemble this shit before the baby comes home?" Jax says, crawling over toward Luca to help him attach the side of the crib.

"Clearly we should've planned better," Luca responds. His glasses have slipped down his nose, and he pushes them back into place. "But we've been a bit overwhelmed, Jax."

Jaxon sighs and places a kiss on Luca's cheek. "I know, baby. But we have to focus on Dasom now." He grabs the screwdriver from Luca's fumbling fingers, locking the pieces into place. "You're doing the right thing, you know. Bringing them here."

"I hope so." Luca picks up the other side of the crib, and they work to attach it. "It will only be until Misun can care for her alone. Not that *I* know what I'm doing with a baby."

Jaxon stands up, admiring their work. "So cute! We did it!" He lifts the mattress and sets it inside the pretty pink crib. "Listen, we'll figure it out. Just like everything else. Victoria and Heidi said they'd help."

"Yeah they've been great," Luca responds, as he starts to wheel the crib into his spare room. "Noah said that they've gotten a ton of baby stuff for us. They're coming over tomorrow to set the nursery up while I'm at the hospital."

Luca places the crib by the window, as Jax sets the new rocking chair next to the plush double bed where Misun will sleep. "See?" Jaxon says. "It's already coming together."

Luca steps close to his boyfriend, placing his strong hands on Jax's cheeks, stroking the soft skin with his thumbs. "How are you even real? Anyone else would have been long gone by now. After everything I've put you through, how are you still here?"

Jaxon closes his eyes, placing his own small hands on top of Luca's. "I already told you," he responds. "I'm not going anywhere. I was meant to come into your life when you needed me, Luca. I honestly believe that." Jaxon puts his arms around Luca's neck, and Luca sighs as Jax continues. "Did I expect everything to be this hard so soon? Of course not. But we're strong together."

"We *are* strong together." Luca agrees. "And things can only get better. What else could possibly happen?" He leans forward and places gentle kisses on his boyfriend's lips when the door buzzer interrupts them.

Jax pulls away from Luca. "I'll get it!" He heads into the living room towards the door, addressing Luca over his shoulder. "This has to be the changing table we ordered." Jax throws the heavy door open, surprised to see that it is not the delivery.

"Hello, you must be Jaxon." The regal man standing there extends his hand.

Jaxon accepts it graciously. "Mr. Blackwood! It's an honor, please come in." Jaxon gestures toward the living room and quickly moves to push the boxes to the side.

"I see that you're busy preparing for my great-granddaughter. And please, Jaxon, call me Dalton." He takes a seat on one of the Italian leather chairs, silently noting, once again, that his grandson shares his taste in decorating. Jaxon sits on the matching leather couch across from him, leaning forward.

Luca hears his grandfather's voice, and freezes, dread seeping through his bones. He can hear his boyfriend talking with Dalton in the other room.

"I'm so pleased to finally meet you, Jaxon. Although your face is very familiar to me. Your work with Blackwood has been excellent thus far." Dalton's face is tense, and he looks exhausted. "My family admires you, and I am so pleased that you and Luca have chosen to work things out."

"Thank you so much," Jax replies. He quickly gets up when he sees his boyfriend enter the room.

"Grandfather," Luca addresses Dalton, who stands and embraces his grandson.

"Can I get you a drink?" Jaxon asks as he and Luca share an anxious glance.

"A bourbon would be nice," Dalton replies. Jax nods and heads to the kitchen, pouring Maker's Mark into three crystal glasses. "Luca, congratulations on the birth of your daughter. My first great-grandchild," Dalton continues, and takes his drink from Jax. "Let's have a toast to beautiful Dasom." The three men clink their glasses together, Dalton's hand noticeably shaking as he raises the glass to his lips. Luca downs the entirety of his drink, and Jax gets up again to get the bottle and refill Luca's glass. He knows that Luca needs it to take the edge off of his anxiety. "She's a gorgeous girl. All that black hair. Noah showed me a picture. She looks just like you, Luca." Jax can see Luca's eyes well up, and he knows exactly what his boyfriend is thinking.

"Grandfather, you should have waited to come all this way until you could meet her. You don't look well," Luca says. Dalton is pale and is beginning to perspire.

"Luca, I need to discuss something with you." Dalton clears his throat, holding back his tears.

"What's wrong?" Luca braces himself. *Here it comes.* Jax sits right beside him, grasping his hand tightly.

"Your father is dead, Luca." Dalton sets his glass on the mahogany coffee table and rubs at his temples with his shaking hands.

"What do you mean, he's dead?" Luca asks. Jax sits frozen, not sure how to respond even though he knew it was coming.

"Your mother called me," Dalton continues. "She was notified by the police that he was found beaten. She identified him by a photograph from the coroner."

Luca shakes his head. "We always knew that he'd end up dead. All of that scum he associated with! He was a despicable man."

"Luca, he was your *father*," Dalton is almost pleading, wanting a different reaction from his grandson. But Dalton didn't know. He didn't know half of what his own son had done, what he was really like.

Luca stands, raising his voice to the man that he respects so much. "My *father*? Really, Grandfather? He was *never* a father to me. *You* made me the man that I am, not *him*!"

Jaxon reaches up to grab Luca's hand again, squeezing it.

Tears are streaming down Dalton's cheeks. "He was my *son*, Luca. I know that he was a terrible father, but he was my son." Dalton begins to sob, leaning forward with his face in his hands.

Seeing the strongest man that he knows fall apart is more than Luca can handle. He rushes to his grandfather, dropping to his knees in front of him. Luca grasps his hands and begins to sob. "I'm so sorry, Grandfather. I'm so sorry, this is all my fault."

Dalton wraps his grandson in a tight embrace. "Luca this is not your fault. Your father made his own choices. God knows we've all suffered for it, but he was my child, and I wish that I could've done more."

Jaxon watches the two embrace, his tears wetting his cheeks. After several minutes, he walks quietly around the coffee table and gently pulls Luca up and into his arms. Jax leans down and places a soft kiss on Dalton's cheek. "I'm so very sorry, Dalton," Jax whispers, his words meaning so much more than he can actually say.

Dalton composes himself a bit and continues. "I have your father's ashes, Luca. Your mother didn't want them. I will have them buried privately next to Grandma Mina. It will just be your Aunt Bella, Uncle Alexander, and myself unless you wish to be there." Luca shakes his head, tears streaming at the mention of his beloved grandmother. Dalton nods. "I understand." He stands to leave, embracing his grandson once more. "I love you, Luca."

"I love you too," Luca whispers into his collar. Jaxon walks Dalton to the door, closing it quietly after he has gone. Luca drops to the floor, his back against the wall as he hugs himself. Jax sits on the floor in front of Luca, placing his hands on his boyfriend's knees. Luca looks at him with so much pain in his eyes that it breaks Jaxon's heart. "I killed him, Jax. I took him away from my grandfather."

"You did what you had to do, Luca. You saved me. He was going to kill me." Jax squeezes Luca's knees and then traces circles on his thighs with his fingers. "He was a very bad man, Luca."

"But we should have gone to the police!" Luca cries out. "I should have taken responsibility!"

"And what would that have done, Luca?" Jaxon responds. "How would your grandfather deal with that all over the news!"

"You're right, I know you're right, Jax. I just need to learn to live with this." Luca takes off his glasses and closes his eyes. "He deserved to die. If he took you away from me I..."

"But he didn't," Jaxon cuts him off. "You didn't let him. Now come on. Let's take a hot shower and go to bed. You have a long day tomorrow. Dasom is coming home."

Luca nods and lets Jaxon lead him to the bathroom. He starts the shower, adjusting it to a comfortably hot temperature, and helps Luca remove his clothes. He then strips himself down and they step into the shower together. Luca lets Jaxon suds him gently, trying to wash away his stress and anxiety.

Should We?

The familiar smell of the sandalwood soap and Jaxon's gentle touch start to relax him. Jaxon takes his time massaging Luca's scalp as he washes his hair, and Luca groans at the feeling.

Once Jaxon has completely washed his boyfriend, he opens the shower door, grabbing a fluffy cotton towel to wrap him in. "Okay, baby. Go get into bed. I'll wash up and be right in." Luca nods drowsily as he grabs his glasses from the marble countertop and heads into the bedroom.

When Jax finishes his shower, he steps onto the plush carpet in the bedroom. He runs the towel over his head, expecting to see Luca sound asleep. Instead, Luca is laying on his side, looking at his phone. When he sees Jaxon, he lifts the black satin sheet next to him; an invitation for Jax to join him. "Whatcha looking at? I expected you to be asleep." Jaxon says as he climbs in to face Luca. Luca holds up his phone for Jaxon to see the beautiful picture of Dasom on the screen.

"She's so perfect, isn't she?" Luca says.

Jaxon nods. "She is a beautiful baby." Jax trails his finger down the side of Luca's face, admiring his features. The soft curve of his jaw and small, perfect nose are such a contrast to his sharp pewter eyes and strong brow. "And you're beautiful too, Luca."

Luca brushes his nose against Jaxon's cheek. Jax gently removes Luca's glasses, setting them carefully, along with his phone, on the bedside table. Jax pulls Luca closer, placing tender kisses on his cheeks and lips. Luca gingerly swipes his tongue along Jaxon's bottom lip, and Jax parts them to allow Luca to taste him. They enjoy languid kisses, tongues teasing each other. Luca starts to ease Jaxon onto his back, reaching down to gently tug on his nipple ring.

"No, Luca," Jax says in a breathy voice. "Let me take care of you." Luca allows Jaxon to gently push his shoulders against the silky bedding, hovering over him. "Do you trust me?" Jax questions, as he brushes a few dark strands of damp hair off Luca's forehead.

"More than anything," Luca answers, and Jax gives him a demure smile.

Jax takes Luca's earlobe into his mouth, tickling his tongue along the lobe, then tracing it along Luca's neck. Luca tips his head back against the pillow, closing his eyes. Jaxon continues to move his lips and tongue along the milky skin and over his collarbones, as he buries his fingers into the hair on Luca's chest.

As Jax follows the trail of hair down his abdomen with his fingers, he takes Luca's nipple into his mouth, lightly scraping his teeth along the sensitive skin. His fingers tenderly brush Luca's cock, and he feels him respond to the touch. As he continues to caress Luca, he leans over to the side table drawer, pulling out the bottle of lubricant.

Luca strains his neck to see what Jax is doing and raises an eyebrow.

"Shhhhhh," Jax murmurs. "Trust me." Luca breathes deeply, nodding. He closes his eyes, laying his head against the pillow again.

Jaxon gently pushes Luca's legs apart, positioning himself between them, taking Luca's nipple into his mouth once more, rolling the other between his fingers. Jax presses his own smooth skin against Luca, the hair tickling him as he glides his body down until his head hovers over Luca's erection. He tongues at the tip, breathing in Luca's natural scent mixed with sandalwood.

Jax lowers his hand between Luca's legs, placing gentle touches to his thighs. "Now hold your legs for me," Jax instructs, guiding Luca's hands to keep his knees bent up.

Jaxon squirts some lube onto his fingers, rubbing them together to warm it. He kisses and sucks Luca's inner thighs as he tentatively circles his finger against his rim. He feels Luca tighten up. "Luca, we can stop at any time. Are you okay?" he asks.

"I'm fine, Jax. It just feels different. I want to keep going," Luca reassures his boyfriend.

Jaxon applies a bit more pressure before slipping one finger inside. "Still okay?"

"I'm good. Move a little," Luca says.

Jax gently pushes his finger in and out, flicking his tongue along Luca's entrance.

"Shit, Jax. Add another." Luca is breathing faster.

Jaxon removes his finger, replacing it with two, and Luca's breath hitches. Jax moves his other hand up below the base of Luca's cock, and gently massages there on his perineum. He hears Luca groan, and twists his fingers inside him, gently searching until he feels a fleshy bump. He gently massages the spot, and Luca cries out.

"Fuck! Jax, right there. That feels so good." Luca begins to move his hips and reaches down to stroke his cock. Jaxon pushes his hand away and uses his own palm over the head of Luca's erection, as he continues to massage his prostate. "Jesus, so close, Jaxon, so close," Luca calls out.

"Okay. I know," Jax says, griping Luca's length firmly and stroking as he moves the fingers of his other hand to the same rhythm. "Doing so well for me Luca. Come for me."

Luca tenses up, his body spasming as he spurts come up his stomach and chest. "Fuck! Oh my god!" Jaxon slowly strokes him through his orgasm, letting his breathing slow down before slowly removing his fingers. Luca wipes the sweat from his forehead. "Jax, that was...holy shit!"

"That was a prostate orgasm, baby. I think you liked it!" Jax chuckles and goes to the bathroom for a warm washcloth. He cleans Luca's chest and stomach, folding the cloth before gently cleaning away the lubricant. He climbs into bed and kisses Luca gently before laying his head on his chest. Luca wraps his arms around him.

"Jax, let me touch you," he says, even as his eyes drift closed.

"I'm just fine, Luca. This was about you. Now sleep." As Jaxon finishes his sentence, he hears Luca's slow rhythmic breathing, smiling as he realizes that Luca is already asleep. He reaches over to shut off the light, then snuggles back into Luca's chest. "I love you, Luca." he whispers.

Chapter 25

Opening the heavy door to the apartment, Luca grins at the group of his family members standing there. They all look extremely excited, their arms loaded with gifts and teddy bears. He can't help but laugh at the bunches of pink balloons floating above their heads with Jayce begrudgingly holding them.

"Come in, come in," Luca says, stepping to one side to let everyone into his place.

Victoria notices Misun curled up on the couch in her pajamas with her phone clutched in her fingers, too busy scrolling through her screen to acknowledge everyone properly. Victoria glances at Heidi, who shrugs, not really expecting anything else.

They give Luca a quick hug before heading over to where Misun is sitting, attempting make an effort with her. Jayce, Harrison, and Noah stay with Luca, shaking his hand and congratulating him. Sitting down next to her, they can see that Misun really doesn't want company, but they had made a promise to Luca to try and make her feel more welcome within the family.

"Hey," Victoria says, striking up a conversation, "how are you doing?"

Misun scrunches her face up. "Yeah, I'm good." She barely looks up from her phone.

Victoria tries again. "How are you recovering after the birth? Are you feeling okay?" She places a warm hand on Misun's arm, but notices that she tenses slightly, so Victoria removes her hand.

"I'm fine." Misun speaks quite coldly. "Thank you for asking."

Heidi looks around the room noting that there is no sign of the baby. "Where's Dasom?" "She's with Jaxon," Luca interrupts, the men joining them. "He's changing her."

The girls give one another a little raised eyebrow look again. Victoria sees Jayce sit on the arm of the chair next to Misun and her demeanor changes when she sees the young man beside her. She smiles up at him, and he returns the look, a gentle smile on his lips.

Jax appears with a tiny bundle in his arms. Victoria and Heidi let out a little squeal of joy. He passes her to Luca who lovingly kisses her on the forehead a couple of times.

"Here," he says in a sweet and soft voice, passing her to Victoria, "Go to your auntie." The two ladies coo over Dasom.

"Right, can I get anyone a drink?"

Noah stands up and offers his seat to Jaxon. "I'll come and help you," he says as Jaxon sits down.

"I want a glass of wine please," Misun says while Heidi stealthily looks at the time on her watch, noting that it is a little too early for alcohol.

Luca doesn't even seem phased by the request, as if it were normal, and takes everyone else's orders heading off towards the kitchen with Noah.

Victoria beams at Dasom in her arms and turns back to Misun who is back to browsing on her phone again, completely uninterested with everything going on around her. "So," she says, trying her hardest to engage Misun in some form of conversation, "how is the breastfeeding going?"

Misun shrugs, screws up her face a little and scoffs. "That's going nowhere! I gave that up pretty much as soon as I left the hospital. It really isn't for me."

"Oh, I'm sorry to hear that," Heidi says, twirling her forefinger in Dasom's tiny palm.

"Don't be sorry." Misun laughs, pointing to her plump and full breasts. "I'm perfectly happy for these to be used for different purposes."

Victoria gives a small, fake giggle at the

response, inwardly cringing at how cold Misun is being towards the baby and her attitude about being a mother.

In the kitchen, Luca starts to make the various drinks that people have asked for. He puts on the coffee percolator, scooping rich beans into the top. Grabbing a glass from the cupboard, he examines it, before putting it back on the shelf and reaching for one much bigger. Opening the fridge, he pulls out a bottle of wine and Noah notices quite a few bottles stacked up in there.

"How is she settling in?" he asks, leaning one palm on the black marble countertop.

Luca uncorks the bottle and places the corkscrew to the side. The only sound around them is that of the coffee bubbling in the machine. "Dasom is doing amazingly well," he says, quietly.

Noah touches his cousin's arm softly. "I didn't mean the baby, and you know it."

Casually pouring the bubbly liquid into the glass, Luca puts the bottle down and sighs. "I don't know, Noah. She's not really bonding with her. Jax and I do most of the work and we are clueless as well. Jax wasn't even planning on meeting her yet until everyone had settled, yet we seem to be doing it by ourselves. It's like she has no interest at all."

"That really isn't good, Luca." Noah sighs.

"I know," Luca says, grabbing some mugs

and pouring out the coffee. "But what else can I do? Hopefully she'll do better once she has her new apartment for them both. She'll be more secure then."

"I assume that you're paying for it?" Noah asks, and Luca nods in a defeated manner. "Luca, isn't that a little premature?"

"What do you mean?" Luca pulls out a modern looking wooden tray and starts to load the cups and glass onto it. "I'm just giving them both a helping hand."

Noah pulls at his cousin's shoulders so that they are facing each other. "You know exactly what I'm talking about, Luca. You could be doing all of this, which is absolutely amazing by the way, but she could be some random dude's child."

Luca bows his head, his voice faltering and shaky. "Noah, you don't understand. It's not as simple as that."

"Well help me to understand," Noah says in frustration. "I want to help you. Why are you so hell bent on helping this woman before you know exactly what the truth is?" He rubs his hands up and down Luca's arms, and lowers his voice to a gentler tone. "Luca, I know that your family has been shit, but you have Jaxon now. You don't need to cling on to a family that may or may not be yours."

Tears start to fill Luca's eyes. He knows that he has to reveal the truth to Noah. "But, she is family regardless." He looks up at Noah's extremely puzzled face. "She's either my daughter, or my sister."

"Dasom?" Noah asks, still not understanding what his cousin is trying to tell him. "But, how can that be unless Misun slept with..." He looks harder at Luca, who tilts his head to indicate that he is along the right track in his thoughts. "Uncle Max? She slept with him?"

"Yes," Luca says, quietly, "She had an affair with him. And now he's dead. So I have to look after them."

Noah releases Luca's arms and rests back onto the table, running his hand over his furrowed brow. "I can't believe it. I always knew that his morals were lacking. But to sink this low?"

"He was the one threatening Jaxon too." Luca spills out more details. "He was behind it all. He was jealous of me in the company and wanted what I have."

"Fuck," was all that Noah could say, crossing his arms against his chest. "I'm truly...I don't even know what to say."

Luca gives a small laugh. "There really is nothing to say, Noah. It is what it is."

Noah pulls him in for a hug. "I guess so. A lot of things make sense to me now."

Victoria comes into the kitchen at that moment and sees her fiancé and his cousin in a warm embrace. "What's going on in here?" She laughs. "I had to come and see what you were both up to!"

The men release each other from their grasp, Luca fully appreciative of having some support and comfort. He knows that he has Jaxon fully by his side, but he doesn't like to burden him more than he already has.

"How is everyone in there?" Luca asks her.

"It's fine," she says. "Misun doesn't seem interested in talking to anyone apart from Jayce."

Noah grasps Victoria's hand, pulling her closer, and then curls his arm around her shoulders. "Luca, I think that you should tell Victoria too. She may be able to help you."

He kisses his wife-to-be on the cheek and slides the tray off the side, leaving them both to talk about things. Victoria listens intently, her lips parted in disbelief while Luca explains everything that has been going on, and the situation that they are in now.

"That bitch!" She blurts out in an annoyed manner, making Luca chuckle at her response. "I can't believe that she would do that. Well, I can, but with your dad?" That is off the scale!"

Luca shrugs. He's accepted the situation now, and the fact that his father is no longer in the picture to give anyone more trouble is a relief. "It's done now. I just have to wait for the results I guess."

"This is very true, Luca, and you will make an amazing dad or brother regardless" Victoria ponders things for a moment. "I have an idea that may help matters with Misun and the baby."

She locks her fingers with Luca's and leads them back into the room with the others. She sits on the floor beside Noah's legs, and Luca sits on the arm of the sofa next to Jaxon who is cooing over Heidi holding the baby. He glances up at Jayce and Misun who seem to be deep in an almost secret conversation. He shakes his head knowing that he is reading far too much into what he sees.

"So," Victoria says, trying to act casual. "Are you looking forward to your new place, Misun?"

Brushing her dark hair to one side, Misun turns to her, the expression on her face bordering on agitated, like she is not happy about being disturbed. "Yeah, I suppose."

"It's not going to be easy, on your own," Heidi adds.

Misun visibly rolls her eyes and takes a large gulp of her wine, emptying the glass. She holds it out to Luca for him to refill it. "I'm not going to be on my own." Luca takes it from her and heads to the kitchen. "I have Luca and Jaxon to help me." She glances up at Jayce and her face softens. "Plus, I have all of you," she adds.

Noah throws his fiancée a concerned glance at the flirty nature between his cousin and Misun. It is bad enough that she has duped and cheated on one of his family members, without luring in another.

Victoria clears her throat. "Well, obviously Luca and Jaxon have to work, so they won't have all of the time needed to take care of the baby. I'm sure that they'll do whatever they can, but maybe a bit of extra help would be good?"

Misun turns to Victoria, her eyes cold and dull. "What do you suggest?"

Luca returns with another glass full of wine and begrudgingly hands it to Misun who instantly places it to her lips. He looks at Victoria and nods his head for her to continue with her suggestion. He knows that they need all of the help that they can get.

"Well, my sister is a nanny. She just finished with a family because they moved to Europe. Maybe she can help you out for a while?"

Misun scoffs. "I can't afford that."

"I'll pay," Luca says a little too quickly.

Misun whips her head quickly in his direction. "Are you implying that I'm not capable of caring for my own daughter?"

"He's not saying that, Misun." Jayce attempts to reassure her. "They just want to help."

"We really do, Mi," Luca says patiently, knowing that he has to try and get through to her in order for his potential daughter to have a better start in life. "Honestly, you are doing great so far. I just think that it will be a good idea to have a bit of extra help. No first-time parent knows what they're doing. I know that I don't have a clue." He laughs and points to Jaxon. "And I bet that he doesn't either."

Jax shakes his head. "Not any idea at all."

Misun looks around the room at the faces of her ex-boyfriend's family staring back hopefully at her. She knows that they have virtually no positive thoughts about her capabilities as a mom. She even knows for herself that she could do with a little extra support to deal with all of this.

Smiling at Luca, she says softly, "Okay. Thank you."

Chapter 26

Taylor holds the photographs up to the light streaming through his apartment window, his mouth open in awe at the images he is seeing. Black and white stills of various materials and patterns, along with dress making equipment. "Wow Jasper, these are seriously incredible." He turns to the new man in his life. "Honestly, you have some serious talent."

Jasper blushes, still getting used to taking compliments for doing the work that he loves. "Thanks. I'm glad that you like them."

Heading back towards the table, Taylor places the photographs down, still barely able to take his eyes off them. "These will look fantastic in my studio at Blackwood. I just need some amazing frames for them."

He wanted the pictures without color to stand out in his otherwise bright and patterned workspace. Plus, the fact that Jasper has taken them, makes them more pleasurable to admire.

"I know someone who does amazing framing. I should take you to their gallery so that you can see if there are any that you like," Jasper says.

"That would be great." Taylor places a slow and gentle kiss on Jasper's lips. He never tires of tasting him.

Jasper reciprocates, parting his mouth a little to allow their tongues to tease each other. Pulling back, Taylor sighs and smiles at him fondly, before turning back to the photographs. Jasper is so grateful to Taylor for being so patient with him and taking things slowly. Coming out as gay has been a little hard to adjust to. He wishes that he could be as open and comfortable with it as Luca is, but he is just happy to have found someone like Taylor. He enjoys being around him and is willing to go at whatever pace that Jasper sets.

"What do you feel like doing this evening?" he asks. "Do you want to go out somewhere?"

"Sure," Taylor says. "Or I can cook for you here as a thank you for the photographs. I don't think that Jaxon will be back here any time soon with everything going on."

"You don't have to thank me, but yeah sounds great. I've yet to sample your cooking skills." Jasper laughs.

"You've yet to sample *a lot* of my skills." Taylor winks at him playfully.

Jasper flushes red once more and pulls off his black leather jacket, swinging it behind him to hang off the back of his chair. Taylor can't help but stare at Jasper's muscled physique in his tight-fitting black t-shirt, his arms exposed and revealing the tattoos that trail down their length.

"Question," Taylor says, curiosity getting the better of him. "Do those..." He nods towards the impressive ink on Jasper's body. "Do they go up any further?"

Jasper looks to where Taylor is indicating, and glances back up. "Maybe you'll find out one day."

"I hope so," Taylor says, running his fingers down some of the lines on his skin, skimming the outline of the intricate pattern until he reaches Jasper's many bracelets adorning his wrist. "Do these all have a special meaning?" He weaves a couple of them through his fingers.

"Not really," Jasper laughs. "I just like how they look."

"Me too," Taylor tells him. "In fact, all of you looks amazing." Jasper looks away, seeming very shy. Taylor lifts his chin to meet his eyes. "I mean it. You are an amazing person with an incredible body and the most beautiful face. I am so glad that you want to spend some time with me."

Jasper melts into staring at Taylor's jawline. His gorgeous amber eyes draw him into what seems like a magic spell. He lunges forward a little too eagerly and pushes his lips onto

Taylor's, getting lost in the sensation of their kissing.

Taylor lets Jasper take the lead as he runs his hands through his hair, pulling them both closer together. Their raspy moans fill the air, their motions getting more frantic. With an instinct that takes over, Jasper lets his hand drop to Taylor's lap and he starts to tease Taylor's hardening cock through the material of his sweatpants.

Hearing Taylor groan out, Jasper discovers a newfound confidence, and slides himself off his seat to rest on his knees in between Taylor's legs.

"Are you sure about this?" Taylor asks him.

"I've never been more sure of anything," Jasper says. "If that's okay?"

Taylor smiles down at him. "Of course. I've been waiting for this." He shimmies himself to the edge of his seat. "If you're sure that you're completely ready."

Jasper nods and pulls at the elasticated waistband. Taylor can see that he is visibly nervous, his hands trembling, so assists in adjusting his clothes until his cock is released for Jasper to explore.

Running his hand along Jasper's brow, sweeping his hair to one side, Taylor gives him a comforting smile knowing that this is all brand new for his man. Jasper is a virgin in all ways aside from kissing, so he appreciates that this is a really big deal for him.

"Let me know if I'm doing anything wrong," Jasper says quietly, tentatively taking hold of Taylor.

"You will do just fine," Taylor reassures him. "Just do it as you would want it done to you. That way it will give me some future pointers too."

They laugh together and Jasper takes a deep breath in preparation, trying to ignore the thudding in his chest. He looks in awe at the sight before him. Taylor with a happy smile, his t-shirt hitched up over his toned stomach, his briefs pulled down enough to expose all that he needs.

Wrapping his hands around the bottom of the shaft tighter, Jasper lowers his head to lick at the tip, so grateful for his teenage years of gay porn watching giving him an insight into what to do.

Teasing his tongue around the slit, the sound of Taylor gasping out helps Jasper to calm down a little and relax with his movements. He can't believe that this feels even nicer than what he has imagined, especially in his alone time in his apartment.

Sinking his lips to reach his fingers, he takes Taylor in as much as he can, amazed at how big he is now fully erect; in some respects, intimidatingly large. Twirling his tongue around the shaft, he appreciates every bulging vein that lines his skin.

Taylor's moans increase, his deep tones filling the otherwise silent room, spurring Jasper on to do more. He clenches his lips further for a tighter grip, his pace quickening along with Taylor's sounds.

Ignoring the burning in the back of his throat, Jasper works harder to please him, lapping up all of Taylor's salty juices and enjoying the new sensory experiences that are overwhelming him.

Jasper's confidence grows as Taylor starts to move his hips up to match his hungry movements. He feels Taylor grasp at the material of his t-shirt in desperation, like he can't hold out any longer.

"Fuck, Jasper. I'm gonna come. Ah, I'm gonna..."

Thick, warm liquid shoots to the back of Jasper's throat, the forcefulness of the stream making him jump ever so slightly. Slowing his pace as Taylor rides his orgasm out, he experiences another first, swallowing all that Taylor has given him.

Giving a few more licks to Taylor's now sensitive tip, he kneels up and embraces the sight in front of him. Taylor with his head resting back, his eyes softly shut with beads of sweat forming on his brow. His breathing is slow but heavy. He wipes his mouth with the back of his hand and waits for Taylor to recover.

He raises his head to see Jasper with a shy, yet pleased grin. "Did you enjoy that?" he huffs, straightening his clothes and using his arm to wipe the perspiration from his forehead.

Jasper nods. "Was it okay?" he asks the inevitable question, hoping that he'll get some sort of verification that he did a good enough job.

Taylor sits forward, resting his elbows on his knees, and kisses Jasper softly on his lips, tasting himself. "Jasper, it was incredible. You are a natural."

Blushing, Jasper smiles. "I'm so glad that you were my first."

Taylor laughs, pulling him in closer. "Me too." He winks at him. "Give me a minute and I'll return the favor, giving you another first."

**

Jaxon looks on with concern at Luca pacing back and forth in his apartment. "Please, Luca. Come and sit down. You'll wear a hole in the floor."

Luca looks at his watch yet again and sighs. "Where is it, Jax? The mail is never this late. I was assured that it would be today."

Jaxon uncrosses his legs and gets up from the couch, making his way over to Luca and slipping his arms around his waist from behind. "It will be here, babe. I know it will."

Luca rests his head against his boyfriend's. "I feel sick. What if it's not what I want to hear?"

Squeezing his arms tighter, Jax kisses Luca's neck. "You know that there's nothing you can do about it. If she's not your daughter, that doesn't mean that you can't still love her. She will still be related to you either way."

"I know, I know," Luca says, trying to ignore the huge twisted knot inside his chest. "This wait is killing me though. I just need to see it for myself."

Jaxon turns Luca to face him and cups his face in his palms. "I'm here for you. Always." He places a soft peck on his lips as the room echoes with a tapping on the door. "That will be Taylor, Jasper, and Jayce."

Jax heads to the door and lets them in. Luca checks his watch again. "I can't go out until this mail gets here."

"Oh, Jayce is talking to the mail guy now downstairs," Jasper says, entering the room. "I think that he's getting it."

"Shit." Luca starts pacing again.

A few minutes later, the door taps again, and Jaxon lets Jayce in. Luca looks at his hands and notes that he is only carrying his phone and keys. He looks up to see Luca staring at him, his face pale.

"What?" he shrugs.

"The mail?" Luca says in agitation. "Did you pick it up?"

"Oh, yeah." Jayce reaches into his pocket for the envelopes. "Sorry I got distracted with an email from work."

He hands the small bundle to Luca who immediately starts to rifle through it. "It's not here." His voice sounds desperate. "Why isn't it here?"

Jax rubs his arm. "I'm sorry, Luca. It will probably be tomorrow then."

"But they assured me that it would be today!" Luca shouts in frustration. "I need to call them."

He makes his way hastily out of the room and everyone left standing there glances at each other, not really knowing what to say. The awkwardness hangs in the air between the men.

"Um, I'm just going to head to the bathroom," Jayce says, breaking the silence.

Shutting the door behind him and clicking the lock, Jayce lets out a nervous breath and wipes the sweat from his brow with his jacket sleeve. Revealing an inside pocket, he tentatively removes another envelope carefully hidden there. He examines the name of the DNA testing laboratory and Luca's name on the front.

Should We?

Carefully turning it over, he casts his eye over the seal. Sliding his fingernail under the corner, he tries to lift up the adhesive, but the paper starts to tear. He huffs and tries the other side which does the same. Clenching his fist in annoyance, Jayce sighs. He really needs to get this envelope open. An idea comes to mind and he turns on the hot tap. The water warms up and steam starts to fill the room. He looks at his reflection in the mirror as it starts to fog up, not appreciating the person staring back at him.

He waits a short while before holding the envelope as close to the water as possible, praying that this will work. A bang on the door startles him resulting in him almost losing grip of the paper.

"Come on, Jayce," Jasper shouts through the wood. "We're still going out."

Jayce sits on the edge of the bath and reaches to turn off the tap. He shakes his head at how crazy he's acting. "I'll be out in a second," he says back.

Admitting defeat, he leaves the bathroom and trails after the boys filtering out of the apartment. Luca has a look of devastation after the lab had assured him that the results were sent and that he should have them. Jax throws his arms around his shoulders, giving him as much reassurance as he can.

Once outside, Jayce bends down with the envelope in his hand pretending to pick it up off the ground. "Oh, look, Luca," he says as casually as he can. "This may be them. Maybe I dropped it."

Jaxon gasps and Luca practically snatches the envelope from his hand. "Oh shit. It's the results."

"Well, open it then!" Jasper laughs at his cousin.

The group goes quiet as Luca tears it open and unfolds the documents inside. Tears start to stream down his face. Jasper and Taylor exchange concerned glances and Jaxon throws his arm around his boyfriend.

"What?" he says. "Is it bad news?"

Luca can hardly control himself, the tears falling faster now. He shakes his head. "No, Jaxon. It's good. Dasom is mine."

Chapter 27

Anna covers her hand with her mouth, tears running down her cheeks. "Oh Victoria, you look like a princess. Just wait until Mom and Pops see you."

"Ahhh, my sweet baby sister. Don't cry! It's not even the wedding day yet!" Victoria says, touching the lace bodice of her wedding gown.

"Well turn around and look at yourself!" Heidi says her hands on her cheeks and a huge smile on her face.

Victoria turns and faces the towering mirror in Taylor's work studio. Her hands fly to her face as she takes in her reflection, turning side to side, swishing the tulle of her gown. "Oh my god...Taylor! It's the most beautiful gown that I have ever seen." Her own tears trail down her cheeks, just as her sisters are. "It's absolutely perfect. Better than perfect."

"I'm so glad that you love it," Taylor says to Victoria as he pinches the lace at her waist.

"You've lost a few pounds." He takes a few pins from the cushion on his wrist, securing the fabric that needs altering.

"I'm not surprised!" Victoria replies. "Between my dissertation and the wedding, it's been a bit stressful. But I'm finally done. All of my hard work has finally paid off. *And* I'll be Dr. Blackwood in a week! I can't believe it!"

"It's going to be amazing!" Anna replies. "But I worry about you. I wish that I could help with the wedding a bit more."

"There's really nothing to do! Noah's mom has done everything with the wedding planner. I'm grateful that I haven't needed to do a thing but nod my head and say yes or no." Taylor turns Victoria to the side and continues pinning. "My stress isn't from the planning, but I'm so anxious about how elaborate everything is going to be!"

"Well Mrs. Blackwood doesn't have a daughter, so this is her time to shine," Heidi adds.

"I'm just glad Mom is okay with it. You know our family could never afford a wedding like this," Anna says. "But she is just so happy for you, Victoria. And so proud. Pops too."

"Anna, I'm not sure when you'd fit wedding errands into your schedule anyway," Taylor says. "You're with Dasom twenty-four hours a day!"

"What do you mean?" Heidi says with a confused look. "I thought you just helped Misun during the day!"

"No," Anna says quietly. "She has me staying nights too. She's just not confident with caring for Dasom."

"It's more than that and you know it, Anna," Victoria says with frustration. "You do everything. She has no motherly instinct whatsoever."

"Well the baby is five months old!" Heidi proclaims. "Hasn't she gotten any better at caring for her?"

Victoria already knows the answer but waits for Anna's response.

"Well, I'm doing my best to get her involved and to teach her. I encourage Misun to bond with her daughter, but she's just not that interested. She'd rather have me care for her." Anna continues, "It doesn't help that Dasom doesn't really want Misun for comfort. She only settles down for me and her dad."

"And Jax!" Taylor pipes in.

"Yes, and Jax." Anna nods in agreement. "Jax is amazing with her. They adore each other. Jax has her right now so that I could come here!"

"Well why the hell doesn't Misun have her today?" Heidi asks, bewildered.

"Yeah what does she do while you have the baby all the time?" Taylor inquires, hands on his hips as he examines Victoria's gown for anything that needs adjusting.

Anna feels a bit awkward discussing this since she works for Misun, but this is Dasom's family and she has been uncomfortable about the entire situation.

"Well, I'm going to be honest with you. I'm not sure what is going on with Misun." She takes a deep breath, twisting her honey blonde ponytail into her fingers. "She's been drinking. Like, a lot. She sleeps most of the day, and when she *is* up, she's on her phone." Now that she's getting things out in the open, Anna feels relieved and continues. "She leaves at night too. I have no idea where she goes, but when she gets home, she's a mess."

Taylor raises his brow. "What do you mean by a mess?"

Anna stands up from the floor where she was sitting cross-legged, and paces. "Just a mess! Usually she's been drinking. Her make-up is all smudged, and her clothes are all disheveled."

"Is it a man?" Heidi asks, standing up and approaching Anna. "I bet she's meeting a man! What the actual fuck? Leaving her daughter to do god knows what!"

Victoria lifts the bottom of her dress and steps off the elevated platform with Taylor's help. "Anna, you never told me it's this bad. What does Luca say about this?"

"He doesn't really know, Victoria," Anna is getting upset. "He never really sees Misun! They communicate by text or through me.

The days Luca has Dasom, I drop her off at his place before I come to stay with you and Noah."

"Anna, you need to tell him!" Heidi says. "This really isn't good. Misun has always been a disaster, but she has Dasom now!"

Anna nibbles at her nails, thinking before she replies. "I haven't wanted to betray Misun's confidence, and Luca and Jax are so happy! I just don't want to cause Luca anymore stress than he's already had with Misun."

Victoria grasps her sister's hands. "We have to tell him, Anna. He has a right to know."

Anna nods, and Heidi adds her support. "It's the right thing, Anna. As much as we all dislike Misun, she is Dasom's mother. It would be terrible if something bad happened to her."

"You're right," Anna agrees. I will tell him everything. Let's just get through the wedding first, Luca has a lot to deal with as Noah's best man."

"Well Anna," Taylor says. "Dasom is so lucky to have you. So is Luca. I know how much you love that baby girl."

"Oh, I do," Anna replies with a smile. "She is the sweetest baby. I adore her."

"Ok ladies," Taylor says, clapping his hands together. "It's your turn! Let's get you into your bridesmaids' dresses! They're gorgeous.

My assistants have them all completed. Wait until you see them!"

Heidi and Anna giggle, excited to try their dresses on.

"Taylor, you are absolutely amazing! I can't wait for Noah to see me in this stunning creation of yours!" Victoria embraces him.

"Hey! Watch the pins, beautiful! And you are very welcome. Your wedding is going to be the talk of New York!"

**

"Here it comes, baby girl" Jax has a jar of mashed peas in one hand, and a tiny plastic spoon in the other.

Dasom is sitting in her highchair, banging her rattle on the tray, as Jax brings the spoon airplane style up to her rosy lips. Dasom smiles and babbles at Jax, until the peas reach her mouth. She promptly blows raspberries, spitting them out, speckles of green hitting Jaxon's cheek.

"Dasom, you think that's so funny, don't you!' Jax grins, wiping his cheek with the back of his hand. "Daddy wants you to have your veggies, baby. You can't have peaches and bananas all the time. Jax will get in trouble with Daddy!"

The door buzzes and Jax hears heels tapping on the wood floor, followed by an enthusiastic voice.

"Auntie Bella is here, Dasom! Where's my baby?" Bella clicks her way theatrically into the kitchen. "Look at you two!" she says. "Is Jax making you eat those yucky peas, princess?" Bella makes a disgusted face, kissing Dasom on the head. She leans over and places another kiss on Jax's cheek, getting a bit of peas on her lips. "Ugh, those are simply awful."

Bella walks to the fridge, taking out the organic yogurt, scooping a bit into a dish. "Here, princess. This is much better." She brings the dish to Jaxon, who defeatedly puts the peas aside.

"Are you checking up on us, Bella?" Jax asks.

"Of course, I am, darling. With all the boys away, I wanted to pop in on my way to the penthouse," Bella replies.

She sits down next to Jax, and he hands her the yogurt and spoon, then heads over to the sink to fill it with warm water for Dasom's bath.

Bella feeds some yogurt to Dasom, who smiles happily now that the offensive vegetable is gone. "It looks like you two are getting along perfectly well. Really, Jaxon, you are amazing. Fatherhood comes so naturally to you!" Bella praises.

Jax checks the water temperature on his wrist, setting a bath towel on the counter. "Well thank you, Bella. I don't know, I just really enjoy taking care of her. I love her so much. Sometimes I forget that she's not my own daughter." He walks over and unhooks Dasom from the highchair as Bella puts the tray aside.

"Well, darling, it seems to me that you and Luca could be in it for the long haul. And Dasom certainly loves you! She even looks like a combination of you and Luca with her Asian heritage!" Bella says.

Jaxon smiles sweetly and kisses Dasom all over her messy face. She giggles, reaching her little fingers up to grab at his cheeks. "Oh, you silly girl, you're getting me just as grubby as you are!"

Bella watches as Jax expertly holds Dasom in one arm and strips off her onesie and diaper with the other. He places a hand towel at the bottom of the sink, checking the water again before placing Dasom in for her bath.

Bella strides over to the sink, tickling her great-niece's belly. Dasom splashes happily, cooing as Jax lathers her with baby soap. He sings to her softly as he takes out the little pigtail on top of her head, protecting her eyes as he rinses and sudses up her curly black hair.

"You look really happy, Jax. Content. Are you happy?" Bella asks.

Jax looks at Bella and smiles. "I am. I'm very happy. I never expected my life to change so drastically in such a short amount of time, Bella. But I feel like I'm right where I belong."

Bella holds up the towel and Jax places Dasom in her arms. She bundles up the little princess and looks at Jax. "You are Jaxon...You are."

**

"Good afternoon to all of you Mr. Blackwood." The young lady behind the counter flashes a big smile at the group of men as they place their bags down onto the floor. She motions to one of the assistants nearby to collect them. "Here, Scott will take these to the changing rooms while we arrange for you to be taken to your table."

Scott scuttles off with their gym bags containing comfortable clothes for later, and the bubbly receptionist leads them to the spa's opulent restaurant, handing them over to the concierge who shows them to their table.

"We have prepared a special lunch for you today, sir," he says to Noah. "As a thank you for picking our establishment for your bachelor get together before your wedding."

Noah smiles and nods at the kind and aging man, who rushes off to prepare his team for the V.I.P. meal. The Blackwoods are well respected in the spa for being regular customers, but today is even more special. The staff knows that the Blackwoods will spend more money than usual. The five cousins Noah, Luca, Jayce, Harrison, and Jasper all relax at the table.

"I'm so glad that you didn't go to a strip club or something." Luca laughs. "That would have been awkward, considering two of us have boyfriends."

Noah takes a sip of his chilled sparkling water. "I'm too old for that shit now.

Besides, as easy going as Victoria is, I'm not sure she'd be too thrilled with me stuffing dollar bills into young women's G-strings."

The waiter places their food in front of them, and the cousins get straight to enjoying the luxurious salmon dish.

"How are things with you and Heidi?" Luca asks Harrison. "She seems sweet."

"She really is," Harrison says. "I'm so happy."

"Maybe it will be your wedding next then?" Jayce teases his brother, who playfully punches his arm. He turns to Luca. "And how is fatherhood? Is Dasom doing okay?"

Luca grins. "It's so amazing. Don't get me wrong, it has its hard moments, but I love her so much. She's my little princess."

"What about Misun?" Noah says. "Is she behaving herself?"

"Seems to be." Luca shrugs. "I think she's managing Day pretty well with Anna's help."

"Good, good." Noah finishes off his last mouthful. "Hopefully things will settle down now and there will be no more drama."

Luca laughs. "This is Misun we're talking about. Trouble follows her around."

The group joins in the banter, aside from Jayce who remains a bit quiet. Jasper notices his half-hearted attempts to be included in the conversation.

"What's up with you?" Jasper says, nudging Jayce's arm.

"Nothing," he huffs.

"Oh, yeah, I forget that you always spring to Misun's defense," Luca says with slight annoyance.

"I do not!" Jayce protests, playing with his fork. "I just think that the subject should be dropped." He shuffles in his seat.

Noah senses discomfort around the table and diffuses the topic before it goes any further. "So, Jasper. How's Taylor?"

Jasper coughs, a little embarrassed. "It's good. We're good. He is incredible. We're just taking things slow. I'm not used to it all yet. And he is so, so patient with me."

"It is new. Just take your time. When the time is right, things will happen." Noah reassures.

Jasper addresses Luca. "So, you and Jax. Can I ask you a personal question?"

Luca flushes crimson. He knows where this conversation is heading. He takes a deep breath. "Go on, ask me about sex with another man."

Noah laughs loudly. "How did you know he was going to ask about that?" Luca raises a brow, shooting him a look indicating that it was obvious. "Okay, yeah, I'm curious," Jasper says. Is that so wrong?"

Shaking his head, Luca smiles. "Of course, it's not. What do you want to know?"

"I want to know if it hurts." Jasper blurts out. "The thought scares me a lot, I'll admit that."

Luca is grateful that they're all so close and comfortable talking to each other. He doesn't think that he'd be able to speak so freely to anyone else about such personal matters. "Okay, so Jax and I have had sex a few times, but I've done it to him. I'm not brave enough to try being a bottom yet." He chuckles as he becomes aware that his cousins are silently staring at him for more details. "It's different than being with a woman, but not in a bad way. You need to prepare your partner first and go slow. Jax has been guiding me through it. He's amazing, I really love him."

Luca gets quiet after revealing so much detail without thinking. When it comes to Jaxon, he can't help himself when he speaks.

Jasper asks another question. "So, it doesn't have to be, you know, like both people taking it?" He coughs in embarrassment.

"Of course not, that's something you discuss with your partner," Luca says.

"Just take your time. If Taylor is as patient as Jaxon is, which I suspect is the case, then he will wait until you're ready."

Jayce rubs Jasper's arm. "Does that make you feel better?" Jasper nods. "Good, I'm glad."

**

Once their food has settled and they've enjoyed a good conversation, the five men get changed for their various spa treatments, starting with massages. Jayce and Noah settle on tables next to each other as their treatments begin. The conversation flows, their faces squished into the holes of the massage tables, as they lay face down staring at the fancy ceramic floor tiles.

"I'm not used to this sort of pampering except from Victoria," Noah says, as the female masseur sets about loosening his muscles.

"I am," Jayce says with a groan as he relaxes. "It's such a good feeling." Noah closes his eyes and embraces the firm touch until Jayce speaks again. "That is until they get too high on your legs and you have to try and stop yourself from getting a boner." The room erupts with laughter, and Jayce shrugs. "True though."

"Shit, don't tell me that!" Noah whines. "I'll be conscious of it now."

"It's okay, Mr. Blackwood. I'm in professional mode," the woman says. "We have seen it all before."

"Wait," Noah says, leaning himself up, "so he's not kidding?"

She laughs and gets back to work. The door opens and the men can hear someone talking on the phone. Jayce tenses up at hearing the voice but casually stays where he is, listening at the same time.

"Yeah, It's me again. Why aren't you answering my calls or texts? I'm in town for two more days and I really want to see you. There's no reason you can't see me now. Call me." The man ends the call.

"Oh, hey Korian. Trying to set up a hot date while you're in town?" Jasper says. "What are you doing here?"

Korian shakes his head. "Yeah something like that. I'm in town for a shoot. What are you guys doing here?"

"Not here to see my Mum then?" Harrison teases, making Jayce cringe at his brother's words.

Korian laughs loudly. "As much as I love Bella," he says, "I'm here for other purposes." There is a pause before Korian pops his head underneath Jayce's table, meeting his eyes. "Hey, Jayce. Nice to see you here."

"Um, yeah, you too," is all that Jayce can

respond with, trying to act as normal as possible.

Korian stands back up. "Right. Well, I'll leave you all to it. Enjoy." After bidding them all goodbye, he leaves.

Sitting up, Noah looks at his cousin who has turned onto his back on the table. "Well, Jayce, you didn't make that awkward at all."

"What?" Jayce protests.

"I don't know why you act so jealous of Korian," Harrison says. "You *are* more famous than he is."

"I'm not jealous!" Jayce says.

"Okay, okay," Jasper jumps into the conversation. "Let's forget about Korian, Misun, and everyone else and just enjoy the day."

Jayce sighs and resumes his previous position, trying his best to relax for his massage, but struggling with the thoughts going around his head. *Forget about Korian, Misun, and everyone else...*

Chapter 28

Victoria stands on the terrace of the Penthouse Suite of the Plaza Hotel. She sips her champagne as she takes in the view of Central Park below her, the afternoon sun reflects off of the pond and the skyline beyond. As a young girl growing up in Buffalo, she dreamed of the day her prince charming would sweep her off her feet, and of the fairy tale wedding they would share.

She and Anna would spend nights giggling under the covers on the top bunk of their tiny bedroom, creating stories about their handsome grooms and princess wedding gowns. Now here she is, on her wedding day, and her dreams are coming true. Victoria sighs, thanking the Universe for bringing Noah to her. She knows how blessed she is to have this love, and although she imagined modest life, she is so grateful that she is here.

"It's princess time, Sis," Anna steps out to join her on the terrace, resting her cheek on Victoria's shoulder. "The makeup artist is ready to get started and Heidi wants to work on your hair."

Victoria tips her head to the side, resting it on Anna's already curled blonde hair. "Hmmm, I know. I just wanted a quiet moment. I can't believe that I'm here."

"But you are," Anna replies. "Just like we always dreamed about. I'm so happy for you, Victoria."

"And I'm so happy that you're here to share it with me." Victoria kisses her baby sister's head, and they silently take in the view for a few more minutes until Anna takes her hand and leads her inside.

The living room area of the suite has been transformed into Victoria's bridal room. Full-length mirrors have been brought in by Harrison's assistant stylists, the elegant glass tables covered in makeup palettes, brushes, hair products, and curling irons. Victoria's favorite makeup artist from Blackwood beacons her to sit on the sky-blue velvet couch, sitting beside her to prepare her skin.

"Okay beautiful, as soon as your makeup is done, I'll get started on your hair," Heidi tells the bride as she busies herself organizing what she needs.

Anna sits on a nearby chair, another makeup artist applying shadow to her lids. Victoria and her bridesmaids all wear satin robes and feathered slippers, sipping cocktails and nibbling canapés that the Penthouse butler has served them. A ring at the door draws their attention over the relaxing music, and Heidi rushes toward the door.

"Oh! That must be Taylor with your dress!" Heidi says, flinging open the door. Her excitement quickly changes to surprise when she sees Misun standing there, with Dasom in her stroller.

"Misun, what are you doing here?" Heidi asks, squatting down to kiss Dasom on her head.

Misun is already dressed for the evening. Her black hair hangs sleek and shiny down her back and her makeup is perfectly done with an elaborate cat eye and red lipstick. Her floor-length dress is silver lamé, tightly hugging her curves. The fabric at her neckline drapes low, showing off her ample cleavage, held up by spaghetti straps.

Misun pushes Dasom into the room, not waiting for an invitation. "I'm so sorry to bother you, but I really need Anna. Dasom is so fussy."

Dasom is wearing her pajamas, trying to tip her bottle up to get a drink. The formula is dripping down her chin, soaking her front. She wiggles in her seat, whining in frustration. Anna stands up and rushes over, unhooking her and cuddling her close. She tips the bottle up and Dasom guzzles it down.

"Misun, did you feed her any jarred food this afternoon?" Anna questions.

"I tried but she just spits it out. I figured she was fine with the bottle," Misun responds. "I needed to get ready."

Anna sighs deeply and strokes Dasom's cheek. "Well, she needs food and a bath! Where's the beautiful little dress that Luca got her to wear tonight?"

"It's here in the diaper bag," Misun says, rummaging through the bag looking for it.

"Misun, listen. I'm sorry," Heidi walks over to Anna, taking Dasom from her arms. "Anna can't help you today. She has other responsibilities right now. You're Dasom's mother and I'm sure that you'll manage." She hands Dasom to Misun, who holds her away from her body to protect her outfit.

"Here we are!" Taylor's voice rings out from the doorway. He is holding up Victoria's dress which is wrapped protectively. Jax is behind him carrying another cotton garment bag containing her veil and shoes.

"Misun, you look lovely. What are you doing here?" Jax asks.

Taylor enters the suite heading toward the bride, and Heidi takes the package from Jax. "She was just leaving," Heidi says. "Anna can't help with Dasom right now."

Jaxon takes Dasom into his arms, kissing her forehead. "My sweet girl, you're a mess! Come on Misun. I'll help you get her ready. Ladies, we will see you at the wedding. I'm sure that you'll all look gorgeous. Please kiss Victoria from me." He carries Dasom out of the room, motioning Misun to follow.

Heidi and Anna exchange looks. "Thank god for Jaxon," Heidi says. Anna sighs and nods in agreement. They walk back to assist the bride, relieved that Dasom will be well cared for.

**

"Are you ready to do this?" Luca asks, as he adjusts Noah's bow tie and smooths down his black velvet lapels.

"Never been more ready for anything in my entire life," Noah replies.

Luca nods, squeezing his cousin's shoulders. "Noah, I want to thank you for choosing me to be your best man. It means so much to me. I couldn't have gotten through these last months without your support."

"Luca, you're not just my cousin, but my best friend. We're here for each other. We always have been." Noah replies, pulling Luca into a tight embrace.

Luca responds, pulling back from Noah to check on his appearance one last time. "Well, I'm so happy that I'll be at your side when Victoria becomes your wife. Wait until she sees you. You look great. Taylor was right about these suits."

"Yeah well, I wanted to go traditional black, but he wouldn't have it. He was right, of course," Noah says.

The Blackwood men are dressed in slim-fitting custom tuxedos. The traditional black pants, ties, and white shirts Taylor had dressed them in are complemented by elegant jackets. Noah is wearing a deep eggplant purple, single-breasted jacket. The jacket is flocked with an intricate pattern in black velvet. His groomsmen have the same design, but their jackets are charcoal gray accented with black velvet.

"Noah, everyone is seated. Mum and Dad just went in," Jasper informs him.

Jasper's hair is gelled back off his beautiful face. He had removed his lip ring and several earrings at his mother's request. A hint of his tattoos is still visible above his collar and on his hands, above his ring clad fingers.

Noah nods as Harrison and Jayce join them, looking like they have just stepped out of the pages of Blackwood Magazine. Their brown eyes shine with excitement as they approach the groom.

"It's time to get married, Noah! Let's go in," Jayce says, placing a hand on his cousin's shoulder.

The men enter to the familiar refrain of Vivaldi's Spring being played by an eight-piece orchestra. The Terrace Room looks like something out of a dream. Golden ambient light dimly illuminates the archways surrounding the towering room and its intricate ceiling. Victoria's favorite flowers adorn the space; pale blue hydrangeas, lavender, pink peonies, and white and coral tea roses have been elegantly arranged and scattered throughout. Six-foot crystal candelabras are placed on either side of the center aisle, the marble flooring covered in a royal purple satin runner to lead Victoria to her groom. Guests are seated in golden gilded chairs placed in rows on either side of the aisle. Noah takes in the sight of his family around him, his parents looking at him proudly.

Standing beside Noah, Luca looks at Jax sitting next to Taylor, gorgeous as always. His eyes sparkle when he meets Luca's gaze. His beautiful little girl is sitting on Misun's lap behind Jax.

She looks adorable in a lacy lavender dress. A little ponytail with a purple bow bobs on top of her black curls. Luca raises his eyebrows in concern as he sees Dasom reaching out for him, starting to cry. Misun is bouncing her daughter on her lap trying her best to calm her but is unable to do so. Jax turns around, whispering to Misun, who hands Dasom to him. Dasom fusses for a few more moments, then calms, sucking on her pacifier and gently touching Jaxon's face. Luca smiles at the sight, amazed at the way his daughter is looking at his boyfriend as he gently whispers to her.

After a brief pause, Vivaldi's Autumn begins to play, and everyone directs their attention to the aisle. The bridesmaids begin their walk slowly, looking beautiful. They carry hydrangeas that complement their dresses, a shimmery amethyst with indigo undertones to the intricate lace appliqué bodices and knee-length tulle.

The orchestra plays a bit louder, and everyone stands as the bride begins her walk towards Noah, accompanied by her father. The diamanté accents adorning her long loose braid and stunning dress sparkle in the candlelight. Her bridal bouquet compliments the arrangements around the room, composed of her favorite blooms. Victoria walks gracefully, a joyous smile on her face as her cathedral veil trails behind her.

When she reaches Noah, her father places their hands together, and they look into each other's eyes with pure love and adoration. Noah cannot believe how unbelievably gorgeous Victoria is. As he takes in her beauty, he sees nothing but a glorious life together for them as husband and wife.

**

Victoria looks around the grand, dimly lit room and sighs with contentment. The high, exquisitely painted ceiling displays an elaborate hanging chandelier sparkling in the center, casting twinkly patterns on the tables below.

Large round tables are set away from the dance floor, draped with crisp white tablecloths that drape to the floor. Towering floral centerpieces sit in the center of each table, with candlelight flickering from crystal candelabras. Victoria glances around at everyone who has attended and smiles at how happy they look. *Maybe this big, fancy wedding wasn't such a bad idea after all.*

Holding her hand up to inspect the new jewelry adorning her finger, she beams. The gold band sparkles with emeralds and diamonds matching perfectly with her engagement ring. *Victoria Blackwood,* she repeats in her head, trying to get used to her new title.

"Wow, Victoria," Heidi says, plonking herself in the seat next to her. "It's so warm in here."

"Well, you *have* been dancing for a while with Harrison." Victoria laughs out loud at her tipsy friend. "Are you enjoying yourself though?"

Heidi throws her hands up in the air. "Have you seen this place?" She points around at the drapes hanging from floor to ceiling, and the marble floor. "It's amazing!" Kissing Victoria on the cheek, she jumps up to join her boyfriend for the next song.

Victoria picks up her sparkling crystal glass and takes a sip of the champagne. She lovingly gazes at her new husband talking to other members of his family. *My family too.* She looks at the couple standing beside her husband. Luca's arm is wrapped around Jax's waist, his hand resting on the leather of Jax's belt, his thumb tucked into the waistband.

She is so happy to see Luca in a better place.

She knows that he deserves it after everything that he's been through. Feeling eyes staring, she sees Noah facing in her direction. He calls Victoria over, and she gracefully makes her way to him, exchanging small talk with friends and associates of Blackwood, that she doesn't know too well, along the way.

When she finally reaches her new husband, Noah pulls her in close, his fingers gently gripping her hips. She lazily drapes her arms on his shoulder, teasing her fingers through his perfectly styled hair.

"Sorry," he says, apologetically, "I didn't mean to leave you alone."

"Don't be silly." She carefully places a small kiss on his lips, their lips gently brushing together. "I was enjoying a little moment's break from the madness."

Taking a step back, Noah looks her up and down, taking in the image of his wife before him. "I still cannot believe how beautiful you look." He turns towards Taylor who has just joined the group. "Honestly, Tay, you couldn't have done any better with this." He points to her dress.

Taylor flushes red and beams with a big smile. "Thank you. But I would say that it is more down to the stunning woman that is wearing it."

Noah swoops Victoria back into his

Should We?

arms again. "You are correct, Taylor. She is just something else." They embrace closely, kissing each other hungrily.

"Get a room, you two." Luca teases over the music. "I've just eaten some really expensive food. I don't want to see that again."

Everyone laughs, and Victoria strokes his elbow. "Like you two can talk. You never keep your hands off each other." Jax and Luca look at each other fondly, and then back to Victoria. "Seriously though," she says. "I am so, so glad that you're both happy now that things have settled down." She scans the room until she spots Dasom being bounced very enthusiastically on Bella's knee, wearing her pretty dress and a little bow in her growing black hair. "And look at how big she is now. What is she? Five months?"

Luca nods his head. "She is, and she is so cute."

"She certainly is," Jax says, I just absolutely adore her."

"That's great." Victoria gives them both a quick hug. "At least she has some stability in her life. And she can't ask for more than you two." She checks around the room again. "Speaking of... where is that mother of hers?"

The group all eye around the guests until Jaxon spots Misun over in the corner, flirting with a waiter, showing off her curves in her long silver dress and very exposed cleavage. "Typical," he tuts.

Luca shakes his head. "I can see us ending up looking after Dasom all night." Jaxon nods in agreement.

"I can't believe that Misun even wanted to come," Noah says. "I mean, why would she?"

"For the room paid for by Luca and the elaborate party! She's used bringing Dasom as an excuse, I'm sure." Taylor rolls his eyes.

Jaxon hums, nodding his head again. "She absolutely does play on it."

"At least she has been trying to be more friendly?" Victoria attempts to give Misun the benefit of the doubt. "There haven't really been any issues since Dasom was born, aside from needing a little assistance to look after her."

"Baby care assistance, or financial assistance?" Noah raises an eyebrow. Victoria taps his arm, indicating for him to drop the subject. "I know, I know. I'm sorry."

"It's fine," Luca says, taking the last chug of his beer. "I am fully aware of how it is. But I guess that I'm stuck with her now as long as I have that little girl to raise."

Jaxon kisses his cheek. "And what an amazing

job you do with her."

Luca smiles, resting his head on Jax's shoulder. "We." He looks up, his eyes narrowing with suspicion. "Where is she going now?"

They all turn to watch Misun make her way through the wedding reception guests, over to where Jayce is sitting near his mother. Bella turns to her and attempts to pass Dasom back, but Misun refuses. Bella pauses in surprise and sees the group looking over in her direction. She shrugs her shoulders. Misun sits next to Jayce and strikes up a conversation.

"What is that woman doing?" Heidi says, joining the others. "Like, seriously, she will flirt with anyone."

Luca and Jaxon exchange a knowing glance, and Jaxon heads across the hall to take over from Bella and babysitting duties for a while. Luca turns to Noah and Victoria. "She has a bit of a thing for Jayce, doesn't she?"

"It would seem so," Noah says, huffing at Misun, obviously pushing her breasts closer to Jayce's face to get his attention. "I'm just glad that he's sensible enough not to go there."

"He wouldn't dare!" Heidi laughs, grabbing another glass from the waiter as he passes with a tray. "Anyone would be crazy to go with that woman." Her eyes widen when she realizes what she has blurted out. "Oh, shit,

Luca. I'm sorry. I didn't mea..."

Luca laughs and places a hand on her shoulder. "It's fine. It's in the past. She will find her next victim soon enough."

"As long as it's not my cousin," Noah states, watching as Jayce stands and walks away from Misun, leaving her looking a touch offended. Bella and Jaxon share a smug smile.

Chapter 29

"Hey, baby, baby, baby," Jaxon says in his softest lullaby voice, carrying a sleepy Dasom in his arms through the corridor. "Let's go and see if we can find your mom. If not, it's back with us." He kisses her on the forehead. "Which is fine..." he continues to talk to her as if it were possible for her to answer back, "except we have none of your things." He knocks repeatedly on Misun's door with no response.

Sighing, he proceeds to Bella's room to see if she knows where Misun is. Bella hasn't seen her. He thinks it best to leave Victoria and Noah alone for a while, considering it *is* their wedding night. Luca has gone back downstairs; in case they have missed Misun in some of the rooms.

"Here we go," Jax smiles sweetly at her. Dasom coos back at him. "It's so late for you to be up. If your mom isn't in your room, then we can try Heidi." He knows that Heidi and Harrison are further down this corridor in one of the other suites.

He knocks on Heidi's door, but there is no answer. Jaxon sighs. As much as he loves

Dasom, he knows that he needs her supplies. He knocks again a little louder. Nothing.

He smiles again at the bundle in his arms. "Not to worry, little one. We can sort something out." Glancing at his phone, Jax sees that Misun still hasn't responded to his messages. He makes his way along the carpet, considering where to look next.

As he does, Misun's door finally opens, and he expects her to be waiting for her own daughter. Instead, she bundles out of the room in a robe, clearly wearing nothing underneath. Her arms are draped around a man. He straightens his shirt and fastens his belt, looking like he is trying to get away swiftly. Misun laughs, not seeing Jaxon standing there, trying to kiss her latest conquest. The man pulls back from her, clearly recognizing the mistake that he has made.

"*You?*" is all that Jaxon can get out, his lips dry.

They both stop abruptly, turning to face Jax. The other guy's eyes widen in sheer fear upon seeing him. Heidi's door opens, and she steps out too, not realizing what is going to greet her. She looks at the couple, Misun with messy hair, her robe not leaving much to the imagination, and the man almost glued to the spot knowing that he has been caught.

Heidi's face pales. "Harrison?"

The icy pause that hangs in the air can almost be cut through with a knife. The group standing in the corridor exchange glances for a moment. Jaxon pulls Dasom closer to him and takes a step backward, knowing that this isn't going to be pleasant.

Harrison looks at his girlfriend, his eyes wider than they have ever been before, his hand still thrust into his waistband midway through tucking his shirt in. "Heidi. I..."

"Oh, you found her..." a voice begins from behind them, before trailing off. "Um, what's going on? Why is everyone out here?"

Jaxon turns to see his boyfriend heading towards them along the carpet and can see him taking in the sight before him. Misun in her robe, Harrison looking very flustered and unkept, Heidi with a red face looking ready to explode. Finally, his eyes rest on Jax and his daughter when he reaches them.

"Luca," Harrison says. "I'm sorry..."

Heidi cuts him off, marching to stand in front of him. "Are you seriously apologizing to your cousin before me?" Harrison can hardly look her in the eye. "Please tell me that this isn't what it looks like?"

"Misun?" Luca asks, still not quite believing what he is seeing. "What are you playing at?"

Shrugging, Misun leans smugly against the door frame, her robe sliding off her shoulder and exposing her bare collarbone and the slope of her chest. "Well, he looked good as he was walking past. How could I resist?"

Heidi's face turns purple as the rage consumes her, the anger waiting to burst from her system. She flies towards Misun, a loud and pained shriek escaping her lips. Luca manages to grab her waist swiftly to stop her.

Dasom starts to cry at the noise. Jaxon pulls her in tighter for comfort as Luca struggles to hold on to a distraught Heidi. Harrison comes to his senses and assists his cousin in attempting to calm his girlfriend.

"Get your fucking dirty hands off me," she shrieks at him, shrugging his arms off. Misun scoffs, a smirk on her plush lips. "Nice," she teases. "I showered beforehand."

"Right, that's enough." Luca lets go of Heidi. "This is Noah and Victoria's wedding. We are not going to ruin this for them." He motions towards Heidi. "You get back in your room with Harrison and talk." He turns to Jaxon. "You take Day back to our room. I'll be there soon."

Jaxon nods, his face pale with shock, and heads off in the direction of their suite, still gripping the little girl firmly in his arms firmly. Harrison glances up at Heidi, and she motions him into their room. He follows her sheepishly.

"What?" Misun says with a contemptuous grin. Luca grips her arm and pulls her back into her room. "Owwww, Luca. Easy!"

He slams the door behind them and faces her. "What the actual fuck, Mi? What the hell are you playing at?"

"Oh, come on, Luca," she sneers at him, folding her arms indignantly. "Am I not allowed a bit of fun?"

"Misun, don't treat me like a fool. Of all the people that you could have gone anywhere near tonight, why him?" Luca snaps. "Out of everyone in this entire building."

"Did you see how hot he looked?" Misun continues with her bravado. "He was just in the right place at the right time, and I took my chance." She fiddles with her nails, pouting. "It's not my fault that he was so easily persuaded."

Luca sighs. "And what about your daughter? *Our* daughter?"

"She was fine with Jaxon, wasn't she?" Misun speaks as if she believes what she's saying. "He could handle her."

Luca grabs her shoulders, almost shaking her in frustration. "But that's the point. He shouldn't have to. *You are her mom*, it's *your* job to look after her, not everyone else's!"

Misun grins at her ex and tries to snake her arms around his neck. "It's been a while since we were this close, Luca. Do you miss me?"

Luca pushes her away. "You are fucking unbelievable, Misun. Really you are."

She laughs out loud and sits seductively on the edge of the bed. Her robe opens a little to reveal her legs right up her thighs. She leans back, her palms resting on the bed. Tilting her head, she gives Luca a familiar look. "Come on, Luca. Come to bed. For old times sake."

Luca can't believe that she is still up to her same tricks, although he isn't really surprised. Spotting Dasom's changing bags on the dressing table, he reaches for them, before addressing Misun again. "I really don't know what game you're playing, but it's a dangerous one and people are getting hurt." He steps back toward the door. "You are putting a wedge between my family, and I don't know why." He throws his hand in the air. "Fuck, Mi, I don't even think that you know why. But it has to stop."

She realizes that he is leaving and stands. "I'm sorry, Luca. I really am."

Grasping the door handle, he turns to her. "I'm not falling for that again. You've done enough damage and I have to put my daughter first. She's going to stay with me and Jaxon until you sort your shit out." He gives her a sympathetic glance. "If you ever sort your shit out."

**

Harrison paces around the room. "Please talk to me, Heidi."

Heidi sits cross-legged on their bed, staring blankly at the luxurious bedding beneath her, her mind swirling, her thoughts dark and defeated. "Why?" Is the only word that she can manage to whisper, her lips dry.

Sitting beside her, Harrison tries to take her hand, but she snatches it away. "Look, Heidi, I made a mistake. A stupid fucking mistake. I've been drinking, and she was just there."

"I was next door," Heidi says without emotion. "You went into her room while I was a few yards away waiting for you."

"I know, I'm a fool." He tries again to take her hand, and she allows him. "I can't tell you how sorry I am."

"Did you fuck her?" she says with more venom.

Harrison shakes his head, "No. Kind of. Well, no."

She turns to him, a frown on her pale face. "Kind of? Either you did or you didn't."

"Well, no then. I couldn't, you know, keep it up," he stutters.

Heidi swiftly stands up and becomes the one pacing the floor. "Actually, you know what? I don't want to know. I don't want any details. The fact of the matter is, you went in there in the first place."

Harrison joins her and grasps her fingers. "Please, Heidi. I don't know what came over me. Really, I don't. Please forgive me?"

Heidi laughs, startling Harrison. "Forgive?" Her temper is flaring at his seeming lack of understanding of the seriousness of the situation. "Are you joking?" She brushes his hands off and starts to grab his bags. "You went into another woman's room, right next door to ours. You attempted to have sex with her or even did have sex with her, I don't fucking know. Yet you want me to forgive you?"

Thrusting his things at him, he realizes that she wants him to leave the room. "Heidi, please. I'm sorry."

Tears are streaming down her freckled cheeks as she starts to push him towards the door. "I don't want to be around you. How can you even think that I would share a bed with you after you've had your lips and god knows what else on that slut. I want you to go."

Pleading with her, Harrison tries to reason with her. "Heidi let's talk. Please. Don't do this. Where am I supposed to stay?"

She pushes past him and opens the door.

Luca is just passing outside after leaving Misun's room. He stops to see Heidi shove Harrison into the corridor.

"Get out," she shouts at him. "I don't want you here. Go and fucking sleep next door. I'm sure that she will have you."

She slams the door, and Harrison's body slumps in shame. Luca sighs and places an arm around his cousin's shoulder. "Come on, you idiot. You can bunk in our room tonight. We can talk about this mess in the morning."

Chapter 30

Anna grasps Victoria's hand and admires the sparking emeralds on her finger.

"I can't believe that you're married! How is it being Mrs. Blackwood, or should I say, Dr. Blackwood?" she asks her sister.

"Mrs. Blackwood is just fine," Victoria responds, taking a sip of her pink martini. "I like being a Mrs. It is strange though; the way people look at me when they see my name. I'm still getting used to it," she continues, swirling the seeds in the bottom of her glass. "It's like I'm expected to dress up to go get groceries! If I wear my sweats, I get weird looks."

Anna rolls her eyes, sipping her drink. "Hmmm. It's such a shame having to look presentable when you're part of an iconic fashion family."

"Hey, you know what I mean!" Victoria responds, giving Anna's arm a playful slap. "I guess now I'm gonna have to start giving a shit about what I wear."

"Well, you look cute tonight!" Anna gestures to her sister's outfit. Victoria is wearing a grey pencil skirt and heels, with a ruffled peach silk blouse. Her golden hair is styled into a high ponytail that hangs down her back. "Why don't you ask Heidi to help you put together some outfits?" Anna suggests.

"Yeah, great idea." Victoria checks her phone for messages. "She should be here any minute," she says.

"Victoria, have you spoken to Heidi since the wedding? What a nightmare for her." Anna shakes her head, finishing the last of her cocktail.

"Just a few texts. She didn't want to bother me on my honeymoon." Victoria sighs. "Oh, here she is now." Victoria raises her hand to get Heidi's attention.

Heidi waves back and heads over to join her friends, looking lovely in a short floral blue dress and bohemian lace-up brown leather boots. Her strawberry hair is loosely piled on her head, a few stray curls escaping to frame her pretty face.

"Hi," Heidi says, and places kisses on her friend's cheeks. "God, I've missed you girls." She takes her seat and grabs Victoria's cocktail for a sip.

"Pomegranate martini," Victoria tells her, waving over the server.

"Yum, count me in," Heidi says, and the women order more drinks.

Once the server has gone, Anna grabs Heidi's hand. "We've been really worried about you, Heidi. You should have returned my calls!"

Heidi accepts her drink from the waiter with a nod, taking a sip, and raising an eyebrow at its sweetness. "I just needed some time," she replies, "and I knew that you both had your own shit going on. Now before we go *there*, Victoria, I want to hear all about your honeymoon."

Victoria smiles warmly. "Well, it was amazing. Sunny skies, beautiful beaches, blue ocean, and it was hot. *Very* hot, in more ways than one."

The girls laugh, clinking their glasses together. "So, lots of sex then!" Heidi giggles while scooping some pomegranate seeds from her glass with a spoon, teasing them onto her tongue suggestively. Anna covers her mouth with her hand, feigning revulsion, but bursts out laughing instead.

Victoria interrupts, "Well, Noah *did* bring these silk ropes and…"

"Oh my god, Victoria," Anna exclaims." That's my brother-in-law! The visual! Stop!"

"Don't stop!" Heidi chimes in. "I need details, lots of details…"

The women continue to talk about Victoria and Noah's trip, laughing, drinking, and admiring photographs on Victoria's phone. Once Heidi has started on her third martini, she's ready to talk about what happened with Harrison.

"So what actually happened, Heidi? Noah and I missed everything," Victoria asks quietly as she takes Heidi's hand.

"Fucking *Misun* is what happened. And my idiot boyfriend who had shitty judgment in his drunken state." Heidi shakes her head, thinking of Misun half-naked all over *her* man. "And of course," she continues, "that bitch is still hot as ever even after having a baby."

"So, did they sleep together?" Anna asks.

Heidi trails her finger along the rim of her glass, bringing it to her lips to lick off the sugar crystals. "He says no, that she pulled him into her room as he was stumbling to ours."

Victoria's green eyes gleam with suspicion. "So, you don't blame Harrison for any of it?"

"Oh, I blame him alright," Heidi scoffs. "He drank too much and fell for her advances. They got close to having sex; I know that."

Anna leans toward Heidi. "But he said they didn't?"

"He *said*," Heidi continues, "that she opened her robe and they kissed. Misun pulled him to the bed and tried to undress him. Supposedly, he never got hard and came to his senses and tried to leave. *That's* when Jax and I saw them." Heidi shakes her head indignantly.

"But *come on*! I know damn well at the very least he felt her up. With those tits right in front of him? Please."

"What the fuck is with Misun and the Blackwood men?" Victoria shrugs her shoulders. "I mean there are plenty of rich men she could have! I just want her to stay away from them. These are smart men; I just don't understand how they keep falling for her game."

"I don't either. It's like Luca's situation all over again." Heidi shakes her head. "Harrison and I are working on things slowly. Obviously, I can't avoid him with work. I'm pretty sure I believe him, but there's still some doubt there. It's going to take a while to build up that trust again."

Anna nods in agreement but looks silently at her glass. "Anna, you're quiet," Victoria says.

"Yeah, you are," Heidi adds. "I'm sure this is uncomfortable for you since you work for Misun."

Anna looks up and makes eye contact with both women. "I'm just feeling sad for Dasom. You know, she's pretty much full time with Luca now."

"No, I didn't know that," Heidi replies, surprise showing on her face.

Victoria nods. "Yeah, Anna is pretty much always at Luca's. She sleeps in the spare room with Dasom on Luca's workdays."

"Misun has only seen the baby a few times since the wedding incident. Luca just doesn't trust her," Heidi explains. "I just want Dasom to have a mother who loves her and can care for her. It makes me sad. Luca and Jax are amazing, but Misun is her *mother*."

Victoria's eyes go wide as she sees someone enter the bar. Anna follows her gaze and sees Misun, fucking Misun of all people. She teeters on her heels while walking over to the bar, sitting on a stool near the most attractive bartender.

"Shit," Victoria whispers.

Thinking quickly, Anna speaks up. "Hey, I'm getting hungry. A new Thai place opened down the street, and Jax says the food is authet..."

"I thought we were eating here!" Heidi interrupts. "The food is good, and I don't feel like leaving."

"But Thai sounds so good! Come on Heidi, let's go." Victoria tries to persuade her.

A loud laugh at the bar causes Heidi to turn her head. Her eyes open wide as they land on Misun, leaning seductively over her drink and playing with her long hair as she flirts with the bartender.

"Shit," Victoria and Anna both say at almost the same time.

Heidi turns back to them, her face flushed. "You have *got* to be fucking *kidding me!*" she says through clenched teeth. "This *cannot* be a coincidence."

Anna brings her hands up to her cheeks. "This is my fault. Misun called me to bring Dasom over, but Luca said no. I told her I was going out with my sister as an excuse. Misun knows we always come here." Anna reaches out to Heidi. "I'm so sorry."

"Don't apologize, it's not your fault," Victoria says. "You didn't know she'd show up here."

"And we're *not* leaving," Heidi says firmly. "She is not going to ruin our time together."

The waiter comes over to their table with more drinks and takes the women's dinner order. Victoria sighs, sipping her martini. They've all been drinking on empty stomachs, and Victoria feels that her head is a bit fuzzy. She's sure that Anna and Heidi feel a little tipsy as well.

After a few more minutes of conversation, Victoria sees Misun look over, their eyes meeting. Misun smiles, turns on her barstool and grabs her drink.

"She's coming over girls, get ready," Victoria announces. The three of them watch as Misun slowly approaches their table, gripping chair backs for balance on the way. The wine in her glass sloshes side to side with each step she takes, some of it spilling over the rim. When Misun reaches their table, she takes the available seat with no invitation.

Should We?

"Hello, beautiful ladies, you look like you're having a nice time over here," Misun says in a pleasant voice.

"Yes, we're enjoying each other's company, Misun," Anna replies tensely.

"That's lovely," Misun says. "I wish I had some girlfriends to spend time with."

"Well, Misun," Heidi says in a sugar-sweet voice. "You might have more luck with that if you stayed away from other women's boyfriends!"

"Oh, Heidi, I'm so sorry about that. Harrison just looked so delicious all dressed up," Misun responds. "He seemed more than happy for me to help him out of that suit!"

"Enough, Misun!" Victoria shouts at her. "Why are you here?"

Heidi looks like she's ready to slap Misun across the face. The waiter comes over with their meals. "Actually," Heidi says to him, "can we have those meals to go?" The server nods and walks back to the kitchen.

"I'm sorry for ruining your meal," Misun replies. "Anna mentioned that you'd be here, and I thought I could spend some girl time with the family."

"You are *not* part of our family. Dasom is our family." Victoria points her finger toward Misun. "You will *never* be a Blackwood."

"Well, that remains to be seen," Misun says smugly.

Anna places her hand on Misun's arm. "How much have you had to drink today, Misun?"

Misun downs the rest of her wine. "I may have had a few drinks before coming."

Anna squeezes her arm. "Misun, I'm worried about..."

"Actually, I really shouldn't be drinking at all," Misun interrupts, smiling sweetly at the women. "Considering my period *is* two weeks late." Misun stands up from the table. "So nice seeing you all. I'll just catch a cab home. Anna, please kiss my baby for me." She turns on her heel and walks away, leaving a stunned Anna and Victoria to console Heidi.

Chapter 31

Bella's toes curl into the plush carpet of her enormous bedroom suite as she strides around preparing things. It's been a while since Aiden has come to her place, but today is perfect. Jayce and Harrison are attending meetings to discuss plans for Jayce's upcoming shoot in Chicago, and then they'll head directly to Noah and Victoria's for the evening. Bella folds down the luxurious red damask comforter and drapes a black silk sheet across the bed, assuring that it is free of wrinkles.

She places a small wooden table near the bed and walks to her closet to retrieve the items that she will need for today. Setting them neatly on the table, she then covers it with a matching black silk scarf. Bella checks her watch as she walks to the kitchen. She places a few water bottles into a silver bucket and fills it with ice. Next, she cuts some cheese and apples placing them on a silver plate with an assortment of crackers. After covering the plate with a silver lid, she takes it along with the ice bucket, into her ensuite bathroom and places both items on the marble surround next to the sunken tub.

Bella's hair is almost dry from her earlier shower, but she pulls out the blow-dryer and brushes through the silky black strands. Once her hair is dry, she pulls it up into a high ponytail. She adds a bit of gel to the front, securing any loose wisps of hair. Bella touches up her makeup, applying another coat of crimson to her lips, and then changes for her guest. After zipping up her stiletto ankle boots, she tosses on her red silk robe and heads to the living room to wait.

Bella sips on sparkling water and catches up on a bit of computer work. Quiet jazz music floats through the apartment from the speaker system, relaxing her. When her driver messages her that he has dropped off her guest, she puts her computer aside and takes a quick look in the mirror, awaiting his arrival. Bella's attention is directed to a quiet knock on the door. She takes another sip of her water, letting him wait. She knows that he won't knock again.

Bella finally walks to the door, opening it to see Aidan standing there. He looks enticing, as always. His shoulder-length blonde waves are half pulled up into a messy bun. The loose button-down he's wearing is partially open, revealing his muscled chest and the traditional style tattoo there. It is a portrait of a beautiful woman's profile. She has blood-red lips and, ironically, chestnut-colored eyes and long raven-colored hair which is adorned with pearls. Aidan is wearing soft brown leather pants; which Bella can see are already tented with his half-hard erection. Aidan waits for Bella to invite him in, his eyes trained to the floor.

"Come in, Aidan," Bella invites. "Now look at me, baby." Aidan meets her eyes with his ice blue ones. Bella can see that his gaze is somewhat hazed over. "Aidan, have you had any alcohol today?" Bella asks as she traces her nails down his cheek. He shakes his head while staring at Bella. "Use your words please," she says.

"No Bella. I know the rules," he replies.

"Good boy, you're already getting into your headspace. Are you that excited to see me?"

Aidan nods and then remembers his words. "Yes, Bella. It's been a long time."

"Oh, my poor boy," Bella responds and places a tender kiss on each of his cheeks. "Do you remember everything we discussed yesterday?"

"Yes, Bella, I remember."

"Are there any changes you'd like to make? Remember, we only have a few hours to play today. You know I have a dinner to attend," Bella reminds him.

"Yes, I remember. And I'm fine with what we discussed."

"Okay, that's good, Aidan. Is there anything else you want to talk about before we start?"

"No Bella, I trust you."

"Okay then, go ahead to my room and wait for me," Bella instructs. Aidan walks hurriedly to the bedroom while Bella locks the front door and sits back down on the sofa.

After ten minutes, Bella enters her room. She locks the door and directs her attention to Aidan kneeling at the side of the bed, fully naked as he's been taught. His hands are placed on his muscled thighs. Bella walks around the room, lighting candles to indicate the start of their scene. When she's done, she stands directly in front of Aidan and discards her robe. His eyes stare straight ahead.

"Aidan, you can look at me now." He gazes expectantly into Bella's eyes. "Do you remember your colors, baby?" Aidan nods. "No, I need you to tell me."

Aidan takes a deep breath and responds. "Green for all good, yellow for slow down, red for stop."

"Good boy," Bella praises him. She walks over to the table and removes the scarf, placing it to the side. She lights the pillar candle and stands back in front of the beautiful man. "Did you prepare for me, baby? I see that you shaved," Bella asks. "You can look at me."

Aidan meets her eyes again, trying not to shift his gaze to the red corset she wears, her beautiful breasts just waiting to be touched. "Yes, Domina. I'm wearing what you sent."

"And did you touch yourself when you put it in, baby boy?"

Aidan drops his gaze. "I did, yes."

"Yes, what? Look at me," she demands.

Aidan looks up again. "Yes, Domina. I touched myself."

"What did I tell you, baby?"

"You told me no touching, Domina."

Bella takes the toe of her boot and traces it over Aiden's erection. "You were very naughty, weren't you? I'm not happy about that." She pushes her boot firmly into his crotch and he whimpers. Bella walks over to the table and retrieves the scarf. She folds it and places it over Aidan's eyes, tying it behind his head. "Color?"

"Green," he replies.

"Now stand up. On the bed, all fours, baby boy," Bella commands and he complies. "Now what should I do to a bad boy who doesn't listen to me?"

"Punish me, Domina," Aidan whimpers.

"Hmmm, I'm not sure. It seems like you really want to be punished," Bella teases. Before she finishes her sentence, she places a firm smack on Aidan's muscular ass, rubbing over it gently afterward. She places two more smacks on the other buttock in quick succession, watching the skin redden. Aidan groans. She follows up with three more hits, caressing the reddened area afterward.

"Please, Domina, harder!" Aidan cries out.

"No. No paddle today. You will take what I give you. Color?"

"Green, green, please!" He begs.

Bella delivers three final spanks and withdraws her hand. Aidan turns his head searching for her although his eyes are covered. She lightly traces her fingers down his back for reassurance, dragging them closer to the plug she has instructed him to wear. She grasps the end of it, pulling it out a bit before pushing it back in. She repeats the action, and Aidan brings his hand up to grab his erection. Bella quickly releases the plug and pushes his hand away. "No touching. You know the rules."

"Please, Domina, touch me, please!" he begs.

"Now, now baby. So desperate. We've only just gotten started. I can't have you coming already," Bella scolds. She walks to the table, picks up her phone, and selects an app. When she pushes a button, the plug begins to vibrate. She watches Aidan squirm from the stimulation. She waits for a few seconds before increasing the intensity. Aiden slumps to the bed, seeking friction for his aching cock. "On your back," Bella commands, and he complies, his glorious dick fully hard and straining toward his chest. She checks in again, and Aidan tells Bella that his color is still green.

She picks up a large feather and traces it down his chest, circling his nipples and tickling down to his toned abs. Aidan's breath hitches in anticipation of some stimulation to his neglected cock. Instead of using the feather, Bella traces her tongue over the head, and down the length of his penis. She briefly takes the head into her mouth, sucking and licking.

"Ahhhhh, I'm going to come!" Aidan cries out, and Bella places a firm pinch on his thigh.

"You will not come until I say you can," she says sternly. Bella reaches to the table, grabbing an item, and returns her attention to Aidan. She slips the cock ring onto his erection, sliding it to the base.

"No, no, please!"

Bella places a few kisses on his chest and stomach. "You can do it, baby, I know you can. You're such a good boy for me, aren't you?

"Yes, I'm good. I'm a good boy for you." Aidan is panting. Bella takes in the sight of him and turns off the vibration to the plug. She pulls at it a bit, twisting it around until he moans as his prostate is stimulated. His cock twitches but he's unable to come with the ring in place.

"How are you baby, still okay?"

"Green, I'm green, just..." he says between deep breaths.

Bella reaches for the candle, sitting back on the bed next to Aidan. She strokes his sweaty skin and places gentle kisses on his cheeks.

He reaches for her, and she kisses his hand, before gently placing it back at his side. "Just a little longer, baby. You're doing so well." Bella lifts the candle above Aidan's chest, making sure to hold it high enough not to burn him. She gently tips the candle.

As the wax hits his chest, Aidan cries out and his erection twitches again. Bella drips more soy wax on his nipples and moves it over his torso, dripping in an erratic pattern so that he can't anticipate where the wax will land. She travels to his inner thighs, and he opens them wider, groaning at the sting of the hot wax on his skin, feeling both pain and pleasure intertwined.

Taking her time, Bella finally drips the wax above and around the base of his cock onto the shaved skin there. Aidan is shaking, and Bella sets the candle to the side. She straddles him, reaching up to remove the blindfold. Bella runs her fingers through his long hair as he blinks, looking at her as his eyes adjust to the candlelight. "You can touch me now, baby," she tells him. "You're such a good boy."

Aidan whimpers as he touches the soft skin of Bella's shoulders with shaky hands. "Please, can I come? Let me come."

"Just a few more minutes. Don't touch yourself." Bella grabs a condom and her phone back off the table. She takes the cock ring off and rolls the condom onto Aidan. She positions herself over his erection, and he tries to push up into her. "No," Bella tells him.

"Wait." Aidan shutters as she turns on the plug again.

Bella grasps his erection and places it inside herself, moaning at the feeling after so much build-up. Aidan touches her breasts and pinches her nipples, lifting himself to nibble at her neck.

"Wait for me," she says, and Aidan nods, trying his hardest not to come yet. Bella holds him tight, using her thighs to control her movements, and bounces to reach her climax. Before long, she reaches behind herself, grasping the base of the plug, pushing it firmly against Aidan's prostate. "Come with me," she pants.

Aidan shouts out as he pushes his hips up to meet Bella, finally able to reach his release. His climax is intense, as it always is with Bella, and he fills the condom as they ride out their orgasms together. Bella reaches around and gently pulls out the plug and lays her head on his chest.

"So good for me, baby. Such a good boy." She places gentle kisses on his neck and cheeks as they lie there.

"Thank you," Aidan replies, kissing her forehead.

"Just tell me when you're ready." They stay in that position for a while until Aidan nods, indicating that he's ready for after-care.

Bella gently lifts off him, pulling off the condom to dispose of. She covers him gently with the top sheet, grabbing the toy to clean, and heads to the bathroom. Bella fills the tub with warm water, adding some jasmine bath oil. When the bath is ready, she returns to Aidan and gently leads him to the bathroom.

"Sit here for just a minute," she instructs him to sit next to the tub.

She gently scrapes the wax from his skin using her fingernail and checks for redness on his skin. She takes Aidan's hand and helps him step into the warm water. She strips down and joins him in the tub, sitting behind him to hold him close. Reaching for a cold water bottle she tells him to drink and grabs a bottle for herself. Bella takes her time washing Aidan and feeding him the food she prepared earlier.

"How are you feeling?" she asks.

"Amazing. Sleepy. I missed seeing you."

"I know, baby. We're both busy, though. You'll get sick of me if we see each other too often!" Bella teases.

"Never, Bella, you know that."

"Well, we'll find our time to play. But you're a young man. You need to find a nice girl your age."

"I know, I'm dating a bit. But I don't want to give *this* up. Give *you* up." Aidan reaches behind him, pulling Bella close for a tender kiss.

"Well, you'll know when you find someone. We can have *this* until that happens. The bath is getting cold. Let's get some cream on that gorgeous ass of yours, then I'll clean up the bed and tuck you in. I'll lay with you a bit until I have to leave. You can stay and sleep."

"Hmmm, I'd love to. Jayce will be pissed if he sees me, though. You know he gives me the cold shoulder when we work together," Aidan replies.

Bella laughs as she drains the tub. "Well, he has no say about whom I spend my time with. Stay the night if you want to. He won't bother us." She wraps Aidan up in a soft, fluffy towel and presses a kiss to his cheek.

"Okay. Thank you, Bella. I missed you," he says.

"I missed you too, baby." Bella pulls him into a tight hug.

Chapter 32

Noah looks up from his book and smiles fondly at his new wife bustling around the large, brand new dining table. "Do you need any help, sweetie?"

She fluffs up one of the red and gold cotton napkins and adjusts the silver cutlery that she has researched about, and where it should be placed. "I just want it to be perfect."

Noah makes his way over to Victoria and slips an arm softly around her waist. "It already is." He turns her to face him. "Besides, we've entertained them before, and you've never been this stressed before."

She brushes a few strands of hair away from her brow and takes a big deep breath to try and relax. "I know, I know." She puffs her cheeks out. "But this is the first time since we got married. I want it to be memorable."

He gives her a slow, reassuring kiss on the lips and feels her shoulders ease their tension. "Relax. It will be just fine."

Looking down at her apron covered in splashes from cooking the sauces and realizing that her hair is still in a messy bun, she gasps. She has spent so much time preparing the food and the table that she has forgotten about her own presentation. Rushing off, Noah can't help but chuckle at her panicking. As if his brother and cousins would be so fussy anyway.

Pausing to look out of the window, he gazes across the city skyline that is dimming as the sun is setting behind the buildings. Letting out a contented sigh, he thanks his lucky stars for giving him such a perfect wife and an amazing family. Overseeing Blackwood now just makes life even better, and he couldn't be happier.

The buzzer from the intercom echoing around the room pulls him from his thoughts. He goes to answer it, but Victoria practically runs out, pinning the last of her clips into her newly done hair and sliding on her stocking feet. She answers it and then brushes herself down.

"How do I look?" she says to her husband.

"Absolutely beautiful," he answers. And he means it too. She looks radiant as usual.

The family all start to pile in through the door and Victoria goes instantly into fuss mode. She starts taking jackets and offering drinks out. Luca hands his over to her already full arm, leaving her chatting to Jaxon and Heidi, and goes to speak to his cousin.

"Why is Victoria so jittery?" he says to Noah. "I'm not used to her being like this."

"She's just nervous, I think. She wants to hold more dinner parties now that we're married. But she wants to make an impression."

Luca looks in awe at the neatly laid out table. "Well, she has certainly done that."

Everybody settles down on chairs, and Victoria hands out some glasses. "No Bella?" she asks, scanning around the group and spotting one of the empty chairs. "I know that Anna will be here soon."

Almost immediately, the buzzer sounds again. Victoria answers it and Anna bustles in with Dasom in one arm and bags in the other. Luca jumps up to take his daughter from her, and Jasper takes the bags from her arm.

"Wow!" Anna says, looking at everyone. "How did you manage to fit this many people around the table?"

Victoria laughs and pours her a glass of wine. Luca gives Dasom cuddles and stands as she yawns. He reaches for the bags.

"I think someone is tired," he says, flinging the strap over his shoulder.

"I set up the crib in the spare bedroom, Luca." Victoria points in that direction forgetting that he knows the layout of the apartment.

He nods politely at her before going to settle Dasom off to sleep. The buzzer of the intercom echoes for the third time and Victoria opens the door. Bella glides in loudly, saying her hellos to everyone in the room.

Sitting at the table, she immediately reaches for a glass of wine. "Sorry that I am late. I was, you know..." She winks at everyone looking at her. "Busy."

Jayce makes a groaning sound, burying his head in his hand, while Harrison scoffs. "Mum, seriously. Do you have to?"

She laughs loudly and takes another gulp of her drink, slinging her other arm over the back of the chair. "Stop it, you two. I'm allowed to have fun as well."

Jayce shakes his head, smirking in pretend disgust. He secretly loves how open and honest his mother is over such matters, it's just a shame that it's with someone that he isn't too fond of. Victoria eyes the bottle almost empty and knows that Bella will at least need another.

Grabbing it, she turns to make her way to the kitchen. Anna gets up too. "I'll come with you."

Once in the kitchen, Victoria checks the food in the oven and stirs the sauce that is simmering on the stove. Anna skulks around behind her.

"Um, Sis," she says quietly. "Can I talk to you?"

Victoria faces her sister with a concerned expression. "Sure, are you okay?" Anna smiles to reassure her. "Yes, yes, I'm fine. It's Misun."

Rolling her eyes, Victoria sighs and leans on the marble counter. "What has she done now?"

"Well," Anna explains. "She has been drinking. Like a lot. So, I have been looking after Dasom a lot more. Every day she's been sick."

"Dasom has?" Victoria is confused.

Anna shakes her head. "No, Misun."

"I'm not surprised if she's drinking that much," Victoria scoffs. "She is a disgrace."

Taking a step closer to her sister, Anna shakes her head again. "No, you don't understand. I found a test in the bathroom trash bin. Misun is pregnant again."

"What the fuck?" Victoria yelps a little too loudly.

"What did you just say?" A voice behind them makes them spin around. Heidi is standing in the doorway, her face pale.

"I am so sorry," Anna says, rushing over. "I was going to get Victoria to speak to you."

Heidi flees from the room and the other girls follow. Luca is just making his way back into the dining area with the baby monitor in his hand. She races over to Harrison, her face contorted in anger.

"You fucking liar!" she spits in his face. "You lied to me."

Harrison sits up in his chair, his eyes wide. "What's the matter? What have I done?"

Heidi is crying now, big tears streaming down her cheeks. Bella, who is beside her, stands and pulls her arm gently to look at her. "Sweetie, what is it? What has he done?"

Verging on hysterics, Heidi can't even bring herself to say the words, and Bella draws her in for a hug. Victoria speaks for her. She approaches Harrison. "Misun is pregnant again."

"You have got to be fucking kidding me," Luca says. "Harrison, you said you didn't sleep with her."

He holds up his hands in protest. "I didn't. I couldn't. I was too drunk."

Heidi sees red and flies at him, banging her fists at his arms as he protects himself. "YOU LIAR!" She shouts as Taylor and Luca pull her away from him and Taylor holds her by the waist while she sobs. "I don't believe this," she repeats into Taylor's shoulder, drenching his shirt with tears.

Bella addresses her son. "Harri? Are you being completely honest about all of this?"

"I am!" he insists. "We didn't do anything like that."

Luca pulls his phone from his pocket. "I'm going to get her over here." He scrolls through his phone until he finds her number. "We need to figure this out."

He calls her, informing Misun that he needs to speak to her and that he's sending Tony to pick her up. She agrees, and the group mulls around while they wait. The air in the room is filled with tension and distress. Victoria abandons the food, figuring that no one has an appetite anymore anyway. Heidi continues to cry, completely convinced that her boyfriend is lying, while Anna comforts her. Harrison tries his best to get her to talk to him, practically begging her to believe him.

Bella wraps her arm around Victoria's shoulder. "I'm, sorry, darling. Your evening has been ruined."

"By that bitch. As usual, she ruins everything," Victoria says, sadly. "But I'm really not surprised."

A long forty minutes pass before Luca gets a text from Tony to say that they've arrived. The door buzzes for the last time of the evening. Noah puffs his cheeks out and answers it. The group glances awkwardly around at each other.

"Ohhhh, look at this. A Blackwood family gathering." Misun enters the room as if she's a celebrity. "I'm glad that you invited me to join in the fun."

Luca grabs her arm a little too aggressively, fed up with her antics, and pulls her towards everyone else.

"Easy, Luca," she says with a smile on her face. "It's been a while since we had a little rough play."

"Misun!" Bella has had enough of the games. "Just shut up for once, and act like a grown-up."

"Jeez." Misun flicks her hair back off her shoulder. "Okay, what is this all about?" She sits on one of the vacant chairs, crosses her legs, and reaches for a glass of wine.

Bella snatches it from her, much to Misun's surprise. "Is it true?"

"Is what true?" she asks, innocently.

"That you are pregnant again?" Luca says.

Misun flashes Anna a nasty look knowing that she's the one who said something. There is no one else who could possibly know.

"Yeah," she shrugs. "And?"

"Seriously, Misun. What is your problem?" Luca addresses his ex with disgust. "What game are you playing?"

Heidi starts to cry again upon hearing the words come from Misun herself. Everyone else is looking at Misun not really knowing what to say.

She sinks back onto the chair and crosses her arms across her chest. "I'm not playing any games." Tilting her head at Luca, she smiles. "I had a little fun, and obviously it didn't go as planned."

Luca rubs his eyes in frustration and starts to pace around the room. "This is insane, Misun. Day isn't even six months old yet. And you are drinking."

"Oh, like you give a shit about me, Luca," she spits sharply. "You've not given a damn about me in a long time. Why do you care about it anyway?"

Luca crouches beside her chair and takes a deep breath. "Misun, things may have changed, but you are still the mother of my daughter. I don't want to see you destroy yourself."

"Please," she smirks, sitting so that her nose almost touches his. "As if you're bothered. You just want our baby." She points towards Jaxon. "With him."

Luca sits back on his heels and glances towards Bella. He knows that someone has to get through to her and is hoping that his aunt will help him. She turns her chair towards Misun.

"Listen, sweetie," she says to her. "We want to help you. Let us do that."

Misun grins at the elegant lady in front of her, jealous of the fact that she'll never be as rich and successful as her. "Well, you will have to," she shrugs, reaching for the wine glass again. Bella pulls it from her and gives her a confused look. "Seeing as the father is your son. This baby is another Blackwood."

Bella spins towards Harrison, and Heidi let's out a distressed wail. Anna and Victoria comfort her. Harrison's jaw drops and his eyes widen in disbelief.

"But, but..." he says to Heidi, "It didn't happen, Heidi. She's lying."

Heidi jumps from her chair and runs to grab her coat. Misun laughs out loud at the dramatics unfolding in front of her. "Wait!" She shouts at Heidi, making everyone stop again. "Stop being so dramatic. He's right. It didn't happen. He was useless in that department."

Harrison faces Heidi who is wiping her tears on her sleeve. "See, I told you."

"Then why are you lying about it?" Heidi shrieks at her.

"I'm not," Misun shrugs again. "I'm having a

baby with Bella's son. That part is true."

"But, I don't underst..." Luca stops mid-sentence and tries to catch his breath as the penny drops. He slowly maneuvers himself to look in the direction of someone else who has been sitting very quietly on the other side of the room. "Jayce?"

Dropping his shoulders, Jayce stares at the floor and nods. "Yeah, it's me."

"Fuck," Noah and Jasper say in unison. Taylor and Jax make cringe faces at one another.

"Are you serious?" Bella's voice booms around the room as she approaches her eldest son. "Jayce, please tell me that this is a joke."

"I'm sorry, Mum." He bows his head even further. "I knew that she suspected that she was pregnant, but I didn't know that she actually is."

Bella grabs her head and runs her hands through her hair. "I cannot believe that you have been so irresponsible, Jayce." She lets out a groan. "Have I not taught you to be safe?"

He can see that his mother is getting ever increasingly angry. "Look, Mum, I'm sorry. It wasn't supposed to happen."

Luca laughs in disbelief. "Please somebody wake me up from this nightmare."

The room is silent. Everyone is frozen in place, no one knows what to say. Harrison and Heidi stay awkwardly by the door. Noah and Victoria stare at the mess that their dinner party has become, ending in such a dramatic twist. Jasper, Jaxon, and Taylor shuffle awkwardly in their seats not knowing what to do. Bella and Luca are trying to process the unexpected information that they have just received.

Jayce is the first to make a move, and stands, making his way towards Misun. "I think that we should go and talk and let everybody calm down."

"You are not leaving this room until we have discussed this." Bella tries to speak with authority, but the words choke up in her throat.

Jayce races over to the most important woman in his life, drawing her into his arms. He isn't used to witnessing his mother in such a vulnerable state. She is always the strong one who holds things together.

"Mum, I'm so sorry that this has happened. I really am. But for now, I think that everyone needs a little time to process things. I'm going away for work, remember. Let's just take some space for reflection."

Bella bows her head in defeat. She has no more words to say right now or any solution to the mess that the family is in, yet again, due to this woman. He gives her a gentle kiss on her cheek. Releasing her from his arms, he makes his way over to a smug-looking Misun and takes her by the hand.

Leading her to the door, he stops in front of Heidi and Harrison. "I'm sorry," he whispers to his brother. Opening the door, he steps towards it before facing Bella and Luca. "I'm sorry."

Chapter 33

Jayce closes his eyes and leans his head back against the leather of his first-class seat.

He boarded the plane early, anxious to get the fuck out of New York and the nightmare he's created. Thank God the magazine shoot is in Chicago. Jayce and a few models from Blackwood were asked to participate, as well as some from other agencies around the country. Staff and stylists from the publication are handling everything, so thankfully his family and Blackwood staff are staying in New York. He needs this escape. Badly.

The music through his headphones plays softly, and Jayce can hear shuffling as his seatmate settles in. Jayce opens his eyes, glancing over to the right. *Just fucking perfect*. The man meets Jayce's eyes, nodding before buckling his seatbelt and busying himself with his phone. Jayce sighs deeply before he decides to address the blonde sitting next to him.

"Hey Aidan, I didn't know that you were coming to Chicago."

"Hi, Jayce. Yeah, there were some last-minute changes and Treeva and I were added to the shoot. I'm surprised Bella didn't warn you." Aidan laughs uncomfortably.

Jayce's face gets warm when he remembers his last encounter with his mother. They haven't spoken since. "No, she didn't tell me."

Aidan nods and quickly turns his attention back to his phone. As the plane ascends, leaving New York far below him, Jayce thinks about all the times he's voiced his disapproval to Bella about who she takes to bed. A sudden realization hits him. What gave him the right to criticize his mother? She has never hurt anyone with her choices. He wishes he could say the same.

Jayce turns to the handsome man next to him. "Aidan, I think I owe you an apology."

Aidan looks at Jayce with a puzzled expression. "What?"

"You've been seeing my mother for a while now, and I've treated you like shit." Jayce rubs his temples and continues. "I've made no effort to get to know you, and I've made it clear that I disapprove of the two of you."

Aidan places his hand on Jayce's shoulder. "I understand. It must be difficult for you. I'm only a couple of years older than you."

"No, it's really not okay. You're a grown man. I have no right to judge you or my mother."

"Thank you for saying that, Jayce. It means a lot. But really, there's nothing serious between us. I've hardly seen her these last several months." Jayce can see a pained expression on Aidan's face.

"Really? I thought you got together almost every week?" Jayce realizes that he really has no idea about Bella's personal life. Other than shaming her when he sees her with a lover, he's never actually asked her about it.

"I've really missed her," Aidan says, rubbing his hand on his knee while looking at his lap. He meets Jayce's eyes again. "I'm sorry Jayce. I shouldn't talk about this with you. I just care about her so much, but she wants no part of a relationship with me."

Jayce raises an eyebrow. "And you want one with her?"

Aidan closes his eyes for a moment before he continues. "I do. We were spending a lot of time together, other than, you know, just physically. We made a real emotional connection, but then she pulled away."

Jayce is surprised to hear Aidan's confession. He always just assumed that his mother was happy without a relationship. Thinking back, he can never remember her having anyone serious in her life. She never spoke about ever being in love, and he never asked.

Aidan speaks again. "I wanted to have a relationship with Bella, to be exclusive. I know she has feelings for me, Jayce. But as soon as I made it clear what I wanted, she told me she wasn't interested in pursuing anything serious."

"Do you know why? Is it the age difference? Twenty years is a lot," Jayce asks.

"That's what she said." Jayce's stomach sinks when he sees the sadness in Aidan's eyes as he speaks. "She said she wanted me to find a nice girl to have a family with. But it doesn't matter to me, Jayce. I know it's a cliché, the age is just a number thing, but for me it's true. You can't help who you fall in love with. Honestly, I think she's just afraid."

Jayce nods. "I'm sorry Aidan. I hope things work out; I really do. I want my Mother to be happy."

Aidan gives Jayce a sad smile and squeezes his arm before reclining in his seat and closing his eyes. Jayce puts his headphones back on and looks out at the clouds. *I wonder if Mum is lonely, if she's holding back from loving. Aidan's right, you can't help who you fall in love with.*

Jayce's thoughts return to his own fucked up situation, and he shakes his head. He and Misun have barely spoken since the showdown at Noah's place. She's avoiding the entire situation, and honestly, so is he.

He's trying to wrap his head around the fact that she's pregnant again. Pregnant with his child. *Fuck.* How did this happen? He thought that he'd been careful, always using condoms.

However, for the last few months, Misun's drinking had escalated, and Jayce usually joined her when they were together.

Being sober would mean facing his obsession with being near Misun. He's spent countless hours rationalizing the reasons to stay away from her, but his resolve fades whenever he sees her name appear on his phone screen.

I don't love Misun, there's no love between us. We're using each other in some messed up co-dependent nightmare. What am I going to do? I'm not ready to be a father, not with Misun. What the fuck have I done?

Jayce closes his eyes trying to clear his troubled mind during the short flight. He knows he only has a few short days before he needs to face reality, to talk to Misun and his family, to Luca and his mum. Until then, he's going to push it away.

I'll deal with this when I get home. I have no choice.

Chapter 34

Luca paces the floor of his office giving his watch yet another glance, even though he only looked a minute or so ago. "Where is he?"

Jaxon reaches over from where he sits on the desk and strokes his boyfriend's arm. "He will be here. I'm sure he will"

"But, he should have been back from his trip hours ago, Jax, and this shit all needs to be cleared up." He slumps into his leather chair. "He can't keep running away from this."

Leaving him in his thoughts, Jaxon gives Luca's arm a reassuring squeeze. Luca's phone pings with a message, and he pulls it out of his pocket to read.

"Anything?" Jaxon asks, hopefully.

Luca sighs and shakes his head. "No. Noah hasn't seen him either."

Jax slides off the desk and crouches next to his man, clutching his fingers. "Look, I know that this is eating you up and that you need answers, but Jayce can't stay away forever. I'm sure you will get to have it out with him soon."

Luca taps his foot in frustration. Even though he needs to speak to his cousin, he'd been willing to let him go on the work trip without any trouble. Now, he needs to get this inevitable confrontation over with. He has to find out the truth.

Another notification sound fills the air and Luca looks at Jaxon hopefully as he checks it. Jax looks at his phone and sighs. "It's Heidi. Harrison hasn't seen his brother either."

Luca runs his fingers through his hair and closes his eyes, breathing deeply as he tries to relax. It's bad enough that his cousin is having a baby with his ex-girlfriend without being left in the dark.

Standing up, Luca grabs his jacket from the back of the chair. Jax slowly rises and follows, as Luca quickly exits the office. Sacha attempts to speak to him, but he ignores her and Jaxon nods an apology in her direction.

"Where are we going?" he asks Luca, scuttling behind him to keep up with his quickening pace.

"I have an idea," Luca says.

**

Arriving at the apartment door, Luca rubs his hands together in front of his chest trying to prepare himself for what he might find.

"You really think that he is here?" Jaxon says.

"He has to be, Jax." He knocks on the wooden door. "He isn't at home or at work. No one has seen him, and he won't return our calls. He has to be here."

After a pause, the door opens and Misun steps out. She leans against the door frame and folds her arms.

"Luca," she smirks. "What are you doing here?"

"Mi, come on. Is he here?"

She glances between the two men. "Possibly."

Luca barges past her, fed up with the games. He finds Jayce sitting in the living room looking sheepishly at him. His designer luggage is by the couch, making it obvious that he'd come straight to Misun's after returning to New York.

He stands to face his cousin and holds his hands up. "Look, Luca..."

"Seriously, Jayce? You came here first?"

Jayce can see the pain and hurt etched on Luca's face, and the guilt twists his stomach into knots. "I'm sorry. I was scared."

"Scared?" Luca can feel his anger rising and Jaxon grabs his hand. "Of what?"

"Of you, of this," Jayce says with desperation as he reaches out to his cousin. "This is so fucked up. I'm fucked up and I don't know what to do."

Luca looks away from him. "I can't even look at you right now, Jayce. At least with Harrison we talked it out the next day and he dealt with his own issues with Heidi. What's your excuse? You weren't even drunk that night."

Misun scoffs and joins in. "Oh please, Luca. Even I have *some* morals. Two men in one night? Nah."

Taking a step back, Luca tilts his head in confusion. "So, you didn't sleep with Jayce on the night of Noah and Victoria's wedding? Well, when was it then?"

Misun smirks again. "Which time?"

Jaxon's hand flies to his mouth to try and hide the shocked gasp escaping his lips. Luca's jaw drops open wide and he places his hands on his cheeks to let those words sink in a little.

"Luca, I'm sorry. I can explain." Jayce pleads. "I was stupid."

"Oh, thanks," Misun says. "What? Every time?"

Jayce glares at her. "Misun..."

"What?" she says, shrugging. "He may as well know."

Jaxon holds on to Luca's arm tighter, seeing his face turning red. "Right, please tell me that you two..." he says, pointing between them, "haven't been having an affair for longer?"

Jayce stutters, struggling to get the answers out.

"Luca..." Misun tries to speak.

"Shut up, Misun. I wasn't asking *you*." Luca shuts her down instantly. He needs to hear this from his cousin. "Jayce?"

Jayce knows that he has to come clean, and his shoulders slump. "Yes. We've been seeing each other for a while."

Jaxon rubs his eyes with his fingers. Luca takes a step closer to Jayce and Jaxon pulls his arm, trying to hold him back. Misun has her hand on her hip and she flips her hair over her shoulder. The smug grin on her face makes it obvious that she's loving every second of the unfolding drama,

"How long?" Luca asks the question that Jayce has been dreading. "How long, Jayce? Since before the wedding, right?" Luca's voice is shaking as he tries to hold his anger back.

Jayce nods. "Yes, before then."

Luca frees himself from Jax's grasp, standing two feet away from the man that is not only his cousin, but his friend too. "Before Dasom was born?" He is desperately trying to get a timeline of the relationship.

Jayce bows his head again, and Misun dramatically throws her hands in the air and rolls her eyes. "Yes, Luca. Before Day. Now be quiet, she's asleep." She motions in the direction of the bedrooms.

"Tell me when!" Luca is angry now as the betrayal is starting to sink in. "Surely not when I was with her. My own father was bad enough, and I hated him for it. But you... You wouldn't do that to me, right?"

Misun laughs and leans right into Luca's face. "Yes, Luca," she hisses through gritted teeth, pleased to spill the venomous truth. "When I was with you. In fact, nearly the whole time that we were together."

"I'm sorry," Jayce says quietly, the words sticking in his dry throat.

Luca loses control. He can't handle this devious behavior from yet another member of his family. He flies at Jayce, knocking Misun forcefully to the floor in the process, and slams Jayce up against the wall, grabbing his collar.

"You bastard!" he screams at him in a high-pitched growl. "How could you?"

"I'm sorry," Jayce repeats, as Dasom's cries start to echo in the room after hearing all of the commotion.

Misun is gasping on the floor, trying to regain her breath after having the wind knocked out of her. Jaxon helps her to her feet, and then races to try and pull Luca off of Jayce.

"Why would you do this to me?" Luca snarls, pushing his body in harder, desperately trying to resist the urge to lash out at him. "What did I ever do to hurt you?"

"Nothing," Jayce says softly, trying to remain calm. "You didn't do anything. It was about me and all of my shit,"

"You? What are you talking about?" Jaxon pulls him back a few steps.

Jayce holds his hand up in defeat. "Luca, I need to tell..."

A piercing scream fills the apartment, and the men turn to look at Misun, her face white. Together, they notice the red liquid running down her legs. "Jayce, help, I'm bleeding."

**

The atmosphere in the emergency waiting room is cold and tense. Jayce and Luca sit side by side, the vending machine coffees going cold in their hands.

Luca clears his throat. "Jayce, I am so, so, sorry. You know that I never meant this."

Jayce's eyes pool with tears, and he rips at the cardboard of the cup. "I was just getting used to the idea of being a father."

"It's all my fault," Luca says with sadness, the guilt aching in his heart. "If I hadn't gone at you, she wouldn't have fallen and lost the baby." His voice falters saying the last words.

A tear falls down Jayce's cheek. "Will Dasom be okay with Jaxon?" He changes the subject.

Luca nods his head, "She's fine," he says. "She loves Jaxon."

"He's a good father figure to her," Jayce sniffs. "You know that I never meant to hurt you, Luca."

Sighing, Luca puts a hand on Jayce's knee. "We don't need to talk about this now. You've just had bad news. This can wait."

The silence returns between them. Luca takes a sip of his drink before recoiling at the fact that it's cool now. Wincing, he throws it into the trash. Observing Jayce sitting with his head bowed, swirling his coffee cup, Luca's heart sinks even lower. He knows that he has caused this and wonders if his cousin will ever forgive him.

A nurse appears in the doorway and Jayce stands to address her. "Misun is comfortable. She will be okay," she says with empathy. "She's sleeping right now, so it's probably best to leave her be. I should let you know that she had a large quantity of alcohol in her system. Has she been drinking throughout the pregnancy?"

Jayce nods solemnly.

The nurse continues in a comforting voice. "That may have contributed to the miscarriage, or it could have been a combination of factors. The baby may just not have been viable. Misun may feel a lot of guilt from this loss, so she's going to need your support." The nurse hands Jayce a packet of information. "There is some information here on counseling options and support groups she may need. We have contacted her next of kin. He will be here soon. I am so sorry for your loss."

Jayce nods a thank you at her and she leaves. Luca turns to him. "Wait. Next of kin?"

Luca is confused. As far as he is aware, Misun has no close relatives, especially close enough to be an emergency contact. He was that role when they were a couple.

Sighing, Jayce sits Luca back onto the plastic chairs. "Yeah. There is something you should know. It's what I've been trying to tell you."

"What is it? I don't understand."

He grabs Luca's hands and maneuvers them to face one another. "Misun has a brother, Luca. She was estranged from him at a young age."

Luca screws his face up in confusion. "A brother? Since when does she have a brother?" He stands up, shoving his hands into his jacket pocket. "And why do you know about this and I don't? I was going to marry this woman. I have a baby with her, for god's sake." He is increasingly agitated at being left in the dark. "I know that I said this could wait, Jayce, but I think that you had better start talking."

Jayce rubs his eyes before running his hands through his hair. "Her family life growing up was shit. You know that. Her brother left home at the first opportunity that he could, and she did the same. They have had contact on and off since, but it's very strained between them. They rarely speak."

"How do you know all of this?" Luca says his mind swirls as he tries to process this new information. "I still don't get that. I know you've been seeing her, but why didn't she talk to me?"

Knowing that he has to come clean, Jayce takes a deep breath. "Because I knew him first." he speaks quietly.

Luca is even more confused now. "What are you saying? You aren't making sense."

Jayce starts to spill his story. "I met a guy. Through work. He was the most beautiful man that I have ever seen, and, well, I fell in love with him. We fell in love with each other."

Luca holds his hands up. He has never seen Jayce with a man before, only women. "Hold on. You... with a guy?"

"Yes," Jayce continues. "We had a secret relationship. I was totally besotted with him. He told me about his family. His sister."

Luca's guard comes down seeing his cousin look so sad. He sits beside him. "Hey, I have no issues with these things. I think Jax and I prove that. So, what happened? Why didn't you say anything?"

"We split. He left. He said that he couldn't be around me or the company for some reason that he wouldn't say. I don't know if it was just excuses. But he walked out on me. It broke my heart."

"You could have come to me and talked," Luca says softly.

Jayce shakes his head. "I couldn't. I was shattered into a thousand pieces. Then you met Misun and I knew who she was. She made a move on me and just looking at her, all I could see was him. The hair. The dimples." He starts to cry, whiney sobs escaping his lips." She was the closest that I could ever get to him again." He looks up to see Luca's bemused expression. "I know. I really do. It's stupid. I was drawn in. Then when I finally came to my senses and realized how stupid it was, she kept threatening to tell you. So I kept going back. She has a way, you know?"

Luca half laughs. "Believe me, I do."

"I never meant to hurt you, Luca. I'm so sorry." His shoulders start to shake as the tears fall. Luca draws him into a tight hug, knowing that Jayce is releasing a lot of emotions that he has kept bottled up inside for a long time.

They stay that way until Jayce has calmed somewhat and they pull apart.

"This is all a bit of a mess," Luca says, rooting around in his pocket for something that he can give to Jayce to wipe his face. He doesn't find anything, so Jayce uses his own sleeve. "Well, Jayce, I've certainly learned a lot today."

"My shit hole of a life!" Jayce half jokes. The men smile at each other. "This is going to be fun explaining to everyone."

"It is," Luca says. "How do you feel about seeing this man again?"

"The same way that I do every time I see him." Jayce shrugs his shoulders.

Luca frowns. "What do you mean?"

"We know him, Luca. All of us. I'm surprised no one else has noticed it."

A man enters the room and it takes a moment for Luca to piece things together. He looks at Jayce who nods, indicating that this is Misun's brother. Luca has no words.

Jayce stands to acknowledge him. "Hi, Korian."

Chapter 35

Jayce sits quietly as Luca and Korian talk. He feels an uncomfortable mix of emotions. The love of his life is here, in front of him. The person that he had once pictured being with forever, now seems like a stranger to him. That combined with mourning the loss of his baby with Korian's sister, it is almost too much for him to take. Luca tells him that they are going in to speak to Misun, and Jayce tells them that he will follow them soon. He needs a moment with his thoughts.

They leave and Jayce buries his head in his hands, letting out a pained groan. This is not how his life is supposed to be. He has everything he's ever wanted; an amazing family, perfect job, fame and fortune. What he doesn't have is Korian. And it's killing him inside.

He thinks back to meeting Korian all those years ago. It was purely by chance. Blackwood had been collaborating with other companies for a promotional photoshoot in New York. Jayce, being the lead model for the company, was the obvious choice to take part in it. He had seen Korian in photos before considering he was the main model for another company but seeing him in the flesh had floored him. It was literally the most breathtaking moment of his life.

Remembering the moment that he laid eyes on Korian, Jayce sighs. He hadn't been able to take his eyes off him as he ran his hands through his thick, dark hair while getting ready. He wore simple jeans and a crisp white shirt, unbuttoned to reveal his toned chest. They had been placed next to each other for the shoot, and Jayce could pick up Korian's scent. He breathed it in deeply trying not to be too obvious. It was intoxicating. The session went well, and many of the models went for drinks together afterwards. Korian was the only reason that Jayce tagged along when asked. He had originally planned to go home rather than make small talk with strangers, but something had enticed him to agree.

They sat opposite each other and Jayce had hardly been able to take his eyes off him. It had been quite obvious and when Korian met his gaze across the table and smiled, Jayce's heart had skipped a beat, not to mention the other feeling going on inside his boxers.

Jayce gets up and pours himself water from the cooler next to the vending machine, trying to get the images from the past out of his head. He knows that Luca and Korian are waiting for him to go and see Misun, but he can't stop the memories from flooding his mind. Taking a drink, he sits back on the uncomfortable plastic chair and remembers the moment that his life had changed.

After leaving the bar after a few drinks, Jayce was walking home, his hands stuffed into his pockets, when he heard footsteps behind him. Turning in case he was about to get mugged; he came face to face with Korian who had been looking for him. Staring at each other for a moment, Jayce had fallen into his deep brown, almond eyes. When Korian smiled, alluring dimples appeared on his beautiful cheeks. Jayce had never believed in such things as love at first sight until that moment. He was instantly besotted. Korian had told him that something had urged him to follow Jayce when he left.

They had spent their time getting to know each other slowly. Korian had insisted that their relationship remain a secret. He made excuses, saying that he would be in so much shit if it came out. Jayce had been so captivated by him that he did as asked. He was also happy to not have the family giving him the third degree about being with a man, which is quite ironic, considering that Luca and Jasper now have boyfriends.

Jayce's phone pings, snapping him back to reality. It's a message from Luca telling him to hurry up, but he's so wrapped up in his memories that he needs a little longer to reminisce.

He recalls the moment that they had first kissed. They had been enjoying an indoor picnic at Korian's. He had laid out a spread of food in front of the fire in his apartment, and the two men had spent the evening laughing, talking, and eating together. They had both opened up about their lives; Korian had been through more than he had. He had remained quite closed off when talking about it, giving little detail, but from what Jayce did hear, it had been a very unpleasant childhood. That's how Jayce had found out about Misun, having no idea about the tangled web that he would get caught up in when it came to these siblings.

The night had passed amazingly, and they had both ended up lying next to each other on the Persian rug in front of the burning logs. Jayce can still remember Korian's creamy skin flickering orange as the flames cast shadows around the dim room. His heart had been beating so fast with anticipation. He wanted things to be perfect, and so far, they had been.

Jayce screws his eyes up at the next memories. The moment that their lips had touched for the very first time. The feel of Korian's soft lips against his own as he allowed the most beautiful man that he had ever seen to tease his tongue over his, before trailing kisses along his jawline and onto his neck. Korian had been so confident as he unfastened Jayce's jeans and grasped hold of his cock.

Jayce's eyes spring open as his dick throbs in his pants and he ferociously shakes his head. He is annoyed with himself. This is highly inappropriate. He's in a hospital and down the corridor is the woman who has just lost his child. He is desperately trying to ignore the burning in his groin as he imagines again the feeling of Korian's fingers on his skin.

Jayce's emotions are running so high. A mixture of sorrow and pain over what has happened, combined with confusion and desire at seeing Korian again. Tears stream down his face as he races to the closet bathroom, his phone sounding for a second time. Locking the stall door, he rolls out some tissue around his hand and dabs his face, but the sobs are escaping him quicker than he can wipe them away.

His mind goes back to that night again. He can't shake it. The most perfect time of his life. Wishing that he was back there with Korian and that the hurt had all gone away. Without even realizing it, his hand slips into his boxers as he tries to mimic Korian's actions from that night, picturing the look on his face as he stroked him. He runs his fingers up and down the shaft, his skin tingling under his fingers, pre-come leaking out of the end. He doesn't even care at this point if somebody else comes into the bathroom.

Jayce pulls at his cock, needing some emotional release to rid himself of the consuming tension that is taking over him. He pumps faster and harder, desperate for it to be over until he wails out as he comes into the tissue, the pressure giving him a short spell of relief, streams of tears rolling down his face at his own disgust.

He takes some deep and long breaths to calm himself, and throws the wads of paper into the toilet as the guilt begins to set in. *What am I doing? What was I thinking?* He leaves the cubicle and washes his hands. Looking up in the mirror, he examines his puffy and red eyes, his cheeks flushed. *No wonder he walked out on you.* He tortures himself further with the memories of that night. The moment that Korian had said that they needed to part ways. Jayce had never believed his feeble excuses about conflicts of interest and his company having a problem with it. He just remembers feeling like he had been stabbed repeatedly in the heart as he watched Korian walk away for the last time, knowing that it was over for good.

Yet more tears start to fall as a disgruntled Luca enters the bathroom looking for him. He sees the devastation surrounding his cousin and pulls him into a huge hug, Jayce sobbing into his shoulder. Luca has never seen him this distraught before.

**

Korian checks into the corridor to make sure that Luca is out of earshot. He goes and sits beside his sister's bed again and tries to take her hand, but she pulls it away.

"Why are you here?" she asks, quietly. Her face looks tired and pale. She smooths down the sheets around her.

"Because I'm your brother," Korian says, touching her shoulder and she flinches.

She rolls her eyes. "Korian, I can manage just fine without my big brother."

He motions to her in her hospital nightgown. "Really? Look at you."

Her eyes pool with sadness at the reminder of what has just happened. She wasn't keen on being a mother again at first but had started to accept the idea.

Korian sighs and reaches for her hand. She allows him to take it this time, her vulnerability showing through the tiny cracks in her hard exterior. "Mi, what are you going to do now?"

She shrugs. "There isn't much that I can do. Go home and look after Dasom."

"How is she?" he asks with a little sadness at never seeing his niece.

Seeing her brother's face falter, she asks him to pass her phone that Jayce has left on the side table. She scrolls through the photos, ignoring the hospital wristband twisting around her wrist. She stops at a picture Luca had previously sent her, and hands the phone to Korian.

He takes it from her and examines it. Smiling, he looks up at his sister. "Misun, she is beautiful. Of course, she is, she's a mixture of you and a Blackwood. I can't believe how much she looks like you when you were a baby."

"You remember me as a baby?" she says with surprise.

"Sure I do. Only vaguely, but this picture could be you."

She takes it back from him and stares at the image of her daughter, a heaviness in her heart. She knows that she isn't doing right by her but can't seem to drag herself out of the destructive hole that she has dug for herself. She has a lot. A nice house, a stunning daughter and an ex-partner willing to do anything in his power to help. Which he does. More than enough. From money, to paying for Anna. Being there whenever she needs, and she knows that she has abused that too.

"How does it feel seeing Jayce again?" She changes the subject.

What do you mean?" Korian acts innocently. "I see him often with work."

"Don't bullshit me Kay," she says.

He falters a little when she uses his childhood nickname. She used to say it when she couldn't pronounce his name properly and it has been a long time since he's heard it. She gives him a knowing look.

"How?" he asks.

"Jayce told me, of course. He tells me most things with a little persuasion. I have to admit, I was a little surprised by it."

Korian bows his head, remembering the man who has touched his soul more than anyone else has. "It still hurts. I don't want to talk about it." He too, changes the topic of conversation. "So, are you going to tell the father that you have lost the baby."

Misun's eyes widen, and she pulls herself to sit up a little, wincing at the aching in her stomach. "Did Luca not tell you?"

Korian shakes his head. "No, why would he?" He gasps. "Wait, is it his again? Fuck, Misun."

"No, no," she says. "It isn't... wasn't his. But still a Blackwood."

"What?" Korian stands up, clasping his hand to his mouth. "Please tell me that you don't mean..."

She bows her head in shame, and slowly nods.

"I don't believe this." Korian's voice is high pitched. "My sister, having a baby with my ex-lover. Oh, this is fucked up, Mi."

"I know," she whispers. "I'm sorry." She genuinely means it too. She never had any intention of hurting her brother. She just got caught up in the game.

"Right," he says, very matter-of-factly. "I can't even begin to process that right now. We need to get you well first."

"No, Kay. You know we can't see each other."

He approaches his sister. "Yes, we can. We don't have to worry. We don't need to be scared."

"Yes, we do!" she shouts, trying to make him understand. "We need to stay away from each other."

"But he's gone now, Mi." Korian protests.

"He," a voice says from the doorway. "You mean my father?"

The siblings turn to Luca standing there. Korian sighs. "Yes, Luca. Your father."

"What about him?" Luca joins Korian at the side of the bed. "What about my dad?"

Korian glances at Misun who shakes her head, then looks at Luca. "There is a lot that you don't know about your father."

**

At Misun's apartment, Korian sits on the edge of Misun's bed stroking her knotted hair as she cries.

"What aren't you telling me, Mi. Why are you making me go? I want to be here for you."

"I can't, Kay. I just can't do it. Having you here is just a reminder of the past. I need to forget." Misun wipes her puffy eyes with her hands before tearing off her hospital bracelet and throwing it to the floor.

"But we can work through it together, Mi. It can be a new start for us. I want to be here for you and my niece. I want us to be a family again. He's dead, Misun." Korian can't understand why his sister is pushing him away.

Misun shakes her head. "No! It's too late now. You have your life in LA. It just won't work! Leave!" Misun is yelling as she weeps and pushes her brother away. "Just go Korian! Please!"

Korian sits quietly for a few moments, holding his sister's hand. She won't even look at him. He shakes his head sadly as tears stain his cheeks. "Okay, Misun. I'll go. But this is your choice, I want you to remember that." Korian stands, brushes his sister's hair off her face, and places a gentle, lingering kiss on her cheek.

Korian walks into the living room and sits across from Jayce, who has his elbows on his knees, and his fingers threaded through his thick raven locks. Jayce lifts his head and looks at the despair on Korian's face.

"I'm leaving. Going back to LA. She doesn't want me here." Korian shakes his head, grabbing his phone to book a flight.

"You're leaving me, *again?*" Jayce says bitterly. He stands and walks to the window, gazing out but seeing nothing. "Why did you leave me, Korian?" he whispers, not quite ready to turn around yet.

Should We?

"I told you Jayce. My company..."

"That's bullshit and you know it!" Jayce spins around to face his old lover. "You never reached out to me again! I had to see you at all those events, Korian. Do you know what that did to me? Pretending that we were nothing to each other?"

"Stop, Jayce. Just stop. You've clearly moved on. With my sister, for fuck sake." Korian strides towards Jayce, gripping his shoulders. "My sister, Jayce. You did this to hurt me."

"To hurt you, Korian? You're the one that hurt *me*. I wasn't with Misun to get back at you." Jayce pulls away. "She appeared in Luca's life and I couldn't fucking believe it! I couldn't stop myself, Korian. I see *you* when I look at her. I needed to be with her because I wanted a part of *you*!"

"What the hell are you saying, Jayce?" That doesn't make any sense." Korian replies with bewilderment.

Jayce turns to face him again." No Korian, it doesn't make sense, but my heart was pulling me to any part of you I could get. I don't love Misun. I love you. I never stopped loving you, Korian. Never."

Korian slowly approaches Jayce, placing his strong hands on Jayce's flushed cheeks. "You think it's been easy for me? I *never* wanted to leave you. I had no choice. I still love you too, Jayce. I never stopped."

Jace reaches one hand to the nape of Korian's neck, pulling their foreheads together. He traces the fingers of his other hand down the side of Korian's face. Korian rubs his nose tentatively against Jayce's cheek, taking in the familiar scent that he's longed for. He places his lips against Jayce's, guiding him into a tender kiss. It's so intimate, so vulnerable. Neither man wants to pull away, but they do, the moment ending too soon.

"Why, why didn't you have a choice? We can start over, Korian. Please stay."

"It's too late for that, Jayce. I'm so sorry. I have to go." Korian pulls away, leaving Jayce standing there, numb. Korian grabs his jacket and his suitcase and walks to the door. Glancing over his shoulder, he looks at Jayce; the hurt and remorse are evident in his eyes as he leaves Jayce...again.

**

Luca enters the apartment finding Jayce sitting on the sofa with a drink in his hand and a blank look on his face. "Where's Korian?"

Jayce shrugs his shoulders. "Gone."

"What do you mean, gone?" Luca is shocked.

"Gone, back to LA. Misun told him to go."

"What the fuck, Jayce? He owes me an explanation about my father. He can't just leave."

"Yeah, well he did." Jayce stands, setting his empty glass on the counter. "Luca, I'm exhausted. Can we talk about this later?"

Luca nods, taking in his cousin's weary state. "Yeah, okay. Go home, Jayce. Get some sleep."

Jayce nods, approaching Luca who draws him into a tight hug. "I'm so sorry, Luca. I don't deserve your forgiveness."

"We'll talk later. Everything is too much right now." Jayce nods and Luca walks him to the door and watches as he puts on his coat and shoes.

"She's asleep. I'll call you tomorrow," Jayce says before he leaves.

Luca quietly opens the door to Misun's bedroom, expecting to find her sleeping after her traumatic ordeal. Instead, he sees her sitting up with her bare feet dangling towards the floor. She has a bottle of wine on her side table and she's refilling a glass.

"Misun, stop. Where did you get that?"

She looks at Luca, startled to see him there. "I always keep a bottle by my bed. I need it to sleep."

"You shouldn't be drinking, Mi."

"Stop, Luca. Not now. Please." She takes a few sips, then sets down the glass and climbs under the covers, pressing her cheek into the pillow as tears spill onto the pink satin.

Luca sits down on the edge of the bed, not really knowing how to begin. "Misun, I'm so sorry. It's my fault you lost the baby."

"No, Luca, It's not." Misun doesn't meet his eyes. "I'm a terrible mother. I've been drinking the entire time. This is my punishment for all the shit I've done."

"That's not tr..."

"You know it's true. I'm a mess. I just keep hurting people."

"Mi, what does this have to do with my father?" What did Korian mean?"

Misun sits up again grabbing her wine. She stands up, wincing as she cradles her abdomen, and begins to pace. "Drop it Luca. Nothing good will come from this conversation."

"Misun, I have a right to know. How did your brother know Maxwell?"

"It's complicated, Luca. Max knew my father."

Luca stands approaching her. "What are you talking about?"

"Enough, Luca! Your father is dead! You have to let it go!"

Luca grabs Misun's arm and she pulls away from him. "No, Misun. I need to know! How long did you..."

"Years! We knew him for a long time! It doesn't matter, Luca! He's gone!" Misun is approaching hysterics. "He's gone and my baby is gone!"

"Calm down, Mi. Please, sit back down."

"No! It's my fault! I ruin everything! I'm toxic. I should never have been a mother, Luca. I'll ruin Dasom like I ruin everything!" Luca tries to comfort Misun, but she is agitated and won't allow him to touch her. "I'm done, Luca. Done ruining your family. I won't see Dasom anymore."

"You're her mother, Mi. Don't say that. She needs you."

"No, she doesn't need me! I can't even care for her on my own!" Misun rushes out of the room and Luca follows her into Dasom's nursery. She grabs a bag and starts to shove the baby clothes into it.

"What are you doing?" Luca watches her frantically rushing around the room.

"Take it! Take everything!" Misun shoves the bag, more clothes and anything she can grab into Luca's arms. Suddenly she stops and grabs Luca's shoulders, looking into his eyes. "I want you to raise Dasom with Jaxon. I can't be in her life. Please Luca. Do this for me."

Luca stands shocked as Misun runs back to her bedroom, locking the door. He drops the items in his arms and tries to get Misun to let him in. She's silent. Sighing deeply and rubbing his temples, he finally gives up, exiting the apartment and locking the door behind him. He needs to get home to Jax and Dasom, to his family.

Chapter 36

Luca looks around the massive great room of his apartment. Hundreds of balloons, mostly pink, are gathered into bundles to frame the cityscape from the wall of windows. Gigantic stuffed animals are scattered throughout the room; a lion, tiger, giraffe, monkey, elephant ... all of Dasom's favorites from the Central Park Zoo.

It's her special place to visit and Luca and Jax take her any chance they get, entranced by her wide-eyed excitement as she babbles and reaches out to the animals. Anna takes her often during the week as well. Dasom never tires of it; every time she goes to the zoo she's just as excited as she was on her first visit there.

Luca pulls Jax close, placing one hand on his lower back and the other threaded through his thick blonde hair. "Angel, this is amazing. Thank you so much for doing this."

Jax wraps his arms around Luca's neck and pulls him in for a gentle kiss, their lips brush gently until Luca teases his tongue against Jaxon's bottom lip, and Jax pulls him even closer, deepening their kiss. Their tongues play languidly together, and they enjoy the quiet moment before the guests arrive. When their lips reluctantly disconnect, the men rest their foreheads together.

"I loved doing it. Anything for our girl. I can't believe it's been a year already."

Luca rubs their noses together. "Yeah, a year since the best and worst night of my life."

Jax holds him tightly and whispers in his ear. "How are you feeling about everything? Overwhelmed?"

"I'll be okay, it's just a lot. The memories of that day...but I won't let anything ruin this. I just wish Grandfather was coming."

Jax nods and pulls back a bit to meet Luca's gaze, slowly tracing his ringed fingers down his cheek. "I know Luca, but it's a difficult day for him. God knows we understand that. We'll see him this weekend at the estate. It will be a nice getaway."

Luca's next words are interrupted by Anna coming into the room with Dasom bundled in her arms. Heidi and Victoria trail behind them.

Upon seeing Luca, Dasom holds out her arms. "Dadadada!" Luca takes her into his embrace, placing quick pecks all over her rosy cheeks. She smiles widely, her cute little teeth on display, her darling dimples appearing on her chubby cheeks.

"My beautiful birthday princess!" Luca coos as he tickles her side."

"Oh my god, Anna. She looks so adorable!" Jaxon's hands fly to his face as he takes in the sight of his precious girl.

Dasom is dressed in her party dress. The top is cheetah print with a pretty pink bow at the neckline and a pink frilly tulle skirt that poofs out around her. She's wearing tights and little black party shoes, and her unruly black curls, now chin-length, are held back by the cutest headband with cheetah ears pointing up.

Dasom sees Jax looking at her and she reaches for him, squealing, "Paaaapa!"

Jax takes her into his arms and kisses her forehead while fluffing up her curls. Dasom's eyes go wide when she looks around the room. Jax and the girls had decorated during her nap, and she has an expression of absolute wonder on her face. She wiggles to get down, and upon reaching the floor, immediately crawls over to the towering stuffed giraffe and pulls herself up by holding onto its leg.

"Shuuuuuuuuu!" she cries cutely, her word for 'zoo'. She bounces up and down happily, before crawling over to the lion. The adults all fuss over her cuteness.

Anna heads to the kitchen and starts to help Luca bring the food over to the table. Jax grabs the long submarine sandwich that's set on a tray, curved into a snake shape with olive eyeballs and a pimento tongue. He'd also made a veggie tray; the dip in the center has a cute lion face and sliced carrots, orange, and yellow peppers surrounding the dip make the mane. Luca sets down a big bowl of animal crackers, Days favorite, next to it.

Victoria and Anna have made an elaborate fruit display, with a watermelon sculpture shaped like an elephant. Jax had insisted that they prepare the food instead of hiring a caterer, and he and Anna had scoured the internet for fun ideas. Luca had only ordered a large sushi tray, in the shape of a fish, of course, and a tall tower loaded with adorable animal cupcakes.

Anna arranges some of the platters and cute decorations on the table, laughing at the metallic balloons on the wall that Luca had picked out. "WILD 1, how appropriate for our little sassy girl."

"Isn't it?" Luca replies. "She certainly has her mother's personality!" Luca notices the frown on his boyfriend's face. "What's wrong, Angel. You okay?"

"I'm okay. It just makes me sad that Misun won't come. It's her daughter's first birthday and she should be here," Jax replies quietly.

Anna shakes her head. "You both did everything you could to get her to come. I called her too, but she said that she'd ruin everything."

"I just wish she would see Dasom," Jax says. "She's only seen her a handful of times, and only with Luca and me there. It's not fair that Dasom doesn't even know her."

Luca sighs and rubs Jaxon's shoulders. "I'll go see her tomorrow. She's back working at the bar, and she can't avoid me if I just show up."

Jax nods. "Thanks, Luca," Anna says. "I'm worried about her."

Their conversation is interrupted by loud voices by the door. "Where's my birthday girl!" Taylor shouts. He walks in with Jasper, arms loaded with gifts.

Luca looks them up and down and bursts into laughter. "Oh my god, you two."

Jax looks over and giggles. "Awe, look at you! So cute!" Taylor gives him a big smile and sets the gifts down, while Jasper shoots him an annoyed look.

"Taylor's idea." Jasper mumbles.

"Of course, it was!" Jax covers his mouth to stifle another laugh. Jasper is wearing a tiger pajama onesie, tail wiggling behind him and ears poking up from the hood. His boyfriend wears a matching outfit, a brown kangaroo with a huge tail, and a little pouch in front with a baby kangaroo peeking its head out.

"I love you two, you're the best!" Heidi shouts from across the room.

Taylor kangaroo hops over to Dasom, who giggles and claps her hands. He drops to the floor in front of her, and she pulls herself up clutching onto him. Her almond eyes go wide when she sees the little stuffed joey peeking from the pouch, and Taylor pulls it out and presents it to the giggling girl.

The family starts to arrive, followed by a few co-workers with their kids. Luca makes a point of arranging playdates on the weekends so that his daughter has other children to interact with. Jayce and Harrison arrive, and Heidi rushes over, planting a kiss on her boyfriend's cheek, and takes the gifts from him.

Luca embraces his cousins. "Guys, you know I said no gifts. Day is spoiled enough. I don't want her to become a brat!" Luca and Jax had made a large donation to the zoo in Dasom's name and asked his family to consider their own donations in lieu of presents. Of course, they had done both.

"It's her first birthday, Luca. The Blackwood Princess deserves it." Jayce pats his shoulder and joins the festivities.

Noah arrives soon after, kissing his beautiful wife on the cheek as she flits through the guests with Jax, passing out drinks. He greets a few colleagues on his way to see Luca.

"Wow, I can't believe she's a year old," Noah says, helping himself to a Jameson.

Luca sighs, "I know. So much has happened."

"You have a great life, Luca. You and Jaxon are amazing fathers," Noah says, placing his hand on his best friend's shoulder.

"Thanks, Noah. I mean it. Thanks for helping me through all the shit. What about you and Victoria? You ready for kids yet?"

"No, not yet. Not for a few years. Victoria is setting up her practice and I need time to really dig in at work. My hours are too long right now."

"Well, the company is doing remarkably well under your direction. Taylor's line has been an unprecedented success and the new one is almost complete. Grandfather made the right decision." Luca claps Noah on the shoulder.

"Now, no more work talk. Let me go see my sweet little Day," Noah says as the men walk into the great room.

Anna and Heidi are trying to get the older kids involved in some simple games, while the adults chat and nibble on the food. Jayce and Taylor are on the floor playing with the younger kids, who are climbing all over them. Dasom is sitting on Jaspers' back as he lays with his stomach flat against the floor. She's bouncing up and down and grabbing at his tiger ears. The sight is absolutely adorable, and Luca snaps a few photos with his phone.

Noah sits beside his wife on the comfortable leather sofa, wrapping his free arm around her shoulders as he sips at his drink. Jax takes over helping Heidi with the games, and Anna plops exhaustively on the sofa next to her sister.

"Ready for a drink, Anna?" Luca asks. She nods and he heads back to the kitchen to get her a glass of wine.

The door swings open and Bella makes her usual grand entrance, striding toward Dasom when she sees her on top of her favorite nephew. Her guest lingers behind, chatting with Luca who presents him with a beer.

"Hey Bella," Victoria greets her from the sofa. "You look stunning as usual."

"Thank you, darling, cheetah to match the birthday girl." She places kisses on Noah and Victoria's cheeks, then greets Anna, who's always been a bit intimidated by the beautiful woman. "Anna, how are you sweetheart?" Pretty as always, I see." She grips Anna's hand gently and takes a seat on the arm of the sofa."

"I'm fine Bella, a little frazzled from all the party preparations," Anna says a bit timidly.

"What an amazing job you did, girls. It's so much fun for my special baby." Bella notices Anna looking toward the kitchen, her eyes widening as she sees the man chatting with Luca, and Jayce, who has joined them.

"Hmmmmmm. Handsome, isn't he?" Bella teases.

Anna breaks her trance, looking up at Bella. "Who is he?"

"Oh, he's a special friend of mine." Bella tips her head back and laughs.

"Oh... OH!" Anna stumbles over her words. "I'm so sorry, Bella. I didn't mean to stare."

"No, no, darling. He deserves to be stared at." Bella stands and takes Anna's hand, pulling her gently up from the couch. "Come on, come with me." Anna's eyes open wide, and before she can protest, Bella leads her toward the kitchen and the blonde adonis.

"Hello boys. We've come for more wine," Bella says casually, taking Anna's glass to refill.

"Hi," Anna says shyly.

"Aidan, I'd like you to meet Anna." As Bella stands near the two, a somewhat uncomfortable silence settles as Aiden looks between the women.

Finally, he extends his hand, grasping Anna's gently. "Hello, Anna. It's always a pleasure to meet a beautiful woman." Anna blushes, and before she comes to her senses, she sees Bella grab Jayce and Luca guiding them to rejoin the party. "We'll just let you two get acquainted."

Jayce gives his mother a quizzical look, and she whispers in his ear. "No questions, darling." He raises his eyebrows in response. He knows better than to ask.

Jayce and Luca resume their conversation. "So," Luca begins, "you haven't reached him?"

Sadness overtakes Jayce's face, as it has so often over the last few months. He shakes his head. "No, nothing. He's even cancelled attending a few events where he knew I'd be."

Luca squeezes his cousin's shoulder in silent commiseration, when the door buzzer interrupts them, and Luca's eyes light up. "It's my surprise. Come help me, Jayce."

As the men head to the door, Luca addresses the guests. "Everyone! I have a special surprise for my beautiful birthday girl. Can I ask you all to keep your voices down and move to the sides of the room?"

The guests follow Luca's instructions, and Heidi looks at Jaxon, who shrugs his shoulders. Attention remains on the door as several zookeepers begin bringing in various cages and containers. Oohs and aaahs are heard as the cages are placed down for presentation. A huge snake, turtle, meerkat and several unidentifiable animals are visible, and, in one cage is a precious baby tiger.

Jax gasps, rushing over to his boyfriend with Dasom in his arms. Her eyes are wide, and she laughs excitedly when she sees the animals. "You didn't!" Jax whispers in Luca's ear.

"I did!" Luca replies, kissing Jaxon's cheek.

"You're amazing, you know that?" Jax lays his head on Luca's shoulder, while their daughter wiggles in his grasp.

"You are too, Angel. You are too."

Chapter 37

Resisting the urge to cry, Misun lets out a huge sigh. She pulls her phone out of her apron pocket and stares at her lockscreen. Her daughter. Her baby. Dasom's pretty little face looks back at her on the illuminated screen. An image that Luca has sent to keep her updated. He has been so good at trying to keep her involved, but she has resisted most of the attempts.

"Misun," the voice of her bar manager booms in her direction. "We have customers to serve you know."

She is startled, and clicks the picture off quickly, flinging the phone on a wooden shelf behind her, forgetting that she has a pocket to store it. Returning to the customers, Misun pours a beer for one of the regulars. She's only been back working there for a few months and always sees the same patrons.

Handing it over to the man known as Hank, he grasps her fingers. "Fancy a drink later, Misun?" he asks, slurring after a few too many. "I can make you happy, you know. Let me treat you nice."

Shaking her head, she pulls her hand away from him. "No, thank you, Hank. You know that I'm not interested," she says, firmly. "I'd like to ask you to leave me alone please."

He shrugs and slides drunkenly off the stool. "Fine. Your loss. But it won't stop me trying." He goes off to sit at a table.

She watches him take a seat, regretting all of her previous flirting in order to gain some tips, before looking over to the other side of the room to see what her manager is doing. He's sitting with a trashy blonde lady, too busy looking at her cleavage heaving out of the unbuttoned gaps in her blouse. Taking the opportunity, Misun quickly grabs a glass and unscrews the bottle of wine. Pouring a small amount, she turns her back away from everyone and gulps it back.

She closes her eyes as she swallows the liquid that gives her some short-term relief, and rests against the counter. Her heart is heavy, trying not to think about it being Dasom's birthday and that she is missing out on being with her, but she knows that it's the right decision for her to be with her two fathers. They and the rest of the Blackwoods can give her a much better upbringing. She was invited by Luca, but she declined.

Tears start to fall, guilt tearing her up inside. She has no one. Nobody that will love her. A waitress appears beside her and sees her distress. She pulls her in for a quick hug and tells her to go and have her break to get some fresh air. Thanking her for being kind, she heads out into the darkness, purposely avoiding going past her manager's table in case he gives her yet another lecture about being unprofessional.

Once outside, she takes a big deep breath before patting her apron and cursing that she has left her phone on the counter inside. She does, however, realize that she still has the glass in her hand. She moves into the darkened car park and sits down on one of the outdoor wooden benches. Glugging the last few mouthfuls of wine, she puts the glass on the gravel next to her feet.

Slumping back, she lets her head drop onto the backrest behind her and focuses on the stars twinkling in the clear sky. She picks the brightest one that she can find and declares to herself that it's her lost baby's star. Something to look at forever.

Her mind wanders back to that awful time. When her life was in complete chaos and everyone hated her. She knows that people have tried since, but she just can't allow people to get close. *You don't deserve someone to love you.*

Luca has been amazing. He has tried to keep her so involved in Dasom's life. Sending her updates and videos. They are her pride and joy to sit and watch when she is feeling lonely. She just knows that she can't be part of her life. Dasom needs good role models and someone to look up to. *And that isn't you. You are worthless and she is better off without you.*

Angrily wiping a tear from her cheek, she sits up and rests her arms on her knees. Looking up in the dim light, her eyes widen when she spots the man leaning against a car, silently watching her. He crosses his arms in front of his chest, and she sits up straighter. She didn't even hear him getting out of the car or closing the door, too lost in her own dark thoughts.

"What do you want? I don't have anything to say to you." She puts on a braver face than how she feels, unnerved by being out here in the dark with no one around.

"Don't be like that," he says with a smirk. "I'm only being friendly."

She stands and tries to make her way back in the direction of the bar, but he clasps her arm swiftly. She tries to shrug it off, but he grips firmly.

"Get your hands off me," she says, her heart racing.

"Misun, come on. You know that we are meant to be. You know that you need me. You have no one else." He seems to take delight in bringing her down. "Just accept it. I'm the only man for you. Everyone else walks away from you." The words cut Misun deep like a knife and she hangs her head. He continues his persuasive mental assault with a determination to make her back down. "Look, I just want to do right by you. By us. You deserve someone to look after you, and I can. Go on, Let me."

He releases his grip but still stays close, waiting in the evening air and giving her time to mull it over. She is so tired of battling with life. Struggling to allow people in and love her before being rejected and even hated. *He is all that you have and all that you deserve.* She finally meets his eye, her face dark and sorrowful. "Okay," she whispers.

"Great." He smiles, clasping her tensed up hand. "Let's go."

"What? Now?" she asks him, and he nods, pulling her in the direction of the waiting car.

She struggles with him, her anxiety levels rising. "Wait, I need to go back and get my purse and phone!"

He opens the door and starts to shove her inside. "Misun, don't worry about that. You don't need them."

Misun starts to panic thinking about her contact with Luca and all the photos of Dasom that he has been sending her. Her only source of happiness. "No, please. Let me get them. I need them." She cries, her stomach flips, realizing that she isn't strong enough to get away.

**

Luca takes a few steps into the door and glances around, scanning the people in the bar. It's busy, lots of customers watching the game on the ancient TV in the corner. Everyone is hollering and cheering.

He heads over to the bar and leans over to the man pouring a bourbon. "Hi, I was just looking for Misun, if you've seen her?"

The guy gives him a suspicious look. "And you are?"

"I'm Luca, Misun's ex. We have a daughter."

He smirks. "The infamous Luca Blackwood, hey? Well, we are honored."

Luca ignores his sarcasm. "Well, is she here?"

"She should be," he says, shrugging. "She was supposed to be on shift tonight, but as you can see, she didn't show. In fact, she just walked out yesterday evening."

"It was our daughter's birthday yesterday. Did you call her?"

The guy scoffs, lifting something from the shelf. "Of course, I called her." He shows Luca the cell phone. "But she left this here, and her purse. One of the girls went to her apartment and it's empty."

Luca is becoming increasingly worried about her after hearing this information. He knows that Misun has a self-destruct button in her hand, but this is so out of character, even for her. "And no one is concerned about this?"

"Look, buddy," the man says, putting down the glasses he's drying. "I have enough to do around here. I'm in charge of this place. I haven't got time to chase some two-bit, no good waitress around."

Feeling his anger escalating Luca takes a deep breath and thinks for a moment. He has an idea. "What about the security footage?"

Rolling his eyes, the manager motions to a man that has just approached the bar. "Fine, can I serve him first?" Luca nods and the manager turns to the customer. "Hank, what can I get you?"

When he has finished, he ushers Luca into his office in the back. Once inside, he fumbles around looking for the remote for the security cameras. After finding it, he skips to the previous evening, stopping at approximately the time that Misun walked out from the bar. He enlarges the images of the car park.

The two men squint at the grainy images filling the screen. They witness Misun leaving and sitting on the bench. Luca's heart sinks at the sight of how sad she looks. He has no ill feelings towards her now. Just a strong sense of pity. Of course, he loves having Dasom to bring up with Jaxon and the three of them are very happy, but he wishes that Misun wanted to be a part of their daughter's life. Wishes that he had tried harder to keep her involved.

Luca is pulled swiftly from his thoughts, when he spots another figure appearing in the frame. He leans forward to get a closer look. A man, in a cap. He can't make anything else out.

Suddenly, the image moves around, and he sees Misun being dragged toward the car. He lets out a soul wrenching gasp causing him to stumble back into the filing cabinet, the clatter of metal echoing around the room. "No," he says, "it can't be. This cannot be happening. He is supposed to be dead."

The manager is shocked at Luca's reaction, and pauses the frame. "Is everything okay?" he asks with genuine concern.

Luca composes himself and peers at the frozen image on the small screen, not quite believing what he sees. "No way. I don't believe it. That's my Father."

To be continued...

Character List

Dalton Blackwood ~ Iconic designer, founder and patriarch of Blackwood.

Maxwell Blackwood ~ Dalton's eldest child and Luca's father; removed from the business and estranged from his family.

*****Luca Blackwood*** ~ (age 29) Dalton's eldest grandchild and Maxwell's son; director of marketing and photography for Blackwood.

Bella Blackwood ~ Dalton's only daughter; former model and creative director for Blackwood. Mother of Jayce and Harrison.

*****Jayce Blackwood*** ~ (age 28) Bella's eldest child; head model of Blackwood.

*****Harrison Blackwood*** ~ (age 26) Jayce's younger brother; senior stylist at Blackwood.

Alexander Blackwood ~ Dalton's youngest child; sibling to Max and Bella. Retiring as CEO.

*****Noah Blackwood*** ~ Oldest son of Alexander; assuming CEO position of Blackwood.

*****Jasper Blackwood*** ~ Noah's younger brother and youngest heir; new photographer for Blackwood.

Taylor King ~ Fashion designer; contestant on Aspire to Design.

Jaxon Somsi ~ Dancer; Taylors best friend and roommate.

Misun ~ Luca's ex-girlfriend.

Victoria ~ Engaged to Noah; doctoral psychology student.

Heidi ~ Junior stylist at Blackwood.

Korian ~ Rival model; works for different company.

Anna ~ Victoria's sister.

** *The Blackwood Heirs*

About the Authors

Samantha is a busy mum of 10 who lives in Warrington, England. She recently began writing and her online works have been well received.

Beth is a mother of four and an RN who lives in Buffalo, NY. She is a first-time author.

Sam and Beth met online through common interests and have become close friends. They decided to write their first novel together after collaborating for some of Sam's stories. They have never met in person but cannot wait for that day.